James Long was a BBC TV news correspondent until the end of the 1980s. After two years of starting and running an international TV station out of Zurich, he returned to England to concentrate on writing, which has always been his first love. He has three grown children and lives in Bristol.

You can discover more about the author at www.jameslongbooks.com

THE BALLOONIST

Running from a troubled past, Lieutenant Willy Fraser, formerly of the Royal Flying Corps, has chosen the most dangerous job on the Western Front — a balloon observer hanging under a gasbag filled with explosive hydrogen, four thousand feet above the Ypres Salient, anchored by a slender cable. Swept across enemy lines after his balloon is damaged, Willy is hidden by Belgian farmers, whom he grows close to during his stay; with their aid, he manages to escape across the flooded delta at the English Channel and return to his duties. But once he's back in the air, spotting for artillery and under attack, Willy can only focus on his own survival — until he is forced to make an impossible decision that threatens the life of the woman he has come to love.

JAMES LONG

◆

THE BALLOONIST

Complete and Unabridged

CHARNWOOD
Leicester

First published in Great Britain in 2014 by
Simon & Schuster UK Ltd
London

First Charnwood Edition
published 2015
by arrangement with
Simon & Schuster UK Ltd
London

A catalogue record for this book is available from the British Library.

ISBN 978–1–4448–2634–0

Published by
F. A. Thorpe (Publishing)
Anstey, Leicestershire

Set by Words & Graphics Ltd.
Anstey, Leicestershire
Printed and bound in Great Britain by
T. J. International Ltd., Padstow, Cornwall

This book is printed on acid-free paper

For Denis Avey, for my father Bill Long and
for all the other heroes I have known.

Introduction

The odds were stacked against you on the Western Front but nowhere more than in the air above it. Much has been written about the pilots on both sides but little attention has been paid to those who undertook the most dangerous aerial task of all — the balloon observers.

Why were they needed? Because the grim cartography of war demanded accurate artillery, guided to the target by eyes in the sky. Because the flimsy aircraft of the time had limited endurance and poor communication with the ground.

Why was it dangerous? For so very many reasons. The only lifting gas available was hydrogen and hydrogen burns fiercely when hit by incendiary bullets or exploding shells. A balloon makes a fat target and when the balloons went up, the enemy did its best to knock them down again by every means available.

For that reason there are very few first-hand accounts of the hazardous life of the balloon observer. I have trawled the archives to find them and I owe a great debt of gratitude to those who were able to commit their experience to paper. For so many of them, their life ended in a greasy smear of smoke down a hostile sky.

PART ONE

1

Monday, 29 June 1914. South-western Scotland.

The mourning had been brief and almost devoid of affection, stiff with Scottish formality, and Gilfillan minded that. They had hardly known the Colonel, not as he had once been before he was shredded by war, injustice and a dearth of love.

The motorcars left first, lurching down to the Raider's Road before the clock struck three. A Rolls-Royce, a Napier and two foreign cars — modern things. Unpopular. The people of Galloway considered internal combustion to be a passing and poisonous fad. Most of the guests took another cup of tea and waited ten silent minutes before setting off in their carriages, hanging back long enough to make sure that backfiring motors would not frighten their horses on the slow way down to Newton Stewart.

Gilfillan watched the last of them go then he took the teacups to the scullery. Morag would be coming presently to wash them. He stacked the unused cups back in the cupboard, noting that they outnumbered the used ones, and he went in search of the new owner of Grannoch Castle.

There was no point in checking the ground floor because that was where the thin scattering of guests had briefly settled in their sombre

3

knots of politeness and the boy had evaporated as soon as he had gone through the minimal motions with each of them. The boy? Gilfillan corrected himself. He was no boy any more. Gilfillan was not at all sure he should approve but when he heard the local stories he smiled inwardly at most of them. Willy had gained a powerful reputation in the short years of his adulthood before he had left to join the cavalry.

Gilfillan sniffed the air as he trod softly through the rooms. He wondered yet again that a sixty-year-old house built on the slope of a windy hillside could manage to smell quite so sour. He considered the stags' heads on the walls and wondered if the fault lay in their dead breath. The Colonel had given up all forms of killing after they came back together from the South African war, but he had left the heads there because he wasn't one for too much change.

Willy was another matter. He was one for the chase. Gilfillan had never known a lad so skilled at dancing with danger in so many forms. That frightened child had transformed himself into a man who shied away from nothing. No one could match him in riding, in shooting and in the pursuit of life in all its forms. The great houses of the Galloway Forest and the women inside them were scattered over a hard terrain of crags and bog and burns and rock. It took a determined hunter to winkle them out. Gilfillan heard the stories. As he had served the tea he had watched the couples in the room. Even Lady Livermore allowed a softening in her painted granite face when she talked to Willy. Surely she was too old for that to have gone any further but he had seen the way that young Mrs McCann looked at the Colonel's son and knew that story at least must be true. He had also seen from the way Mr McCann looked at both of them that the same rumours had clearly reached his ears.

Gilfillan might have worried. An accident with a shotgun or a hunting rifle out on the hills would leave only suspicion behind in place of proof, but there was something about the boy that had served as protective armour so far. Even the men smiled at the way he talked. Willy had a spellbinding way about him, a happy trick for relating every challenge and mishap with such humour driving through it that all those within earshot howled with laughter and the rest stepped in closer to find out what they were missing. You would think he had been born to be king of the world unless you were Gilfillan and had seen the hard path that brought him there.

Soaked in the painful knowledge that a predictable age had now ended, he unlocked the study door, not because the boy might be in there but because it was an excuse to spend a few more moments in his dead master's inner sanctum.

The long sand-tray filling the bay window had been rearranged one last time. Gilfillan studied the Colonel's final evolution of the Battle of Groenfontein. The emptied man had been fighting it one way or another for all of the dozen years since they had both come back from that ragged war. He studied the lead soldiers ranked along the line of the hot sand slope and nodded slowly. That would have done it. The Colonel had spent these past years looking in vain for the tactics he might have missed — anything for a better outcome. This time he had simply conjured a battery of field artillery out of nowhere to enfilade the Boer positions. Wishful thinking had perhaps been better than nothing but then Gilfillan thought of what the Colonel had done next after this false final victory and knew the desperate trick had not provided him with any real comfort.

The first-floor bedrooms were empty. The Victorian staircase of fine, turned oak ended there and he climbed the next, narrow shoddy flight to the attic storerooms and the long-deserted staff quarters at the top of the castle. Gilfillan breathed in as he looked around him, his eyes now searching more for problems in the fabric than for the boy. There was no longer any smell of damp up here for this was nearly July and the effects of the wet winter gales had finally been removed by a thin Scottish sun. He knew it would not last.

Gilfillan had come to believe that there is a place, a physical location, in everyone's life where they can be most of the ages they have ever been and sometimes all of them at once. For him that was the solid cottage he had been born in and where he and Morag still lived. He was in no real doubt where Willy would be. For the boy, he knew that place lay behind the brown painted door at the corner of the second-floor landing. He eased it open, trod gently up the tower's spiral staircase and as soon as he stepped out on

6

to the roof, he saw the man sitting sideways between the fantasy Victorian battlements, staring down towards the River Dee lost in the depths of the valley. Once the boy had been able to sit in the battlements' slots with his legs out straight in front of him but now he filled the gap with his knees drawn up tight to his chest.

'They have all gone,' said Gilfillan. 'It is only the two of us.'

Willy turned his head sharply and stared at him. The eyes tricked Gilfillan for a moment — those same wide eyes, brown and shining with unshed tears so he saw the child's smooth face and not the man's. Then Willy blinked twice, allowing the present to replace that past, and Gilfillan saw how his hair had bleached from brown to sand while his skin had weathered to meet it, tightening over the cheekbones, the jaw so much stronger — something Nordic about him from his mother, but so unlike her in every other way. He was relieved to feel the strength of the man though he could not entirely stop himself fearing for the boy.

'Tell me true, my old friend. Was it because of me, do you suppose?' Willy said.

'Because of you? Oh come, whatever makes you say that?'

'I wrote him a letter. Did he not tell you? I am quite sure he did. He told you most things. I wrote that I had resigned my commission, that I had left the regiment. Six days later your telegram told me he was dead. That's what makes me say it.'

Wedged, as Willy was, in the battlement space,

7

Gilfillan could not take him into his arms as he had done many times during his childhood. Instead the steward of the house sank down on the stone slabs and leant back against the parapet so he was next to Willy but looking away.

'It was not that,' he said slowly, hoping he was right. 'I believe he approved of your decision. I am sure he was proud of you for sticking to your guns. He had been through it himself, after all.'

'I did not tell him why I left.'

'He guessed you had too strong a spirit to tolerate a poor commander. As I say, he had been through that himself.'

'But I had a choice. He was given none.'

'Oh now, listen to me. He carried his sadness inside him for many years. You knew that. It swelled up inside until it left him no other way.'

'And that was nothing to do with me?'

'He had tried it before. You know that only too well.'

'But why now, if it was not prompted by my letter?'

'None of us can know,' he said slowly. 'I think perhaps he had enough of being alone but that was how he had chosen to live and he did what he did for his own reasons. You must not take on the burden of that. You were not the cause.'

There was no immediate answer and Gilfillan knew that Willy was staring out at the hills again, north-west towards the high and distant loom of the Merrick.

'You used to draw your pictures up here,' he said and Willy's head turned sharply back to him.

'Pictures?'

Gilfillan had sometimes watched him, unseen, from inside the doorway, making sure of how he was, perched high above the causes of his misery, checking that he was safe.

'Oh, I am sure you must know what I mean.'

Willy looked at that kind face, only the eyes smiling, then he turned and stared down at the flagstone path bisecting the bleak garden. In his mind's eye he could see his mother, beating at his father's retreating back then hurling flower-pots and clods of earth as she howled her anger at him. He could feel a pencil in his hand, remembered his discovery of how to improve the scene, sketching his parents back towards love, putting them hand in hand, not hand against hand.

'You saw that?'

'I did. You always drew well but however good the artist may be, a picture does not change the way life runs its course. Even from the loftiest of viewpoints.'

'Yes. I liked being up here, looking down.' Not nearly high enough, Willy thought. I wanted to be as high as an eagle so that I could not hear what they were doing to each other down there.

'Your mother would not agree, would she? She has no head for heights,' and Gilfillan knew that was another reason the boy had chosen to spend so much time up here. It had been a safe refuge. That last steep staircase had been his protection against furious discovery.

'I wish she had seen the view from here. It might have made her less willing to condemn

Scotland,' said Willy, 'and I confess I am concerned about you and Morag. Grannoch will be hers now and I know you never found her easy. Will you stay?'

'Stay?' said Gilfillan, surprised. 'Why would we leave? Oh, I see. No, that is not right. It will not be hers at all. Did you not know?' and he saw Willy shake his head. 'It is to be yours. That was your father's decision. He knew she would not come back from America, nor did he want her to. That is her place if it is anywhere, back with her people. He has left all this to *you*.'

Willy was surprised to find he didn't care one bit about his sudden inheritance. It felt no better than a burden, not a place he would ever choose to live. 'How did you know that when I did not?'

'Your father told me last year. I presumed he had told you the same.'

'All mine? So you will stay, won't you?'

'I'm sorry to tell you there is no getting rid of me. He has left us the cottage. Your estate is smaller than it was. Do you mind?'

'I am delighted, Mr Gilfillan. What could be better?'

'Ceasing to call me Mr would be better, for a start. Now I work for *you*. You are my master and I must simply be Gilfillan to you, sir.'

'I won't call you Mr if you agree not to call me Sir. I am too young to feel like a Sir. Were they ever happy, do you suppose?'

'Oh, I'm sure they were. For a while. When they first came here together.'

'For how long a while?'

'A month maybe.'

Willy gave out a short, shocked laugh and Gilfillan shrugged. 'You did ask,' he said. 'She was beautiful and he was besotted with her, but . . . '

'But?'

'It is perhaps not her fault that she was as mad as she was beautiful, but that is the sorry truth of it. What will you do now? Will *you* stay?'

'No.'

'What then?'

'You heard what they were all talking about when we got back from the burial?'

'The two people shot, you mean? The Austrian duke?'

'Seven separate stories in *The Times*.' Willy shifted and pulled the creased and folded newspaper out from under his bottom. 'He was an *Arch*duke, whatever that may be. Grander than a mere duke. Why seven separate stories do you suppose?'

'I know nothing of the place where it happened but I presume that means it must matter a great deal.'

'One man and one revolver. Two bullets and seven stories all saying that his death might send Europe tottering. I think I will go and take a look for myself.'

'Well, that does not surprise me,' said Gilfillan. 'You were always one for wanting to see everything that was going on. You will go there, to the Balkans? Will there be anything still to see?'

'I have a fancy to take the pulse of all of Europe.'

'You will be missed.'

'By you?'

'I meant by a young lady.'

Willy looked baffled. 'Really? Which one?'

'I do have eyes. Miss Wakeley is clearly very fond of you. Did you not notice that today?'

Willy laughed. 'Lorna Wakeley? She is not much more than a schoolgirl.'

'She is twenty-four years old. Near enough your own age.'

'Oh Mr Gilfillan, she is far too young for me. I am fond of women who have had time to develop a character. Lorna only acts out what she thinks might be her part in life. She thinks of what she should and should not say. There is no red meat to be found in her.'

Gilfillan wished he had kept silent. He knew what Morag would say. 'That poor boy has suffered from a dearth of love. You would not expect him to be normal now, would you? That is why he goes for the risky ones.'

'Forget the Wakeley girl,' said Willy. 'She might grow up in another twenty years. If she misses me, I'm afraid I shall not miss her. Will you look after this place for me?'

'Just as I have done until now. The place and the horses. Unless, that is, you would like me to come too?'

Willy looked at the man. 'I know you would like to, but Morag would not like that at all. She suffered enough when you went to war to protect my father.' The knowledge that Gilfillan had been a truer father to him rang in his head. 'Anyway, you wouldn't like it. I know you don't approve of the way I travel now.'

2

You grind magnesium powder mixed with potassium chlorate to make *Blitzlicht* but that is a dangerous business. Thierry Dardel's father lost both his eyes in the process and a portrait photographer does need his eyes above all else. At twenty-two years old, Thierry had been obliged to take over the family business and he wielded the pestle and mortar much more gently. In consequence his flash powder was of very indifferent quality. The couple in front of him held their pose as the first tray sputtered and failed then they waited in silence while he replaced it with mixture from a different jar. The two of them stood in position, side-by-side between the aspidistra on its wooden stand and the half unfolded Japanese screen and they looked into the camera again. Thierry had seen love and sweet happiness in their newly married faces when they first came in and he envied them a little. He knew his father would have arranged things so that all of that would be kept fresh, captured on the plate and transmuted to the final print. His father would have known just the right words to say to keep their happiness alive for those vital seconds.

He didn't.

They looked very different, these two. Thierry

13

had already begun to realize that the average newly married couple displayed surprising similarities in subtle ways — in the proportions of their face, the shape of the jaw or the spacing of their eyes. Lieutenant Claude Tavernier and his bride Gabrielle were an exception. She could have passed for Dutch, with fair skin and fair hair pinned up in a bun, except that she had that more sculpted face. From northern France perhaps? The dark-eyed lieutenant looked almost Spanish, so lean and saturnine that, remembering him afterwards, Thierry thought him the shorter of the pair though the photograph proved them equal. They had talked non-stop, these two, until the serious business of photography reduced them both to silence. Thierry had listened to them, also with a touch of envy, because sharp and unexpected humour flashed between them and lit up the room as his flash powder so resolutely refused to do.

The apprentice Miko held the refilled tray up at full arm's stretch but the powder failed to ignite for the next three or four seconds and by the time it finally did its job with a puff and a bright flash the couple were both holding onto only the tight skeletal remnants of that joyful expression. Thierry knew the whole event had slipped beyond the point of no return and that was the best he could hope to get. He assured them the photograph would be perfection itself and that he would rush it to their house by messenger as soon as it was ready. Later that day, as the prints slowly emerged, his worst fears were realized. The following day, when they had dried without any miraculous overnight improvement, he put two of them into a stiff envelope, sighing gently, and sent Miko off to the upper reaches of the Rue de la Dodane to deliver them.

The house stood at an angle to the narrow road, sheltered by a high brick wall and surrounded by a peaceful and generous garden. The street wound downhill to the bank of the River Sambre, on its way to merge in mid-town with the mightier Meuse. Claude was lying on the grass, his back propped against the wide trunk of a shady tree, utterly at peace. Gabrielle, his wife of three days, teased his lips with a small, ripe plum, bending down over him with her hair brushing his face. He nibbled at the plum with his eyes closed, reaching both arms around her to pull her close and that was when he heard the front gate creak open and footsteps on the gravel. The footsteps changed course and softened as the new arrival headed across the grass towards them.

'The photographs,' said Claude as he opened his eyes and let go of Gabrielle, but he stood up, alarmed, as he took in the approaching soldier — a young infantryman of the 4th Division, hot and bothered with his high shako hat firmly on his head and his blue jacket buttoned up tightly.

'Lieutenant Tavernier?' he asked, his eyes on Claude's loose civilian shirt, stained by drips of plum juice, then wandering towards Gabrielle before he fought them back.

'Lieutenant Tavernier *on leave*,' said Claude, 'feeling more of the Tavernier and less of the lieutenant. You're looking for me?' They had sent this poor boy across the bridge from the citadel, that was clear, and Claude glanced at the envelope the boy extended towards him hoping it might be late congratulations from some other officer — a curious misuse of a military messenger.

'Urgent, sir — straight from old Ironchops . . . I mean from General Leman.' The boy's face paled at what he had just said.

Claude lifted an eyebrow and felt his heart sink. 'Thank you. Have a glass of lemonade before you go. Cook is in the kitchen.'

He pulled his knife out of his pocket by its thin leather belt-lanyard and cut the envelope open. The paper was pale yellow, pasted with strips of typing from the military telegraph.

'Please rejoin my staff with all possible speed,' it said. 'My personal apologies to your beautiful wife and my hopes that I may soon return you to her for the remainder of your wedding leave once this emergency has passed.' It was signed 'Leman'.

Gabrielle was reading it over his shoulder. 'Is this a joke?' she said. 'Please say it is.'

'Who would joke like that?'

'Your strange friends in the regiment. The ones who tied the gun dogs to our carriage at the cathedral.'

'Oh my dear. It is no joke. This is real. Leman must see trouble coming.'

'What trouble? That is not possible. This is Belgium. We are a neutral country.'

'And he is a wise and cautious general.'

She stepped back and watched him straightening, turning back into a soldier before her eyes, away from the Claude she had seen for the first time in a market place only months before, brought into collision by the world's wondrous and random benevolence.

'I am an officer in the army,' he had said at that first unexpected meeting, then saw her surprise and immediately amplified it as if she might have mistaken him for a Frenchman. 'The *Belgian* army.' He had not realized that her surprise was not about his nationality but about his age. She had taken him for a college boy. Later he told her that was down to the blood of his Moroccan grandmother, a woman who still looked thirty when she was sixty. That was after she told him about her childhood in the Lorraine metal works but the point was the talking itself as much as the meaning because by that time both of them were dancing in the sound of each other's words.

His duty in Brussels and her home in Namur had kept them apart too much in these few months but he laid siege to her with a ring of proposals and, though she knew he had some slightly indefinable growing-up still to do, she also knew that whatever crackled between them was undeniable.

When they had walked out of the Cathedral of St Aubin under an avenue of crossed sabres, he had sighed with happiness and said, 'May this last forever.'

She had squeezed his hand and said, 'Nothing lasts forever. That is not the point. Our task is to make the most of every second that it does last.'

'I love that about you, Gabrielle Tavernier. You are half brave dreamer and half brutal realist. Oh, did you hear what I just said — *Gabrielle Tavernier*.'

'That is my name, husband. Get used to it. I already have. I think it fits me quite well.'

They had three days of bliss in the old house, talking, talking and talking, and it was meant to last a week. Gabrielle's parents had gone to stay elsewhere to give them space. He found proof of what he had already suspected: wisdom, bravery and humour running through and through her. She delighted in his joy, his keen interest in the world and wondered only at some lack of belief in himself. That, she thought, was something she could help put right but then the messenger arrived.

Nothing lasts forever.

The soldier went on his way, leaving the two of them in a numbed silence that was broken almost immediately by the arrival of Miko, the photographer's apprentice, with another brown envelope — this one, briefly, more welcome than the first. It disgorged the shining prints and they studied them in silence.

'Who are these two people?' said Claude.

'The one on the right is clearly your long-lost brother. He is quite like you but he looks younger and he's just starting to think he might be about to vomit,' said Gabrielle, 'but I haven't the first idea about the woman on the left. I don't think I want to meet her. I would say she has strong religious opinions of a very puritanical

18

nature and she would see a frying pan more as a weapon than the start of any culinary process.'

'Don't be so horrible about the woman I love,' said Claude. 'Do we have time to make him do it again?'

'I don't know. Do we?'

They both knew they hadn't.

'You look fine,' they both said at exactly the same moment. 'No,' said Claude. 'You do. It's me I don't like.'

'Neither of us really looks like that,' said Gabrielle, practical and accurate as always, 'but it doesn't matter at all. This photograph is no more than the hook on which I shall hang the beautiful hat which is my memory so just in case my memory does not last, make sure you hurry back to me when this fuss is over. I have hardly seen you. First Leman sent you off to England and now this. You tell your wonderful General that I have only lent you to him and, like a library book, there will be a fine for late return.'

'What sort of book am I?'

'A romance and an adventure story mixed together.'

'Not a history book?'

'A very short one,' she said, regretting the words immediately and then reminding herself that she did not believe those who talked of tempting fate.

The message had said 'with all possible speed' and to Gabrielle that meant tomorrow but she saw that it meant today to Claude and knew that if she tried to hold on to him, she would be stretching him thin. She helped him pack his

19

bag, tidied his uniform around his spare frame, offered to walk with him to the railway station, knew he was right when he said he could not bear that sort of parting and held him instead for a long silence at the gate which she had to bring to an end because he could not.

3

Saturday, 1 August 1914. Berlin, Germany.

The afternoon sunlight of the Unter den Linden gleamed on a plate glass window flanked by tall Corinthian columns. Above the glass, gilded letters set into black slate spelt out WELTREISE-BUREAU UNION but the real business of the office was contained in the name lettered across the precise centre of the window itself. It was the pride of Herr Direktor Maschmann, the largest one-piece shop window in the whole of Berlin when it had been installed six years earlier. The lettering proclaimed that the Union World Travel Bureau was the Berlin agency for the world famous company of Thos. Cook & Son. Herr Maschmann had fussed over the signwriter's work, watching to ensure that the edges were sharp, the lines straight and the curves perfectly regular. For all the years since then, his bureau had been full of Thomas Cook's customers, exchanging money, booking tickets or embarking in their Daimler-Benz charabancs for tours to the Tegeler See or up to Wandlitz. Herr Maschmann had been very proud of his English connection.

At tea-time on Saturday, the butt ends of three rifles shattered the plate glass.

Tomas, the trainee, was the front-of-house man that day — his first time on duty as greeter after a year's training and it had been quite hard

21

enough even before that brutal moment. Saturdays were always busy but this one was quite mad. The salon, as Herr Maschmann preferred to call it, was crowded as never before with nervous foreigners trying to leave Berlin. They had spilled over from the leather sofas onto the dark brown benches that ran along the walls and now twenty or more were having to stand and wait for the harassed agents at the tables to attend to them. Tomas's head was full of lists and intelligent guesses. *Café au lait* for the French couple, certainly. Mineral water for the Italian lady with the white gloves and the giveaway 'Bad Reichenhall' spa sticker on her leather valise? Safe enough. Black coffee for the fat Yankee in the awful suit. He was confident of that one because the man had been in yesterday and rejected the offer of milk with abrupt American dismissal. They had all taken their drinks from his tray and he was quietly delighted that Herr Direktor Maschmann had noticed. Herr Maschmann set high standards. He believed that the best travel agents must be able to identify their customers' countries of origin, take an informed guess from their demeanour as to the nature of their problem and be halfway to solving it before a single word had been spoken. The greeter was first in the firing line and offering the right refreshment without having to ask was the test to show that a trainee could grow to be an essential cog in the Weltreisebureau's machine.

Then the street door opened again and Tomas was at a loss. He tried to mask his uncertainty, baffled by the latest arrival. The man was quite young, dressed curiously informally with a jacket of thin leather, chamois perhaps, over an open-necked plain cotton shirt and whipcord trousers cut a little like riding breeches. He was the tallest man in the whole room by a hand's breadth, tanned in a working man's way by regular exposure to the wind and sun but Tomas could see he was not a working man. The clothes were expensive despite their informality. They looked as if they could take a beating and still hang smooth. A man of action, he was confident and alert, cleanshaven in a city where moustaches were the universal badge of trust and dignity. His hair was short, wavy and the yellow side of brown and as his eyes searched the rooms whatever he saw there had brought a slight smile to his face. East Coast American, thought Tomas? Perhaps. Doesn't give a pfennig for our old-world ways. English? Less likely. The English came dressed for city business and always seemed uncomfortable as if they might be made to look absurd by not understanding something. Scandinavian? A wild idea. He had never had to deal with one of those and had no clue what they preferred to drink. If it had been later in the afternoon, he would have poured a small glass of the Glenfarclas malt whisky but Herr Maschmann would not allow alcohol before six so instead he prepared a cup of Thomas Lipton's Ceylon tea, added a slice of lemon on a saucer, another cup of Mocha Sidamo coffee and a small Meissen-copy jug of milk and went towards the man.

'May I offer you refreshment?' he asked in

English and watched as the man took the cup of tea.

'Thank you,' he said. A friendly smile but nothing to help him tell for sure. Some strange burr in those two words.

'How may we help you?'

'I have a circular note to exchange.'

A circular note. Thos. Cook's ingenious paper certificate, proof against thieves and exchangeable for whatever currency the holder desired.

'Our Herr Wildberger at the far end table has three clients waiting but he will be with you as soon as possible, Mr . . . ?'

'Fraser,' said the man.

Not quite English, thought Tomas and saw Herr Maschmann frowning across the room at the insurance cup of coffee left on his tray, but the next moment that joined the mass of small irrelevancies which history constantly wipes from its memory because that was the moment the window came bursting in.

The glass split across its centre with a crack, held briefly together by the laminating layer that had doubled the already massive cost of the window, then sagged inwards as the customers nearest to it scattered in alarm, women inside screaming and men outside shouting. One heavy slab felled Herr Maschmann and Tomas stared through the space where the glass had been to see a crowd of grinning, cat-calling soldiers on the pavement outside. One of them, a beefy country lad who stank of beer, stepped in through the gap, holding his rifle in front of him.

'Engländer!' he shouted, 'Komm sofort hier.'

The customers watched him warily. Two more of his fellows stepped inside after him. Tomas looked down at Herr Maschmann but he was inert on the floor. This is Berlin, he thought, not Montevideo or Shanghai. These things do not happen in Berlin. Our soldiers are disciplined people not beasts. Everyone in the room stayed silent. No one was admitting to being English.

'You,' said the soldier, grinning at the fat Yankee. 'Papieren. Papers.' He prodded the man in the lurid tweed suit. 'English, no.'

'Don't do that to me,' said the Yankee. 'I'm an American.'

The soldier slung his rifle over his shoulder and tried to grab the man's briefcase from him but the man hung on grimly, his face flushing. 'Let go, you bastard,' he said. 'What the hell's got into you guys?'

The outrageous and unexpected violence had frozen everyone else in the room. The other staff were gaping from behind their desks. Tomas's moment came and he stepped forward, shaking with fury and the adrenalin of action. 'He is our valued customer,' he said firmly in German. 'He is to be respected. You are drunk. This is a disgrace.'

The soldier ignored him and punched the American in the side of the head with his right fist while he tugged at the bag with the other. Tomas went for the soldier with his hands and feet, flailing away to no apparent effect, slapping him on the side of his face. The man had the look of a street brawler and began to laugh. Then a rifle butt hit Tomas from behind and he went down hard on the floor, face first, to the sound of a breaking nose. He lay still and a trickle of blood ran out from under his head.

That was when the new arrival, the mysterious Fraser with no tie and no moustache and no clear country of origin, stepped forward and ripped the rifle from the first soldier's shoulder. He swung it round into the midriff of the boy's attacker, lifting his knee sharply into the man's face as he doubled up so that the soldier dived to the floor, then held it like a club. In a second, the rest of the drunken troop watching from the street outside came leaping through the window into the room. He held them off for a few moments, felled another one with a blow to the forehead then four of them grabbed him. The first soldier let go of the American's bag, turned and punched the mystery man Fraser, now pinioned by the rest of the gang, in the stomach. The man lifted both feet and kicked him hard. He stumbled back and at that moment a voice barked a harsh command from the broken window. All eyes turned to a German officer who stepped through the broken glass into the room, looking around him, frowning. He was young and by himself but he was bursting with outraged authority and he grabbed the first soldier by the arm. The others fled.

'Was ist hier passiert?' he demanded. 'What is going on?'

'You speak English? These goddam hoodlums of yours are busting the place up,' said the fat American. 'See what they did?'

'I do speak English,' said the officer. 'As well

as you do and very possibly rather better. They are responsible for all this?' He looked at the wreckage of the window. Tomas was getting to his knees, shaking his bloody head. Other men of the Weltreisebureau went to lift the heavy glass off their Direktor.

The officer was still gripping the ringleader by the arm. He barked a question at him, listened to the answer and gave a derisive snort. 'He says they were arresting English spies,' said the officer. 'He believes this office is a meeting place for such people. Let me see now, are there any English spies here?'

'Me, I'm a newsman from the US of A,' said the fat man in the ugly suit, 'Chester K. Hoffman, and you can bet your last dollar that the citizens of New York are going to be reading all about this.'

'And you, sir?' asked the officer, turning his head to the man who had stepped in. 'You are surely English but are you a spy?'

'I got my US papers right here,' said the man, dusting down his jacket. 'The name's Fraser. Are you going to deal with these guys or do I need to make a formal complaint through the American authorities?'

'I am truly sorry for what has happened here. It is completely unacceptable and I can assure you they will be dealt with under military law. I am arresting this man and it will be easy enough to trace his fellows. They will certainly all be in the same unit. This is not the way the German army normally behaves, that I can promise you.'

27

'You sure of that?' said the fat American. 'This ain't the first place they wrecked since I been here.'

'There are always some who get over-excited,' said the officer. 'I expect your army is the same. Soldiers on their last day of leave. They hear the latest news and they respond badly. You have to understand that the mobilization is quite disturbing. Our men feel threatened by France, by England, by Italy, by Russia. They are told over and over again that enemies want our land and are massing at almost every frontier.'

'You're kidding me,' said the American. 'You believe that?'

'Me? I am fortunate enough to see more than one side. I was educated in England, you know.' He looked hard at the other man and something unexpected passed between them. 'And you, Mr Fraser, you too are American?' said the officer. 'Really?'

Fraser nodded and the German officer smiled. 'Wait here one moment,' he said. 'I will find a fellow officer to lock up this idiot then I will return. I will come back to make sure this mess is sorted out properly.' He smiled. 'Seventy-three not out if I remember correctly,' he said. 'Not bad for an American.' Then he dragged the drunken man away. Fraser watched him go then turned to inspect the recovering Herr Maschmann. The newspaperman joined him. 'What did he mean by that?' he said.

'I think you would have to ask him.'

'He's right. You're no American.'

Fraser shrugged.

When Herr Maschmann and Tomas had been dealt with and the glass cleared out of the way, the staff by common consent attended to the circular note and the American's cable first of all.

'Let me buy you a drink,' said Hoffman afterwards. 'Guess I owe you that. It's early but could you eat some supper? I'm at the Adlon. They do good food.'

'I know, I'm staying there too,' said Fraser but as they reached the pavement and turned towards the hotel, he glanced the other way. 'Give me a few minutes,' he said, 'I have some business to conclude. I'll join you there.'

The American walked off and Fraser stood there watching the approaching German officer. The German had a smile on his face. 'I insulted you, didn't I?' he said when he came up. 'It was seventy-four, not seventy-three.'

'It was,' said Fraser, offering his hand. 'And as you know, these things do matter. I remember your first name is Otto and your bowling is terrifyingly rapid but I'm afraid the rest of your name is lost to me, save that it had a lot of syllables.'

'It is a very German name,' the other man said, 'and anyway my pals at Oxford preferred to call me Freddy. A bowler and a batsman, they quickly find out what truly matters about each other so let us accept those two small lies, that I am really Freddy and you are really American Are we friends?'

'I think we may be, strange though that may be.'

'Then as one friend to another may I make a suggestion?'

'Please do.'

'Leave Berlin. Leave Germany. Go back across the narrow Channel to that very pleasant island of yours, so pleasant that I wish it were still my own home. When you get there, close your ears to news from Europe.'

'Why?'

'Do you have to ask that? I don't believe so. You did not come to drink our beer and eat our sausages and I hope your papers will stand up to close inspection because, believe me, they will soon need to.'

'Can I get a night's sleep first?'

'One. Possibly even two, but not three.' He frowned and took out a very English pocket watch on a very English chain. 'I am on duty,' he said. 'I have no more time but please don't take anything I have said as a pointless threat. It is an anxious and respectful warning from a terrifying bowler to a redoubtable batsman. Run fast and keep your wicket intact.' He saluted, turned on his heel and walked rapidly away.

★   ★   ★

'Let's start over,' said the American when they were sitting down in the Adlon's restaurant. 'Chester K. Hoffman, like I said. Special Correspondent for the *New York Sentinel*. The finest newspaper of that name anywhere in the whole world.'

'K standing for what?'

30

'K standing for the space between J and L.'

'William Fraser,' said the other, putting out his hand, 'with nothing that need detain us between the W and the F. My friends call me Willy.'

'Okay, Fraser. Come clean. You're about as American as my wife's piano.'

'She has a half-American piano?'

'No, it's all Polish. You mean to say you're half-American?' He looked the other man up and down. 'Which half?'

'Bottom half. I have an American mother.'

'English father?'

'No, he's . . . he was Scottish.'

The American did not seem to notice the hesitation. 'Same thing.'

'If you insist on saying such insulting things, you will have to eat by yourself.'

The American grinned and Willy began to relax. It was two weeks since he had last stopped moving and several more since he had sat down to talk to someone just for the sake of talking, especially someone who understood that wit and irony may be a good recourse in a tight corner. He looked at Hoffman and saw a worried, determined man dressed for a different continent, entirely out of place in this city at this critical time. 'It's good to meet you, Chester,' he said and found he meant it.

'So come clean. You really got US papers?'

'I really have. It comes in handy when my English ones don't work so well.'

'Listen, pal, what are you doing here? Whole place is about to blow in our faces. You don't sound like a citizen of the US of A and you don't

31

look like one either. There's going to be a lot more crap like that flying in a week or two. Anyone with any sense already got out of town.'

'People keep telling me that. You think war is coming?'

'Hell yes. The red glutton is stirring.'

'An unusual expression.'

'Only wish I'd invented it. My pal Irvin S. Cobb of the *Evening Post* has a felicitous way with his words. Well, I tell a tiny lie, he ain't my pal yet. Probably never will be. Guy like that, he's the competition, see? Friendly when there ain't nothing happening then liable to rat on you the minute the story gets going. You know why I'm staying in this goddam two dollars an hour hotel, which runs out at twice my daily limit so I'll be paying back the *Sentinel* for ten years by the time I get home? Because that's the only way I can keep my eye on Irvin S. Cobb, not to mention Walter Watling of the *Tribune* who is even more likely to get the best story. I'm happiest when I can see what they're up to. Then I play catch-up.'

'Have you been over here long?'

'Me? I'm the new boy. One week. First time out of good old New York. My usual beat is the East Side murders. This is a whole new piece of wax and they don't even speak my language here.'

'Did they give you a choice?'

'Kinda choice that goes 'you ever want to get anywhere in this office, you shift your ass on to that boat tomorrow morning.' They don't give a rat's ass one way or the other.'

32

'Difficult for you.'

'So, give me something to go on. Who are you anyway, Mr Willy Fraser? Were they right back there? Are you maybe some kind of spy?'

For a moment Willy wondered if perhaps he was. He no longer knew quite what he was. 'As I understand it,' he said, 'and of course you're the authority on the use of the English language, you're a spy if you're uncovering secrets in one country on behalf of the government of a different country. Would that about cover it?'

'I guess.'

'Then, no. I'm not a spy. I'm finding out stuff entirely for myself. I'm seeing the sights.'

'Makes no sense. I see a good-looking guy who looks like he might be a soldier risking getting his face mashed saving folk he never met before and here he is in a country that's fixing to fight the whole neighbourhood and where you only have to know ten words of German to know they hate all Englishmen right now. You telling me that's a holiday?'

'I already told you, I'm a Scot. We hate the English too for at least five days a week. I'm travelling for the sake of it. That doesn't make me interesting.' He stared at Chester who was inspecting his plate of cold meats with even more suspicion than he had levelled at his companion.

'Don't they know about pastrami around here?' he said. 'What I'm saying is you interest me in a whole bunch of different ways. Makes me want to tell your tale. The hero who saved our correspondent — that kind of story — so

33

why don't you just come out with it and tell me why you're here?'

'Why would I? I live in a universe of one at the moment and that suits me.'

The American took a swig of lager and scowled at the glass. 'Hey listen, Willy. You really don't mind me calling you Willy? Fact of the matter is, I'm out of my depth. Put me in a Brooklyn courthouse and I can look at the guys in the dock and give you their life story word perfect. I can tell by their clothes and the shine on their nose and the way their shoulders hang even before they open their mouth. I'm never wrong — famous for it. Don't even need to hear their names — I know if they're Sicilian mob or Italian hoods or Corsican bandits or just plain old Irish boyos out for a light-fingered evening to help them buy their beer. I can spot the loan sharks and the numbers boys. I could write their family trees, every one of them going back two generations, maybe more. Over there, I look at people and I just know the truth of them. Here, I'm floating face down in the water — no idea what I'm staring at. Might as well be on the moon. The boys on the desk back home spiked every single goddam word I filed so far, so this afternoon's little upset is the best story I got except it don't work without you in it. Give me a break. There's this word I rarely get to use. Hurts my lips just to say it.'

'What word is that?'

'Please?'

Willy laughed and sliced off a fine piece of leberwurst. He speared a gherkin and swallowed it down. He found himself liking the fat man for his honesty and the game might drive away the sour residue of the afternoon's violence. 'I'll offer you a deal,' he said. 'Let's see how good you really are, Chester. You can tell me ten things about me from what you've observed so far and every one you get right, you can ask me a question and I promise I will answer it truthfully.'

'Done. One. You're . . . let's see now, you have to be around about thirty years of age. Am I right?'

'That depends what you mean by 'around about'. I could say you're around about forty. Would that be right?'

'Hell no. I'm thirty-seven next month.' Chester sounded offended.

'So three years out equals wrong? Then you're wrong. Nine to go.'

'You ain't married.'

'And you say that because?'

'Because look at you. You're not dressed right for the city. Look at me. I got a good suit on and a necktie that matches the suit. See that?'

'You mean your wife chooses your clothes?'

'Sure she does. My Ruthie, she walks past this shop window and she says, 'Hey, Chez.' That's what she calls me see, Chez. She says, 'Hey, Chez, you'd look damned fine in that one. So I go in and I buy me this first-class tweed suit and you know what, it fits me like a glove straight off. She has a keen eye for colour, that girl. I picked a good one.'

Willy looked at the suit reflecting the glancing

sunlight from the window with a faint sheen of metallic purple. His childhood had been spent in close contact with tweed. Shorts that chafed, jackets that hung heavy on his shoulders as they sucked in the mist on the slopes above the house. Gilfillan always had the best tweed, strong and soft and old, matching the colour of the mountain slopes.

'That's tweed, you say?'

'Sure. You should know that. Scotch tweed cut by a master tailor in Brooklyn.'

'Brooklyn's your neighbourhood?'

'Lived there like my father before me. Met Ruthie in school.'

'In sight of the bridge?'

'Only if you climb on the roof. West side of Vinegar Hill.'

'Next?'

'You're in the military.'

'Wrong.'

'You kidding me? I watched you back there. You looked like a soldier to me.'

'In what way?'

'You watched what they were doing then you did what you had to do. Controlled. Straight to it. One against ten. That was brave.'

'Chester, I have a strong sense of injustice. I have always found it hard to stand by at times like that.'

'Ah, I get it. You *were* a soldier once.'

For a moment Willy felt like denying it but truth seemed more important than his personal feelings. Putting soldiering into a box marked 'the past' disconcerted him. It was a loss he did not yet want to acknowledge. 'Correct,' he said.

'Until when?'

'You only get to ask direct questions at the end. You have to earn them first.'

'Your father was in the military.'

'Also correct. Do sons usually follow their father's trade in Brooklyn? Was your father a newspaperman?'

'Hell no. My pop was in the rackets. That's why I got my break with the *Sentinel* on the courts beat.'

'Was?'

'He got snuffed. Tried to quit. They didn't like that. How many guesses I got so far?'

'Three right. Five facts to go. Are your sons going to follow you into your trade?'

'I got one kid and she's a she. Only four years old so, no way. Listen, I know jack shit about Scotland so help me out. Which city do the rich folk live in?'

'Edinburgh.'

'So here's number six. You live in some kind of fancy town-house in Edinburgh.'

'Wrong in all respects. Four more.'

'All right, all right. You came here by train.' Chester looked smug. He was sure that was an easy one.

'Wrong.'

'By automobile.'

'Wrong again.' He was quite sure the American would not guess this one.

'Goddam. What else is there?' Chester cast around for a more promising line of enquiry.

Willy glanced up and saw a woman sit down

37

by herself at a table across the aisle, an unusual enough sight in the Adlon even without the Italian elegance of her long silk dress and the fierce, tanned beauty of her face.

Chester followed his gaze. 'Jeez,' he said, 'that's something.'

'Back to work, Chester.'

'All right, all right. You don't have no brothers and sisters.'

'Interesting. True if I ignore the double negative but I wonder how you knew?'

'I told you, I'm good. Me, I got two older brothers, Louie and Isaac. They gave me a hard time but I kinda live more in the world than you do. I'm right there alongside my fellow men. You? You got an outsider feel about you, like you've always watched it all from somewhere else.'

That's clever, thought Willy. This man I have only just met has seen something I know to be true but did not know to be obvious. He looked at Chester with renewed interest, reminding himself not to judge on first impressions.

'Louie and Isaac? Are you on good terms with them now?'

'Isaac, yeah, so far as it goes. Ruthie don't like his wife. Louie? He's in the rackets, down in Jersey City. He got no time for me and what I do.'

'All right. Last one.'

Chester smiled. Willy knew he had been storing this one up.

'Okay, this one counts double. The German officer back there at the Reisebureau. He knew who you were and you knew how he knew.'

Willy nodded slowly. 'Yes, that's true.'

'Gonna tell me how?'

'Only if you ask me as one of the, let me see, six bonus questions you have somehow managed to earn.'

'Somehow? Hell, I've found out a whole bunch of stuff about you. I told you I got the skill. You should try that on me sometime. Know where you'd get? Nowhere. I'd be a mystery to you at the end just like I am right now. So answer it. That's my first question. How do you know each other?'

'Because we played on opposite sides in the Varsity Match of 1908.'

'What in hell is the Varsity Match? Don't count that as extra. You gotta give me full answers.'

'Oxford versus Cambridge at Lord's.'

'What kind of sport is Lord's? Is that like baseball?'

'Lord's is a place and the sport practised there is cricket, Chester, you vulgarian. The annual university match at Lord's cricket ground. I had no idea he was German at the time. Then I saw on the scorecard he was listed as Otto followed by something horribly complicated. He took six wickets for Oxford in the first innings and got me caught behind for thirty. We almost had them in the second innings, but he wasn't quite right. I was seventy-four not out.'

'So were you some kind of professional cricket guy?'

Willy shuddered. 'It's an amateur match,' he

said patiently. 'I was up at Cambridge — that means I was a student there. He was up at Oxford.'

'And you say you remember him from that?'

'Of course. When you've stared at a man hurling a hard leather ball at you at a hundred miles an hour, their face does tend to stick in your mind.'

'And now he's all dressed up in soldier gear and you're on different sides?'

Willy considered that and it seemed bizarre.

'There'll be no tea in the pavilion afterwards,' he said quietly but Chester looked blank.

'Okay, okay. Next question. The military thing. What happened?'

'I was an officer in the Hussars. That's part of the cavalry. I had, shall we say, a misunderstanding with my Colonel and I resigned my commission.'

'What kind of misunderstanding?'

'It was to do with the way I hunted.'

'You mean the red coat, tally-ho British thing?'

'We call the colour 'pink', my dear chap. He wasn't just my Colonel. He was my MFH, Master of Foxhounds of my hunt, the Galloway — much more important than a mere colonel. He didn't like me much. He used to swear at me for riding too near the hounds.'

'Ain't that the whole idea?'

'Not the way I did it. I prefer to see what's coming up and where we're going. I hate following the crowd. He was always complaining I got in the way.' He could see the Colonel, bright red in the face, shouting at him in front of

40

everybody just like a sergeant-major insulting a raw recruit on a parade ground. All of his friends in the hunt, watching him to see what he would do and what could he do? Military privilege being misused in the civilian world — a higher officer using his invulnerability to insult a junior — so Willy had to bite his lip.

'That's why you quit your regiment? Jeez, everything they say about the Brits is true.'

'Well, not just that. It was a matter of what I was hunting.'

'Not just foxes? You got wolves over there?'

'No wolves.'

'What then?'

Willy had a brief distracting memory of Marion under him in the thicket, of mud and scent and their horses panting. 'Something he didn't approve of,' he said softly. 'Let me ask you a question. Fair exchange. What were you doing at the Thomas Cook office?'

'Sending a cable. I needed to wire a story. The guys here . . . ' he hunched forward and lowered his voice. 'Our embassy guys, they say don't trust the hotels. They copy the overseas wires to this Abteilung outfit.'

'Abteilung?'

'Yeah. Abteilung IIIb. Bad, bad people. They're the ones who look for spies. Dungeons and nasty tricks. My guys said go to Thomas Cook, it's safer. My turn. What's the real reason you're here in Berlin at this precise moment?'

'No mystery. I told you. I've been touring around.'

When they finished the food, they moved to

the leather sofas in the room beyond and talked amiably of not much in particular.

'I saw this guy downtown,' Chester said. 'In a toy store. He was the proprietor, I guess. Made me think. He took this set of lead soldiers out of the window. What do you call those horsemen with the lances?'

'Uhlans.'

'It was a crying shame. They were bright red and gold and green and he was painting them grey. What was that about?'

'Accuracy. You must have seen the new uniforms. They call it *feldgrau* and it's not quite grey and it's not quite green but you put a man dressed in that into a wood or a field and you're going to have a lot of trouble seeing him.'

'But these were for kids. You telling me they wouldn't like the bright colours better?'

'German kids? They want what they see marching past out there. I can explain about the bright colours.'

'You mind if I take some notes?'

So Willy sipped his wine and told Chester about military days gone by, about old-fashioned black powder and swirling smoke and how bright uniforms were the only thing that could separate friend from foe in that lethal fog. All the time he was talking, half his mind was in Scotland, in his teens, with his father still interested enough to explain the smoke in the picture, telling him how they finally learnt the advantage of khaki when they had to fight the Boers in the drab and dusty veldt.

'Smokeless propellant, you see,' he said to

Chester. 'That's what made the difference — the end of black powder. No more thick walls of smoke rolling across the battlefield. You don't need bright colours any more. The duller the better.'

They drank more wine and at the end of the first bottle Chester started talking about Ruthie and the halfway point of the second bottle took him to his childhood, but perhaps both of them were thinking about toy soldiers because Chester suddenly said, 'I was given one. Bronx Benny gave it me when the cops took my dad,' and Willy knew he meant a soldier. 'It was all made out of wood,' said Chester. 'Only toy I had. I guess you had soldiers?'

Willy shook his head. His father had soldiers. He didn't. 'I stopped playing when I was little,' he said.

Chester went on with an interminable tale of Bronx Benny and some complex fraud and Willy drifted back again to the Highland silence. He had jigsaws, not soldiers, and he could remember them in the order of their arrival in his life. The first was a blurry landscape he hated because it was cheap and the pieces weren't well cut. The second was that battle scene of cannon firing in some Napoleonic war, men peering fearfully into the dense smoke of the barrage and falling to their knees wounded by invisible musketeers hidden from their view. It had always disturbed him and he had turned it over, painted his own picture on the back of the view from his high bedroom, looking past the Victorian battlements and the park down to the river which marked the place where the rocks and heather rose to the sky beyond. The third jigsaw was his favourite, found loose in a bag in Aunt Rose's cupboard when he went to visit and given to him when he reluctantly went back home.

He could see it now, an explorer in proper explorer's clothes, pockets all over his jacket, strong boots, a good leather bag over one shoulder. The man was perched on a high pinnacle of rock staring across a great plain below him to a distant sea, pointing with a long outstretched arm to a place near the horizon where, of course, one piece was missing. It was the piece on the far-off coast that must have held the mystery to explain the delighted excitement on the explorer's face. Later, when Willy had to live with Aunt Rose in Inverary, he had searched the cupboards for the missing piece with no success, so he had carefully cut one from card, glued together in layers to the right thickness. He had painted it to match the coast and tried to think of something good enough to paint on it, something to justify the man's expression. He was still thinking.

'You gone away somewhere?' said Chester.

'Sorry. What did you say?'

'I asked where you live when you're back home.'

'Nowhere really.'

'You don't have a house?'

'There's a family place. It's called Grannoch. I suppose it's mine now but it doesn't feel like it. I don't plan to live there.'

'Big house?'

44

'No, no. Not really.'

Chester screwed up his eyes. 'I had you figured for a rich guy,' he said.

'Oh I see. No, I mean it's not really a house at all. I suppose it's what you would call a castle.'

'You got a *castle* and you don't live there? Why the hell not?'

Willy was saved from answering by the appearance of the Head Waiter proffering an envelope.

'From the lady over there,' he breathed quietly into Willy's ear.

Willy glanced across the room and there was the exotic stranger sitting in an armchair looking at him with a slight smile. 'Freeze, Chester,' he said. 'Don't look round.' He opened it, drew out a note and glanced at it.

'I have a fine bottle of Krug,' it said in a bold, slanted hand. 'I am not strong enough to open it by myself. Are you? Room 207 in one hour if so.'

'What are you doing this evening?' asked Chester. 'I'm catching a late show. Want to come?'

'I'm afraid I have a prior commitment,' said Willy.

4

Sunday, 2 August 1914.

'Any messages?' Chester K. Hoffman had checked at the desk three times already that morning and the clerk simply shook his head without even troubling himself to look at the pigeonholes. Chester had been trying to find Willy since soon after nine. There was no answer when he pounded on the door of room 315 but Willy had not left his key at the desk. Chester was in a state of profound unease. The news was all bad. He had no idea where Irwin S. Cobb had gone but there was no doubt at all about the movements of Walter Watling who had left Berlin in a big hurry. Chester had a sinking feeling that events were leaving him far, far behind. He was heading back to his room along the second-floor corridors when a door opened and Willy came out, looking back into the room, saying something. Chester stopped short and stared at him in surprise. The number on the door was 207. He walked up to Willy, looked past him into the room and saw a woman in a silk dressing gown, the woman from the restaurant.

Willy closed the door behind him and turned to see Chester watching him with raised eyebrows.

'Something wrong?' he said.

'What were you doing in there?' said Chester.

46

'That ain't your room.'

'An acute observation but somewhat indiscreet. Perhaps I was advising a friend on her investments.'

'Since last night? I been looking for you.'

'Chester, there are some questions better left unasked. Her portfolio is complex.'

'Jesus, Willy. I gotta talk to you. Not here. I need a beer.'

Chester turned away from the lifts and led Willy down the stairs. 'You got no self-preservation about you?' he said, stopping halfway down. 'Can't you see trouble when it's staring at you? That lady spells set-up to me.'

'You have very little confidence in my charms, Chester.'

'I didn't take you for an idiot. She has to be with the bad guys. I lay you fifty bucks they went through your room while you were busy advising.'

'Of course they did. That was the whole point. There's nothing in my room they would find remotely interesting so now perhaps they'll leave me alone.'

'The whole point?'

'Well, most of it.'

'Let's get out of this place,' said Chester. They walked through the foyer and the doorman stared at them as they approached. He came from Munich and he had seen every sort of mismatched pair pass through his hotel but rarely so mismatched as these. He suppressed a shudder of distaste at the sight of the fat American, sweaty and ill-dressed, scuttling along

47

on fast-moving legs to keep up with the man next to him. The man's eyes were too close together and his chin was a purplish blue that almost matched his suit. As for the companion, what was he doing with a schmuck like that? The doorman was a movie fan who found more pleasure in male leads than vapid females. This man made him think of John Barrymore in *An American Citizen*, with his aquiline face and wavy hair, but he was fairer than Barrymore and he had the wide eyes of Hoot Gibson. Hoot Gibson featured in the *Shotgun Jones* poster the doorman had filched from the cinema and pinned up on his bedroom wall. He opened the door and let them out on to Pariser Platz, appreciating the way the tall man loped along, one stride to the Yank's two.

Excited crowds were milling around the Unter den Linden, waving flags and watching the cavalry squadrons clip-clopping through the side portals of the Brandenburg Gate, stiff Uhlans with their lances held perfectly at the vertical.

'Do you see that?' Chester said. 'It's a rule now. Only the Kaiser gets to use the middle arch.'

'And do *you* see how they're dressed?' said Willy. 'No more bright colours. That's the new field uniform. Grey means business. Your toyshop man with the paintbrush was keeping up with the times.'

The breeze carried bursts of song wrapped round the smell of wurst and onions frying on coke braziers. A horse lifted its tail and the moment the shit slapped on to the road a youngster in a leather jerkin darted between the

48

columns of lancers to shovel it into a bucket, still steaming.

'These fellas think of everything,' said Chester. 'Now you see it. Now you don't. That's what I call organization.' He put on a Homburg hat, the same colour as his suit.

Over two steins of beer in a side-street bar he said, 'Something you need to know. It's all on the move. The wires say they crossed the Moselle River into Luxembourg.'

'Who did?'

'These guys. The Germans. Who the hell do you think? Wouldn't be much of a story if it was the Luxemburgers. It's a big deal. Listen, I'm in trouble. Cobb and Watling have both left town. I got no idea where Cobb's gone but I know exactly where Watling went and that's worse cos I don't have the slightest idea why.'

'Where?'

'I don't know how you say it. I got the busboy to write it down for me.' He opened a notebook and showed Willy.

'Liège?'

'Lee-age, is that it?'

'Almost.'

'So where is that?'

'Belgium, near the German border.'

'What the hell? This is how it happened, see? I booked to see the same show as Watling last night. First night of some musical cabaret thing with a long German name.'

'A strange way to spend the evening with a war looming.'

'Like I said, I'm playing 'follow my leader'

49

here. Watling went and that was good enough for me. Anyway, he don't even wait for the end of the show. He gets up halfway through, runs back here, packs in a big hurry and goes off with his tame snapper, little Al, in a very expensively hired Benz automobile.'

'To Liège?'

'That's what I said.'

'You left the show when he did?'

'Course I did. You got some kind of thinking look going on there. I need a second opinion on that show. Whatever Watling saw changed his mind. It's the only hook I got. He saw something on that stage and he went.'

'What sort of show was it?'

'It's got all kinds of army stuff in it, like it's some kind of burlesque version of a military pageant. Willy — still okay if I call you Willy? You know about that kind of thing. You were a soldier just like Watling. I never did that stuff.'

'*Was*, Chester. I *was* a cavalryman. I quit. There are many things I would much rather be doing.'

'Like what?'

'Like sticking ginger up all these horses' arses.'

Willy looked at the little American and the sweat on his face and his anxious eyes. He tried to put himself in Chester's garish shoes, thousands of miles from all that was familiar, missing his Ruthie, on the edge of flunking his first big opportunity to make his mark, and he felt that old familiar slide inside him towards helping an underdog. He tried to resist it. 'Maybe Watling has a girl in Liège.'

50

'He ain't like you. Walter Watling got no time for girls. All he has time for is work and he's been three steps ahead of me all the way so far. Famous for it. He was in Sarajevo, for Christ's sake. How did he know to be in Sarajevo that day? Okay, he wasn't on the corner where it all happened but he was only two blocks away. Claims he even heard the shots. If he's spending the *Tribune*'s dollars on fast cars there's a reason because, believe me, he will have to justify every cent to the guys in the back office when he gets back home.'

Chester was at least a brave underdog. He had taken this assignment and he wasn't giving up on it. Willy began to analyse the situation. 'And you think this was because of something he saw in a *musical?* Anyway, how can I go? It's Sunday. The theatres are closed.'

'Oh yes? So closed that I'm holding the ticket I already bought you right here. They're making a special exception for reasons of patriotism. I need you to see the matinée. Curtain's up in two hours. 'Vo-ran-veer something or other.' Just do this for me, Willy. You can walk round there. It's close by. You go down Glinkastrasse and Behrenstrasse runs right across it. You can't miss the Metropol. It's big. Take care. Merge in with the crowd. Don't draw any attention.'

A group of women waving flags broke into lilting, mournful song, their faces rapt, ecstatic.

'*Lieb Vaterland kann ruhig sein*
Fest steht und treu die Wacht
Die Wacht am Rhein!'

51

'Attention? Me?' said Willy. 'Wouldn't dream of it. Oh look, you remember you asked me how I was travelling? Excuse me, gentlemen.' A mob of young soldiers was clustered around something just ahead of them by the kerb. They turned at the sound of his voice and revealed a very large white motorcycle. Chester stared at it. The shining paintwork of the frame cradled a big silver engine. A short mast was bolted to the handlebars.

'Goddam,' Chester said. 'Please tell me that thing's not yours.'

'You should be proud. That *thing* is best quality American iron from Aurora, Illinois — that is a Thor motorcycle, the fastest *thing* on the road today. I bought it for that very reason. I had it shipped from America all the way to Scotland and I rode it here without it breaking down once. Bow down and worship.'

Chester shook his head so hard that his belly wobbled. 'Are you mad?'

'Engländer?' asked the nearest soldier, his eyes suspicious above a walrus moustache.

'English? Oh good heavens no,' said Willy. 'What an absurd idea. Nein, nein, nein.' He reached into the bike's leather pannier bag, pulled out a rolled-up flag and clipped it to the handlebar mast. The Stars and Stripes fluttered in the breeze.

'Amerikanischer,' said Chester loudly, then grabbed his sleeve and hissed at him. 'Don't mess with them. They got guns. You're travelling on *that*? You want everybody to notice you?'

'Yes I do,' said Willy, 'I want them to notice

me in a very particular way. What's the matter? It's an American bike. I have American papers.'

'And an English accent.'

'Scottish. I told you.'

'Try talking more like me and less like Lord Kitchener.'

'Oder vielleicht wäre es besser, wenn ich so spreche?' It felt a little like showing off but Willy was proud of his accent. His mother's main contribution to his upbringing had been her insistence that the tutors who came to stay at the castle for the long summer holidays coached her son in all the skills he would need to be a citizen of the world. He had done well with the German and French but his course in Italian had been abruptly terminated by events. He didn't like to listen to Italian.

'Okay. You never told me you speak German.'

'Just like a well-educated American with a slight Boston accent.'

'You mean all the time, you been listening to what these guys were saying and not letting on? Like, back there in the travel bureau?'

'Of course.'

'You're a tricky guy.'

'Just cautious. I keep my aces close to my chest.'

'All the same, don't make a big song and dance at the show. The Kaiser's tough guys are looking out for foreign snoopers.'

'We're not at war, Chester. Not yet.'

'Don't hold your breath. I give it a week, maybe less.'

'Give me the ticket. I'll go and see your show.

53

I think I'll go and take a look around the city first.' Willy grinned at the soldiers, swung his leg over the motorcycle's saddle and heaved his weight backwards onto the kickstart. The engine spat, coughed and rumbled to life. Chester had to shout. 'There's a bar close by the theatre, the Weinstubenhaus Trarbach. Got that? T-R-A-R Trarbach. Meet me there after.'

Half an hour into the show, Willy was wishing he were almost anywhere else. The Metropol theatre was packed with sweating Germans roaring their approval from the hard seating. The show's laborious title translated as 'What is in our minds — tableaux from a greater past'. On stage, a man dressed in a metal cylinder waltzed awkwardly with a truly beautiful girl, as fragile as he was solid. He wore a conical silver hat. She wore a nun's habit with scalloped wings attached to her sleeves, all in pale fawn. He stamped and she glided as they sang a love song to each other. 'I am delicate and slender,' she sang, 'I fly above the clouds as light as a feather and elusive as a breath.'

The metal man roared a bass response. 'I blast the air with roaring smoke, the youngest child of mighty Krupp.'

The man next to Willy turned and blew a gale of beer across him. His eyes were gleaming. 'Gefällt Ihnen der Brummer?' he asked.

'Der Brummer?'

'Ja, der dicke Brummer. Sie sind nicht Deutscher?'

'American,' said Willy.

'So? I speak your tongue a small part also.'

'What is this Brummer?'

'I work for the Krupp,' his neighbour said proudly. 'It is the, what do you say, *auf Deutsch, der zweiund . . . Ah!*'

He broke off and twisted round. The man sitting behind him was leaning forward and his hand had gripped the other German's shoulder. He was looking hard at Willy. 'Ignore my drunken friend,' he said. 'It is just a shell . . . an ordinary artillery shell.'

'Nein,' said his neighbour. 'Es ist . . . '

'Sei still,' cut in the man behind him.

A Prussian, Willy thought and surely not there just by chance. Now he understood that metal suit and the shining conical hat. 'The new shell,' he said and nodded as if he knew what his neighbour was talking about. That earned him a sharp look.

★   ★   ★

Chester had commandeered a table in the Weinstubenhaus Trarbach and the wine bottle on the table was already almost empty. Around the bar, a crowd of soldiers bawled out another song. Willy listened.

'Was schiert uns Russe und Franzos?
Schuß wider Schuß und Stoß um Stoß!'

They pounded earthenware beakers on the bar to beat out the time. On and on it went and each verse ended in a roaring chorus,

55

'*Wir lieben vereint, wir hassen vereint,*
Wir alle haben nur einen Feind,
England!'

'That doesn't sound too friendly,' said Chester. 'What exactly are they saying?'

'That they don't give a damn about the Russians and the French. They'll trade blows if they have to. They say there is only one real enemy who crouches behind the dark grey flood, full of rage and envy. They will swear an oath cast in bronze that they will keep their single-minded hatred for England, their only real foe.'

'Keep working on the accent,' said Chester. 'Piece of luck you can sail under Yankee colours. Now let's talk about the show. Did you catch on to anything interesting?'

'Maybe. There's just one scene that made me think. The man dressed as a shell, the one who falls in love with the *Taube.*'

'*Taube?*'

'*Taube* means dove. That's what they call the aeroplane, and she calls him her '*Dicker Brummer*'. That means something like the thick, heavy grumbler. He's supposed to be an artillery shell.'

'Yeah, I got that. A shell made by Krupp but we know Krupp makes shells, right? No surprise there.'

'I don't have the complete answer but I think we had better change the subject because there was a Prussian gentleman taking a close interest in me in the theatre and right now he's heading our way. The tall man in the green coat.' Willy waved a welcoming hand at the man squeezing his way through the crowd of drinkers.

'He looks like trouble. What does he know about you?' said Chester.

'Nothing. Only that I'm American. Watch out, he speaks good English.'

'My friend,' said the Prussian as he reached them. Willy pulled out a chair and he sat down. He had the trim look and the clear eyes of a sailor or a man used to outdoors and hard riding.

'This is my friend Chester,' said Willy, and Chester reached a hand out to him.

'Chester K. Hoffman, travelling correspondent for the *New York Sentinel*,' he said. 'So you've already met my snapper, Willy.'

'Snapper? What is a snapper?'

'You might call it a photographer. I write the words. He's gonna take the pictures. I didn't quite catch *your* name.'

'I am Heinrich von Lettow.'

'A soldier? You look like you might be a general.'

Von Lettow shook his head. 'No, merely a background worker in affairs of government. A writer and a . . . snapper you say. Well, well. What do you think of our city?'

'Impressive,' said Chester. 'Getting more like my hometown every day. You got telephones all over, you got vending machines, you got electricity, electric trams, subways, department stores and boy, oh boy, you've got factories.'

'You have visited our *Fabrikstadt*?'

'That's factory land, right? I passed that way.'

'People are calling our city Elektropolis now.' Von Lettow smiled but his eyes did not. 'So, do tell me, gentlemen, are you the sort of Americans who are independently minded or are you perhaps still holding on to your old English heritage?'

'English heritage? You kidding? With a name like Hoffman, you can guess where my folks came from. English heritage is one of many things I do not have. That blue-eyed Anglo-Saxon apple pie, covered wagon pioneer history is so much bullshit anyhow. You should know most of us came from somewhere else.'

This time, the smile spread to von Lettow's eyes. 'And you, sir? Are you as independent as your colleague?'

'Independent?' said Willy in his best Boston accent. 'My mother's ancestors helped to win America's independence with rifles and cannon.'

'Ah! My felicitations. So I wonder, do you think your fellow Americans will support us if we are forced to protect our borders against the aggression of the English and their friends?'

'There are many Germans in America and most of us already showed what we thought of the British Empire by leaving it,' said Chester.

'Ah yes. The British Empire is what it is all about, I think. The British have taken more than their fair share of the world and now they want our share too. So you think America will stay out of it if there is some trouble?'

'I think America is a long way away.' Another bottle of Mosel arrived at the table and Chester filled three beakers. 'What was that song they were singing just now?' he asked.

'That? That was the '*Hassgesang gegen England*' — how would you say it? The hate song against England. It is very popular at the moment. It is written by the young Jew, Lissauer. I think it would not be good to be an Englishman in this city today. As I came here they were tearing down the signs on the English shops. You would not want to be mistaken for English. You should be thinking of leaving Germany perhaps.'

'Leaving?' said Chester. 'We got a job to do.'

They talked politely of Berlin, of restaurants, of good and bad hotels for the length of two more bottles then Willy shifted in his chair. 'How did you enjoy the show?' he asked the German. 'That girl was something, wasn't she? Very beautiful.'

'You have an eye for beautiful women? The *Taube* girl? You saw her wings? They are shaped just like the wings of our new scout aeroplane, a very graceful machine.'

'I did. I prefer the girl to the aeroplane. How about the guy with the shiny hat? He was big. That must be quite some piece of artillery.'

Von Lettow shrugged. 'Every army has shells. You have heard this evening's news I expect? We have been forced to declare war on Russia.'

'You have?' said Chester, shocked. 'Hell.'

'I guess they gave you no choice when they mobilized,' said Willy. 'We should have seen that one coming.' He reached to pour out more wine but the other man shook his head.

'Gentlemen,' he said. 'Will you visit me in my office tomorrow morning? We must, I think, discuss how we ensure your safety in these troubled times. Shall we say ten o'clock?' He handed Chester a card, stood up and saluted them. 'Please make sure you are there. I feel responsible for your safety and will make arrangements to protect you. If you do not come I cannot be responsible for what may happen to you. You will not be departing before then?' They watched him go.

'Did that sound just a little bit like a threat to you?' said Chester, looking at the card. 'I thought so. Bad guy. Our embassy people told me about that building. It's Abteilung IIIb. He works for Colonel Nicolai.'

'Meaning?'

'Meaning like I already told you, Abteilung IIIb are the hard men who catch spies. You're really not a spy, are you, Willy?'

'Not again. Suddenly it seems I'm a snapper. Where did that come from?'

'Seemed like a good idea at the time. My permit was made out yesterday. They got the word wrong. It was meant to say I could take a camera but they wrote down 'photographer' instead.'

'Do you want a ride back to the Adlon?'

'On that thing of yours? It would be safer to dance back naked shouting 'I love England'.'

★　★　★

Willy found a quiet table at a corner of the hotel bar and waited. The American was out of breath

60

when he arrived and clearly rattled.

'It's all going off,' he said, 'and I'm stuck here.'

'What happened?'

'You didn't see them? A whole train of trucks going down the road, stuffed full of soldiers. They got decorations all over, flowers and tree branches.'

'That bothers you?'

'The signs on the trucks bother me. There are slogans all over them.'

'Saying what? Did you understand them?'

'Listen, friend, even I can understand *'Nach Paris'*. They're heading for Paris and what's worse, Walter Watling has gone to Belgium which is, as we all know, a neutral country and I still don't know why.' He stopped and frowned. 'But before we get any deeper into this, I got a question for you because you and me are set to march into von Lettow's office tomorrow and that might not be the wisest thing I will ever do. They already locked up three of your guys.'

'Yes, they certainly did. Trench of the Marines, Brandon of the Royal Navy and Captain Bertrand Stewart of Stalcaire Castle. Stewart served under my father in South Africa. All imprisoned quite wrongly. Disgraceful.'

'You're kidding, right? They caught Stewart with plans of the Bremen dockyards.'

'An academic interest in naval architecture is no crime.'

'That's like you and investment portfolios is it?'

'Chester, it was your idea to say I was your camera person. Otherwise you could have denied any knowledge of me.'

'Hell, I'd just say the office hired you. Speaking of which, I see no sign of your lady friend. I guess she and von Lettow are comparing notes. Did you say anything to her which might not work too well with the fact of you being my snapper?'

'I took great care to distract her whenever she asked me a question. Anyway, stop worrying. Happily all three of those men have now been released.'

'Only because your King twisted his cousin the Kaiser's arm.'

'It's all right, Chester. Calm down. Nobody sent me and I'm not racing home to report back. As I said, I needed a break. Always thought I'd be in the cavalry for life. It came as a shock. I wanted something to distract me.'

'Needed to get away from a woman as well as the Colonel?'

'A little of that maybe.'

'She leave a hole in your heart or are you such a lady's man they just come and go?'

Willy shrugged but Chester wouldn't leave it. 'You gotta find the right woman while you got time. I got Ruthie. Life would be a bitch without her.'

'It's not for me. Not yet. Maybe not ever. I'm fine by myself so long as the adventures keep coming.'

'So you came looking for a war. Did your poppa take it hard, you quitting the service?'

'Yes, he took it very hard. As I said, he's dead.'

Chester looked momentarily nonplussed. 'And your momma too?'

'She left Scotland some time back. She lives in the Hamptons where her people come from.'

Chester sniffed. 'American aristocracy. Leaving you a castle to look after?'

'It's nothing grand. Fake arrow slits, weak battlements, leaking roof, that sort of thing.'

'Yeah but, Jeez, my Ruthie would have given anything to be raised in a castle.'

Really, thought Willy, even her childhood? Gilfillan's weekly letter was sitting in his pocket, sent to Berlin Poste Restante.

'*You will be surprised perhaps to hear,*' Gilfillan had written in his precise, slow lettering, '*that you had two visitors last week. Miss Wakeley rode over to ask if there was news of you and I told her all I could which did not take very long. She looked very fine and was anxious for your safety in such a troubled time.*' A long section about fencing followed and an unremarkable report on the health of the horses, then Gilfillan returned to the subject. '*The smith's visit puts me in mind of your other visitor. The lady wife of the Colonel came at mid-day on Tuesday. I am sorry. Her name has eluded me. I was left with the impression that she did not believe me when I told her you were overseas. She left in a great hurry on a chestnut mare with little apparent awareness that it was in sore need of reshoeing.*'

That was as rude as Gilfillan ever got, Willy had thought as he read it, profoundly glad that he had not been there. So, Marion had come to see him. The Colonel must be safely far away. He could imagine the stern set of Gilfillan's face.

'You're not really going to write about me, are you?' he asked Chester.

'I plan to, but I guess that depends what happens now. Broken glass don't do a whole lot to grab the front page when there's a war starting. Hey, what was all that garbage you gave von Lettow about how your mother's folk fought on the rebel side?'

'That's not what I said.'

'I'm a reporter. I remember these things. You told him they helped to win America's independence with rifles and cannon.'

'They did. That was because they fought on the English side and they were bloody awful soldiers. They only decided they were Americans after the English lost. Lucky I take after my father's family. The Frasers know how to shoot straight.'

Chester nodded. 'And my ancestors were hounded out of Germany for their beliefs, so let's get working. Tell me about this artillery stuff.'

'You know about howitzers? Big guns that fire big shells way up in the air at a steep angle.'

'Sure, so they can get through armour and concrete.'

'Yes. Everyone knows the French have a line of fortresses down their border strong enough to stand up to the biggest German guns. At the time, those were the twenty-eight centimetre howitzers. They're a bit worried because the Germans have been buying a new Skoda weapon they call the mountain gun. That's a thirty centimetre howitzer. Now the man next to me in the theatre was in a very breezy state, a few too many steins on the way in. He told me he works for Krupp and began to say the new shell is a 'zweiund' something. I guess he was going to say 'zweiunddreissig' but von Lettow reached over and stopped him halfway through. 'Zweiunddreissig' means . . . '

'I know what it means. I know enough German to pay a bar bill. It means thirty-two, right?'

'Yes. A thirty-two centimetre howitzer would be a mighty big shell and if it's true, those French forts down the Alsace border could well be in a lot of trouble.'

'Four centimetres more? You telling me they could stand up to a twenty-eight but not a thirty-two?'

'Perhaps geometry wasn't a big part of your curriculum. You raise the diameter by what is it, one-seventh? The shell's going to be fatter and longer.' He did rough sums in his head. 'That's half as much explosive again coming down out of the blue yonder with a whole lot more punch behind it.'

'Meaning the Germans could blast through the French forts and march right through to Paris? So why didn't Watling go to the French frontier?' Chester looked at Willy but Willy was staring at the floor, frowning, shaking his head.

'A thirty-two would be a monster. It would have to weigh, what, thirty tons at least?' He was thinking hard. 'You couldn't drag that through the Ardennes — too hilly by far. Anyway, what would a big howitzer's range be? Seven or eight miles? Try getting that ready for action anywhere near the French forts. The French would knock it out long before it was anywhere near ready to shoot, but Belgium?' He snapped his fingers. 'Neutral Belgium where nobody expects them? They can take it there by train, get it all ready on the German side of the border and nobody will spot it. Do you see? That's why your man has gone to Liège. It's got the roads and the railways and it's the bung in the bottle. Chester, they're going through Belgium.'

'And the Belgians don't have an army?'

'Certainly they have. I came through Liège on my way. That's the border town. It has a ring of huge forts five miles out from the centre. They're even better than the French. Those Belgian forts are buried in hilltops and they're bristling with ordnance — big guns, small guns, machine guns, all that stuff. Remote-controlled cannon on hydraulic lifts. One minute you're looking at a smooth steel dome. The next, there's a hissing noise and you're looking down a ruddy great gun barrel.'

'So the Germans won't get past them easily?'

'Chester, think about it. They were designed twenty-five years ago and the Germans must have been thinking all this time about how to get past them. If Krupp really has a thirty-two centimetre . . . ' He trailed off, shaking his head.

'Jesus, Willy. How do I get to Liège?' asked Chester. 'Germany's on the march somewhere. If that's where Watling's gone, I should be there.

Do you think they'll still rent me an automobile?' He looked around anxiously. 'Von Lettow might have someone watching us.'

Willy felt that old urge to see over the next fence. He had finished with Berlin. This was not where the answer was to be found any more because the question had just changed. 'How much baggage have you got?' he said.

'Not a lot that matters. Clothes I can buy anywhere. Just my notebooks and the camera and its sticks.'

Willy had seen the varnished wooden box. 'It's huge. Why did you bring such a big one?'

'Same reason as you ride that goddam machine of yours, because nobody could miss it. No spy would be insane enough to take sneaky photos with a thing like that. Oh Jeez. I know what you're thinking. No way.'

'Come on, Chester. Time to be brave. If you want to catch up with this war, it's time to try two wheels. Let's get out of here before von Lettow and your Colonel Nicolai can stop us.' It was a hard, hard ride. The headlight's acetylene ran out just after Kassel but they rested by the roadside until the rising moon, fat and waxing, came to their rescue. By 2 a.m. it was high enough in the sky to paint the road ahead silver. Behind his goggles, Willy's eyes scanned the glistening surface for potholes and loose gravel as he held the throttle wide open. The night air of early August was cool enough to keep him alert. The engine coughed and he reached under the tank to switch over to reserve, wondering where their next fill-up would come from.

67

Behind him, Chester lurched and the motorcycle wobbled. The American was a terrible passenger, perched on makeshift padding on the luggage rack behind him and unable to keep still. He complained constantly and after two hundred miles hard riding, he still had no concept of how to lean with the bike into the corners. The square wooden camera on the American's lap dug hard into Willy's back every time he braked.

Dawn was just touching the sky behind them when they rounded yet another bend, the back tyre skittering across the road surface, and saw a dozen guns pointed straight at them.

5

'Keep your rifle to yourself,' said Willy, 'or I'll bend it round your head.' The soldier behind him had jabbed the muzzle into him once too often.

'Sit down on the log,' said the man in good English. 'Keep still and shut up.' A ring of taciturn men formed around them, each one with a weapon held ready. A motorcycle despatch rider rattled off to seek instructions. His machine left a blue haze behind it and Willy sniffed.

'What?' said Chester.

'Too smoky,' said Willy. 'Burning oil. I thought they were good engineers.'

The nearest soldier scowled. 'You know very little,' he said. 'It is meant to be just so. The oil flow has been increased to incur less wear while the army is on mobilization. It is in accordance with the deployment orders and absolutely deliberate.'

'You speak very good English,' said Willy, 'though perhaps more pedantically than one might choose.'

The man looked at him blankly. 'I should do,' he said. 'I was a waiter at the Criterion for the past eight years.'

The despatch rider was back within minutes, conferring with the other soldiers.

'There's no way they could know about us, is

there?' muttered Chester.

'Von Lettow won't know we've gone yet, not until we don't show up at his office.'

'Would he guess we headed this way?'

'I did my best to confuse the issue. He should get reports that we went north-east.' Willy had taken them out of Berlin on the Bernau road, taking care to rev his engine going past the police post, then circling back on lonely lanes all the way to Magdeburg.

'Get in the truck,' said the Criterion waiter, walking back. 'We will bring your machine behind.' It took two soldiers to push Chester up over the tailboard. They passed up his camera with wary politeness and Willy climbed up after him.

'You have gasoline?' he said to the German.

The man turned his head towards a truck a hundred yards away. 'Yes.'

'You'll need to put some in. My tank's plumb empty.'

He watched and as he expected, standard soldier psychology came into play. The man fetched a can from the truck, poured a little in the motorcycle tank then thought better of carrying the heavy can all the way back again so he poured the rest in after it. The despatch rider kicked the Thor into life and Willy watched carefully as they set off until he was sure the man knew what he was doing. The sun had come over the horizon, lighting up cathedral woodlands on both sides, trunks wide apart under a high canopy. They emerged on a long straight road through open country and Chester let out a whistle. They were staring at what looked like the entire German army.

For perhaps five miles they drove between lines of military vehicles parked nose to tail all along both sides of the road and in the fields wherever there was a gate. There were horse wagons, with their shaggy-haired teams grazing next to them, towering motor lorries with canvas covers, ambulances, and two carts with unfathomable loads of piled yellow fabric showing through gaps in their tarpaulins. Open grey touring cars had steel rails curving from the front of the chassis irons up and over the passenger area.

'What are those for?' Chester asked.

'To keep their heads on their shoulders. A retreating force might string wires across the road.'

There were hundreds upon hundreds of wagons and vehicles of all sorts — thousands even, Willy realized, only outnumbered by the vast army of men lying in the fields on their ground-sheets or just starting to get up and wander towards the rows of mobile kitchens, chimneys smoking.

He ran a wondering soldier's eye over the men and their equipment as he passed: the grey uniforms which seemed to melt into the background, the high boots in fine brown leather, the cobblers' wagon with men already lining up to have the stitching on those boots repaired and the medical truck next to it where men in white gowns were examining bunions and blisters. By a barber's wagon, a man was shearing soldiers' hair with an electric clipper. That was the gentler side of this perfectly orchestrated horde but it was a tiny part of the whole. He saw field guns by the hundred, limbers piled with shells, two-wheeled carts mounting linked machine-guns and a score of great siege guns on massive wheels. Willy craned round to look at the ends of their barrels — the muzzles shrouded by canvas covers — but none looked anything like a match for the monster of the musical. The vast, wheeled army went on and on and on, its disparate parts connected together by telephone wires strung along the side of the road. Soldiers everywhere were sorting out their gear and getting ready to move, delving into tough backpacks backed with panels of red ox-hide. It was like no other army he had ever seen, utterly prepared, utterly modern and utterly suited to an implacable purpose. By the time they came to their destination, the sun was fully up.

The truck stopped near a dun-coloured marquee where the despatch rider pulled the Thor up on its stand and the soldiers marched them to a table at the entrance. An officer rose to his feet, studied them and requested that they show their papers. He inspected Chester's passes, read a long letter stamped with wax seals and raised his eyebrows. 'You saw General Ludendorff last week in Berlin?'

'That's right.'

'We expect he will be here with us soon. He says in these papers that we should provide help within reason subject to your acceptance of such restrictions as we may need to place on your movements. Do you understand that?'

'Yes, but General Ludendorff told me he is anxious that the American public should see the great advances in the quality of the German army and the steps they are taking to protect their borders against aggression,' said Chester smoothly.

Willy produced his US papers but the officer gave them no more than a cursory glance. He was a man used to hierarchy and here Chester was clearly the master and Willy only the servant.

'We will show you a little of our army, Herr Hoffman, then I am sorry to say that you must return to Berlin. All civilians are banned from travelling further into the border region under edicts issued yesterday. It is not safe for you under the current circumstances. We may be attacked at any moment by the French. Now, my General wishes to make your acquaintance.' He got up and put his head inside the marquee entrance for a moment.

The man who emerged was an impressive old man with a curving moustache, waving silver hair and a broad face. He looked at both of them and lifted one quizzical eyebrow. 'My name is Otto von Emmich,' he said, 'and I did not expect to find the American press here where my army is on manoeuvres. How has that come about?'

'By chance, General,' said Chester. 'Just passing through. We didn't know you were here. I have some stories I need to write in Belgium.'

'In Belgium? Well, that may prove difficult. This area is now out of bounds. You will understand that military manoeuvres can be dangerous for civilians.'

'Your man there said you were expecting to be attacked by the French.'

'Ah. He is taking the scenario for our exercises a little too seriously perhaps.'

'So can we carry on through?'

'I do not say that. We will have to see. Until then, please accompany the Feldwebel here and he will show you those parts of our corps which are suitable for such inspection.' He turned abruptly to Willy, looked him up and down then reached out and grabbed his wrists. He examined Willy's hands. 'So? A horseman, I think?'

'I was once, sir,' said Willy, and nodded towards the Thor. 'Now I am a motorcyclist. They go faster, they have brakes and they usually do what I tell them.'

The General studied his face then smiled. 'But they have no soul and no love for their master,' he said. 'Ride carefully, Mr . . . ?'

'Fraser.'

'Did you serve in the American army?'

'No, General.'

The Feldwebel told Chester to leave the camera behind. He showed them the catering arrangements, the field hospital, the mobile laundry and the pay office. He kept them away from the guns and the soldiers. They were walking back towards the marquee after a pointless half hour when Chester said, 'Tell me now, what's that going on over there?'

On the edge of a small wood, soldiers were

gathered around a cart. They had taken off the tarpaulin to reveal one of those enigmatic piles of yellow fabric. Removing the load carefully they began to unfold it, spreading it out across the ground, unravelling a network of ropes as they did so. It soon became clear that it was all one single enormous oval construction made from some strong fabric. A motor lorry snorted up beside it, laden with stacked grey cylinders each the height of a man and the soldiers rushed to unload it, two to a cylinder and struggling with the weight.

'That is what we call a *Drachen*, a balloon used for observing,' said the Feldwebel. 'We employ it to guide our guns. This is an exercise to see how fast they can fly it up into the air, you see?'

'May we look closer?'

'It is no secret, I suppose. Other armies have the same balloons. Do not light any cigars please. That is hydrogen gas in the cylinders. We will all go bang.' He seemed to find that very funny.

The gas was already flowing into the balloon envelope as crouching men with copper spanners coupled up more and more of the cylinders to a manifold. Three or four minutes passed and the top surface was just beginning to lift and ripple.

'They will alert us when it is ready,' said the Feldwebel. 'Come. We will drink coffee while they do their work.' And he led them away through the trees to a mess tent the far side.

They didn't need any alert. The drab yellow whale-back of a vast sausage rose slowly into view from behind the sheltering belt of trees. It was zebra-striped with darker brown panels. By the time they walked back to it, the long cylinder of the balloon was ready for flight. Fifty men were hanging on to lines dangling from it. A dozen more were securing its rigging ropes to a cable from a lorry-mounted winch. A wicker basket hung underneath, sandbags hooked around the rim helping to keep it down on the earth as it writhed in the breeze.

A man in a long leather overcoat walked up and saluted. He addressed the Feldwebel in German and Willy pretended not to understand.

The Feldwebel looked amused. He turned to Chester and said, 'This officer who is the chief observer of the ballooning detachment wishes to know if you would like to ascend with him?'

'Me?' said Chester. 'Really? Er . . . '

'He says it is delightful. They will not go higher than perhaps one thousand metres today.'

'One thousand metres?'

The *Drachen* had a tail in the form of a smaller sausage, like a fin curling down under the main body. They could smell rubber as they came closer, the whole balloon writhing now and tugging at its lines as the wind gusted.

The basket was a tall cube with a gap in the side halfway up as a step. The man in leather climbed nimbly in, slipping between the rigging ropes. Chester looked doubtfully at the remaining space, and tried to hoist his foot high enough to reach the rung. He staggered backwards.

'My legs don't bend like that,' he said. 'I don't think I'm built for this.' The officer in the basket shrugged and pointed at Willy. 'Go on,' said Chester in relief. 'You go. Tell me all about it afterwards. My readers won't know the difference.'

Willy was in the basket before Chester could change his mind. It was a snug fit. A narrow canvas seat slung across the middle of it separated them but any movement meant contact. The handling crew began to unhook the sandbags. He saw a telephone headset and a pair of binoculars suspended from the rigging above them on elastic cords. He looked over the side and was utterly astonished to see that the ground was rushing downwards away from them. There had been no sense of movement at all but now he could see all the upturned faces getting smaller and smaller. He found that he loved it.

He leant over, looking down again, and was lost in complete fascination. They were much higher now and the ground was still falling fast. This was the world as he had always longed to see it — the golden eagle's view with everything laid out plainly for inspection. His old perch on the castle battlements had showed him a small circle of Scotland, blinkered by surrounding hills, in which little of interest ever moved unless his mother had just thrown it. Now there was nothing between him and the whole truth of the land below except for two thousand feet of clear air. From up here all was in plain sight. No mysteries lurked beyond the hedges and the shrinking woods. No cannon smoke could hide the shape of the battle from here. Anything bad would be revealed long before it could reach you.

There was no hiding place and he could see it all, even a fox flowing through the grass at the edge of a field. Up and up they went, drawing church spires towards them like fishing floats, their villages clinging to them, in from the distance, rolling the horizon back. Still further up, perspective changing and the huge curving circle of the world surrounded their calm centre. It reached through to touch him in a deep and unsuspected place. He gloried in it and knew this basket was where he had always wanted to be.

Except, that is, for his companion. The man in the leather overcoat addressed him in German. 'You do not speak a word of my language?' he asked. Their faces were only a foot apart and Willy felt a fine spray of spittle on his cheeks.

Willy looked at him, smiled apologetically, gestured hopelessly and said, 'Do you speak any American maybe?' There was no glimmer of understanding so, just to be completely sure, he added, 'I hate everything about you and I plan to set fire to your balloon.'

'I don't like the sound of your voice,' said the man, again in German, 'but then you are an ignorant foreigner from a childish nation. My countrymen in your land will take command of it one day and then they will oblige you all to speak our language.'

Willy smiled again, shrugged and ran his eye along the road stretching ahead of them, pointing west towards Belgium, empty. Then he looked to one side of the road and there, perhaps half a mile or so further on, was a railway siding, running down from a distant mainline. Eight wagons stood on the rails surrounded by a ring of soldiers, as clear as toys on the floor. Six of the wagons were sheeted over but men were working on the other two and they were loading dozens of stubby cylinders. Four men were struggling to lift just one of the cylinders on slings between them. An officer on horseback seemed to be superintending them but something spooked his horse and it started jibbing as the rider struggled to control it. The horse danced around and caught one leg in a rope loop trailing from the tarpaulin cover of a rail wagon. The horse backed away, panicking, and pulled half the tarpaulin sideways off the load.

It revealed by far the biggest gun barrel Willy had ever seen. It was only twice the length of the horse prancing next to it, but its girth was astonishing. The fat barrel swelled into an even fatter breech — so much steel that he could see why it needed rail transport and that was only one part of the dismantled weapon. The rest had to be on the other wagons.

The worker-ant soldiers down below dragged the tarpaulin back into place and the German next to him craned over to see what he was looking at.

'Ah!' he said. 'Der Brummer.' He glanced westward. 'Belgien und dann Frankreich,' he said 'Nichts kann den Zweiundvierzigen stoppen.'

Zweiundvierzig, thought Willy, fighting to keep the vacuous smile on his face. Nothing can stop the *zweiundvierzig*? That thing down there isn't a thirty-two. Good God Almighty, it's a *forty*-two. 'Lovely day for a flight,' he said. 'How high are we? Understand?' He said it again, louder, 'How high? Er, what is that? Vee hike? No, vee hoke?'

The German stared at him. 'Wie hoch?' He glanced down, 'neunhundert, tausend Meter.'

Willy looked down again and thought of all the mountains he had climbed, of the view from the summit of Ben Cruachan on a clear summer's day, but that was nothing. The angled sides of a mountain disguised the truth of a thousand metres, more than three thousand feet of height. Even the edge of a precipice left solid ground beneath your feet but here he was with only an inch of wicker-work between him and all that depth of air below. He found the clarity exhilarating. It was very quiet in the balloon. He had expected to hear sounds from the ground below but the layers of air insulated them in remarkable calm. Then they came to the end of the winch's run with a sharp jerk and as soon as they did, the world went mad. Held in the wind, the *Drachen* changed from a boat on a calm ocean to a game-fish fighting madly on a tight line. The basket swayed and creaked as the sausage buckled, flapping and crackling. They rocked violently as a gust heaved the writhing gasbag up at a steep angle then nosed it down in a stomach-churning plunge. Willy held on to the rigging with both hands but immediately saw the other man glance at his knuckles with contempt so he let go quickly.

'Frightened, are you?' said the German. 'So much for Americans.'

Willy looked down at the road more than half a mile below them and followed its line west, wondering how far he could see clearly. He imagined the triangle in his head, tried to come up with a rough estimate. Ten miles certainly. He reached for the binoculars. 'May I?' he said.

The German nodded with a knowing smile and Willy found out why as soon as he tried to focus on the ground below. The balloon was gyrating and snatching at its cable and he tried to brace the binoculars against the rigging ropes but the ground below, magnified massively by the lenses, refused to cooperate, darting backwards and forwards so he could hardly see a thing. It made his stomach heave. He let go of the ropes, flexing his knees, and tried his best to stay vertical in spite of the basket, like changing a foresail on a rough day in the Firth of Clyde. He began to get the hang of it and studied the road, seeing the roadblocks on the way to the howitzer siding, taking in the details of the countryside around them.

The motion of the balloon quietened as they were dragged back down to calmer air and now he could hear the rattle of the winch engine and the shouts of men. The horizon was shrinking fast and he regretted every moment of the descent, then they bumped on the ground and a squad of soldiers ran to hook the sandbags back on the basket. His sour companion climbed out and walked off without a backward look. Willy rejoined Chester and the Feldwebel.

'How was that?' said Chester.

'Quite extraordinary. I was promoted to the world of the gods.'

'It looked wild at times.'

'There was a touch of the bucking bronco about it.'

'The old ones were worse,' said the Feldwebel. 'We used round ones and they would spin all the time. Very sick-making. The *Drachen* is much more steady. Now come, please. My General wishes to speak with you again.'

The table outside von Emmich's marquee was laid with plates of cakes and flasks of coffee. The General came out of the tent to greet them. 'Do eat,' he said. 'You will be hungry after all your exertions. I am still puzzled as to why you risked travelling at night on such a dangerous conveyance.' He glanced at the parked Thor.

'Needs must in the news business, General. Europe's going wild and I'm supposed to find out what's going on,' said Chester. 'Can you help me there maybe?'

'There is only a little news. Italy has announced it will stay neutral and that is good,' said von Emmich. 'We were asked to enter Luxembourg to ensure its protection.'

'Asked by who?'

'The people of Luxembourg, of course.'

Chester raised his eyebrows. 'All of them?'

Von Emmich smiled. 'What happens next does not depend on us,' he said. 'It depends rather on the French and more importantly on the British who would like to portray us as the aggressors. We have been threatened for so very long, you know. I can tell you that we have politely requested permission from the Belgians to enter their country, only to protect them from a French invasion of course, but their King has not yet seen fit to oblige us. It is their mistake.' He pointed down the road. 'Any aggression against us will have to be punished. This army you see here is a small part of the whole. For ten years we have been making ready for the moment when our enemies move to threaten us.'

'I've got to say it's an impressive sight,' said Willy.

'I am one of those who have worked hard to build it. It is now complete and ready and I would be glad to see it go to work before I am too old to take part.'

'On manoeuvres, you mean?' said Chester, 'or would you like to have a war?'

The General laughed. 'Of course,' he said. 'Only on manoeuvres, but in the unfortunate event that war is forced upon us then we are very well prepared. You should write that, Mr Hoffman, so nobody is in any doubt about it. Now, gentlemen, if you have eaten enough, you will be escorted back to Berlin. We have a vehicle ready for you and your precious American motorcycle will be loaded into the back of it. It has been a pleasure to meet you. May I suggest, Mr Hoffman, that your snapper here, as you call him, takes a picture of us together for your newspaper? Here is your camera.'

The Feldwebel handed the camera to Willy. It was all brass and varnished wood with a series of levers and buttons around the lens. He had absolutely no idea what any of them did.

'No problem,' he said, 'but I need the tripod. I'll go get it.' He walked calmly across to the Thor, thirty yards away, and made a show of trying to loosen the lashing holding the folding wooden legs to the side of the luggage rack. He gave up and called across to them, 'Anyone got a knife?' Without waiting for an answer, he kicked the Thor into life and swung his leg over the saddle. As he saw the Feldwebel's hand go to his holster he let the clutch in and gently trickled the bike towards them. The Feldwebel relaxed and that was when Willy twisted open the throttle, hauled the handlebars around and slewed onto the road west towards Belgium, catching a glimpse of the Germans standing there with their eyes like saucers.

6

He held his breath and crouched low over the handlebars, hearing shouts behind him. The absurd possibility of being shot made his shoulders tense as if firm muscles might stand a chance of deflecting a bullet. They wouldn't shoot in full view of an American reporter, would they? The bike snaked from side to side under hard acceleration and no shots came. He was already beyond accurate pistol shot but still far inside the range of a well-aimed Mauser rifle. Then he was round a kink in the road with hedges barring their view but it felt safe only for a moment because of course they had other ways. The army's new copper voice ran alongside him, telephone wires strung on poles along the road towards the outposts and towards the howitzer siding ahead. He knew the soldiers manning the checkpoints there must already be answering their buzzing phones but the balloon ride had done him a great service. It had revealed the local geography like the most magnificent of maps. The farm track he had seen from the basket branched off to the right and he swung off the road, the bike's wheels bouncing in and out of potholes. He dismissed a twinge of remorse for Chester and hurtled through a deserted farmyard straight on down the track, seeing the church spire he had identified from the balloon half a mile ahead. They wouldn't know where he had gone.

Yes, of course they would.

He twisted in the saddle and there it was, the dirty yellow balloon just rising above the trees behind him. Idiot. That would be their first response, sending up the balloon, the all-seeing eye, and in a moment its eye would fall on him. He saw a barn ahead and slowed to swing the bike in through the open doors. They couldn't see him here. He stopped the engine but once again it felt safe only for a moment as he realized this was now a whole new game. If they couldn't see where he was, they could very easily see where he wasn't. It would only take a moment to identify all the possible hiding places and the telltale dust from his passage would still be hanging in the air along the track. The observer up there in his leather coat would be scanning every inch of this small sector of countryside and men would already be fanning out because that thing rising behind him was the lord of all it surveyed. He was caught between the devil of staying under cover and the deep blue sea of the hue and cry.

He got off and moved to the barn's entrance, taking care not to show himself. Peering between two slats of wood, he saw the balloon was already several hundred feet up and still rising fast. Would they even bother to send soldiers? They had field guns. What was the destruction of one barn compared to stopping a spy? He might be better off as a moving target and he was weighing up whether to make a break for it when the balloonist's abrupt misfortune gave him an unexpected chance. They must have been unrigging when the urgent call had come for its services and speed had got in the way of efficiency because one end of the wicker basket lurched down as a suspension rope came undone. He saw the man, so far up in the air, slide half out, grabbing wildly at nothing and fetching up with a jerk, hanging upside-down below the skewed basket as a rope caught around his leg, his black coat falling down to cover his face. Willy could vividly imagine what that must feel like, head-down over a long drop to death. The man flailed his arms around, hooked one of the handling ropes trailing down and wrapped it around his body but he still dangled precariously. They must have put the winch into reverse because the balloon nosed down as they sought to retrieve him and Willy didn't waste another moment. He was back on the bike and away down the track before ten more seconds had passed.

Two hours later, navigating by the sun and keeping to the smaller lanes wherever he could, he came upon a faded wooden signpost pointing ahead to the town of Bonn. An aeroplane buzzed the sky a mile ahead of him, a clumsy biplane moving slowly across against a head wind, and in case it was searching for him he moved the bike in under the trees at the side of the road. He used the minutes until he was quite sure it was out of sight to rub a sticky mixture of earth and engine oil all over the white paint. When he had finished it felt ready for war and so, he realized, did he. He took off the stars and stripes, rummaging among the other stand-by pennants in the leather panniers to find a tricolour in red, white and black with the German Imperial Eagle at the centre. Squashing a felt forage cap on to his head, he found his way through the cobbled streets of the small town to an old bridge over the Rhine where, of course, a pair of soldiers stood ready to stop every vehicle. They looked at him curiously as he approached and one held up a hand. Could they have been alerted? He slowed to walking pace and shouted as loudly as he could.

'Aus dem Weg! Ich habe Versendungen vom General.'

Was *Versendungen* the right word for despatches, he wondered for a moment, or did it mean shipment? His peremptory tone of voice and the Imperial tricolour combined to do the trick. The soldiers stood smartly aside and saluted him. After that it was almost easy. He took to the smallest roads he could find, by way of Stotzheim, Mechernich and Hehrhahn in the wilds of the Eifel forests, steering by the sun when he could see it, always watching the road ahead for soldiers but seeing none. The armies clearly needed easier routes than this for their vast mobilization plan and there was hardly a soul to be seen. After another spell of hard riding he saw a hut ahead and a striped pole across the road and braced himself for trouble, but the German side of the frontier was deserted. The Belgian side was another matter. Two dozen Belgian soldiers were very busy building a bank of earth and stone across the road beyond the pole. A flagstaff flew a vertical tricolour of black, yellow and red. He braked to a halt, seeing the men snatch up their rifles as they stared at his German flag. Reaching out, he tore it off and threw it down on the road. 'Je suis très heureux de vous voir,' he said with feeling.

They searched him, inspected both sets of his papers with increasing suspicion, emptied out the contents of the panniers and then locked him in the hut. His sudden sense of safety let exhaustion in to make up for lost ground. It was more than thirty hours since he had last slept and he curled up on the wooden floor until he was shaken awake by a puzzled officer wearing red trousers and an ornate blue jacket.

'Who exactly are you?' said the man in English. 'We cannot tell if you are an American or an Englishman, if indeed you are either.'

'I am neither,' said Willy, getting to his feet. 'I am happy to say I am a Scot with an American mother.'

'Scottish? And they tell me you are asking to see my commanding officer because you claim to have information?'

'Correct. It is very urgent.'

'What sort of information?'

'I have come from Berlin. If you don't mind, I will keep the details to myself until I see him. Who are you?'

'Excuse me. I am Lieutenant Claude Tavernier of the Mounted Rifles. Your papers say your name is Fraser. We will need somebody to vouch for you. You must give me more details so that

89

we can send a message to whichever ambassador you answer to. You will have to stay in our custody until then. These are dangerous times.'

'How long will that take?'

'Perhaps a day or two.'

'We don't have that much time.'

'There is no other way. You could be anybody. You could be an assassin for all I know. Now, please give me your full name.'

'To a fellow cavalryman? Certainly. I am Captain William Fraser, formerly of the Queen's Own Hussars.'

The Belgian lieutenant stared at him. 'You mean that?'

'Of course.'

The man went on staring and began to smile. 'Then perhaps I can save some of that valuable time. Did you recently do something a little strange to your Colonel's horse perhaps?'

'I gave it a shave,' Willy said slowly, staring at the Belgian in wonder.

'Just a shave? No more than that?'

'Words. I shaved a message into its flanks.'

'And tell me, what exactly was that message?'

'It said 'aiming point' with an arrow pointing up at the saddle. Not all that funny really.'

The Belgian's smile became a broad grin. 'And just to be quite sure, you also named the two pets in the officers' mess? The dog and the cat?'

'You mean Bach and Magnificat? How on earth do you know that?'

'I met them. Your identity is quite clear to me. You are undoubtedly Wild Willy Fraser.'

'Good heavens. How did that news spread to Belgium?'

'My friend, do you not know how famous you are? I have recently spent two weeks with your regiment. I arrived soon after your abrupt departure. They talked of nothing else and it was not just within your regiment. Afterwards, whenever other officers asked where I had been, the conversation soon turned to you.'

'I hope you didn't believe it all.'

'I certainly hope that every word of it was true. It is an honour to meet you.'

'Why were you over there?'

'You know we are a neutral country so we cannot be seen to be cooperating with the foreign military but some unofficial liaison was thought to be very timely. I believe I was supposed to be discussing humane field treatment for ailments of the horse's hoof or some such nonsense. You really do have information?'

'I really do.'

'Then I will escort you to Liège immediately. I came in a staff car but it has despatches to deliver elsewhere. Is there space for a passenger on your machine?'

'For you? Easily.'

Half an hour and twenty miles further on, the city of Liège seemed to contain as many cows as men. Every small park and grassy square was packed with them. 'They have been coming in since yesterday,' said Tavernier as they got off the bike in the early evening. 'When they heard of the German ultimatum, the farmers brought

91

their animals into town. If any army is going to eat them, they thought it should be ours. More to the point, we at least are quite likely to pay them for the privilege.'

The chimneys of the mills and factories along the river had the smokeless look of a pious Sunday but this was Monday. 'Where are all the men?' said Willy. 'Have they joined the army?'

'They live out in the villages. They stay in town for their week's work then they go back to their wives, their pigs and their vegetables. Today they chose to stay home. Even the coalmines have stopped. Now, Willy Fraser, I know you don't like the brass hats but please try to be pleasant when you meet my General. He is a good man and a very good soldier but he has already had a hard day. We only arrived here this morning at dawn.'

'I always like generals who know what they're talking about,' said Willy. 'Though I haven't met any so far.'

There were guards at the entrance to the decaying citadel high up in the town. 'The old man's at his look-out,' said Tavernier after talking to the guard commander. They climbed a cobbled alleyway to a terrace where a tall house stood by itself. Willy found himself shaking the hand of an elderly Belgian with the standard luxuriant moustache before he noticed the General's insignia. He stepped back and saluted.

'I am Gerard Leman,' the officer said. 'Lieutenant Tavernier assures me you really are who you say you are. He tells me that you wish to speak to me. You do not mind if he listens to this as well?'

'Sir,' Willy said. 'I have come to tell you that many thousands of German soldiers are heading in this direction under the command of General von Emmich and I am quite sure that they intend to invade your country.'

'That, mon capitaine, is your news? It comes as no surprise to any of us. Kaiser Wilhelm has already informed our King that he intends to bring his troops through Belgium to reach France. My King did his best to explain that a brief study of any map will show him that Belgium is a nation, not a road, but the Kaiser seems quite unable to comprehend that. It is not just a question of von Emmich however. You have seen only one German army.'

'Oh.'

'Oh indeed. There are also the hunting packs of von Massow, von Oertzen, von Hulsen and several other vons besides out there. My brave scouts tell me there are at least eighty thousand German soldiers already approaching the frontier and with all the new railway lines they have been busy building in our direction I am sure that is just the beginning.' He paused and frowned. 'We do not have a large army here in Belgium and many of my soldiers are more what you would perhaps prefer to call militia men. However, there is no going back. France has declared war on Germany today and who knows what will follow.'

Willy was shocked despite himself. A further-off part of his mind which concerned itself with

93

speculation had been predicting that with increasing urgency right through his trip but that wasn't the loudest of his inner voices. The day-to-day sensible part assured him that the world would somehow go on as it usually did. It reassured him that this was all sabre-rattling and that common decency would still hold sway. Leman's words silenced that voice and propelled his world into dark certainty.

He looked Willy up and down. 'You are a cavalryman yourself, I understand?'

'I have been, General. I am not currently serving.'

'Captain Fraser is being modest, *mon Général*,' said Tavernier. 'In England he was a very famous soldier, known for his panache, his horsemanship and many other things beside.' Willy gave him a sharp look and he smiled innocently.

'Then I should value your opinion, Captain Fraser, but, as I say, your news is not so new.'

'But that was not my news, General, merely the preamble.'

'What then?'

'Can you stop them if they come?'

'It is my duty to stop them.'

'But *can* you?'

'Step outside with me, my young friend.' From the terrace, they looked down at the Meuse flowing past below the town and Leman pointed to the bridges. 'This is their obvious and fastest way to France. They have to come here because this is where the good roads and the mainline railways run but we have known that for a very

94

long time and so first they have to get past our defences. A concrete ring surrounds this city and blocks their way, twelve truly powerful fortresses, but we are very neutral and fair-minded, you know. Just as many of them face France as face Germany. You have seen them?'

'Yes, I came this way a few weeks ago.'

'What brought you here?'

'Curiosity. The rumours that Germany's more ancient generals were even more keen on war than their Kaiser.'

'So you looked at my fortresses? All of them?'

'Two of them just to get the idea, and of course only from the outside.'

'Then you must have seen that they are formidable. Each fort is protected by massive concrete all around.'

'I know, sir, but exactly how thick is that concrete?'

'How thick? The roofs are four metres deep. The walls of the casemates are one and a half metres. They were built to defeat the heaviest shell.'

'General, that is the burden of my news for you. I am afraid that was true but now the German army is equipped with a new weapon.'

'Again that is not news. We know all about the Skoda mountain gun. It is thirty centimetres bore, they tell me, but it is not so easily moved. Their largest field howitzer is twenty-one centimetres and we can easily cope with that.' He pursed his lips. 'But from the look on your face you are going to tell me, perhaps, that they have made carriages that can move their thirty centimetre gun? I have heard such stories. If so, then they still do not worry me. I believe our good concrete will keep their shells out.' He looked towards the rise beyond the steep valley of the Meuse as if he might see them coming.

'No, sir. I wish it was the Skoda but this one comes from Krupp. I am sorry to tell you that it is far heavier than the mountain gun. Its bore is *forty-two* centimetres,' said Willy.

The General turned sharply. 'That is not possible. There can be no such thing.'

'I have seen it.'

'Where?'

'On a railway line. Only a day or two's travel east of here.'

'Someone has misled you. They could not transport such a thing.'

'I saw it dismantled into its separate parts. I know what I saw. I heard a German balloon observer name it as a forty-two.'

'And they let you measure it?'

'Of course not, but it was huge.'

'No. I cannot allow myself to believe you, Captain Fraser. There is no hope for us if I do. You walk in here and tell me that all the labours of the past months are wasted, that every hour of every day that they have worked to strengthen these defences has achieved nothing.' His voice rose. *'It was huge?* Is that supposed to be a soldierly assessment? Yours is the voice of doom and you must be wrong. You don't agree? Then tell me *exactly* what you have heard and seen in as much detail as you can recall. How did you first hear of this mythical monster?'

'An American newspaperman tipped me off. There's a new musical just opened in Berlin. I went to the second night. It has a dance scene between a girl and . . . ' Willy saw Tavernier's frozen face behind the General and realized how absurd this account must sound. He struggled on, told them of the man from Abteilung IIIb, their dash through the darkness and the encounter with von Emmich's army. He ended with the giant gun he had glimpsed from the balloon.

The General gazed down at the town below them for some time after Willy finished.

'Have you served in war, Captain Fraser?' he asked. 'No, how could you? You are too young. Skirmishes in India or Africa perhaps? Yes? I served in our Observation Corps during the war of 1870. I saw Prussian equipment and organization destroy France so very easily and then hold our neighbours to ransom. You have seen shells fired on manoeuvre, no doubt. You have seen artificial targets explode with a satisfactory bang and a shower of wood and canvas but I suspect you have not watched unfettered destruction sweep away hundreds of years of man's fragile and painful endeavour, have you? Do you see those bridges down there? They are just stone bridges, are they not? You might not give them a second look but it took vast skill and human effort to make each one of those, to cut each block so it fitted perfectly against its neighbour in a peaceful cause and had the strength to stand against the battering of the river in full flood. Not only that, but also to

97

please the eye. If von Emmich's attackers get inside my forts then I must issue orders to blow those wondrous bridges to pieces and that will just be the beginning. Do you understand how very much I want you to be wrong? But I see that you are quite sure you are not wrong.'

'General, I wish I was.'

'Whatever the Germans will bring against us, we *will* hold out because I have sworn an oath to my commander, King Albert.'

'In that case is there any way I can help you, sir?' said Willy.

Ten minutes later, he found himself a serving officer in the Belgian army. 'You will start tomorrow morning at first light please,' the General said. 'I would especially like you to work with Lieutenant Tavernier to inspect each of the fortresses, reporting back to me in person. He tells me you have a rapid machine capable of racing from place to place. It sounds vile to me but you also have a quick mind and fresh eyes and you might see things that have been neglected. Tonight, eat, drink and sleep, for you have work ahead.'

Much later, Willy sat at a bar by St Lambert Square with Claude Tavernier drinking beer.

'So? Do we have a chance?' Claude asked.

'Soldiers create their own chances.'

'I am twenty-six,' said Claude, 'and I married my beautiful Gabrielle only a very short time ago so I am in no hurry to die. How old are you, Willy Fraser?'

'The same age as you, give or take.'

'Married?'

Willy had grown to like Claude more and more as the evening went on. He was a wiry man with immense energy and a wry sense of humour. Willy laughed and shook his head. 'No,' he said, 'not even close.'

'But your friends said you had many women in your life?'

'In my life perhaps but not in too deep. I don't need a woman's love to keep me alive, Claude. I plan to survive all by myself.'

'I have a photograph of my Gabrielle. May I show you?'

'No. If she is not beautiful I will have to lie. If she is, I shall perhaps feel a little jealous.'

'It is a very bad photograph.'

'Then keep it to yourself. Where is she now?'

'We were staying at her parent's house in Namur so she is safe but I have told her to go straight to Brussels if anything bad should happen here.' Claude called to the waitress for more beer. 'And now you suddenly find yourself volunteering as an officer in the Belgian army, Willy Fraser. So were you missing the soldier's life?'

A bit, Willy admitted to himself. Rivals had become the brothers he had often imagined but the Colonel had put an end to that. 'I like your General Leman, Claude, but I'm not very good at being told what to do.'

'That was clear from the stories I heard. Your friends in the regiment missed you.'

Willy thought back to that last day when he resigned his commission and packed his bags. He remembered the suppressed delight on the

Colonel's face and the road stretching away from the barracks gate that suddenly led to absolutely nowhere in particular. 'My superior officers didn't.'

'Willy Fraser, that was peace-time. They will value different skills in war.'

'Oh really? My former commanding officer was quite convinced that the best way to fight off charging Uhlans is to dazzle them with the shine on your brass buckles.'

'I hope I have what is necessary,' said Claude quietly.

'Of course you have.'

'It is not such a simple thing. What do you see when you look at me?'

Willy studied him. 'Not a typical Belgian. Your skin is more like a Spaniard. Your face is more pointed than flat.'

'My Moroccan grandmother. I have her brown eyes too. What I mean is, do you see someone fitted to be a soldier?'

'Stand up. You are, let me see, five foot nine inches?'

'Oh, that English system. The Scots use that too? No, I am more. I am five foot twelve.'

Willy smothered a laugh. 'Five foot twelve?'

'You doubt me? Not as tall as you. You are what we call *une toise métrique*.'

'*Toise?*'

'You would say fathom. That is two metres.'

'Not quite. You are thin but you look strong enough.'

'But do I look like a warrior?'

Willy cast around for something that was both

100

kind and plausible and settled on Claude's whipcord build. 'You look like an Alpine guide,' he said, 'a mountaineer,' and Claude frowned as if unsure whether to be pleased.

'I will make a proper soldier in time,' he said. 'I promise. Do you suppose we will have enough time?' They turned their heads as boots crunched on the cobbles. A long line of soldiers marched past in silence. They looked exhausted, as if they had tramped for days. Only half of them had rifles. It seemed better not to answer the question.

'Do you really want to fight for Belgium?' Claude asked when they had trailed out of sight. 'If England declares war, what will you do then?'

'One thing at a time. I'm prepared to fight for Scotland but England hasn't served me well recently. Let's save Belgium first.'

Claude raised his glass. 'To my Gabrielle. Sleep well, my precious.'

Willy wagged a finger. 'I will drink to her and all her fragrant beauty just this once, Claude, but my strong advice is stop thinking about her if you want to live to see her again. Clear her out of your mind and only leave space for the demands of war. Fractions of a second make all the difference. That is how to stay alive now.'

'Clear her out? I cannot accept that. What ointment can we spread on the blister of war if not love? It is everything.'

'It happens inside your own head, Claude. If you are lucky enough to feel that for a woman who is suffering the matching delusion then you are lucky for however long that lasts but you

101

cannot afford the luxury of that fantasy when bullets are flying.'

'You know that?'

'My father taught me that.'

Claude shook his head. 'No, no, no. You are as wrong as it is possible to be and I am sorry for you, Willy Fraser. Love is a magic ribbon that forms across space and across time between two blessed people. The only reason you disagree is that you are ignorant because for you it has not yet happened. You admitted that. Tell me. In your life so far, what woman has meant the most to you?'

'Queen Victoria,' said Willy. 'Because I saw her standing on a Scottish quayside once and I knew if a gale got up, I could throw my mooring rope round her and my boat would have been completely safe.'

'Please be serious.'

Willy thought back down the line of women in his life. He thought of the swelling excitement of the cross-country hunt, of the surging heat of the horse between your legs, of the ride home afterwards with the woman who had caught your eye, pretending not to notice each other until you were both out of sight of the rest and a copse, or a green lane or a side valley presented itself.

'The women in my life have each chosen to be there for a brief adventure,' he said. 'That is the way I like it and they like it. For me, it seems an honest way.'

'That is so silly,' said Claude. 'It might do for a time but one day you will wake up. I promise you

102

that there are far better ways to live your life than that. What in heaven made you decide to be so lonely?'

'Lonely? I'm not.' Willy stared at him. 'Really, Claude. I'm not.'

'If you say so.'

'Life is a big adventure. I decided a long time ago that was the best way to look at it.'

'How old were you then?'

'Probably about ten. Maybe eleven or twelve. I remember I told my parents that I wouldn't marry until I was very old.'

'Oh, so you did at least have parents? You make that much of an obeisance to normal human relationships? You weren't left under a gooseberry bush by a passing stork, ready to go adventuring? What did they say?'

'My mother laughed.' And that was quite rare, Willy thought. My father was already beyond laughing by then. 'She told me I would forget all about that later, so I climbed up to the top of the turret.'

'You had *turrets*?'

'We lived in a small castle.'

'Just the three of you?'

'Plus one or two staff.'

'So you climbed up into one of the perfectly ordinary turrets of your perfectly ordinary castle and then?'

'I carved a message for myself into a beam.'

'What did it say?'

'It said I, William Fraser, swear I will not get married before I am . . . '

Claude waited. Willy saw the carving vividly in

103

his mind's eye. The two numbers, 2 and 5. 'Get me another beer,' he said. 'Enough of this soul-searching. Let's work out how you and I are going to win this war.'

'Will you teach me what you know?'

'The first thing I will teach you is not to say anything like that again. This is your country and your army. I need to learn from you.'

'Gabrielle says . . . ' he saw Willy's look. 'Just this and then no more of her. Gabrielle says I will soon let the boy inside me meet the man because they both live in me but they do not yet talk to each other.'

'Claude, I don't care if it's the boy inside or the man but will one of you buy us two more beers.'

⋆　⋆　⋆

The next day was August the fourth. The bike now flew a Belgian flag from its handlebar mast, kicking up dust as they raced north-east along the Meuse to Fort Barchon. At Leman's insistence, Willy wore the same colourful brocade uniform as Claude and it made him feel like a giant target. There was no khaki or field grey to be found in the Belgian army and in Fort Barchon, Willy found out why. Barchon was a small town in its own right, a concrete triangle, hundreds of yards on each side, with its point facing outwards from the city. A wide roadway ran inside each of the outer walls and within that was the fort itself, a vast, mostly subterranean concrete redoubt designed to service the hydraulic gun cupolas in which the Belgians had put so much faith.

'Impressive, do you not think?' said Claude.

'I don't trust any of it,' said Willy. 'Give me a saddle and a good horse any day. War should be mobile. Imagine being cooped up inside here when they're attacking.'

He felt more and more out of place as they walked down long staircases into the depths of the fort, through arched corridors sweating with dank breath and generator fumes. Chains of yellow bulbs lit stencilled arrows pointing to command centre 12, magazine 8 or cupola 27. They passed chilly, gloss-painted barrack rooms lined from floor to ceiling with narrow wire bunks and the further they went from daylight, the less Willy liked it. Claude showed him the big guns, housed in pivoting frames of thick steel, ingeniously designed so that they could be automatically dropped down into the bowels of the fort for attention. Always there was the drone and the stink of engines in the background. Everything here relies on power, Willy thought. It's like a warship. If the engines stop, the hydraulics go and the electricity goes and then the battle is lost. The engines ran the ventilation in a precarious balance of fans versus poisonous exhaust.

In the plotting room, Captain-Commandant Hannefstingels was about to start exercising the gun turrets and he bore their visit with the marginal politeness of the over-stretched officer. 'I have three hundred gunners,' he said, 'and practice is almost impossible. What am I meant to shoot at without killing Belgians? In ten minutes' time I will fire four half-charge empty shells into the middle of a harmless field and hope no cow or passing idiot has ignored our red flags. What use is that to anyone?'

When the first of his cannons fired, the crash reverberated down the corridors in wave after wave of echoing sound and it was immediately followed by a cloud of dark and choking smoke.

'Good God Almighty,' Willy said when he could breathe again. 'What the hell was that?'

'What do you think? Black powder. That is what we use in the guns,' said Claude.

'Black powder? Why? Is this some kind of military museum?'

'That is all we have. We are a little old-fashioned, perhaps.'

'A little? That's after one half-charge shot. I can hardly breathe. What would this place be like in a battle?'

'Smoky, I think. Perhaps even very smoky.'

'Let's get out of here,' said Willy and was delighted to reach open air. They made a rapid inspection of the neighbouring forts, Évegnée, Fleron and Chaudefontaine, then onward around the whole perimeter of the city. When they reported back to the citadel they found squadrons of horses saddling up, General Leman in the middle of uproar and staff officers running through the corridors with maps.

'Gentlemen,' he said, 'it has begun. We have had a message from Gemmenich. That is our border post north-west of here, Fraser.' He looked down at the piece of paper in his hand. 'It says: 'Le terroire Belge a été envahi par les troupes allemandes!' They have indeed invaded us. Now, quickly, tell me what you think of my forts and do not pull your punches.'

'You won't like this, sir.' Willy ran through the faults, the weak walls at the rear, the new houses built between some of the forts creating dead ground for the enemy to sneak through and the design faults of the smaller ones which had left open ground for the men to cross between the central redoubt and the latrines, kitchens and water supply built into the surrounding ramparts.

Leman agreed with him. 'Yes. Fort Loncin is the best. The others are not ideal. Is that it?'

'I wish it was, sir. The magazines are located high up within the fort. If German artillery penetrates the concrete, they are vulnerable.'

'Then we must continue to hope that your monster gun was merely a nightmare. Please tell me that is all?'

'Not quite, sir. The worst problem of all is the powder. When the guns are fired, the fort fills up with thick, choking smoke because you are still using black powder.'

'You would have us use smokeless propellants?'

'Yes, sir, like every other modern army.'

'Politicians do not understand war but they do understand money, Captain Fraser. We asked and were denied. They told us it was too expensive. We have tens of thousands of tons of black powder to use up and they insist that will have to do until it has all gone.' Willy looked at him and saw Leman knew perfectly well that he was expected to fight with one hand tied behind his back. 'Captain Fraser, I must also tell you that Belgium has appealed to your own country for its support. We believe Britain will join the war within hours if she has not done so already. I will happily release you from my service if you prefer to join your own forces.'

'Sir, if von Emmich's army gets through Liège where else might you hope to stop him?'

'Namur is next.' Namur, thought Willy, where Claude's new wife is living. 'It will stand for a while but Brussels has no defences,' said Leman. 'The main resistance will be at Antwerp.'

'Antwerp? That is all that would keep the Germans from Dunkirk, Calais and the other Channel ports?'

'Yes.'

'Then I think I serve my own country best by fighting with you here.'

'How do you prefer to fight, young man? Would you like to take your place inside the fortress of Loncin? I think it will be safer there, despite your fears of Mr Krupp.'

'I prefer to see where I am, sir. I am a cavalryman. I like the open country.'

'Then ride with my scouts. That is where Lieutenant Tavernier serves. I would like the two of you to be my eyes and my personal messengers. I would count it as a favour if you would continue to put that noisy American machine of yours into service for me.'

'Certainly, sir.'

'If you are quite sure, I wish you to go as fast

as you can towards the incursion at Gemmenich. Take Tavernier and report back as soon as you possibly can.'

Claude was silent as they made their way to the motorcycle.

'Namur and Brussels,' said Willy. 'You should send a message to Gabrielle. Tell her to head for Antwerp right away.'

7

Halfway to the frontier they found war. Willy longed for a cavalry charger to let him canter from cover to cover, zig-zagging through the hedgerows and the woodland to probe forward. As it was, he was stuck with the rutted road and could barely keep the motorbike under control. The muddy fields to each side were out of the question. Claude was a better passenger than Chester had been, but even his extra weight made it hard to manoeuvre the unbalanced machine.

His mind strayed briefly to Chester. Was he in an Abteilung IIIb cell or had he talked his way out of it? Could he be out here somewhere with the invading Germans? The rotund American made an unlikely foreign correspondent but he certainly had guts and he was hell-bent on getting to the action. Then Willy rounded a bend past an abandoned mill and the war reminded him sharply to practice what he preached on focusing the mind. Dogs were racing towards them from the edge of a small wood two hundred yards in front — flop-eared black and tan hounds, harnessed in pairs to miniature chariots. Belgian infantrymen in grimy dark blue uniforms ran with them. The men's staring eyes and the sweat-streaks down their grim and dusty faces showed they were running for their lives.

The first carts bounced and rattled past them,

the dogs yelping, panting at their heavy load. Fat, snub-nosed machine guns were bolted to metal frames between bicycle wheels.

'*Mitrailleuses*,' said Claude in Willy's ear. 'The Germans cannot be far behind.' He jumped off the back of the bike. 'Stop,' he shouted, but the men and their dog teams ran right on past him as if he wasn't there. One team was trailing, the dog on the left doing its best with a hind leg dragging. That last limping team was still thirty yards short of them when dust exploded in the road and a spinning black cylinder scythed through them like a viciously bouncing cricket ball. One dog dropped in its tracks. The other screamed and twisted to fall, kicking as arterial blood sprayed into the sky. Their gun trailer crashed on its side as the hurtling cylinder bounced once more, hissed between Willy and Claude and thumped, nose first, into a tree trunk six feet from them.

'Shell!' shouted Claude. It was half buried in the tree trunk, wisps of steam curling off it.

'Dud,' said Willy, staring at it in fascination, but Claude was already running forward towards the dead dogs and their toppled gun as riders poured out of the woodland beyond. For one final moment of the familiar peacetime world, Willy savoured the sight of fine horses and orderly ranks of lancers, proud Belgian cavalry. Then he took in the meaning of the grey uniforms and the spiked helmets. Not Belgians after all but German lancers, Uhlans. Enemies. No longer were Germans the people who ran hotels and staged musicals. In that moment they

111

turned into hard-bitten soldiers riding straight at him, intent on killing him with no more compunction than they had just killed these dogs.

'Help me,' shouted Claude. He had hauled the machine gun as upright as it would go and was wiping dirt from the breech. 'That wheel's bust. Brace it. Keep it steady.' He was kneeling, squinting along the barrel, pulling back a cocking lever. The gun erupted into a spitting staccato. Willy crouched by him, staring past the smoky, jumping barrel as all he held dear — fine animals, gleaming harnesses, trained and ordered men — were devastated by a hose of Belgian bullets. Horses danced, screamed and fell, dropping under riders already slumping out of their saddles, their lives stolen by Claude and his gun and though it was the attacked turning on the attacker, the scene filled him with horror. The ammunition ran through to its end in twenty seconds and in the renewed silence he heard the whinnies of a single horse, twisting in circles in the carnage, its reins held by something hidden in the heap of death. In a strange state of detachment, he found it very curious that all those men would never breathe again.

Another field gun crashed from somewhere in the far trees. Stones fountained in front of them, hissing and rattling against the machine-gun trailer. Claude flinched and clutched at his shoulder.

'Come on,' said Willy. 'We should go now.'

Claude nodded and Willy saw blood spreading on his tunic.

'You're hit.'

'I'll be all right. Start the damned engine.'

It took five eternal kicks to bring it to life and in that time another troop of Uhlans had come galloping out of the wood. Willy skidded the bike round and pulled Claude on board, then thundered away with the throttle wide open. Around one bend and then another and a sudden spout of flame sent a flight of bees humming past his right cheek before the Belgian machine-gunner lying in ambush realized his mistake. The gun teams were ready, spread out behind a low pile of logs beside the road.

He shouted a warning as they came level. 'Uhlan squadron. They'll be here any moment,' and then slowed.

'What are you doing?' Claude said.

'We should help.'

'No. Follow orders. Back to the General. He needs to know.'

They hadn't gone half a mile when machine guns opened up behind them but the noise soon died away and Willy could not be sure whether it was death or distance that brought the change.

Claude swayed on the bends on the way back. As they got off at Leman's headquarters Willy saw the dark blood and the two-inch splinter of steel sticking through his uniform. Claude refused to have it dressed until they had reported back to General Leman and shown him on the map exactly where they had encountered the German forces. The command centre was thick with cigarette smoke. Leman gave terse orders. Five minutes later, as Willy was watching nurses

113

tugging the metal out of Claude's shoulder, four booming blasts spelt the end of most of the Meuse bridges. He followed Leman and his staff as they went out on to the terrace.

The old General looked down at the smoke and the rubble where the bridges had been. 'We will hold the others open for the moment,' he said and Willy knew he meant in case of retreat but did not want to say the word. The General turned and cocked his head. A rattling drone swelled in the air behind them.

'Watch out,' called Leman's aide-de-camp, Captain Colland. 'A *Taube*.' He grabbed the General's arm as if to drag him back under cover but Leman shook him off and pointed up at the pale orange monoplane rocking its wings from side to side as it soared over them.

'*Taubes* are painted white. That one is ours,' said Leman calmly. 'It is the magnificent Henri Crombez who has volunteered his services to the Aviation Militaire Belge and that is his own Deperdussin racing monoplane. He has offered to reconnoitre the positions of the German forces and I have accepted. We are not the only ones who can copy the doves but ours is a hawk.'

Exhausted soldiers were digging trenches in front of the forts and haggard scouts told of Germans marching on the city from all directions, from the north right round to the south-east. Claude was ordered to rest and for the next few hours Willy took one of Leman's staff officers from fort to fort instead, handing out orders to men too over-stretched to implement them. He was a pot-bellied irascible

114

major with sour breath that swirled around Willy however fast he went but it was clear that they could not make much difference. Many civilian buildings still stood in the way of the forts' lines of sight and there was neither enough manpower nor enough spare explosive to remove all of them in time.

When they came back, a young man was talking to the General, a man whose aviation goggles had left a clean domino mask of pink flesh around his eyes in an oil-blackened face.

'Fraser,' said the General, beckoning him over. 'This is our intrepid Crombez. He has returned safely and he too has seen your train.'

'They are unloading it at Herbesthal, thirty kilometres to the east, and beginning to assemble a gun,' said Crombez. 'I saw the barrel you described and other parts of great size. They have brought up enormous motor tractors to haul it.'

'Can we attack it before they can bring it nearer?'

'Unfortunately there is a good German road from Herbesthal all the way to Liège and it is already well-protected by their troops.'

'It was the forty-two?'

'Who knows what size it is but it is certainly a large piece of steel.'

'Can you carry bombs?'

'Sadly no, monsieur. The Deperdussin, she is a wonder but she is a very light machine. Our air force has Henri Farman biplanes. The pilot can drop small bombs from those but they are few and they are not here. I can fly and look and swoop down to scare them but that is all I can hope to do.'

* * *

That night Willy went out to the citadel's terrace to get away from the smoke and the tension inside. He sat on a bench looking at a darkened town and a darker horizon, wondering whether the enemy was already inside the ring of forts and whether anybody in this changed world really knew what was happening. Out there men of one country or another were staring into the same darkness, wondering if every little noise was a precursor of sudden death. Every minute, star shells would soar up from the northern forts along the Meuse Valley, Pontisse and Barchon, but he heard no gunfire and concluded that the bright drifting lights in the sky had revealed no creeping grey squadrons on the ground.

He heard slow footsteps in the dark and a voice spoke his name — Claude, pale in the moonlight and shaky but walking carefully. 'Should you be up?' Willy said.

'I think so.' They sat in silence for a while then the Belgian spoke.

'Willy. Tell me. You have been in battle before. Were you afraid?'

'Of course I was. That was my first time too.'

'Really? But the General said . . . '

'Your dear General was guessing. He talked of skirmishes. He was thinking of Africa and India. That was his idea not mine. Yes, I served in India. The most dangerous thing I did there was play polo. That is the first time anyone has ever shot at me — at least, anyone sober and officially on the opposite side. It did feel a little personal. Why do you ask?'

'I don't know what is normal. I am worried that afterwards I felt so shaky.'

'Having steel sticking into you will do that every time. Of course you did.'

'But you did not shake. You showed what we call the cold blood.'

'We call it *sang froid*.'

'Ah! Surprising that neither nation wishes to claim it as their own. You are, I think, one of the fearless. I wish I were the same. How is a man to do it?'

'First, Claude, I *was* scared. Second, you should understand that being fearless does not mean being courageous. I knew a fearless man. It ran down through his family. All the men were soldiers. It was in their blood. The only reason they weren't extinct was that the strong desire to procreate was also in their blood. They mostly managed to have their children early, then they died young, gloriously and usually utterly pointlessly.'

'They were not courageous?'

'The word had no meaning for them. They were simply unable to feel fear. It was a profound lack of imagination. Claude, fear is the thing that keeps us alert. Courage keeps us going. Courage is what counts, not fearlessness.'

'So you truly had fear today?'

'I was terrified.'

'How did you not show it?'

117

'The same way you didn't. Have you forgotten? You ran straight to the gun cart. You gave me orders. You stopped the Uhlans. I have rarely seen such cold efficiency.'

'That was just . . . just drill, the obvious thing to do.'

'We both had more important things to do than waste time feeling frightened, it's as simple as that.'

But it wasn't simple at all. Willy found himself remembering a day many years earlier, a day when he was eight years old and his father took him out with the Galloway Hunt for the very first time. That was his father in the simpler days before Stellenbosch had entered the family vocabulary. In his memory it was early morning and cold and they were among the first to the meet so there had been nobody else to see when his father set him at a hedge far higher than anything he had jumped before. It was a trial that he failed ignominiously. He wanted to blame Frigate for the collective lack of nerve that sent him over his pony's head but he knew it had been his own fault.

'Back on,' said his father, instead of the things he wanted to hear which were more like 'are you all right?' or 'let's wait until you're older.' He climbed miserably into Frigate's saddle and stared at the vast barrier of the hedge waiting there, rustling in an untrustworthy way, poised ready to kill him.

'This time,' said his father, 'remember that you have a hundred heroes galloping with you.'

He twisted round in surprise but there was

nothing behind him but a large grey house, a few trees and one distant man leading a bay horse across the mud.

'No, you won't see them — not until you learn how to look,' said his father, 'but they are there, you know. All your ancestors. Mighty hunters and soldiers, every one. They have come to help you but only if you show them how. Go on. Lead your galloping army over that hedge. Nothing can stop you.' And armed with that, nothing did.

Claude broke in on his thoughts. 'I have my talisman to preserve me,' said Claude. 'Before we left Brussels, I set all my affairs in order with clear instructions for Gabrielle as to every part of it.'

'Why is that a talisman?'

'Because by writing it all down, I think she will not need it.'

'That works?'

'Yes. I knew it for certain today when the dogs came. I could shoot the *mitrailleuse* with impunity. It was given to me to know that was not my time.' He frowned. 'I am wrong. There is one thing I have not yet done. It is all business, that list. I must also write a letter to go with it to my wife, to remind her of my love.'

'Just shoot straight and move fast, Claude. That's better than any talisman. You have to get this into your head. If there is one thing my father taught me over and over again it is that in a war, every thought of home puts you in danger. Live completely in the place you are in. One hundred per cent of your thoughts, of your hearing, your sight and your smell. That is how

119

you survive. Keep home thoughts for when you're back home.'

'It helped your father survive the South African war?'

'Until the army got him.'

'The Boer army?'

'Oh no. Not the Boers, far worse — the English. How is your wound?'

'It will get better. I was lucky. Only flesh. There are many men out there who are not so lucky. I will write to Gabrielle to say she must not stay in Namur. I will tell her to go to her friend Anna in Malines. That should be safer. It is in the north, close to the outskirts of Antwerp. I will not tell her that I am wounded.'

'Why? Is she the sort of person who would burst into tears if she read that?'

'No.' He frowned, irritated. 'Not at all. She is a brave, strong woman. If you won't let me tell you about her then don't make ridiculous guesses.'

'Sorry. All right, Claude, just because you're wounded I'll give you two minutes to tell me about Gabrielle, starting now.'

He turned in his seat, expecting a predictable litany of sweetness, beauty and domestic skill. Claude stared at the ground for a moment then looked out towards the river.

'I first saw her when she knocked down a man who had robbed me.'

Willy laughed. 'No, I'm serious,' said Claude. 'It was in a Brussels market. I took out my wallet to pay for some fish. A man snatched it and ran. He was big. I started after him too late then all at once there she was ahead with her foot out and he was sprawling on the ground. In a moment she was sitting on his shoulders to keep him down, holding his hair and banging his head on the cobbles. How could I not love her after that?'

'So she's a big, powerful sort of woman, is she?'

'If you interrupt me, I demand more time. No, she is slender and lovely and . . . don't yawn. She is good at the things men do. She likes to fish and to shoot and she is better at mending things than I am. Most of all, when bad things happen she finds a way to make them funny. When I asked her to marry me she started laughing. No, stop. I don't mean that was a bad thing. It's just that her responses often surprise me. She knows all kinds of things. Do you know, when I stayed at her parents' house for the first time we were of course in our separate rooms and she started tapping on the wall and at first I thought it was just tapping but then I realized it was the Morse code so I could tap back, except she was better at it than I was. I am very lucky that she chose me and . . . '

'Time's up. Claude, she's lucky too. So that's the mark of a perfect wife, is it, tackling thieves and knowing the Morse code? It's an unusual set of virtues. Now let's get back to the business of war.'

* * *

The fifth of August was a nervous day of waiting. Another month might have made a difference to the Belgian preparations. A single day could do

121

little. He saw nothing of Claude, who had been ordered back to his cot for one more day's rest. Leman was philosophical and appeared to enjoy Willy's company — an opportunity to speak his mind to an officer outside his Belgian hierarchy.

'You wonder why we were not better prepared? We kept saying how neutral we were so our politicians saw little reason to spend more money on our forts,' he said. 'What was good enough for 1900 would be good for 1914. Now we will hold on here. Every extra day is of value. I will give the King the time he needs to strengthen Antwerp as much as possible. He has commanded me to resist and I shall do so.'

'King Albert, sir? You answer directly to him?'

'Don't think he is merely a king, young Fraser. He is my commander-in-chief not just in name but in fact. He is a very fine soldier and I should know. I trained him myself.'

'But the Queen is German, I understand. Does that not create a problem?'

Leman flushed then calmed himself. 'Believe me, Queen Elisabeth has a Belgian soul,' he said. 'And who are you to talk? Your own country is ruled by a family who were German very recently but I am sure you do not think of Queen Victoria's son as an enemy.' He took a deep breath. 'Enough of that. You may be amused to hear that the Germans have demanded the surrender of the city. Equally, you may not be surprised to hear I intend to ignore them.'

Before midnight heavy gunfire drummed in the south and reports began to come in from the Embourg and Boncelles forts that German

122

infantry was storming the defensive ditches, unheeding of the crossfire that mowed men down in rank after rank, lit up by the forts' searchlights. The messages said the Germans had attacked in parade order as if death simply did not matter and they came out of the darkness as if there was no end to them.

It was a warm night and Willy knew he would not rest cooped up inside, out of touch with whatever might happen next in the darkness of the hidden distance. He chose to sleep out on the terrace. Others had the same idea and soon there were rows of officers lying on blankets. He watched the usual firework display of flares for some time. Dull gunfire continued to spit and rumble from some unfathomable violence a few miles to the south-east. He dropped off to sleep but was rocked awake in the early hours of the morning by a fusillade all around him. Field guns, *mitrailleuses*; everything that could shoot was pounding away. Some of his companions began to fire rifles, aiming almost straight up as if they were trying for high-flying pheasants. There was Claude among them, with a Belgian Mauser held away from his injured shoulder, firing and reloading and firing again as fast as he could.

The big guns fell silent and the soldiers around him lowered their weapons. As the echoes cleared from his ears, Willy heard a deep humming from far above his head. It was more than an hour to moonrise. Surely the *Taubes* could not fly at night? How would they land? The humming reminded him of swarming bees, but bees, like *Taubes*, weren't nocturnal, were they? A hiss and a trail of sparks from the slope below the citadel marked the firing of a flare and as it flashed alight in a blue-white glare, it drew a shape out of the night sky above it, the curving belly of something immense, already turning away from the light.

Claude turned to him. 'Zeppelin,' he said. Willy caught a glimpse of engine pods hanging down and the flat surfaces of the giant airship's tail then it disappeared as the flare died and the fierce guns fired again. For a moment his heart lifted in the belief they had hit it because the gunfire flashes lit something black tumbling out of the sky, but the falling object plunged into the houses below him and erupted in an orange fountain of masonry, merging into the renewed uproar of the guns. The Zeppelin had dropped some sort of mine, some explosive charge from a thousand feet or more, and there could be no defence against such an unprecedented attack except for the blind probing of the army's guns, designed to fire at targets on the land, not up into the sky. He stared up for the next half-hour but the Zeppelin's invisible progress backwards and forwards across the city could only be plotted by the noise of its engines and the sporadic orange explosions on the ground below it. He kept count. The great menace in the sky dropped thirteen of its missiles before it droned away to escape the rising moon, leaving burning houses and the memory of terror behind it.

In the strained silence that followed, a trumpet blew a long derisive note in the darkness then

124

broke into ragtime and there was Claude, a polished brass instrument at his lips, playing Irving Berlin's 'When that Midnight Choo-Choo Leaves for Alabam' and all the officers on the terrace cheered when he finished as if it was the best possible response.

'You have talents I never suspected,' Willy said.

'I started as a boy trumpeter. I always carry it with me.'

Nine Belgians died under that Zeppelin bombardment and in the morning, General Leman's staff linked two words into a term that was not yet on the lips of the world. They talked of the 'air raid' and they talked not of aerial mines but of bombs. It might have been the Zeppelin or it might have been the endless reports of more and more German forces pouring in from the east and the south-east but Willy thought the General's face showed a set determination that now had nothing to do with victory and much more to do with stubborn sacrifice.

Then in a sharp moment, the battle switched from somewhere on the outskirts to their very doorstep. Willy was in the sheds behind the citadel where the despatch riders kept their machines. He was checking over the Thor, preparing it for his next task. They were running low on petrol and what was left was very dirty. He had already cleaned brown muck out of the carburettor and was carefully filtering fuel from the tin cans through chamois leather into a series of glass carboys that had once contained battery acid. He had three full jars, corked and settling, and he was bending down inspecting the clarity of their contents when a ricocheting bullet sprayed broken window glass across him. Pistol shots came from the courtyard outside, then shouts and running feet. Through the broken window he saw Claude and two other officers rush from the headquarters' back door across the yard carrying the struggling figure of General Leman between them. He watched, completely baffled, as they threw Leman unceremoniously over the wall into the scrubland to his left then, as they turned, a squad of German Uhlans ran into the yard from the right. Claude fired his pistol and the Uhlans dived behind the shelter of a stone drinking-trough. The Belgians had no cover and no way out of the dead-end except over the wall which now concealed their commander. Willy heard Claude ordering the others to rush the Germans and knew that could not end well. Then one of the crouching attackers struck a match and held it out towards a large, fused canister in the hand of his neighbour.

Willy grabbed the nearest jar, ran to the door and yelled, 'Catch.' All their faces swivelled to him and he hurled the heavy glass container straight at the drinking trough. The glass shattered and two gallons of petrol exploded in a fireball, engulfing the attackers and sending them backwards away from the bursting heat. The Germans' grenade blew up in a second smoky blast from within the fire and that was the end of their attack.

They retrieved Leman from the undergrowth,

Claude apologizing as they pulled brambles from his uniform. 'There was no time, sir. We had to get you to a safer place.'

When there was time to explain, they told how the first group of Uhlans had burst in through the front of the building. Taken by surprise, the guard had been overwhelmed with three Belgians killed, so they had rushed Leman out of the back door almost straight into the path of the second group. Every one of the attackers had been killed but the confusion was such that no one seemed to know who had done what, so Willy went back to the shed, took another carboy from the shelf and filled his tank, taking care to cork the container firmly when he had finished.

Back inside the command centre there was shock that the German attack had come so close to the General. The dead were being carried outside. More than two hundred Germans had reached the edge of the citadel and much of the lower town was in their hands. 'It can't last,' Claude said quietly to Willy. 'The General has ordered most of the army to leave.'

'Where to?'

'To Brussels if the city is to make a stand but more probably to pass straight on to Antwerp because that is the best hope. Only the garrisons of the forts will remain here to fight it out.'

'How many is that?'

'Three or four hundred in each fort. That's their fighting strength. There's no room for more.'

Leman's ADC called for silence and the General came forward. 'We know what we have

127

to do, gentlemen. Most of you will do your utmost to support the King at the National Redoubt. The walls of Antwerp are strong. I will continue to conduct the defence of Liège and after our experience today I have decided the town itself is no longer defensible. I will move my staff with me to Fort Loncin. We will leave immediately. We will fight them from the fortresses. Long live the King.'

He walked past Willy on his way out, stopped and turned to face him. 'My Scottish friend. I am very pleased to say that as yet we see no sign of your threatened weapon. Not that life is easy in its absence but Loncin can stand up to everything we have seen them use so far. I can confirm to you that your country has now declared war on Germany. You are free to take up service with your own people should you choose. If you prefer to stay in our service, I can offer you a certain amount of excitement at Fort Loncin should you decide to accompany Lieutenant Tavernier there. Our defence will depend on communications being maintained between the forts and an intrepid messenger mounted on a powerful machine may still be of great value. Would you like the job?'

Willy looked into the old man's eyes and saw there was still humour dancing there behind the vast fatigue. 'So long as you keep me in petrol, sir,' he said. 'I didn't have any other immediate commitments.'

8

Thursday, 13 August 1914. Fort Loncin, Liège.

By the end of a dreadful week, the Germans held the city of Liège. The old citadel in the centre had surrendered six days earlier but the twelve ring fortresses had locked themselves down for the last battle, planning to protect each other as they were designed to do in a circular chain of fire. That chain was broken after only a day. Fort Barchon, guarding the River Meuse to the north-east, came under heavy assault from twenty-one centimetre guns. Barchon's Commandant Hannefstingels knew the size of the shells because his men had coolly gone outside to measure the girth of one that had failed to explode. At noon that day, he telephoned his General to report that a German delegation had come under flag of truce to request his surrender, adding proudly that he turned them away. In the afternoon a final message came through that Barchon was under intense bombardment, that all his observation points had been destroyed and the air inside the fort was barely breathable. An hour passed and the Fort de Pontisse, next in line, reported that a handful of Barchon's guns were firing blindly from the wreckage of the cupolas.

At 6 p.m., Leman called his officers together in the deep bowels of Fort Loncin. Willy and

Claude squeezed in at the back of the sweaty, airless cellar. 'I have to tell you, gentlemen,' he said, 'Pontisse reports that Barchon has fallen silent after a noble and defiant battle.' He stilled the answering buzz with a hand. 'All our ventilation shafts must be carefully inspected and the fans overhauled. Their defeat was due to excessive fumes from their own gunfire. We must not let that happen again.'

★ ★ ★

At the beginning of that endless week Willy had done exactly as Leman had asked, using the speed of the motorcycle to scout the roads around the city, Claude clinging on behind him, banging his shoulders to indicate a left or a right turn. The two of them worked closely with three improvised armoured Belgian cars driven by young madmen, powerful tourers with machine guns mounted behind steel sheets. Willy and Claude would search out advancing enemies in the narrow streets of the city, using speed and the power of surprise to swing round and make their escape when they came too close. They would tear back to the waiting armoured cars, give them directions and watch the hard-eyed killers, who had so recently been the young and idle rich of Belgian society, hurl themselves, guns spitting, into action. On the second day an unseen German field gun blew their best armoured car to pieces, a Rolls-Royce Silver Ghost which had combined speed with uncanny silence. Two more days of probing, running battles and they lost another, Claude leaping from the moving bike in a hopeless attempt to pull the driver from the burning wreck. The last of the cars went the next day, captured when the gearbox stripped as the driver was reversing at full speed from an ambush in an alleyway. Claude and Willy worked as one entity right through that one-sided struggle, learning everything there was to know about each other's responses in the crucible of the burning streets and whining shards of steel. Then came the morning when Leman barred their way to the gates and told them there was nothing to be gained from taking the battered Thor out of Fort Loncin any more.

'There may soon be a time when I shall need you and your motorcycle,' he said. 'Just wait and be glad that your giant gun has not shown its face, Fraser. It is noisy enough in here without that.'

That was the day Willy realized Loncin was an underground prison and was set to become a tomb. For him, it was the very worst of places. There were only two ways to see what was going on outside. The first, close to suicide, was to climb the endless stairs up through the arched tunnels inside the mound and seek an exit past guarded steel gates secured by vast cogs and bolts. They opened onto the riflemen's terrace girdling the fort halfway up its sloping flanks, a trench with a parapet for sharpshooters as a last-ditch defence to fight off an infantry attack. No one went out there in daylight. The field-gun shells landing in salvoes on the fort could barely dent its gigantic bulk but they deterred casual sightseeing. The only other way to see out was to peer through the periscopes or the narrow eye-slits of the weapons controllers but shifts of staring gunners monopolized those and they didn't take kindly to Willy's attempts to look over their shoulders.

'I'm not sure I can stand this for much longer,' Willy muttered, sitting in near darkness, trying not to breathe the foul air.

As conditions inside worsened, Claude's sense of humour had veered sharply into irony. 'Don't say that, my friend. What could you possibly not like? The regular drips from the wet concrete are predictably soothing are they not? The Loncin metronome could become the envy of musicians everywhere. That sharp smell of burnt explosive and petrol fumes adds a delightful edge to the stale urine and the rat faeces. We will talk to Guerlain or Coty as soon as this is over and have it in the shops of the Champs Élysées in no time at all. As for the accommodation, this could become the style for the grand hotel of the future for those seeking seclusion from the world. Even the finest hotels don't have anything like such thick walls and if you still don't like it, the restrained lighting and the unusually opaque nature of the atmosphere in here means you don't have to look too hard at it anyway and I haven't even come to the food yet.'

The city may have been lost but Fort Loncin's big guns held the key to what happened next because they still commanded the lowlands below and the all-important highway towards

Brussels, the only feasible route forwards for the enemy army. Willy had grown almost used to breathing the haze of exhaust and hot oil that filled the chambers of the fort but rational thought still became impossible each time they fired those guns. The guns blew apart a German *Taube* which had unwisely landed below them on the plain of Ans and they created havoc in the German troop concentrations between the fort and the city. A mist of cement dust spurted out of the ceiling joints at each salvo but the harsh smoke of the guns' black powder charges, billowing through the corridors in acrid clouds, was far worse than the noise and the dust. It was Willy's idea of perdition.

Communications with two more forts broke down that day. There was nothing for Willy and Claude to do except stay out of the way of the exhausted gunners and the teams hauling ammunition from the magazines. Most of the incoming field-gun shells produced no more than a dull thump but once every few minutes a twenty-one centimetre would arrive and the concrete vaults would shiver despite their deep earthen covering. That evening, Claude was very quiet. Willy followed him into the small side room where they had been sleeping. Lime stalactites projected down an inch or two from the seams of the concrete ceiling, each one with a drip hanging from its end. The only light came from a lantern in the corridor outside. Candles and fuel were strictly rationed and the pressure waves of the gun blasts had destroyed many of the electric light bulbs.

'Come on, boyo,' said Willy. 'What's eating you? It's not the lovesick blues again, is it?'

Claude shook his head.

'Tell me,' said Willy more gently.

'There are too many holes now,' said Claude, 'and they can only get bigger.'

'What do you mean?'

'You know very well. The forts overlap their fire to save each other. That was their strength. Now the Germans are picking away at the gaps. We cannot win.'

A voice spoke from the gloom of the doorway. 'We are not here to win.'

A tall man stepped inside. Leman. Claude was aghast. 'General. I did not mean to sound . . . '

'Please resist such defeatism, Tavernier, even when there is only one other man to listen. I think you understand by now that winning is not our objective. The forts were here to deter and they failed to do so. Now our task is to slow the invaders down and we shall continue to do that. Loncin is the key to that plan. This fort of ours is stronger than all the rest put together. From here we control the road to the capital. If we are the last fort still fighting, they cannot reach Brussels without passing us first and every day that we hold them is another day for our King to prepare to face them. We will keep them at bay while there is still powder in our magazine. Mr Fraser, if that prospect appals you then I will happily release you to join your own army. The British are coming to our country's aid.'

'I think I'll stay here and wait for them, sir. All that travelling can be a bit of a bore.'

'*Mon Générale*,' said Claude, 'I am so sorry for my words. How can I make amends?'

The General laughed. 'My friend, I know you would only voice such thoughts to Fraser. There is no need to make amends unless you can find a way to persuade the Germans that the French army has come to reinforce us. That might help.'

★ ★ ★

Claude shook Willy awake at midnight. 'Would you like some fresh air?' he suggested.

'Is there such a thing? I thought it had been abolished. There's nothing I'd like more.'

'There's no shellfire at the moment.'

'Well now, could that be because they can't see what they're shooting at?'

Claude's face was invisible in the gloom but his voice was full of determination. 'I would like to try my luck out on the fire terrace. Would you like to come?'

'That certainly sounds fun,' said Willy. 'How could I possibly resist an offer like that?' They took rifles from the rack and Claude slung his knapsack over his shoulder. The guards at the steel door on to the riflemen's terrace were surprised when told to open it. 'It is on General Leman's instructions,' Claude said.

The heavy door was dragged open just far enough for them to squeeze outside and Willy was trying to control his laughter. 'The General's instructions?' he said. 'You great big fibber.'

'Shhh. Be quiet. You don't know who is out

here. Anyway what do you mean? I did not lie. I am here to do exactly what the General told me.'

'Really? What?'

Claude stared into the darkness. The moon was down and it was black as pitch. 'Do you think they are close by, the Germans?'

Willy looked over the parapet, down the slope to the open ground below. There was a dim gleam moving down there but it vanished immediately. A smothered lantern? It was impossible to say what it was or how far away. 'I expect so,' he said. 'If I was them I would have patrols out looking for opportunities.'

'Perfect,' said Claude. He knelt down and undid the straps of his rucksack. Willy stared out, scanning his eyes from side to side, knowing that the most sensitive part of his night vision was a little to the side of the centre point. He didn't expect to see anything but he didn't much mind. A clean breeze was bringing fresh air from the west, from a direction in which there was as yet no sour stink of explosive destruction. He filled his lungs and felt the air bringing him back to life. This was once again a world worth living in, one where he could go in any direction he dared. No one down there knew he was up here. He held all the cards.

A huge noise split the night, inches from his ear. A shrieking trumpet blast. The first nine notes of the 'Marseillaise', unmistakable and played at maximum volume by Claude, hurling his defiance into the night and at whoever was listening below.

Willy swung round and knocked it away from

136

his lips. 'What the hell are you doing?' he said in shock.

'Fulfilling my General's request,' Claude said innocently, wiping the mouthpiece on his shirt-sleeve. 'Doing my best to persuade any German listening out there that the French army has indeed come to our rescue. Do you think they're listening?' He put the trumpet back to his lips and began again, blowing glory into the night.

The night spat back at him. They certainly were out there listening because a critic somewhere down in the darkness below the fort opened up on them with a machine gun from startlingly close range. He was aiming at the sound and he must have had good ears because the burst hit the very edge of the parapet, sprayed earth and stone over them and sent the trumpet spinning out of Claude's fingers.

'Bastard,' said Claude.

Willy had his rifle to his shoulder, firing towards where he had seen the muzzle flash but the pitch blackness quickly stole his point of reference. It did not matter. A moment later they were given a striking demonstration of how the Liège forts were supposed to work. As the burst of gunfire died away, an armoured searchlight buzzed, clicked and glared into life up above them near the summit of the fort. Two machine-gun cupolas groaned, lifted and rotated. As the searchlight bulb warmed and brightened up, Willy saw five German soldiers running downhill a hundred yards beyond the lower ditch, carrying a machine gun between them. He put his rifle to his shoulder again but as he took aim, the fort's machine guns opened up on them and before he could squeeze the trigger there was no longer any living target to aim at.

'Damn,' said Claude. 'Now I'll have to do it all over again. They won't be telling anyone about the French, will they?'

'You want to sit here until more Germans come so you can play your horn again?'

'Yes. That was the whole point. They need to go back and tell someone.'

'Claude, you're a man after my own heart.'

'Really? Do you mean that? That is the second best thing anyone has said to me this year.'

'What was the best?'

'Gabrielle saying 'I do'.'

They sat down in the ditch and Claude inspected the trumpet. 'There's a hole in it,' he said indignantly. 'Look. Right through the bell. It's not going to sound right. My trumpet. How dare they?'

'It will bear its scar with honour.'

'Yes. If that's as bad as it gets, perhaps I shouldn't complain.'

Willy let that one go and there was a long silence then Claude said, 'Have you really never been in love?'

'Oh good Lord. What now? Please, friendly Germans, shoot me.'

'I know what you said. I should not think about Gabrielle. I know you're right but when it's quiet I can't help myself. She is my guardian angel. Have you?'

'How would I know?'

'Then you haven't. Have you never yearned to be with just one woman?'

'Yes.'

'For how long?'

'Two days. Maybe three.'

Claude punched him on the shoulder. 'Stop it. I don't believe you.'

But it's true, Willy thought, and for just a moment he envied Claude.

'There is a woman out there for you somewhere,' said Claude. 'You will meet her.'

'There's not just one. There are thousands, millions even. How many women do you meet in your life? Suppose you meet one new woman every day. Three hundred and sixty-five women a year. Let's say you're looking for the love of your life for ten years, that's more than three thousand women and you fall in love with one of them. How many people are there on earth?'

'I don't know. I never counted.'

'All right. Let's say you're British and there are forty million people in Britain. Twenty million women. Three million of those are roughly the right age so if you only meet three thousand of them that means there are at least one thousand women in Britain alone you could have fallen in love with and that's without bothering to cross the Channel.'

'You are missing the point,' Claude said. 'It is not a matter of the one new woman you might meet each day. When you're not at war, you pass three hundred women in the street every day, in cafés, in bars, at parties. Then without saying a word, you see one of them across a room or in a market and boom, that's it — that is the one in a million. The whole point is she was meant to be there that day and so were you.'

'Meant to be? You're a romantic. You occupy a beautiful world in your mind but it is not the real world.'

'You're an ignorant idiot, Willy Fraser. I tell you I was brought up by serious-minded parents. My father told me he married my mother because she had good teeth. He said good teeth meant good health and a sensible woman with good teeth would go a long way. He told me I should choose a wife in the same way that I would choose a manager to run my company. I think I believed him then bang, I'm chasing after a thief in a market and a thunderbolt comes out of nowhere. She bowled the thief over and she bowled me over and being sensible didn't enter into it for a moment.'

'All right, if you agree to shut up, I'll agree to leave my wallet sticking out of my pocket in the street and I'll promise to fall in love with the first woman who knocks out the thief. Will that satisfy you?'

'Yes. Well, no. When this war is over Gabrielle will help me find you a wife. I told you about her friend Anna from Malines? The place I told her to go to? You would really like Anna.'

'Because?'

'She is funny and strong and loving and she never gives up.'

'Is she beautiful?'

'In the Belgian way.'

140

Willy was not at all sure that was the same way as the Scottish way but he kept quiet for fear of offending Claude.

'Come on,' said Claude. 'As you say, a penny for them. You are thinking of beautiful women? Are you such a shallow man that only the shape of the cheeks and the lips matters to you?'

'Yes.'

Claude switched from English into French, always a sign that he wanted Willy to take him seriously.

'What is the difference between a beautiful woman you want to be with and one that you do not?'

It was a good question. Too good perhaps. 'Claude, we are out in the open with an unknown number of enemy soldiers out there who would dearly like to kill us. I suggest this is one of those times when we should concentrate on staying alive.'

Claude shrugged. 'We are in no immediate danger. If it suits you to avoid my question then I think I have hit the mark.'

'They have to be bold and ready to break the rules,' Willy said, slightly to his own surprise. 'Meek beauty does nothing for me. The spark in the eye counts for everything.'

'Then you *would* like Gabrielle's friend Anna. She is valiant, almost like Gabrielle. Like you are.'

'And you, Claude. I have fought alongside a truly valiant man these past few days.'

'You mean that?'

'Yes.'

In the long silence after that they both scanned the pitch-dark slopes below for movement. 'How long do you think all this will take?' said Claude.

'For more Germans to approach?'

'No. I meant the war.'

'I have no idea.'

'I think Germany will want another piece of land. The war of 1870 gave them Alsace and Lorraine and then they were very happy. This time they will want Belgium to add to their collection and then they will be happy again. We will be penned up in this fort until we surrender and then kept prisoner somewhere for a long while and finally it will all be sorted out so that I can go home to Gabrielle.'

'To live happily ever after under German rule?'

'Maybe we will escape to France. She has an aunt who lives very close to the border. Do you know Comines?'

'No.'

'It is a small town and her aunt has a farm in the country nearby. It is a place she loves. She spent holidays there as a child. It has a farmyard with old brick barns and a little bridge where you can watch the fish swim underneath in the Mallet stream. They have an empty cottage by the bridge. I would live there very happily. You will come and stay with us when the war is over, so long as you promise to behave yourself and choose Anna from Malines and not let my Gabrielle fall for you.'

'She loves you, idiot.'

142

'I know. I'm joking. So, what do you think?'

'About what?'

'About how long this will last.'

If the Germans take the Channel ports it will all be over by Christmas was what Willy thought, but he didn't want to put that into words. He said nothing and Claude stayed silent for a long time then sighed.

'What?'

'You will not want to hear,' Claude said.

'I have nothing else to do.'

'I can talk of the war ending and of living in France but that is not what will happen.'

'Why not?'

'Because last night it came to me that I will not see Gabrielle again.'

'Oh stop that right now.'

'No, Willy. It is all right. I feel quite calm about it but my time is coming.'

Willy looked out into the darkness towards the dead men down there and the unknown numbers of living men with guns. 'Don't do that. Claude, promise me you will put that out of your mind. You must live in the moment you are in and only that. Take anything that is useful to your survival from your past experience but nothing else. Only look far enough into the future to dodge the next bullet. That way you will see her again. While I am with you, I will do all I can to keep you alive and you will do the same for me. I think you should stop thinking and play the 'Marseillaise' again, but be ready to duck.'

Claude did as he said, playing it all the way through. Twice.

Three days later, Fort Evegnée fell and two days further on Embourg and Chaudefontaine had surrendered in quick succession. In the command centre, General Leman called for Willy and beckoned him to the eyepiece of a periscope. 'Tell me what you see,' he said. 'I understand you have some experience of this.'

It took Willy a moment to take it in. He was looking along the line of the northern forts, each on the summit of its own great mound. Increasing gunfire had stopped him making any more sorties out on to the ramparts and so it was a huge relief to see the outside world again, to discover the astonishing sight of a fine summer's day out there with sun shining down on a wide, bright horizon just as if there was no war. Then he focused on the detail, shocked to see the desolation that was the Fort of Lantin, two miles east. Beyond, columns of smoke were rising from Liers and beyond that again, above the Meuse Valley was the fine sight of brave Fort Pontisse, blazing away from all its turrets and cupolas like a vast battleship firing broadsides in muzzle flashes and billowing black smoke.

'Look north of Pontisse,' said Leman. 'Do you see? Towards Oupeye.'

He had no idea where Oupeye was but he looked a little to the left and there was a familiar shape slowly rising in the far distance, a fat yellow slug with a tiny basket below it.

'That is your German balloon?' said Leman.

'Yes, sir,' said Willy. 'That's it.'

'What is it doing?'

'Directing their guns, no doubt.'

'But why? They are now close to all my forts. They can see where their shells land. Why do they need a balloon?'

Willy hesitated. 'I don't know, sir.'

Leman stared at him. 'You don't know but you suspect something perhaps?'

'You will think I am obsessed by my monster gun, sir.'

'What has a balloon to do with that?'

'If they have moved it and put it together and perhaps even built a concrete emplacement for it then they could not easily move it again. It might be at some distance from its targets.'

'My forts, you mean?'

'Yes, sir. In that case the best way to control its aim would be to have a balloon right by it to direct its fire.'

There was a long silence while Leman considered him, frowning.

'I cannot find fault with your logic,' he said flatly in the end. 'How could it be destroyed?'

Willy considered. 'The balloon is full of hydrogen,' he said. 'Hydrogen is explosive. If it were hit then I guess it would be destroyed.' He thought of high-flying birds and his old shotgun at his shoulder. 'A shrapnel burst close by might do it.'

Leman turned to his artillery officer. They discussed fuse settings, elevation and time of flight then orders were issued by phone to the Pontisse fort. The artillery officer glued himself to the periscope and Willy envied him every

145

second of that view, that release from the oppression of claustrophobic concrete. Minutes passed, then the crouching officer said, 'They're shooting now. Well short.' More silence then, 'High, high . . . over-corrected. Too low. I think they are raising the balloon. What a hard target!'

The commentary went on for fifteen minutes, the Germans raising and lowering the balloon to confuse the aim then the artillery officer exclaimed, 'Bravo. That was close. Yes, yes, yes. I think they are hauling it down.'

'Is it burning?' demanded Leman.

'No, sir. Punctured perhaps.'

Half an hour later, it was up again, patched or replaced, and soon after that they lost contact with Pontisse.

'The wires are cut,' a subaltern reported. 'A shell perhaps.'

'Of course it was a shell,' Leman snapped. 'They must stop firing now. It is their best chance. They should appear to be out of action to draw the Germans to them then open up with everything they have. I must get a message to them. Can we signal them?'

'We have tried the lamps. They do not respond. Perhaps they cannot look this way any more.'

'I could take a message, sir,' said Willy.

'On your motorcycle? No. That is no longer possible.'

'On foot, I think. It's a nice day for a stroll.' Anything would be better than staying in here, he thought.

'Do you know the way?'

'I do, sir,' said Claude. 'I know all the pathways well. I'll go with him.'

'Why hazard two men?' said Leman.

'It doubles the chance of one man getting through,' said Willy.

'And the risk. All right. Go. If nothing else, find out if your monster is a myth.'

9

Willy's vivid Belgian uniform was now unrecognisable, blackened by smoke and oil and nameless stains. Claude's was almost as bad but they were still too bright for the work ahead so they borrowed drab green overalls from the sappers. They left the fort through its main entrance, via a complex series of steel doors, blast traps and ambush chambers which led them to a tunnel and a final steel gate watched over by machine-gun cupolas. Jumpy, staring guards let them out into blessed fresh air. The sound of the outside world was a shock. Artillery rumbled constantly all around them in a great arc from north-east clockwise to the west but at that moment, no shells were falling close to Loncin and the word from the observation points was that no Germans were in the immediate vicinity. Loncin, it seemed, was being left alone for the moment as too tough a nut to crack.

Half an hour and a mile further on, enemy units were everywhere. The two of them were running in the cover of walls and hedges, often doubled over, frequently hiding as enemy infantry and horsemen passed them. Ahead they could see field-gun batteries by the hundred preparing for further attacks all around them. They stayed well away from the city centre, arcing round to the north. Another half hour, and an alarming sight showed itself above the high hedge-line of the curving lane ahead — a row of a hundred or more lances bobbing up and down, held at the vertical by the invisible cavalry hidden by the hedge, coming towards them. Claude beckoned Willy into the courtyard of a deserted house then down some steps into a cellar where six German infantrymen were sitting on boxes, staring at them with rifles across their knees. The rifles were raised and pointed in an instant.

'Where is Feldwebel Ruesch?' demanded Willy in German. He was thankful their overalls bore no insignia. 'Quickly. It is very important.'

'Ruesch?' said the oldest of them, shaking his head but putting his rifle down again. He looked around at the others to no avail. 'We don't know any Ruesch. Which unit?'

'The 18th,' said Willy.

'18th what?'

'Damn it, we haven't got time for this.' He turned and Claude followed him up the steps straight into a yard that was now filling up with horses and Uhlans who stared at them curiously.

Willy barely broke stride, heading into the middle of them towards the way out but one in front of him, a tall, scarred man who had just dismounted, was staring at him and opening his mouth when the older soldier shouted from the top of the cellar steps. 'Go back east, boys. The lad says the 18th might be by the church with the broken spire.'

'Thanks, comrade,' shouted Willy. 'If Ruesch comes tell him Schmidt and Baumer are heading that way.'

The Uhlan lost interest and they reached the lane unchallenged. 'Am I Schmidt or Baumer?' asked Claude.

'Whichever you choose.'

They took still more care after that until they came into sight of the Liers fort. They were looking up from the illusory shelter of a small copse at a low hill ahead of them. It seemed to have been chosen as the site of a fireworks display put on by malignant giants. Salvoes of shells were bursting around the outer ditches in gouts of flame, earth and concrete. They could not see as far up as the domed top of the fort but every few seconds another chain of explosions would signal hits from up there. One of the fort's big guns responded — just a single one. Willy could only imagine what it must be like inside.

'That's twenty-one centimetre fire, isn't it?' Claude said. 'They're having a hard time of it. We need to go south now.'

They could see German troops massing ahead of them for an infantry assault but Claude found them a long diversion through scrubby woodland and empty farms. Willy felt at his most alive. He could see where he was going, he had a Belgian FN pistol tucked out of sight and that was all — just two men's wits and stamina against the whole of the enemy's army. This was a better sort of war.

They reached the edge of a spinney and from there they could see the Meuse Valley to their east and Fort Pontisse holding the high ground of the west bank, belching defiant gunfire from turrets all over the cratered curve of its wide

150

hilltop. They could also see they had no hope of getting any closer. Thousands of soldiers and battery after battery of field guns stood silent and poised for assault in the open fields ahead of them. The main attack on Pontisse was coming from their left and shells were bursting constantly on the fort. The fat balloon was soaring in the wind two miles beyond, tugging at its cable, and Willy imagined the eyes in the basket searching the ground below. He took a step back into the shelter of the trees. The gunners trapped inside Pontisse were making no further attempts to bring it down.

They crouched in hiding, waiting for a miraculous opportunity, but they both knew that even if some Red Sea channel opened up through the enemy below them, getting into the fort through the unrelenting wall of high-explosive bursts would be impossible. There was no safety to be found anywhere around them, only enemies, and no way forward except to death.

'How much bravery have you left in you, would you say?' asked Claude.

'How can I answer that? I don't know what units it's measured in.'

'Enough to make for the balloon site? We can do nothing here but we might find a weakness there.'

Willy studied him and then looked again at the mass of troops beyond. 'There's no possible way through.'

'We could be Schmidt and Baumer again.'

'We wouldn't last two minutes.'

151

Claude stared at him. 'I can be brave when there's a plan,' said Willy defensively, 'but that simply would not work.'

'I wasn't doubting your courage, *mon brave*. I was only thinking that when Willy Fraser can't find time for a joke, it would be a foolish man who ignored what he said.'

The barrage stopped abruptly. Pontisse went on firing but the change underlined how much of its sting had already been drawn. The smoke was still impressive but the defending gunfire was thin and sporadic compared to the attack.

A new sound came to them from the direction of the balloon, a bass drone carving a long, slow arc up the sky. It took several seconds and its passage was so distinct that Willy searched for the source of the noise up there somewhere, feeling he should be able to see it. It peaked and the note rose higher as it began its descent. The first shot was long. It landed somewhere outside the fort's defensive ditch and all likelihood of jokes ended. Even at a mile's distance, he felt the pain of the pressure wave assault his chest and the mayhem of the explosion was so immense that it blotted out their view of the whole central massif of the fort. They could hear faint cheers erupt from the soldiers in the fields near them and earth went on falling around them for a long, long time afterwards.

'Aaaah,' said Claude. 'What in hell was that?'

'That *was* hell,' said Willy quietly. 'Krupp's metal monster, the *zweiundvierzig*. The nightmare has come.'

He had the presence of mind to look at his

152

watch. It took the distant gunners just over three minutes to adjust their aim and fire again but the balloon had done its part of the work well and this time the shell hit the very centre of the summit of the fort in a vast explosion far outstripping anything they had seen so far. There was an eruption of chaos so astonishing that it took Willy seconds to realize that the shape whirling end over end in the air high above the fort was an entire metal gun turret, fifty tons or more thrown up like a tennis ball.

They watched as five more of Krupp's vast shells fell like the end of the world on the disintegrating fort and then had no more heart for it.

'We have to get back and tell them,' said Claude. 'They must prepare.'

Willy thought, how can anyone prepare? He saw the same thought in Claude's eyes but they both stayed silent. Then Claude held out his arms and they hugged each other. 'Yes,' he said. 'Let's go and tell the General.'

'After you, Herr Baumer.'

They took to the hedgerows again. Somewhere behind the Lantin Fort, with Loncin only a mile and a half away, they were listening to the whine of field-gun shells arcing and crossing the sky to their target when Willy heard a shell overshooting Lantin and this time the whine did not traverse — it simply grew in intensity, coming from one place, an unwavering spot in the sky. It took him a moment to understand the implication of this but realization and the shell arrived at the same instant. The earth heaved up and threw him over in the centre of a concussive ball of bright orange heat.

★ ★ ★

When he came back to consciousness, he was lying on a hard cot in a blacked-out room with a pain firing through his head at every beat of his pulse. The smell told him he was back inside Loncin and a slow process of muddled elimination told him only Claude could have got him there. He was still dressed in the sapper's overalls but there was a bandage round his head and someone had taken his boots off. It took him several attempts to stand up and a long time to walk to the doorway, leaning against the wall, and down the corridor towards a dim light. He found Leman and four of his officers talking quietly to each other.

'Major Fraser,' said Leman. 'I am not sure you should be walking around.'

'And I'm not sure I'm a major, sir.'

'I just promoted you and Major Tavernier for your services.'

'Then he has told you what we saw?'

'Yes. He told me you have been quite right all along. We are faced with something beyond our experience.'

'I am sorry to bring you such bad news.'

'It does not help but it is better to know than not to know. Tavernier is sleeping. He carried you and it has opened his wound again. I am considering a sortie. A last throw of the dice. A hundred men to go in darkness and find that gun. What do you think?'

'I will be happy to go with them.'

'I'm sure you will but that was not my question. Would we have any chance of success?'

'There are twenty thousand enemy between here and that gun. Perhaps more. I have to say there would be no chance but we should still try it.'

Leman dismissed the other officers then sat back in his chair. 'I think not,' he said. 'We have a little more information. One message came through from the Fort de Liers while you were out there. They have already tried it. They sent out a patrol to aid Pontisse, a bold attempt to destroy the howitzer. They failed to get close enough but the survivors took a German gunner prisoner. He has told them that it takes eight hours to dismantle the gun for movement and a further eight to prepare it for firing again once it has been transported to a new site. A second gun is not yet ready for use. He said that after the fall of Pontisse, the first will be moved to a new position from where it can fire on us here in Loncin. I believe therefore that sometime around the middle of the day tomorrow we will come under fire here. After that, from all you say, it is simply a matter of time.' He studied Willy. 'If you rest tonight,' he said, 'will you be able to ride your machine tomorrow?'

'Yes, sir, but where to?'

'I am not entirely sure, young man. Probably, I fear, all the way to Antwerp. At the moment we no longer have any communication with the world outside. I must ensure that the army high command has all the information we now possess. You may be the only way I can do that if you are prepared to take it on. You are in a unique position to tell them about the forty-two centimetre.'

He looked at Willy and shook his head slowly. 'I can think of no strategy to combat this situation. Tomorrow we will find out just what Loncin is made of. We may still command the Brussels road and if necessary we will use our guns to clear your way if hostile forces try to prevent you.'

* * *

Claude shook Willy awake early the next morning. 'It is time for you to get ready,' he said. 'General Leman has a despatch for you to take and I have one too.'

'*You* do?'

Claude reached into his knapsack and took out an envelope. 'It is my letter for Gabrielle,' he said. 'You will find a way to get it to her, I am sure. There were things I had to tell her. It has taken me much of the night to write them down in the way I want.'

'Claude, don't start that again. While we breathe we fight.'

'Willy,' said Claude very calmly. 'We Belgians must stay here to the very end and we both know how that will be. This is not a matter of probability. I told you, it has been given to me to know that my time is coming. So may it be. I am only grateful that I can send this to her through

156

you. Please, if you possibly can, find her and look after her for me.'

'Stop it.'

'No, take me seriously. I need to know that you will do so.'

'All right.'

'The General is waiting for you.'

But the General wasn't waiting; he walked into the room and Willy swung his legs out of the bunk and saluted him.

'Fraser, Tavernier. You must get on your way as soon as possible.'

'Me, sir?' said Claude.

'Yes, you. How do you think this Scots person is going to navigate his way through Belgium without you to guide him? For the Lord's sake, man, you didn't think I would entrust a royal despatch to a foreigner by himself did you?'

Willy let out a breath and wondered how long Leman had been listening in the corridor outside.

'Is that an order, sir?' Claude asked doubtfully. 'I would prefer to . . . '

'What you might prefer is neither here nor there,' said Leman curtly. 'You will help Fraser get to wherever the King may be and you will keep that despatch safely in your possession until you can hand it to him in person. Is that understood?'

'Yes, sir,' said Claude and if his spirits had lifted at all on being handed back a chance of survival, his voice did not show it.

'I am sorry to impose Tavernier on you again, Fraser,' said Leman. 'He will slow you down but

157

I think despite that his knowledge of the terrain will increase your chances of getting through.'

'It will be a pleasure, sir.'

★ ★ ★

They were ready to leave at 7 a.m., both stiff and sore but intent on the task ahead. Claude took the General's despatches and tucked them into his knapsack. They put on the sappers' dull overalls again with serge jackets over them and then Willy heaved his weight on to the bike's kick-start. It turned over, spat once and died. Ten minutes of fruitless effort got nowhere.

'Dirty fuel,' he said and resigned himself to dismantling the entire system to clean it out. It took him an hour. There was no incoming fire during that time but the fort was firing for all its worth so he had to contend with choking clouds of black-powder smoke and cement dust falling into the cleaned carburettor parts spread around him. He was tightening the last nuts when the German gunners proved just how hard they had been working on moving their giant gun.

There was no warning. The vast mass of earth and concrete heaped over their heads blocked the noise of the approaching shell but its explosion shook the entire fort and punched the breath out of every man inside. The lights went out and debris showered down from the ceiling. Willy's ears were ringing but he thought that somewhere up the stairs to the next level of the fort a man was screaming and screaming. Only the simplest thoughts seemed possible. He

158

wished the man would stop and wondered if someone should go and ask him to. The lights flickered once and came back on and he saw Claude white with dust as if he had been painted. He looked down at the parts and saw he would have to start all over again. He put the pieces under a cloth after he had wiped each one clean so when the second shell arrived minutes later they stayed clean, although this time a square of concrete a foot across fell from the ceiling, just missing the table. One of the gate guards was slumped on the floor and Willy crossed the chamber to look at him. His eyes were tight shut but he was breathing and a small trickle of blood was running down from one ear.

He put the carburettor back together, working automatically, bolting it back on to the inlet manifold and tightening the fuel pipe just as the next one hit and threw them all on the floor.

Claude was pounding him on the shoulder, pointing at the gates and mouthing. Willy couldn't hear a word he was saying but he nodded and kicked the bike over. He couldn't hear the engine either but the vibration told him it was running.

A fourth shell hit Loncin and this time the fabric of the fort cracked — concrete and steel grinding and screeching above them. The remaining guards dragged open the iron gate but there seemed nowhere to go. The narrow alley from the fort's central casemate to the exit was blocked by a heap of earth and rubble from the explosions. Willy looked at it and knew there would not be another chance. He opened the throttle and sent the bike bucketing up the mound, the back tyre scrabbling for grip and the front leaping across the lumps of shattered concrete and splintered wood. The bike almost pitched them both off at the top but then they thumped down onto the surface of the narrow alley beyond and accelerated out of the fort onto the shell-pocked road.

★ ★ ★

For a moment the war lost its hold, pushed aside by trees and grass, fresh air and fields, a vast expanse of still-undamaged nature stretching away in front of him. The road was clear. At full speed nothing could stop them and they would be gone before the enemy could do anything. Life abruptly surrounded them where there had only been the prospect of a dark and stinking death. Willy let out a yell and now he could hear his own voice. Movement caught his eye. A bloated bumble-bee striped in yellow and grey rose into sight to the north east and it wore a giant Maltese cross on its flank.

The balloon.

Perhaps it saw him and perhaps it didn't, but a dozen soldiers in field grey ran across a field a quarter of a mile ahead. They reached the road and began to set up a machine gun on a tripod. He slowed, cursing the balloon, looking in vain for a way round but deep ditches ran down both sides of the road and he could find no escape from the men in front and the eyes above. 'Crouch down low,' he yelled. He opened the throttle again, swerving the bike from side to side, but the cold calculation in his mind told him that no trained soldier would miss a target coming straight at them, not with a machine gun that could spray bullets like rain. Four hundred yards, three hundred yards and the Germans were holding their fire, waiting for a sure kill while Willy had the choice of racing towards the machine gun's muzzle or slowing and giving them an even easier target.

Gerard Leman had not forgotten his word. Their protectors in the fort behind them were watching their progress. A gun fired once from back there. A shell hummed over their heads and burst in the air with a whip-crack, blasting a hissing spray of shrapnel balls down to send the soldiers tumbling and sprawling as their machine gun and its tripod flew apart. The last barrier to their escape was gone. They slowed down to zigzag through the wreckage but then the sky offered them a far less welcome noise, another grumbling arc to announce the next *zweiundvierzig* shell. The balloon had turned its attention to more important business than this casual squashing of gnats.

Far away, the barrel of Krupp's giant howitzer had been angled up into the air at a steep 75 degrees. A massive charge had fired the 1,800 pound shell out of the barrel at a speed of 880 miles per hour. At the top of its parabola, a mile and a half into its journey, it had nosed over and began to accelerate downwards, screaming towards the exact point in the cratered top of the fort where three previous impacts had already fatally weakened the defences. The energy of the shell's impact melted the steel and vaporized the cracked concrete underneath it, letting the huge projectile through to plunge down the lifting shaft for the main guns. That was when the fuse fired the shell's charge and the focused flaming shockwave of that vast explosion was channelled in a microsecond down into the fort's powder magazine.

In the next instant, Fort Loncin ceased to exist.

They were half a mile away from the fort in a straight line but the blast plucked them both off the bike. While he was still in mid-air, Willy saw the Thor sliding on its side and Claude tumbling over and over. Willy thumped down on his back, the wind knocked entirely out of him, and strained to breathe, almost unable to move but looking up at a sky full of suspended ruin, beginning to tumble down towards him. He struggled to his knees but a violent blow to his shoulder knocked him down again and for a time beyond time after that, concrete, metal and earth rained down on to the road and the fields around him. Where Loncin had been there was nothing. The vast mound itself had lost its shape, the summit no longer there. A boiling tree of smoke spread upwards for a thousand feet or more and as they watched, the west wind began to flatten the top of it into a long smear.

10

After the cataclysm, two more shells hammered down into the fort's wreckage to the slow beat of the distant gun so that Willy and Claude knew for certain they could do nothing for those inside. Willy kicked the motorcycle's bent handlebars straight and they rode onwards with heavy hearts, turning their heads back every mile to see the funerary smoke writing a longer and longer epitaph across the sky. For five miles they made rapid progress on utterly empty roads past isolated cottages abandoned by their inhabitants then, at Waremme, they caught up with the reality of the invasion.

Belgium was a nation on the retreat. The roads were jammed with terrified refugees, all trying to make ground to the north-west, towards Leuven and Brussels and away from the German army. Mixed in among them were the last of the soldiers from the captured city behind them, some still in coherent units, some straggling in twos and threes but all wearing a look of exhausted fury on their faces. They helped an army despatch rider pull his motorcycle out of a ditch and he told them that German units had already advanced from Liège, making rapid progress towards Namur, twenty miles south of them.

Claude was visibly shocked by the news. 'Do you want to go there?' Willy asked him. 'We could try to get there before the Germans do.'

'No, we cannot. She must have left, surely? In my letter I told her not to delay. She will be on her way to Malines.'

If the letter got there, thought Willy, but he kept his mouth shut, knowing the chances of finding a single person in a city under attack were impossibly slim.

Claude straightened himself with his jaw set and a fierce look on his face. 'Anyway, we are under orders.'

Close to Tienen they had rested in a small wood, hoping darkness would bring a clearer road, but it didn't. The crowds inched onwards through the entire night. At daybreak, the motorcycle spluttered and Willy discovered how much of its fuel had been spilt when they were knocked down by the *zweiundvierzig*'s blast. They wasted three hours until Claude flagged down a crawling civilian car and took a two gallon can of their petrol at pistol point, explaining politely that they were on urgent military business.

It took them four more hours to force their way through to the outskirts of Brussels and Willy, wrestling to control the bike at slow speed, could feel Claude twisting from side to side behind him, searching the faces of all the tense adults shepherding crying children and frail old folk as best they could. Willy knew he was looking for Gabrielle.

When they finally reached the centre of the capital, they found it was no longer the capital. Posters lettered out in French, Flemish and

German proclaimed that Brussels was a demilitarised city and called on everyone to respect the safety of the civilian population. Most of that population looked hellbent on getting to somewhere else and a man wearing a civil guard arm-band told them the army high command, the royal family and the government had already gone.

'It is the only way they could save the people,' he said. 'They have moved the court and the seat of government to Antwerp.'

'Claude, explain to me what's going on,' Willy said. 'People keep talking about Antwerp as if it's some kind of magic kingdom. Leman was the same. Tell me as one soldier to another.'

'It is the way our generals planned it. Liège guarded the frontier. Brussels guards nothing. It is an open city with no strong fortresses. The plan has always been that in time of war the army and the government would go north, falling back to Antwerp because there is the sea and the Netherlands at our back for protection. Antwerp is the National Redoubt. It has two rings of fortresses, not just one. Nothing can destroy them.' He said the words with little conviction. 'Malines is just a little south of the outer ring. If we go that way, perhaps we will find both Gabrielle and the King. She will be there, I know.'

The engine had been coughing on the last teaspoonful of petrol when they coasted into the ancient market square of the lace-making town once known as Mechlin, and now as Mechelen to the Flemings and Malines to the French

165

speakers, and were ordered to clear the way by a gendarme. An officer wearing a plain uniform was leaning over a wooden table, studying a map with older and much more ornately dressed colonels and generals. 'Oh my goodness,' said Claude. 'Look. That's him over there, that's King Albert. Come on.'

They immediately found out that you don't just rush up to a king in wartime, especially when dressed in reeking, unidentifiable overalls. In a moment, both of them were flat on their backs on the cobbles, pinned down under a mass of soldiers and gendarmes. Claude spoke rapidly in Flemish and then in French. 'Tell the King we have come from the destruction of Loncin with a message for him from General Gerard Leman.'

The King stared at them then turned away. 'Search them and take them into the cathedral entrance,' he said. 'I will see them when I have finished here.'

They sat under guard on the bench in the large porch. 'This is St Rombaut's,' said Claude. 'You would know him, Willy. I think he came from Scotland or Ireland or somewhere like that.'

'Somewhere like that? First, there is nowhere like Scotland. Second, I have very little personal knowledge of any saints.'

They sat, exhausted, and Claude perhaps mistook Willy's silence for genuine irritation. 'There is a story about this place,' he said. 'The lovely Anna told me. She might still be here somewhere. Perhaps Gabrielle is with her. Can we look for them?'

'Of course.'

'The people here take fright easily. We call them the *Maneblussers*, the Moon Quenchers. Hundreds of years ago, they all ran up the tower with buckets of water because they could see it was on fire but when they got to the top it was only the full moon shining through the glass.'

'Let's hope they don't have to do that again.'

Claude opened his mouth to reply but shut it again as approaching figures flickered the bright daylight at the porch entrance. He shot to his feet and saluted. Willy followed suit.

The King stopped in front of them and looked them up and down. He saluted back. 'And who exactly do I have here?' he asked.

'Major Claude Tavernier of General Leman's personal staff, sir,' said Claude, 'and this is Major William Fraser, though both of us were only appointed to that rank in the field by General Leman and Fraser, as you can tell, sir, is not a Belgian.'

'We will let that rest for the moment,' said the King. 'Do sit down.' He sat next to Claude on the bench and the officers with him gathered round. 'The first thing I want to know,' he said, 'is what happened to Fort Loncin?'

Claude and Willy told the whole story of the *zweiundvierzig* and the Loncin disaster and their audience heard them out in sombre silence. The King grilled them on the survival chances of the garrison but there was nothing they could say, though they both knew that Albert was thinking of his mentor, Gerard Leman.

'That confirms all we feared,' said the King at

167

the end. 'It is hard to imagine that all those forts are now no more than crumpled paper. Those poor men.'

'Sir,' said Willy. 'If I may ask, do the Antwerp forts have stronger concrete than Loncin?'

The King shook his head. 'Antwerp is certainly strong but so, we thought, was Loncin.'

'Then with this new gun against them and only black powder to fire your own guns, the forts are a trap.' Willy took a deep breath, never having contemplated giving advice to a monarch before. 'Can you not fight a harassing war in the open? Attack with cavalry to prevent them bringing the guns close enough.'

'You are a cavalryman, no doubt?'

'I am, sir.'

'I am more modern but, like you, I do believe in that sort of warfare. We have fast cars with *mitrailleuses* as well if that appeals, but of course we are hugely outnumbered and we have little choice but to withdraw to Antwerp and prepare.' He looked hard at Willy. 'I confess, Fraser, I had heard of you already. General Leman mentioned you in two of his last despatches. He had a skilled Scottish hero fighting with him, he said, and a young Belgian officer who was following in his footsteps. Your ranks are confirmed, that is, Major Fraser, if you still wish to help us. This town of Malines must be prepared as a base for your harassing war as a tripwire on the way to Antwerp. It will buy us a little more time. You two will have a roving commission attached to my personal staff. Helping to ready the defences of Malines will be your first task.' His nose twitched. 'First, please go with Lieutenant Claes and he will find you accommodation, bathing facilities and something more closely resembling uniform than those old dishcloths you are wearing.'

★ ★ ★

That was August the eighteenth. They were given rooms above the Cleirens hat shop in the town centre while the King went towards Antwerp to spend the night in the palace of Baron Empain. The next day, Belgian soldiers passed through the town by the thousand, retreating from Namur and heading for Antwerp only ten miles to the north. Late that night, rumours spread that the Germans were only seven miles from Malines. The following morning the shops were shuttered, flags were lowered and barricades went up in the streets. Claude and Willy went to work with the armoured car squadron — another closely-bonded group of young daredevils, transformed from careless rich into grim killers. They identified the locations they would need for fast-moving high-powered warfare — hiding places and ambush points, escape routes, ammunition stores and fuel depots. That first evening they went in search of remaining civilians, knocking on any doors where the windows showed a glimpse of candlelight. Each time, Claude would ask the fearful inhabitant if they had seen Gabrielle or Anna or any of that family. Claude would show them his precious photograph, making them inspect it in the dim light, but all he got in response was shaken heads.

Back in their rooms he stared at the picture. 'How would they know? This is not Gabrielle. This person could be anybody.'

'Let me see.'

'No, because you will have a very poor idea of her. The photographer was an idiot. I can see her but you will just see the woman in the moon. Even her nose has disappeared.'

Willy smiled and kept his hand out until Claude reluctantly passed it to him. The couple in the picture looked startled as if the photographer had said something rude. His light had flattened both their faces so no contours remained. Claude looked like a bad oil painting from a hundred years earlier of the young heir to some blighted estate. There was no evidence of the character that now stamped his face. Gabrielle looked more likely to burst into tears than tackle a fleeing felon. Her eyes were slightly screwed up, her nose was no more than a faint smudge and her lips were tightly compressed, all stamped on to a flat face that could have been made out of rolled-out dough.

'She is beautiful,' said Claude defiantly, 'I can see that but perhaps it is not so clear to you. I wish the picture was true to her.'

'Pass me the writing paper,' said Willy, 'and sharpen those pencils. I can sometimes produce a sort of new truth that way.'

He began by drawing the shape of her face accurately on a larger scale and marking in the centre of her eyes and the base of her nose, then

170

he sketched in the rough outline of her mouth. Claude looked over his shoulder, constantly correcting him. 'No, her lips are fuller than that and she is almost always smiling. Not like that, more turned up at the ends. Her nose is narrower. Yes, that's good.'

After half an hour he had a smudged and altered drawing that Claude accepted as a rough approximation, then he reached for a new sheet and began to turn it into a real person, shading it carefully, bringing out the contours a little at a time until Claude said, 'Stop there.'

It was still a full-face portrait, good in its way but failing to evoke a real person. Willy found he was enjoying this escape from the reality of the approaching invaders, somewhere out there beyond the little town. It took him back to quiet afternoons at the castle when he would sit on his bedroom windowsill, drawing the curtains behind him to push away the house and sketch the fabulous temples and palaces, ships and dragons that might have been on the missing jigsaw piece. He said to Claude, 'How do you remember her? How does she look at you?'

'A little sideways like this, with her head cocked when I have said something interesting and one eyebrow slightly lifted.'

It took much longer, an hour and a half more of trial and error and ten sheets of writing paper to conjure three dimensions out of two and all the time he wondered if Claude was pushing him towards a fantasized version of Gabrielle that no one but her husband would ever recognize. He built into his picture all that he had ever found beautiful in women but Claude pulled him back from his wilder extremes. 'No woman has cheekbones like that,' he said.

'No woman you have met perhaps.'

'Ah, Willy. It is the eyes that matter more. They are too blank. Show me what is inside her head.' And somehow Willy, who had never met Gabrielle but had only seen her reflected in Claude's gaze, succeeded in doing that so that the woman in the final sketch looked out with amused love and sent Claude into a reverie, staring at it until the candles guttered and it was time for sleep.

★　★　★

The next day they were bolting extra metal shields to the upperworks of a Minerva armoured car, trying to give the gunner more protection as he worked the *mitrailleuse*, when a sweating infantryman ran into the courtyard.

'Uhlans,' he shouted. 'They are in the Boulevard du Sablon making for the Chaussée de Lierre.'

'That is the heart of town,' said Claude, shocked.

The engagement was brief and brutal and absolutely as they had planned. Three armoured cars came at the Uhlans from three different directions at a crossroads, forcing them back down the narrow street called Biest into the field of fire of the fourth car, driven by Willy. Claude, at the gun, dealt with the few survivors.

That was the last moment at which either of

172

them felt they had the upper hand. Three more days went by with everyone on edge and no further incursions but the few reports that came in were of huge enemy forces massing at Zemst to their south. They were ordered to stay where they were and guard the town. In the tension of waiting and watching, the streets began to fill again as over-optimistic citizens trickled back from Antwerp to see if they could pick up the pieces of their lives. That included Monsieur Cleirens, the owner of the hat shop where they were billeted, a surprisingly calm man who brought a bottle of wine up to their room and for a moment delighted Claude by telling him, not only did he know Anna, but he had seen her in Antwerp, heading for Dunkerque and a boat to England. He shook his head when Claude showed him the sketch of Gabrielle. 'No,' he said, 'I would remember that one. She was not with Anna.'

When he left them, Claude was withdrawn and frowning. 'Where is she?' he demanded. 'There is nowhere else she could have gone.'

Then Willy remembered a conversation in the darkness of the riflemen's terrace at Loncin in what now seemed another world. 'Yes there is,' he said. 'You told me about a farm. You said it was a place she loved. Where is that?'

'Ah!' Sudden hope came into Claude's face. 'Her aunt's farm. It is outside Comines on the way to Ypres. Do you know Ypres?'

Willy shook his head. 'I have heard of it, that's all. Somewhere west?'

'Yes, all the way to Ghent and then the same

173

again. A whole day's journey in good times. That makes sense. Of course, that is where she would go if she could not reach here. See? The Germans surrounded Namur from the east so she would have gone west. I will write to them at once. You are so, so clever.'

The next morning was Sunday but no bells rang. Instead they were woken by a long barrage somewhere to the south of the town, heavy guns booming on and on. No reliable news came in all day, nor the next day, but just after five o'clock on Tuesday morning the hat shop was rattled by an explosion and for the next hour the little town was dismembered by an artillery onslaught. Claude and Willy and the rest of the armoured car squadron patrolled the edge of the town, expecting enemy infantry to arrive behind the barrage, but the Germans were content to let their guns do the work. Right at the end of the attack, a shell pierced the great cathedral tower of St Rombaut's and the flame that blossomed inside the tower was no trick of moonlight. Once again, the people of Malines took to the long stairs inside the tower with bucket after bucket of water and, this time, they saved their landmark but the crowds in the street below watched aghast as the huge metal clock-face high above their heads, no longer secured to the tower's stonework, pivoted slowly outwards to come roaring down, utterly destroying a house below.

At ten o'clock, as they pulled bodies from the wreckage of the Rue de Beffer, a hand touched Willy on the shoulder and he straightened up, blinking dust out of his eyes to find that King

174

Albert had come to rally his people. 'While Rombaut's tower stands, so does Belgium,' said the King. 'Climb it with me, Fraser.'

Willy followed the King and his guards eastward through the streets to the cathedral, watching him as he stopped for an encouraging word here and there. The tower stank of burnt wood but the damage had been contained and the stairs still led all the way to the top. The King began to climb the stairs and his guards and the officers with him moved to follow but he waved them back. 'Wait here,' he said. 'Just you, Fraser.'

From there, they could see across countryside where only distant puffs of smoke gave any inkling of war. Albert pointed south-west. 'Your own army is in action over there. Fifty miles away from here. Despatches have come through. They fought a brave fight yesterday at Mons to delay the Germans but now they are being forced back towards Paris. It is not at all clear what will happen. If you wish to join them I will make arrangements for you to go.'

'Thank you, sir. You brought me up here to offer me that?'

'I brought you up here for two reasons. First, because all the soldiers and half the civilians in Malines know that there is a Scotsman fighting with us and it is a small but powerful sign to them that we have not been forgotten by our allies. I have made use of you, Fraser. I hope you do not mind.'

'Sir, in my experience it is most unusual to be appreciated by a commanding officer, for whatever reason. If I may, I should like to

175

continue to serve for the time being.'

'Good. The second reason is more complicated. And this is a conversation I can only have with you alone, up here in this curious place which is so unlike normal life as to be almost an illusion — a conversation, one might say, that has never happened.'

Willy nodded, puzzled.

'I am in a curious position, Fraser. I am, as you know, in a very real way, the commander-in-chief. I hope that I have learnt my job well but I am never likely to find out because my senior officers also know that I am their King and that perhaps prevents them expressing themselves as forcibly as they might. I would like to treat you as my fool. Do not look offended. You know your Shakespeare? I mean the fool of King Lear, privileged to misbehave by saying the wise words to the king that no one else would dare to speak. Do you mind being that fool?'

'I like new experiences, sir, and this one is definitely new. You're the first king who ever asked me that. Indeed you're the first king that ever asked me anything, although Queen Victoria once asked me to stop staring at her.'

Albert laughed. 'Gerard Leman commended you to me and sent you here for that very purpose I believe. He said I would appreciate you. It will be a private matter between you and me. Do you accept?'

'Yes, sir.'

'In that case, I want you and Major Tavernier to follow me back to Antwerp. You will please do for me exactly what you did for General Leman.

I want you to inspect our fortresses for any weaknesses that may yet be corrected in the time available.'

'So long as I am allowed to fight in the open, sir.'

'Agreed. From what I hear of your time in Loncin I think you have already served your sentence underground. It was cruel treatment for a cavalryman.'

11

1 p.m., 4 October 1914, Antwerp.

At the railway station, worried citizens were queuing for the few remaining seats on the last trains to Holland. Refugees clutching their portable wealth filled the intricate, cramped alleys of the medieval centre and spread across the wide boulevards of the modern city. Nothing was moving in the docks except for the gun turrets of a lone destroyer which had just tied up alongside. Around the embassies, a strong smell of scorching paper indicated that ambassadors were burning their papers because now they could hear the front-line fighting quite clearly.

Antwerp's outer forts, ten miles from the centre, had begun to disintegrate under the assault of the howitzers and the defending soldiers had coined new descriptions for the enemy's weapons as if by the soothing magic of words they could render them banal. The new gun had become 'Big Bertha' and the dreadful shell it fired was the 'Antwerp Express'. They said a single hit was enough to flatten a whole village and they said it with a strange note of pride in their voices. Citizens cheered as columns of German prisoners were marched into town because the Belgian army was still fighting doggedly for their lost country. The soldiers' numbers were dwindling all the time and the crowds would fall silent again as the ambulances brought in the latest casualties. On the outskirts of the city, a maze of cables fed an improvised tangle of electric fencing hundreds of metres deep through which the defenders planned to switch the city's entire power supply as soon as the enemy reached it. Nobody had the slightest idea whether it would work.

Antwerp's rural suburbs, renowned for their tranquil beauty, had vanished. The woods had been clear-felled, the châteaux blown down into rubble heaps, the villages and ancient churches utterly gone. The defending Belgian gunners now had uninterrupted fields of fire and only the doubters pointed out that the same process had also made their city the clearest possible target for the enemy. The sappers had laid minefields and dug mantraps into the open ground — barrels with their tops knocked out, covered with a thin disguise of laths and earth. The trunks of the thinner felled trees had been sharpened and dug into the ground at an angle just as if some medieval battle was imminent involving knights and chargers, swords and arrows. It was a time for desperate measures.

Roadblocks impeded the flow of people all round the city, nervy sentries demanding the day's password. The Belgian army units kept in reserve for the last desperate defence were buzzing with frustrated energy and determination. That passion had spread down to the next generation. Everywhere around Antwerp, Boy Scouts in short trousers and broad-brimmed hats were running errands, carrying messages, itching to get closer to the action.

Night in Antwerp was a fearful time. The streets were still crowded with jostling, colliding people but hardly a light was to be seen because Zeppelins had come twice in the darkness in the past ten days, dropping bombs to leave civilians dead and houses wrecked. Some said there were a dozen dead, others insisted it was a hundred. The latest scare story insisted that the Zeppelins would lower their bomb aimer in a cage on a long steel cable so that he would not miss and that kept people quiet in the streets at night in case some suspended German was hidden in the darkness listening to their every word. A mismatched assortment of fragile British aircraft of the embryonic Royal Flying Corps had arrived to combat the Zeppelin threat but quite how they were meant to do this with their feeble engines and hand-held guns was far from clear. It was all grist to the mill of newspaper vendors who hawked the latest editions, full of brave generalities and very short on facts.

For the past three days rumours of withdrawal had been growing and growing. Would the French come to the city's rescue? Was it true that English brigades were on their way? Some said King Albert and all his ministers were leaving for Ostend by steamer. Fist-fights broke out as others insisted he would do no such thing.

The Hotel St Antoine had parcelled out its rooms to foreign legations as soon as the capital had moved from Brussels to Antwerp. From its roof terrace Willy had seen the night-time glare of burning villages and heard the growling artillery of the front line. At lunchtime on that early October Sunday, a large Minerva touring car roared up the Place de Meir sounding its klaxon and took the tight turn into the Marché aux Souliers on screaming tyres. It was painted drab grey with the large letters 'SM' newly stencilled on its flanks for 'Service Militaire'. Such cars were now a common sight. The armed forces had commandeered every fast tourer, limousine and even racing cars, sketchily converted for the road. The ditches lining the roads around Antwerp were full of their wrecks.

This one made a theatrical entrance, screaming to a halt in a cloud of tyre smoke outside the St Antoine, its horn sounding to the last. The five men who jumped out were all dressed in British uniform. Three were clearly Royal Navy and one was Army but the man at the centre of the group was neither. He might have passed as a naval officer to the ignorant but he was dressed in a plain dark blue cap and jacket, the obscure uniform of an Elder of Trinity House, ancient providers of lighthouses and navigation marks around the coast of Britain. His smooth face made him look younger than his forty years, given away only by the fair hair that was starting to thin. The crowd on the pavement parted for him, impressed by his style and strong self-importance. The St Antoine was in the heart of the apparatus of government with the Royal Palace, the Hôtel de Ville, military headquarters and relocated ministries clustered around it so the hotel lobby was full to bursting with

181

diplomats, officers, government officials and journalists.

'Lunch first, gentlemen,' said the fair-haired man striding through the crowd. 'None of you need worry,' he announced to the room in loud English. 'We're here to save your city.' His emphatic gestures and penetrating voice attracted stares. 'I see Villiers over there,' he said. 'We'll join him.' Sir Francis Villiers was leader of the British Legation and no sooner had the new arrivals sat down with him than two correspondents from the London papers came to stand politely by, waiting for a moment to ask their questions. The fair-haired man turned on them sharply. 'You people have no business here in Belgium,' he said. 'I advise you to get out of the country at once. Go home where you belong.'

People all around fell silent in embarrassment. He turned to watch them leave the room and his eye fell on a man in Belgian officer's uniform sitting at a nearby table, staring at him and shaking his head. He stared back. 'I don't believe it,' he said. 'Sansom, go and get that feller there. The one in red and blue with the absurd sash thing. No, not him. The one next to him.'

The Belgian officer was brought across to the table and stood there impassively as he was inspected while the other diners watched the sideshow in fascination. The fair-haired man looked him up and down. 'You appear to have some problem, sir?' he said. 'Do you speak English?'

'Of course I do,' said Willy. 'Hello, Winston. How are you? I seem to remember that you were

182

a newspaperman once. South Africa wasn't it? Don't you think throwing out those two was just a little bit hypocritical?'

'Willy bloody Fraser,' said the other. 'It *is* you. I thought it must be a froggy lookalike but here you are dressed up like some fancy dress feller from a minstrel show. I'd like to say it's good to see you but that would be telling a lie and I'm really not interested in all that South African nonsense all over again.'

'Nonsense?'

The Lieutenant-Colonel who had arrived with the naval officers rose to his feet. 'How dare you, sir,' he said. 'This is the First Lord of the Admiralty and you will address him with respect. As you appear to be an Englishman you should be wearing His Majesty's uniform not that absurd dago get-up.'

'I'm not an Englishman,' said Willy curtly, 'and I will leave you to your luncheon.'

★ ★ ★

An hour later, the new arrivals were shown into a dark-panelled meeting room in the Hôtel de Ville. 'No loose talk,' said Churchill while they waited. 'We are here for one purpose and one only, to keep them fighting. That is all that matters. Gentlemen, we have to stiffen their backbones.'

They stood up as the door opened and King Albert of the Belgians made his entrance followed by the city's military governor, the Prime Minister and three army officers. Albert

183

and Churchill were a similar age but you could have made two of Albert's fine-featured face from one of Churchill's and the Belgian King towered over the British envoy. Indeed, he towered over everybody else in the room apart from the final Belgian officer who had come in behind him. Churchill bowed, stepped back and looked again at the tall officer at the rear. 'Fraser,' he said flatly.

'Ah!' said Albert. 'Yes, Mr Churchill, I understand you know my personal advisor. Now, gentlemen, before we go any further can you clear up a small point of British military etiquette with which I am unfamiliar?'

'Certainly, your Majesty,' said Churchill. 'What is it?'

'It concerns the courtesies that should be paid by an officer, shall we say, in one army to a more senior officer in the army of an ally.'

'That, sir,' said Churchill, 'is quite straightforward. As an ally, he should pay him exactly the same courtesies that he would pay to his own superior officers.'

'I see. It is just that word has reached me from several observers that Fraser here was poorly used by a member of your party at luncheon today.'

'It was nothing,' put in Willy but the King waved him to silence.

'It was something that I would like to see corrected,' he said.

'I'm afraid I don't understand,' Churchill replied carefully. 'Lieutenant-Colonel Brotherton was addressing Fraser as a former captain in the

British armed forces.'

'A former captain who is now a brigadier-general in the Belgian army,' said the King, 'a gallant and most highly valued member of my staff who therefore outranks, I believe, all the military members of your party. Fraser and one of my other officers fought their way from the Meuse to join us here. They played a gallant role at Malines and have done me immense service since then. While I do understand that his uniform, or perhaps you would prefer to say 'absurd dago get-up', has not yet caught up with his promotion, I simply require that you accord him proper respect from now on.'

That got the meeting off to a frosty start and it got only a little warmer as it went on. When it was all over, the King caught Willy's eye and motioned him to stay behind.

'Thank you for my unexpected promotion, sir,' said Willy. 'That came as something of a surprise.'

'Yes,' said the King. 'I was annoyed to hear how they had treated you. You do understand it was a temporary promotion? I did rather make it up on the spot, you know.'

'How temporary, sir?'

'Shall we say until an hour after Churchill leaves Belgium? After that you will revert to Lieutenant-Colonel.'

'You mean Major surely, sir?'

'I mean exactly what I say.'

There was a knock at the door and Claude joined them. 'Good,' said the King. 'Tavernier, come and sit down. I have news for you two.' He poured them each a brandy. 'First you will be pleased to hear that General Leman survived against all the odds.' Albert sipped his cognac and chose to ignore the tears that had come to Claude's eyes. 'The Germans have notified us that his legs were badly crushed but they are treating him in one of their hospitals. I am sorry to tell you that the majority of the fortress garrison were buried by its collapse. You left just in time.' He looked at Claude. 'Tavernier, the second piece of news is really for you and you may think it is at least as significant. A letter has been received through military channels from someone who I think is dear to you, a completely improper use of an army despatch rider but as sending him to Comines was my own idea, I am prepared to overlook it.' He smiled and passed Claude an envelope. 'I am sorry it took so very long but he was obliged to take a roundabout route.'

Claude was staring at the envelope with his eyes wide, drinking in the handwriting of the address.

'Go on, man,' said the King. 'Open the damned thing. I will make do with Fraser while you read it.'

Albert turned to stare out of the window towards the double ring of forts that supposedly protected Antwerp. 'I was an idiot to believe this was the way to fight a modern war,' he said to Willy in the end. By now, Willy had fully understood that there was nothing of the ancient hauteur of British nobility about this King. Albert was quick-witted, capable and absolutely

186

determined to save some part of his dwindling nation. 'Now, Fraser, if it does not test your loyalty, I would appreciate your views on your First Lord of the Admiralty and his offer.'

'I may not be the most reliable authority on that, sir. We have, shall I say, a certain history, Winston and me.'

★ ★ ★

That same history was on Churchill's mind when he summoned Willy to his room later that evening.

'I'm not going to call you Brigadier,' he said brusquely, 'because you were a captain when you quit and if I have anything to do with it, you'll be very lucky to be a captain again when you do your duty and return to your bloody regiment. However, you seem to have the ear of their King and therefore I need you.'

'Why?'

'Because if you go on terrifying Albert with stories about the impossibility of resisting the damned Big Berthas, he will pull his troops out of Antwerp and the Germans will get to Calais before we can stop them.' He stared at Willy and crossed his arms. 'You and I both know that if so, the war will be over. We cannot supply an army in France if Germany controls the Channel ports.'

'I'm not terrifying him. I'm simply suggesting he prepares better.'

'And is that doing any good?'

'It would help if you could ship over ten thousand tons of smokeless powder and a hundred thousand new uniforms, preferably in German field grey.'

'Ridiculous. We can barely provide what our own men need. Fraser, for God's sake. All we need is a few days.'

'A few days that will kill many thousand more Belgians. Will that really make a difference?'

'Yes it damned well will. The French have performed miracles. Joffre kept the Huns out of Paris but now it's a race to the Channel. You know damned well we can't pull units away to support Antwerp. We have to stick with the French and every day the Belgians hold their ground gives us another day to block them off.'

'You want him to sacrifice Antwerp then you plan to leave him in the lurch?'

'I'm not leaving him in the lurch. I'm offering him my Naval Division.'

'And what is that exactly? Old Petty Officers recalled to the colours and new recruits who have never seen any action at all?'

'Can't you see the importance of this?' Churchill banged the flat of his hand down on the table. 'What is it about the Fraser family? Why do you people always fail to understand the priorities?'

'This has nothing to do with my father.'

'Oh is that so? I find it hard to believe that. He tried to destroy my reputation.'

'He simply described what you did in Pretoria, Winston. He didn't like it and he had a point.'

'I don't give a damn whether he liked it or not. Just like you, he only understood the half of it.'

'So you took your revenge.'

'He was Stellenbosched. He only had himself to blame for that. You're no damned use to me. Get out.'

There was a letter waiting for Willy, pushed under his door.

'*We were so very relieved to get your note,*' Gilfillan had written. '*You can guess perhaps that after all the shocking news we thought you must at best be a prisoner of the Germans. I have addressed this exactly as you instructed in the hope it will reach you in these most uncertain times. You say you are now fighting with the Belgian army. That seems an extraordinary turn of affairs. This is not a good moment for the news I have to convey to you but a young legal gentleman arrived from Glasgow recently, driven here in a large motorcar which, I am happy to say, burst two tyres while climbing the drive. It would seem the gentleman has been instructed by your mother to contest your father's will. I am certain that you have far more pressing concerns at this present time so I have taken the liberty of instructing Mr Morton to lock swords with him. He is, as I am sure you will say, somewhat slow and undeniably ancient but he has an abrasive tenacity about him that your father always said was very useful for wearing down the flightier sort of legal person.*'

★ ★ ★

Next day, a motley collection of Royal Navy and Royal Marines arrived in a range of unsuitable uniforms and clutching rifles so ancient that they had to be loaded separately with bullets and cartridges. They were sent straight into makeshift trenches and Churchill toured the defences but by that same afternoon, German forces had silenced two of the outer forts and moved through to threaten the inner ring.

Late that evening, there was a knock at Willy's door and a grave young lieutenant said that the King requested his presence in the private chambers. Albert was standing by the fireplace with a brandy glass in his hand. Sitting next to him was a dark-haired woman. She gave Willy a piercing look and a very slight smile. He bowed, wondering what the King had told her.

'Brigadier-General Fraser, I thought it was time for me to introduce you to my Queen while you still have that impressive rank.'

The Queen laughed. 'From what I hear, Brigadier-General, you will happily trade your exalted status for the departure of the First Lord of the British Admiralty. Do tell me why he doesn't like you?'

Willy glanced uneasily at Albert who smiled and nodded. 'It is no secret, Fraser. Churchill made that plain enough.'

Willy turned back to the Queen. 'Your Majesty, it is an old story. You may know that about fifteen years ago, Mr Churchill took time off from his army career to report for the *Morning Post* newspaper in the South African war?'

'Of course. The whole world knows that. He made the most brilliant escape from a Pretoria prison. That is surely how he became such a famous man.'

'Yes. My father was one of the other officers being held in that prison. It had been a school, not an especially strong place and there were barely enough guards. The officers there worked out a detailed escape plan. When they got out, they were going to head for the Pretoria racecourse where the Boers were holding hundreds of other British prisoners, ordinary soldiers. Once they overcame the racecourse guards they intended to free all the men and then they would have had sufficient strength to capture the entire town.'

'What a bold plan! But it did not happen?'

'No.'

'You are reticent. Did Mr Churchill somehow prevent it?'

'Mr Churchill hadn't been there long when he heard the details of the escape plan and he purloined it for his own use, ma'am. Nobody else had the chance to follow him because he climbed out first, made too much noise and they raised the alarm. Not just that but when he reached Portuguese territory he immediately sent the whole story off to be published in newspapers round the world. That removed any remaining chance of escape for my father and all the others. They spent another six months locked up there while Pretoria stayed in Boer hands.'

'But surely Mr Churchill has gone on to greater things. Would you not say he has vindicated himself?'

'My father would not have agreed. He thought

191

Churchill was a dangerous adventurer who should never be entrusted with high office and would never achieve anything of importance. You will find many others in the British army who agree with that opinion.'

'You said, 'Would not have'? Is your father no longer alive?'

'No. He was very badly treated by Churchill's allies afterwards when he aired his views and . . . well, he is no longer with us.'

'I am sorry and I do understand,' she said, 'but I think your Mr Churchill is a force of nature whether you like it or not. We have had to put our trust in him. I hope we are not wrong.'

'Of course we are wrong, my dear,' said the King. 'We are wrong to think Antwerp can be saved but we are also right for our own reasons, not his. We should not give up one single small patch of our country until there is no choice whatsoever. Fraser, we have been discussing our next step. What do you think will happen here now?'

'That, sir, depends on whether you can hold them at the River Nethe. That might give you a few more days at best.'

'France has offered my government sanctuary. I do not wish to accept it. Fraser, I like your soldier's keen eye and your Scottish obstinacy.'

'Obstinacy, sir?'

'I mean your complete inability to accept the views of your superiors without examining every part of them for yourself. I want you to undertake a new task. There is a small corner of our country at the western corner of our coastline that might still have the capacity to keep the invaders out. I do not want to vacate my country and I would like you to assess it for me before I decide on the French offer. Would you please go there for me with Tavernier and report back on the possibilities. You will start at Ostend.'

12

King Albert and Queen Elisabeth left Antwerp on October the seventh only when the savage assault brought the city centre within range of the big howitzers. The drained survivors of Churchill's naval brigades marched out past blazing fuel tanks while a party of his marines, cut off by the attack, were forced across the Dutch frontier into internment. After that, the Belgian royal household moved slowly westward, giving up their country one grudging step at a time. The illusion that Ostend might be a safe haven was shattered within a week as the Germans pushed them out. They retreated west to Nieuport, the last town on their own coast, where the River Yser and the drainage canals of that low-lying land entered the sea through a maze of locks. Soon the Germans were on the east bank of the Yser and the town became far too dangerous so the royal retreat went on to the last possible toehold on that coast, a seaside village in the sand dunes. The Belgian army had given everything it had for the past three weeks — fighting, retreating and dying as they were forced into the country's last small corner, cut off by the Channel and with the French frontier at their backs.

The tiny village of De Panne now became the unlikely capital of Belgium.

For the next few days, Willy and Claude

served as the king's eyes, searching the landscape for any sort of defensive line that might still save De Panne and keep Belgium's King in his own country. They rode from unit to unit on the suffering motorcycle, now scarred, dented and roughly smeared with matt grey paint.

'My commanding officers prefer to tell me the best of the news,' the King said one evening at the simple Maskens Villa in the sand dunes that was now the royal residence. 'You will have heard that the noble baron has chosen to replace some of my closest allies with men of his own.' Baron de Broqueville was Prime Minister and Minister of War. The King made a face. 'The baron maintains we are still a neutral country and can yet come to some understanding with the Kaiser. I am not sure who I can trust any more. So, my friends, I ask you to bring me quietly all the rest of the news I might not otherwise hear because I do know I can trust the two of you. My men are heroes but now they look more like the ghosts of heroes and in particular, I need to know when I must stop asking them for more.'

One night, when they had been sent on separate missions, Willy returned first to the villa and Albert's trusted ADC, Captain Commandant Emile Galet, summoned him to see the King before he could wash away the grime. 'You are wounded?' Elisabeth asked as he walked into the room.

'It's not my blood,' he said. 'The man next to me caught one,' but she sat him down and gently pulled his hair out of the way to inspect him.

'It is yours, idiot,' she said. 'I can tell. It comes out tartan. A bullet graze?'

'Shrapnel probably,' he said. 'I didn't notice.'

'Fraser, I asked you to collect information, not injuries,' said the King.

'With respect, sir, I cannot go into the line just to ask questions when they are hard pressed and then leave again as soon as it gets tricky. That would be most impolite. You would have done exactly the same.'

'Keep still,' said Elisabeth. 'There is half an acre of Belgian countryside in your head that I need to get out. You can trust me, I'm a trained nurse.' She got busy with water and iodine as they talked.

'The guns are worn out,' said Willy. 'Our field guns badly need new barrels. The shells are tumbling in flight. The gunners duck away and hope for the best as they pull the firing lanyard. They say they can't really aim them any more. I saw two gun barrels burst this morning. That tends to make the men a little nervous.'

'What of the infantry?'

'They will still fight. They're very tired and they're weak but they aren't going to give up unless you do, sir, and you're not going to, are you?'

'The French want me to,' said Albert, and Elisabeth snorted as she swabbed at Willy's head.

'Ignore Joffre,' she said. 'He is only interested in attack. We have to defend.'

'Fraser, Joffre wants us to cross into France, then put my men under his command. I would rather take them to England if I have to take them anywhere. Ah, Tavernier. Join us. Do you have news?'

'We captured a German field gun, sir.'

'With shells?'

'Only five.'

'Better than none. Now, I have a different job for you two. Tomorrow I need you to go to Nieuport. There is an argument going on and I need you to cut through it. Do you by any chance know anything at all about drainage?'

'Drainage, sir?'

★   ★   ★

The little town of Nieuport was right by the very end of the front line. It stood a mile inland, connected to the sea at its eastern end by the straight Yser Channel which ran out through sand dunes to what had recently been the select beach resort of Nieuport Bains. On the sea, the two armies were separated by four hundred yards of sand and the river mouth. In the town, only the Yser itself stood between them but the lay of the land helped the Belgians hold the enemy back because attackers had to expose themselves to approach the river. It was an advantage that did not look likely to last.

As they rode cautiously east towards the outskirts of the town they could hear the German shelling. In the distance, an entire building's worth of bricks appeared above the rooftops, lifting into the air still in rectilinear sections, then fragmented before their eyes to fall back down as rubble. Willy found himself counting aloud like a child seeing how far away the lightning was. Four seconds, then the crash of the shell arrived. Not quite a mile. Soldiers stopped them twice at roadblocks in the edge of town but by now word of the king's special scouts had spread and they were waved on their way almost before the password was out of his mouth. The third time, he asked for the *Ganzepoot* and the soldier grimaced.

'The Goosefoot? In daylight?' said the tall corporal with a bandage round his forehead. 'Have you been to confession lately? The Five Bridges road is the fastest route to hell.'

'We're looking for a man named Dingens,' said Claude. 'He's supposed to be there.' The soldier shrugged.

'Dingens, the lockmaster? I doubt it. He's not crazy. He usually comes out in the dark.' He glanced at the motorbike. 'You'd better leave that back here. Running and ducking and hiding is the only way to see the Goosefoot and tell the tale afterwards.'

Nieuport was still recognisably a town. There were shops with glass left in the windows and goods on display. All they lacked was customers. Nine out of ten of the buildings were standing so that the rubble strewn across the streets from the unlucky ones seemed the startling exception and not yet the new order of things. Cats were everywhere, pitiful, mewing in the shadows of side streets, but there were no dogs and Willy wondered if they had all been called up to serve. They came out into the open at the end of a street and saw a harbour basin ahead. The wide

198

Yser Channel came in from the sea to their left and sticking up out of the water was the twisted steel bow of a sunken barge. The Goosefoot was to their right, the starting point for a spray of waterways heading inland from the basin like the spread fingers of a hand. The Five Bridges road curved around to cross over each of them by their massive lock gates.

Claude laughed. 'Five bridges?' he said. 'There are six. Count them,' and Willy did, which made him laugh too. Amusement was a dangerous emotion. For a moment it got in the way of his survival senses so he was just that crucial fraction too slow in registering the rising shriek of a shell from that dangerous, unwavering place in the air ahead that always meant bad news. 'Run!' he yelled and was never so aware of the nightmare lethargy of his legs, accelerating in slow-motion strides before he was felled by a wave of red-hot air and two flying blocks of the square pavé cobbles.

He lay unable to move, winded and deafened as the rest of the screaming salvo burst in the buildings beyond, then there were arms under his shoulders and people dragging him across the broken cobbles. Two people. It hurt. He did his best to help with weak legs as they fumbled their way to a doorway and stumbled down dark stairs into a cellar then a mug was in his hands and he gulped a liquid which jolted him as it bit his throat. It could have fuelled an engine. A hand passed him a damp cloth and he wiped the dust of fragmented mortar out of his eyes. Three dim lanterns lit the low space and now he could see

Claude, his face still dust-covered, sitting on a box and another man staring at them both: a stocky man of perhaps fifty with a drinker's nose bulging over the standard moustache. He wore a torn sailor's smock and a battered skipper's cap.

'How do you like the gin?' he said in rough French that gave away his Flemish origins. 'Strong enough?'

'Easily,' said Willy.

'You're no Belgian. Who the hell are you?'

'He comes from Scotland,' said Claude and the man raised his eyebrows.

'I never met a Scotch before. I thought you wore skirts? Why are you here?'

'We're supposed to find lockmaster Dingens. Is that you?'

'Hah! Don't you dare. Gerard Dingens? Me? I am Henry Geeraert, sailor and man of action — not that office-dwelling, pen-pushing, put-your-hat-on-straight bossy-boots.'

Willy guessed that the gin bottle had already seen some action that morning. 'Where would we find him?'

'He's gone off inspecting ditches. You can ask me anything you want.'

'Are you his deputy?'

Geeraert snorted. 'I'm a tugboat skipper but I know this place frontwards, backwards and upside-down. I reckon I know at least as much as he does and I don't just talk, I get things done.'

Claude and Willy looked at each other, wondering whether to take this unknown man into their confidence.

'Spit it out,' said the other. 'I know what you're here for. It's obvious. You're not the first.'

'We want to know if we can flood the fields.'

'The *polders*, you mean?'

Claude nodded. 'Can we?'

'All *polders* are below sea level — otherwise they would just be fields and not *polders* at all. They have to be drained for farming so it stands to reason they can be flooded for war.'

'Others don't seem to agree,' said Willy.

'That is because they are idiots. Officers have been coming through here all week. Belgian, French, even English but you know how it is, ask the wrong people and you get the wrong answers.' Geeraert took another swig of gin. 'Dingens, he's got his job to do and he has to answer to everybody. He knows seawater will ruin the soil and some day the farmers will demand compensation. They're facing the whole goddamned German army and they're worrying about the money? I'll bet old Monsieur Methodical Dingens is out there right now with some crazy idea that he can do it with fresh water instead.'

'Can he?'

'If he had a month, but he hasn't got a month, has he? It's got to be done right now or we'll all be saying: 'Ja, mein Herr.' We have to let in the sea right now. I know how and I know where Dingens has hidden the tools that open the sluices. Put me in charge and I'll have it done in half a jiffy. Are you in a position to put me in charge?'

Another salvo of shells crashed around the

basin, blowing dust down the stairs. Willy thought he might prefer to face the fire outside than drink any more of Geeraert's gin. 'Maybe,' he said. 'How exactly?'

'The Spring Sluice then the North Vaart gates.' He jerked his head towards the stairs. 'Just up there. Open the gates at the start of the flood for two or three tides. Close them to keep in the ebb and that's the job done. Leave it to me and I'd fix it in no time.'

Claude was frowning. 'Wouldn't the Germans guess what you were doing? They can shell this place any time they want to.'

'They won't because they have made a big, big mistake. See that?' Geeraert pointed to a line strung across a corner. A large map hung over it, drying out. 'Got it off a dead Boche who came floating down the Bruges Canal,' he said. 'Nice of him. It's their area map. Very detailed but as it happens, also completely wrong.'

'How so?'

'All their heights and depths are way out. Their map shows the whole bloody place is *above* sea level so with all this rain, I don't believe they will guess. Not at first.'

He stopped as they heard a new sound from the seaward side, the deep boom of a different gun followed by the whistle of a heavy shell passing over them.

'Now, that is the other good news,' said Geeraert. 'That is HMS *Humber*.'

'I've never heard of her,' said Willy.

'The paint is still wet on her name-plate. I went aboard at first light to give them the benefit of my knowledge. Built by your people for the navy of Brazil to patrol the Amazon but commandeered because she is perfect for this coast. Shallow draft. Big guns. Ideal for close-in work to keep the Germans at bay along the beach.'

★ ★ ★

That evening Willy thought the Maskens Villa needed an injection of Henry Geeraert and his gin. The atmosphere had changed. All the officers of the king's staff moved more slowly, talked more quietly, looked directly at each other less often as if a personal hell was starting to singe the edges of their duty. They had been ushered straight in to see the King. The army was just barely hanging on to the winding left bank of the Yser but suffering losses all the time, losses it could not afford.

Albert had called a meeting. Fourteen officers, crowded into the villa's drawing room. Elisabeth was there too and Willy thought her presence marked some turning point in Albert's mind. The final crisis had arrived. 'What about inundation?' demanded the King.

Galet, his ADC, answered first. 'We have people working on it, sir. The French want one thing, the civilian authority wants another. The men who run the canal system can't even agree on whether it is possible.' He began to explain the technical and political complexities of the problem, the number of culverts that would have to be blocked, the dykes to be blown up, the banks to be raised higher. When he turned to the question of compensation for the farmers, the King lost what was left of his patience.

'Fraser and Tavernier have found a man who can do it,' he said. 'First thing tomorrow morning, get this man Geeraert on to it. Tavernier, go with Galet now and help him prepare the orders. Fraser, stay here with me.'

Everyone left. Albert unfolded maps and beckoned Willy. They stared at the land to the west of the Yser River. 'If we can flood all this,' said Albert, 'we will still need a strong front line, high enough to be above the flood.'

Elisabeth crossed the room to look at the map. 'What is that?' she said, running her finger down it.

'That is the railway line from Nieuport down to Dixmude.'

'Those hatching marks. What do they mean?'

'They mean it is an embankment, a levée. It is raised up to keep it out of the water when the fields get too . . . '

'Wet?' she said.

'Ah! You are ahead of me, my dear.'

'Now, that *is* unusual,' she said sweetly and he shot her a sharp look.

'Fraser,' he said. 'As soon as it gets light, please inspect that embankment. Investigate, if you can, all the land that lies between that and the river. See if it can be flooded to a sufficient depth. Do not get involved in any more fighting. That is an order. This may be the key. If we can flood it, we can hold them back and then, God willing, we can rebuild the army behind the

204

shelter of the water. If it can be done . . . ' He paused. 'Do that for me and then you will have served me quite enough. Whatever happens this week the war will take a different turn for us now. You should perhaps go and join your own people again.'

In the past week a new name had begun to feature on the map of war. The German army had launched an all-out attack twenty miles south of the coast, attempting to seize the ancient town that sat astride the other main routes to the channel ports. That town was called Ypres and the Allied armies were throwing lives by the thousand into the desperate struggle to hold them back.

'I will send Tavernier to Ypres with you. He will command a Belgian unit for me.'

Willy knew that the King knew that Gabrielle was there, at the farm somewhere in the melée south of Ypres. He nodded.

There was still no sign of Claude. Willy shunned the morose group of officers drinking cognac in the garden and lay down on his bed to let his tired body get ready for the demands of the morrow. He thought of writing to Gilfillan but it seemed a pointless burden on the army's overstretched message service and he could think of little worth saying that would have any relevance back in Scotland. Instead he unfolded the map of the Yser region and stared at it, knowing it was the last battleground, that the navy's few ships and the exhausted Belgian soldiers preparing for their last stand would need a miracle if the Channel ports were not to fall.

He folded the map and put it in Claude's knapsack for the next day. His fingers touched the leather folder and he thought of the drawing he had made of Gabrielle. He took it out, wondering if he should, but feeling it was, after all, his own creation.

When Claude came in, Willy was asleep on his bed, still holding the picture, and Claude left it in his hand as he covered him over with a blanket.

13

11.30 a.m., Friday, 30 October 1914. The banks of the Yser River.

For the past three days an autumn storm had blown in from the south-west, soaking the surrounding land and bringing winter early. The gales swept away the smoke from the guns and the burning buildings so Willy managed a quick glance round the shell-shattered remains of the border villages before a spiteful burst of bullets made him duck back down. The broken brown walls of farmhouses stuck out of the sodden farmland like rotten teeth amid the ditches of the beet fields west of the winding river. It was the end of Belgium geographically and to Willy it looked like the end of Belgium in every other way too.

He was sprawled as flat as it was possible to get in the wet grass of the long railway embankment that now formed their last defence. Every time he wriggled up out of the trench to take a quick shot over the buckled steel rails, he drew fire from the mass of German troops in sand-bagged positions two hundred yards beyond, blocking any possible attack on the field-gun battery beyond them. Those field guns had already accounted for half of the men around him. He looked to either side. There were so few of them left, a ragged remainder of the Belgian army spread thinly along the reverse of the banking, a man every five yards and outnumbered by a hundred to one.

In those three days they had quartered the area as the King had ordered. Sheets of rain and wandering walls of fog covered them as they had skirted German raiding parties and tried to avoid the sudden murderous encounters of the desperate men of both sides. They had traced out the path of every dyke and bank and lane east of the low embankment, roaming the *polders* towards the Yser as it twisted across the country, sometimes a mile away, sometimes three miles, finding nothing that made the inundation plan impossible if they could only persuade the water to run where they so needed it.

Voices far more learned, far superior to the gin-drinking Geeraert, still held sway despite the king's wishes. Brave men risked their lives to crank open sluice gates perilously close to the German line. Engineers blocked culverts and demolished dykes but the water was sluggish in its response, restricted by narrow pipes and clogged ditches. The Germans' feet grew a little wetter but no more than they might expect after all that rain.

The two friends could not obey the king's order to avoid the fighting. On this last but one day of October, the weather began to clear and they caught a fleeting glimpse of the sun as they headed for Ramscappelle. The next moment, a burst of German machine-gun fire from somewhere no German should have been took the front wheel clean off the Thor. Willy, Claude

208

and the motorcycle plunged at speed into a sodden ditch. They pulled themselves out from under the remains of the heavy machine and saw that it had taken them on its last journey. The machine gun was still spraying the road but they heard Belgian shouts in French and Flemish then a rattle of rifle fire and the machine gun stopped. They climbed up on to the road and a voice called them across to the trenches dug into the reverse slope of the railway embankment. Two dozen bodies were stretched out in death where they had rolled down the gentle slope so Willy relieved one of a rifle and a bandolier of ammunition and that was when he realized this looked likely to be the end.

'How much ammo?' he asked the Sergeant to his right. The man was Flemish but Willy had a quick ear for languages and had picked up a lot of it in the last weeks — all the vital questions a soldier needed.

'Thirty-two rounds. You?'

'Twenty-eight.'

The Sergeant threw him two cartridges. 'Now we're even,' he said. 'Use them well.' It was past the time to use the word 'sir'. He looked back across the empty lands behind him. 'I suppose this must be it then,' he said. 'They'll rush us any time now and I don't see any hordes of Frenchmen coming to help, do you?'

'To hell with that,' said Willy. 'Who needs Frenchmen?'

Claude wriggled up the embankment and lay next to him. 'I found twelve more rounds,' he said.

Willy didn't need to ask where. The tunic pockets of the bodies lower down the slope were the only place worth looking.

'That's all right, then,' he said. 'We'll be fine now.'

Claude slipped the knapsack off his back and looked inside. Willy had watched him go through that ritual so many times, making sure the leather wallet with the photograph was safe, checking that his final letter addressed to Gabrielle was there, to be found and sent on if the worst happened. This time, Claude drew out the trumpet.

* * *

The German forces facing them east of the embankment knew it was going their way. Captain Karl Neubauer was debating whether to use up his limited quota of field-gun shells in a single salvo before rushing the thin remnant of the Belgians when he noticed something odd.

The glistening puddles in the field around his guns were beginning to join together.

As the rain had stopped five hours earlier this seemed surprising and then very quickly it became alarming. He looked around and saw that a quite unaccountable sheet of dirty yellow water was creeping across the whole landscape and the men kneeling behind their sandbag shelters found it rising inexorably around them. He saw a soldier panic and get to his feet to fall immediately backwards as a Belgian beyond the railway embankment shot him through the head.

It was very inconvenient, he thought. Perhaps some flood-tide at the coast, pushed in by the gales, which would wet their feet and then recede again. In two or three minutes it became more than inconvenient. He saw it was already halfway up to the hubs of the field guns' wheels.

'We'll be cut off,' he said, amazed. 'Pull back. We're getting the guns out of here.'

'Shall we clear the breeches?' asked the corporal.

'Fire the damned things,' he ordered. 'What is the point of taking back shells?'

★ ★ ★

It was as near to a miracle as he had ever seen. Willy raised his head over the railway lines ready to duck back down but not a single shot came his way. Instead he found he was looking at the backs of distant German infantrymen, struggling away through water that was already thigh-deep and still rising.

'They're retreating,' he called to the men in the trenches behind him. They came scrambling up the slope to join him, pitifully few. Two dozen only left in this section.

'How did that happen?' said the Sergeant.

'That happened,' said Willy, 'because someone finally listened to Henry Geeraert.' He could see movement around the position of the distant field-gun battery.

Claude reached across to clasp hands with him, a broad smile on his face. 'They're pulling

211

the guns back too,' he said, waving the trumpet. 'Shall we give them a helping hand?'

'Not the 'Marseillaise',' said Willy.

'No, I thought it might be time to sound the charge.'

The Sergeant grinned. 'Why not?' he said. 'We might as well.'

The trumpet notes of the charge burst into their ears.

'Let's go, lads,' shouted the Sergeant.

They all stood up, running across the rails and down the forward slope of the embankment. The water was shallow for the first fifty yards then it began to slow them down. Willy had his rifle to his shoulder as he waded through it, firing at the distant field guns. He saw a muzzle flash from the centre of the battery and had the briefest moment to realize how exposed they were before Claude seemed to leap back towards him, propelled by a geyser of mud and water, splashing down to collapse next to him.

'Claude, are you all right?' he said.

'Of course he's not,' said the Sergeant, 'look at the poor sod.'

Willy reached under him to lift him clear of the water hoping for another miracle, but the day had used up its quota of miracles. Claude's left arm was twitching. The other was shattered, with a spike of bone sticking up through the flesh, but it was his torso and stomach that had taken the brunt of the shell's explosion. It had split him and it seemed to Willy that no surgeon on earth could have put him back together again. One of his eyes was open and it looked towards Willy.

His mouth was moving. Willy bent over him and put his ear to Claude's lips.

*   *   *

Time moves by its own rules in such circumstances. It might have been ten seconds or it might have been a hundred seconds later; Willy was still kneeling in the water holding Claude when the other guns of the German battery fired their final shells. The baffled Germans, splashing away through the rising flood, were relieved and surprised that no more rifle fire came their way from the Belgian defenders who had held them at bay for so long. They could not see that there was nobody at all left beyond the embankment and that round Claude's body two dozen more now lay bobbing in the rising water, surrounded by spreading blood and the explosive reek.

November 24th 1914
Grannoch Castle
Newton Stewart
Galloway
Scotland

For the attention of William Fraser in the service of the King of Belgium or anyone who may know of his present situation.

William, if you receive this letter then, for the love of God reply to us at once. I am sending it as you directed to the headquarters of King Albert of the Belgians and I am most deeply troubled as each day passes with no good news from you. Morag dreams of you every night and is woken by her dreams and I am little better than that.

I have enquired at the barracks as to whether it is possible for me to travel to the Belgian coast in search of you but I am sorry to say that they took no account of the fact that I am an experienced soldier and well able to look after myself.

It is now three weeks since we received your last letter and that was itself some two weeks in the travelling. The newspaper tells us that the German advance has been

214

stopped by the flooding of the Belgian fields but that concerns us still more as it should make you less busy than you were when you wrote last.

You have made a joke of everything in your letters to us and I thank you for that because it has helped Morag to accept the situation until now but it does not fool me. I know the ways of soldiers in war, of our soldiers at least. In South Africa, humour was the very last thing to fail among the men even more than among the officers. I have known you since your birth and I have seen you find your way from frail child to determined youth to bold man wrapped in the armour of your humour. I salute you for it and hope that it continues to serve you but I share Morag's fears at this moment and confess that I long to hear from you.

If somebody else should be reading this letter and its subject is incapacitated or perhaps taken prisoner, please send us all possible information at the above address. Mr Fraser, though my master, is no less than a son to me and my heart grows heavier with every passing day.

With thanks to you,

Donald Gilfillan,
Steward of Grannoch.

PART TWO

Two Years Later

14

Sunday, 22 October 1916. Royal Flying Corps Kite Balloon Section. Southern Sector. Ypres Salient.

Major Bernard Thompson knew he should count himself lucky that he wasn't stationed just one mile further south. He worked on the very edge of the very worst part of the very worst war imaginable. He had a small wood to shelter them, solid ground underfoot and a cookhouse to make sure his men didn't go hungry. Another mile south and that solid ground ended in churning mud on the deadly approach to the shell-pecked lines where there was no shelter except an even wetter trench and the food got through only when the ration parties weren't killed on the way. Thompson could not ignore the all-consuming noise of the nearby war but the edge of it was blunted by that short distance and German shells only came his way a few times every day. And of course, any time he wanted a closer look at the carnage, he had the best possible grandstand seat available.

The Ypres Salient was shaped like the right-hand half of a shallow saucer, running from north of the devastated city at its centre clockwise round to the south. Since the first Christmas of the war it had been the stage for a tragic stalemate, with the Germans content to hold the drier high ground of the rim in relative comfort while the Allied armies suffered in the morass of the base of the saucer. From that rim, the enemy could look across four miles of lethal chaos at the poor, shattered ghost city of Ypres and they could rain shells down at their leisure. All that the soldiers on the receiving end could do was study the thin line of higher ground along the threatening horizon and wish they were somewhere else. On this side, only the men in the balloons could see beyond the rim.

This morning, Thompson's responsibilities offered him a golden ten-minute hole in the war — maybe even fifteen if he dragged it out. A wagon had finally brought the new balloon and that required a commanding officer's inspection before first use. By the time he reached the balloon bed in its woodland clearing, the petrol fans had blown in enough air to swell the new envelope to a saggy whale-belly approximation of its proper shape. Two air mechanics stretched apart the sides of the filling tube in the nose so that he could wriggle along it, boots and tunic off, into the sanctuary of the interior, away from the cold breeze. The Sergeant followed him in and they stood up in an unspoken mutual accord of silence.

The Salient had disappeared. British batteries were firing six hundred yards away but something about the balloon's air pressure dulled their sound to a thudding beat so that they stood in a cathedral of soft grey-green light, a place of unexpected peace dislocated from the vast arc of mud, guns and death. Thompson wondered if he would always now associate the smell of rubber solution with this sense of respite but then he checked himself. There was no 'always'. There was only 'now' and a few more 'nows' if you were lucky.

They took great care inspecting the fabric, the seams, the pressure relief valve and the rip panel because Thompson's observers depended on all of those to combat the loading of the dice against them. They had done this many times together so the Sergeant left early, knowing his commanding officer would follow when he was good and ready.

Thompson stood thinking of the sheaf of unit mail that had come with the balloon, wishing there was someone left who would write to him as 'Bernard'. The war had taken half his name as well as his whole life. These days he was 'Sir' or 'Major' or, if it was someone senior from Wing HQ, just plain 'Thompson'.

He was in no hurry to get back to the long list of problems on his desk out there in the wider world — a burnt-out winch, a worrying shortage of gas cylinders, a number three balloon so patched and leaky that it struggled to climb above two thousand feet and three of his best riggers on a charge for stealing Belgian chickens. Not that he had a desk any more. The shell that had caved in the end of his hut yesterday had also taken two of its legs off.

The Sergeant's voice emerged eerily from the world out there at the far end of the rubber pipe. 'Wing's on the line, sir,' it said. 'They're holding for you.'

Reluctantly he crawled back to the world of

flying iron and armies dying, crouched in their holes. He walked the short distance through the trees to the patched remains of the shed and listened to the voice on the phone. 'Sir, we do have a heavy task list today,' he said in dismay when he had a chance. 'I would really rather not. Anyway, I thought we didn't encourage newsmen.'

'This isn't a matter of *choice*, Thompson,' Peterson's voice said. 'This comes all the way down from the top. I am told the current view is that the good opinion of our Yankee friends apparently matters a great deal. Can't quite think why but anyway we go along with such things when ordered, don't we? Seems the fella was going to write some sort of article about Radford then we offered him Polito but that didn't work out. Now he needs somebody else and he thinks your man's the best bet.'

Ah yes, Radford, thought Bernard Thompson. Radford had been every newsman's first choice for a subject. Pity, but that explained it. 'When's he coming, sir?' He heard an engine outside and looked out through the remains of the window. A Crossley tourer braked to a halt outside. 'No, don't worry, sir. I think this must be him now.'

It was certainly no soldier or airman in the back seat of the car. The chubby man in the Crossley was craning his head upwards and staring. Thompson followed his gaze from the winch and the slender wire cable — up and up and up in a curve to the tiny shape of the balloon downwind to the east almost a mile above them. He walked across to the car.

222

'Good morning,' he said. 'I'm Thompson. Welcome.'

The American climbed out, peered at his badges and shook his hand. 'Chester K. Hoffman,' he said, '*New York Sentinel*. I'm glad to be here, Major. Is that your guy up there?'

'I'm not entirely sure what you mean by 'my guy'.'

'I mean this guy Taverner.'

'He is, but he's a member of my unit, no more nor less than that.'

'Yeah, yeah, yeah. I know. The service comes first. Pardon me, Major, but I know my business and it's all about people, one at a time, not altogether. Your man up there's no Radford but he's going to have to do.'

'Captain Radford was a great loss to the service. One of the very best of our observers.'

'You knew him?'

'Of course.' Everyone in the service, indeed everyone in Britain knew Basil Hallam Radford. 'A famous man. I'm sure you know he was the star of the West End.'

'You ever see his show?'

'Oh yes, spring of '14.'

'Gilbert the Filbert, the Colonel of the Nuts?'

'That's right. Everybody went to see him. He gave a lot of shows here too, you know. Hard day's work then a quick change. Very snappy dresser. Singing two or three evenings a week, just to keep the men happy.'

'I was there,' said the American and glanced up at the distant balloon again as if afraid of what he might see.

'Where? At a show?'

'No. Beaumont Hamel way, place that went by the name of Couin.' He pronounced it 'kwoin' but Thompson knew exactly where he meant. Everyone in the Balloon Service knew where Radford had died.

'Ah.' Thompson stared at the American, wishing he would go away or perhaps be hit by a very small shell. Civilians who were still sentimental on the scale of a single human life had no place in the Salient.

'I never got to meet him, Major, but I came damn close. I showed up that Sunday evening at headquarters. They began hauling him down. Idea was he'd climb out, do the photos by the basket, answer some questions, you know how it goes. Except it didn't.'

'These things . . . '

'Yeah, I know, these things happen. That's what you guys always say. Big gust of wind maybe, cable snapped. Two of them up there. One guy jumped. Radford had some kinda hitch. They say he was tearing up his maps. Damndest thing. We all saw him climb out and then he got kind of hung up somehow, dangling down under the basket, drifting away, next stop German territory. Next thing, I saw him drop. Still three thousand feet up, they said. Fell straight out of his parachute harness. He came tumbling down. I was counting. I got up to fourteen. He landed on the Acheux road. Nothing left to interview. Snappy dresser, you say? Not when I saw him.'

'Mr . . . er'

'Hoffman. I told you.'

224

They sat down on chairs outside the splintered hut. 'It's a dangerous business, Mr Hoffman,' said the Major.

'So they say. Hanging under a bag full of hydrogen gas with people shooting bullets at you ain't my idea of a good time.'

'Oh bullets aren't really such a problem, you know. They go straight through and out the other side, well . . . except for these new incendiary types. Those are a little worrying I have to admit. Shells are always a headache, of course.'

'A headache? Like 'boom' you mean?'

'Well yes. Hydrogen likes exploding, but you see, it's lighter than air so the flames go upwards.'

'That's not so bad then.'

'Ah, well, it is. The trouble is, the balloon itself catches fire and then it drops straight down on the basket so you have to be a bit nifty about jumping.'

'Major, I think maybe we speak different languages. For the sake of my readers what exactly does 'a bit nifty' mean? Is that like half a minute?'

'Oh heavens, no.'

'A minute then?'

'No, no. More like a second really. Yes, a second does it. Straight over the edge and Bob's your uncle, the old parachute comes to your rescue.'

'When they work.'

'Oh well, they work quite often really. You would be surprised.'

'And I hear the wind blows mostly from the

west round here, am I right?'

'Pretty much.'

'So even if the parachute works, the wind blows you over to the Germans?'

'We certainly do our best to come down this side of the lines.'

'Say, Major, if parachutes are so good, why don't they give them to the guys who fly the aeroplanes?'

Thompson shrugged. 'You would have to ask the higher-ups about something like that. They tell me the pilots would be jumping out all the time instead of trying to bring the aircraft back. Look, old fellow, we don't tend to dwell on these things. That way madness lies. Falling's not the worst thing that can happen, you know.'

'What's worse than falling?'

'Well, burning for example. Captain Radford lasted eight months in the service and that's not too bad really. I don't know if you've had the chance to see much action so far in your . . . '

'Stop right there, Major. Don't you give me that crap. I've done three tours of duty in this war so far. One way or another I've been covering it since the very first day. I've seen everything there is to see from both sides. I've been with the Sikhs, the Diggers, the Zealanders, the Zouaves, the Froggies — every one. I've even been with the Boches, damn it. In point of fact, I started off with them before this war even got going. I've seen men killed in more ways than I could ever imagine but I never saw a musical star fall out of the sky before so I would really like it if you could winch that balloon up there down to

226

earth so I can do my business and get back to somewhere safer, like a front-line trench.'

'I'm afraid Taverner is going to be up there for a little while yet. He's coordinating a counter-battery shoot. That's when . . .'

'I know what that is. It's when you try and kill their gunners before they kill yours.'

'More or less. Anyway, we are a bit short-staffed at the moment. Wilcox caught some shrapnel yesterday, Moreton-Jones is . . . ah! Yes . . . dead. Evans is on leave but Lieutenant Bridges is over there in the mess tent. His balloon is still being rigged. Why don't you talk to him instead?'

There was a whine, turning slowly to the screech of a shell coming towards them and they both stopped talking. It burst two hundred yards short of the wood.

'They're not quite reaching us today,' said the Major. 'Might have to move back a bit if they get the range.'

'How long has Bridges been doing it?'

'Must be all of two weeks now. Three even.'

'What's special about him?'

'Special? Nothing much. He's turning into a jolly good observer. Zeroed them in on an ammo dump in only eight shots yesterday.'

'Does he play the trumpet?'

Oh damn, thought Thompson. 'I haven't a clue,' he said. 'Why on earth would that matter? I think he might play a bit of piano. Come and ask him.'

'I get the feeling you don't want me to talk to Taverner, do you, Major?'

'No, of course not.' Bloody Taverner, he thought, why couldn't they just give me some more nice simple Englishmen like Bridges. What did I do to deserve Taverner? He gave up. 'He'll be coming down quite soon.'

Hoffman looked at the sky. 'So why does someone like this guy do it? He's something special from what I hear.'

'Taverner? Really? Oh, I'd say he's fairly typical of all the observers. What exactly have you heard?'

'He flies higher. He flies longer. He sees further. He jumps later.'

Thompson laughed. 'Really? People do come up with some stories, don't they? The fact of the matter is there are many, many heroes in this service.'

The winch engine revved up and the drum began to turn. 'Ah! You're in luck. Looks as if he's on the way down. He must have done his business,' said Thompson. 'Let's stroll over, shall we?'

They walked across to the big winch lorry, its engine snorting and hunting as the winch mounted on the rear half of its chassis turned a vertical drum to wind in the thin steel cable. The balloon grew gradually larger. After four or five minutes a man crouching by a telephone set next to the lorry shouted and held up his hand and the winch stopped turning. Thompson went over to him. The phone wire ran upwards in tandem with the balloon cable.

'What's up?' he asked.

'Boche fighter,' said the man. 'Albatros.

228

Stooging round south. Taverner says to hold.'

'A German scout? So you're leaving him up there? Why don't you bring him right on down?' asked Hoffman.

'It's his choice. You see, at this height he can still jump if things turn nasty. A bit lower and there's no time for the chute to open,' said Thompson. 'Best to hold on there and see what happens.' They waited for a minute and then a faint and curious noise came to their ears from the basket far above them.

'Ah!' said Hoffman, 'so it's true then?'

Bloody man, said Thompson to himself. Why couldn't he keep quiet just this once? Fourteen hundred feet up in the air, a thin trumpet was blowing the 'Marseillaise'.

'He does that when he's hit the target, is that right, Major?'

'A battery, yes. True. When he knocks out a battery, he does tend to play that er . . . that tune.'

'All clear,' shouted the man with the phone. 'Haul down.'

The winch revved up again and the cable drum slowly filled up. A swarm of handlers reached up to grab the trailing ropes as the balloon neared the ground, pulling it away to one side of the truck and clear of the trees. The basket bumped down on the earth and they hung sandbags all around the rim. The observer was alone. He wore goggles and a leather helmet and he climbed out with difficulty.

'Is he all right?' Hoffman asked, concerned.

'He was injured back in '14. It's cramped in

229

that basket. Cold up there. He'll be fine in a minute. I suppose you had better come over and meet him.'

The observer was looking at his clipboard and talking to the man with the telephone as they walked up.

'Taverner,' said the Major. 'We have a visitor from the American press. Meet Mr er . . . Hoffnung, this is Lieutenant Claud Taverner.'

'Hoffman,' said the American. 'Chester K. Hoffman. *New York Sentinel*.'

The observer turned and stared at him, then pushed his goggles up over his forehead and stared some more and that was when the American gasped, stepped back, clenched his fist and punched the observer as hard as he could on the point of his chin. It took three men to help the Major restrain him as others ran to pick up Taverner from the ground.

'Mr Hoffman,' said the Major, 'restrain yourself or I'll have to put you on a charge.' As he said it, he wondered if he had the power to do that to a member of a neutral country and what Wing HQ would say if he did. Hoffman was flexing his fingers and looking a little aghast at what he had just done. Taverner was helped to his feet, rubbing his chin and staring at the American.

Thompson took Hoffman by the arm and led him off to one side. 'Now would you mind telling me just why you did that?' He had wanted to do something like it himself many times but it didn't seem the right moment to say so.

'Because I've had a score to settle with that

man and I've been watching out for him for the past two years and his name isn't Claud whatever you said it was, it's Fraser. Willy Goddam Fraser.'

15

'Am I under arrest?' asked Chester K. Hoffman five minutes later. 'Because if I am, your name is going to be all over my paper, Major, and I'll spell it M-U-D.'

'No of course you're not,' said Thompson. 'Wouldn't dream of such a thing. Have a glass of something. Whisky?'

'It's not even noon.'

Thompson frowned at him. 'Noon? Oh look here. It's a thirty-year-old Laphroaig. We tend to drink these things while we still can. It would be a dreadful shame to leave half a bottle of this stuff undrunk.' His tone hardened. 'Now, while they're ministering to my valued observer, would you tell me what on earth possessed you to do such a thing.'

'We go back quite some way, him and me,' said Chester. 'I met him in Berlin the week the war started. We ran into von Emmich's army on the road to Liège. Bastard rode off and left me in a whole heap of trouble.'

'Yes, but which bastard exactly?' Thompson asked patiently. 'You see my particular bastard really is called Taverner not Fraser. Hard names to mix up, wouldn't you say? Different number of syllables. No 'v' in Fraser and so on. It's quite plain on his papers. The RFC is most particular about getting these things right, you know. I think we may have what the French would call an embarrassment of bastards here, in which case I suspect you've just assaulted entirely the wrong bastard.'

'Major, I'm goddam sure I did not. There are not many men you can mistake for Wild Willy Fraser. You have to understand, I've been studying the guy ever since then. Came from the badlands of Scotland. Got pushed out of some buttoned-up-tight cavalry outfit for taking his pleasure with the Colonel's wife. Because of him I spent two days locked in a cellar with some goon from Abteilung IIIb detailing all the things he planned to do to my teeth with a set of iron pincers. Uncle Sam's envoy had to kick the door down to spring me out of there. I am not the sort of guy who forgets the face of the rat who nearly sank my ship.'

'And you haven't seen him since?'

'I tracked him when I had the time, which was not too often, then the trail went cold on me.'

Thompson shook his head. 'I really can't fathom this.' He sought safer ground. 'Anyway, Mr Hoffman, perhaps all that can wait for another time? Wing HQ asked me to explain the state of play around here.'

'So, surprise me.'

'I'm sure you've heard the French are in a bit of a ding-dong down at Verdun so it's relatively quiet in the Salient at the moment though we still have to stay on our . . . ' He broke off as someone knocked on the door and then opened it without waiting for an invitation. They both stared at the man who walked in.

'Ah, Taverner. You're on your feet again. I'm

sorry to say it may be a case of mistaken identity. Mr Hoffman here seems to think you're . . . '

The new arrival held up a hand to interrupt. 'Sir, there's a flap on. Our services are in demand.' He nodded to the American. 'No need to apologize. I'm sure it's a perfectly normal way to greet a stranger where you come from.'

'Yes, but hold your horses, Taverner,' said the Major, feeling the need to regain control of a situation he could not begin to understand. 'We seem to have some things to discuss.'

'Perhaps it might wait an hour or two, Major? The artillery boys are in a bit of a rush. There's a Boche battery firing from a new location somewhere near Whitesheet and it's pasting our support line. They're asking for all hands on deck. Bridges is on his way up but they want everything we can put in the air and that seems to come down to just me at the moment.'

'Oh dear. I was about to offer our American friend a flight. Wing's instructions.'

'That's all right, sir. I'll take him up. They're putting on the other car.' He turned to Hoffman. 'It's got more space for two. That's if you like the idea?'

'Car?' said Hoffman.

'It's what we call a basket.'

They stared at each other for a long moment — the journalist sure of his ground, challenging — the observer politely blank. Thompson watched, baffled.

'Hell, I wouldn't miss that for the world,' said the American. 'Up there. Just the two of us.'

'Mr Hoffman,' said Thompson mildly. 'I would

be grateful if you could avoid using profanities such as that when you're outside in front of my men.'

'Did I just use a profanity?' He looked genuinely baffled.

'Hell.'

'That counts as a profanity round here? In the middle of all this shit?'

'They're not used to American ways and they will face punishment if they're tempted to copy you.'

'Hell, yeah. I'll clean up my mouth.'

Two years of chasing the war had made Chester K. Hoffman a lot braver and a little thinner. The men had rigged the two-man basket by the time they reached the balloon and Major Thompson was having trouble believing in everything he was seeing and hearing.

'This is a novelty,' he muttered to the American. 'Taverner never flies with anyone else, not ever.'

'Maybe he's planning to throw me out.'

'Have they explained the parachute?'

'Not yet.'

Thompson patted the fat cone strapped to the side of the basket. 'It's in this bag. There's one each side. We hook you up to it. If you need it, all you have to do is climb over the side right next to it and just sort of drop off really.'

'All I have to do? So long as I do that in under one second, right?'

'Let's say as quickly as you possibly can. Most people seem to find they can suddenly move quite fast under those circumstances.'

'Then what do I do next?'

'Well . . . fall, I suppose. The cap pops off the bag and the cords pull the chute straight out of it as you go down. It only takes a couple of seconds to open.'

'Quite often,' said Chester.

'Oh no, please forget I ever said 'quite'. 'Often' is much nearer the mark. Let's settle on often. You could almost say 'usually'. Whatever you do, don't go over unless Taverner tells you to. The odds are against it but go like the clappers if he does.'

'The things I do for the *Sentinel*.'

'Now, the main thing is you mustn't distract him. He has a map board and binoculars. He'll be wearing the telephone headset so he can spot exactly where the shells land and pass on the corrections, do you see? Here's a headset for you too. Just listen. Don't talk unless you have to. There'll be plenty of time for that when you come down. Remember to unplug it before you jump. Otherwise, these things have a nasty way of tearing your ears off.'

'Before I jump.'

'I meant *if*. If you jump.'

The attending air mechanics helped Chester into sheepskin-lined leggings and a padded leather coat made for somebody a foot taller and a foot slimmer, then pulled the wide webbing loops of the parachute harness up around his legs and tightened the belt. Finally they half lifted and half pushed him up and over the side of the basket and clipped his harness to the rope emerging from the parachute cone. He felt bulky

236

and out of breath, squashed into a corner amid all the paraphernalia as the other man climbed in. Binoculars dangled from a cord suspended from the ropes above. Two more pairs were on the floor. A fat red rope came down from above and its end was fastened to a canvas sling across the centre of the basket. A plywood board with a map on it slanted out from the edge of the basket. Four more with different maps were stacked against one side.

'Hold on to the edge,' said the man they were calling Taverner. 'Wind's getting up. You'll be all right. Whatever you do, don't pull the red cord. It lets all the gas out. Bad idea unless you happen to be on the ground. Bad idea even then if anyone's lighting up a Players in the vicinity.' An air mechanic passed him a Lee-Enfield rifle. He propped it in the corner of the basket. 'It makes me feel better,' he said to Chester. 'I like to know I can shoot back.'

The earth and the drone of the winch drum quickly receded below them. 'Willy Fraser, would you care to tell me what exactly is going on here?' said Chester.

'Do me the favour of taking your headset off for a moment.'

Chester did so and watched Willy move his microphone away from his mouth. 'It would make life so much easier if you called me Taverner or even Claud,' he said.

'Why are you pretending to be someone else?'

'Am I? Not my choice. That's who I am these days.'

'I tracked you. I asked a lot of questions.'

237

'And what did you find out?'

'You got yourself injured with the Belgians. Rejoined your own guys. Did a whole lotta stuff with the cavalry then nix. Silence. Nobody's talking and it's like you went up in a puff of smoke. Now here you are pretending to be someone else. It makes no sense.'

'Blame the brave men with the red tabs who quaff fine clarets in their safe châteaux,' said Willy. 'They have decreed that it must be so and I would be greatly obliged if you would go along with their wishes.'

'Only if there's a good reason.'

'I was Stellenbosched, dear Chester, just like my father before me.'

'What is that word? I never heard it before.'

'It's what can happen when you've been a naughty boy.'

'Like being court-martialled?'

'Far, far worse.'

Willy suddenly frowned and put one hand up to his headphones, listening. Chester put his set back on and heard crackling in the headphones then a voice said: 'Chart room here. Battery ready.'

Willy stared at the map board and read out coordinates. 'Three minutes,' he said into the mouthpiece. 'Two and a half thousand feet should do it to start with. We'll go on up from there. Get ready to shoot on my word.' The basket began to weave and bob under the tension of the thin cable letting it up into an increasingly capricious wind.

Chester was not a violent man and the

memory of the punch he had thrown at Willy howled in his head because he was filled with guilt. Willy's desertion had given him his first published story of the war. The American's brief imprisonment by Abteilung IIIb had persuaded the news desk back home that he was a serious correspondent. He stared at Willy, wanting to understand, but this was no time to ask questions. Willy was intent on his task, focusing on the map, the far distance and his headset.

Chester looked down at the ground below. The woodland had shrunk to a spinney. The lorry with the winch was a tiny toy, the Major's battered hut no more than half a sugar cube on the far side of a table. His stomach tightened. The war was creeping closer across the shrinking landscape, the obscenity of wrecked nature that marked the trenches, erupting in tiny pustules of mud.

Willy snapped his fingers in front of Chester's face and pointed at the map. 'See there? They've moved in a battery somewhere about there. It will be very carefully camouflaged.' He looked out across the lines, pointing. 'That wood over to the east, see where the triangular bit sticks out? We'll be watching for muzzle flashes coming from somewhere there. Keep your eyes peeled.'

Chester stared at the target area and then across to Bridges' balloon, half a mile away and quite a bit higher. A voice in his headphones said, 'Taverner? Bridges here. Nothing yet.' Then the headphones buzzed again. A deeper voice said, 'Claud, do we have the pleasure of your company at last? Better late than never.'

239

'Plot? Is that you?' said Willy. 'Where are you?' He put the glasses to his eyes and looked a little further to the north. 'I see you,' he said.

'Keep an eye out. You might have an Eindecker heading your way,' said the distant voice. 'He's in the cloud.'

'Is it just the one?'

'Yes, all by himself, poor lost soul.'

'Anyone we know?'

'Our friend with the red engine cowling.'

'Him again? Thank you.'

Willy searched the sky. Chester kept quiet until Willy moved the microphone aside again and became quite chatty. 'That was Plot Polito, the best in the business. We can talk to anyone from up here. Our unit, the batteries, HQ, the other balloons. I could ring up a floozy in London if she had a telephone and I had her number.'

'Where is he?'

Willy picked up a spare pair of binoculars and passed them to him. 'There he is, over there,' he said.

Chester put them to his eyes and tried to focus but the whole magnified world began to rush backwards and forwards through the lenses and he immediately felt sick. 'What was he telling you?'

'There's an Eindecker buzzing around somewhere.'

'A Fokker?'

'That's the one. Seen him before. He's quite good. Plane's a bit past it. He'll be a lot more dangerous if they buy him an Albatros for

Christmas. Plot thinks he might be heading over our way. Keep an eye out for anything that's managing to fly without flapping its wings. Do you know Plot claims on a really clear day you can see the top of the Eiffel Tower from here? He must have better eyes than me.'

Chester had put the glasses down. He was staring out trying to see Polito's balloon, squinting in the cold wind. He spotted a yellow-brown balloon in the distance, much lower down. 'Is that him?' he said, pointing at it.

Willy laughed. 'No,' he said, 'That's our good friends the Germans. They have heavier hydrogen. They can't fly nearly as high as we can.'

'It looks just like this one.'

'That's because it is. Back in '14, our lot had dreadful balloons, round ones that spun like tops. Remember von Emmich's *Drachen?* We watched their balloons pointing nicely into the wind and staying there so we copied them. This is exactly the same beast.'

'What does that word mean: Stellenbosched?'

But Willy had abruptly had enough of conversation. 'Another time,' he said. 'Now where's this Fokker got to?'

He saw Chester staring around him with wild eyes. 'Relax,' he said. 'We'll see the bursts of Archie if red-nose comes anywhere close. We've got a couple of batteries looking after us. Now, this is where it all gets a bit busy. We're coming up through two and half thousand.'

Chester looked down. It took a moment for his eyes to make sense of what he saw. As they rose higher, the belt of brown devastation was

241

widening before them, circling around from the south through the east towards the north. He looked that way, away from the sun, and saw the remains of old Ypres centred on the skeleton of the Cloth Hall. He had passed through the shattered town many times as the German shells picked it apart but now he could see the whole of the vast ruin, bone-white down there in the sunshine, and could only marvel that soldiers still lived in that wreckage, crouched in the deep cellars and the cave-like shelters dug into the ramparts. As he watched, an orange burst sent up a spray of stone from what was left of the cathedral, a mincer refining the destruction of what had already been destroyed.

The balloon was now swooping and bucking, buffeting him with its antics, but Willy stood with bent legs, swaying easily with the motion, his eyes glued to the binoculars as he called instructions into the mouthpiece. Chester looked down at that shell-ploughed chaos of the front line, saw midget men crouching in the trenches, fountains of sporadic earth from the shells dropping down into the mud all around them. He was surprised how little he could hear until a rising drone had him staring, searching for a source in the sky. Was this Polito's Fokker?

'Howitzer,' shouted Willy. 'There,' but he was pointing at the sky, not at the ground and Chester followed his pointing finger, astonished to see a huge lazy shell, curving over level with them before plunging down towards the distant town. Willy looked back beyond the German lines. 'I see him,' he said. 'We'll have that bastard too.' He spoke into the mouthpiece. 'Second battery please, coordinates coming. First battery, line's good, go three minutes left.'

He reached for Chester's arm, pointed again, said, 'Watch the wood!' Chester saw five gouts of flame, one after another, almost on the same spot — fragments of timber twisting up into the air. 'Line, one minute right. Battery fire,' called Willy.

They waited. 'I could *hear* that howitzer shell,' said Chester.

'They vibrate, you know, that's why,' said Willy, 'I had one pass so close it almost took my . . . ' Words ended and the war reached out to grab them. The sky in front of them burst open in a ball of flame and a punching wall of heat. Chester buckled, completely deafened, then felt himself hauled backwards by some huge invisible force bent on tearing him right out of the basket. He could see Willy's face in front of him, lips moving soundlessly. Whatever was behind him went on tugging him towards destruction. A loop of rope caught round his neck, strangling him under the implacable weight of the pull, and the wicker basket tilted sharply under his feet. He watched, powerless, as Willy wrapped a line around him, heaving in the other direction so that Chester, choking, knew he was about to come in two, cut through by the bite of Willy's rope or garrotted by the one round his neck. His head was forced round under the strain so that he could see the culprit, his own parachute. It had burst out of the shrapnel-ripped canvas cone, filling in the wind to billow sideways. He gripped the basket lines with two desperate hands but knew he could not hold on against the titanic tug of the gale in the silk. His vision faded to a shrinking disk as blackness came in from the edges.

Then the pressure lessened as one side came free and vanished completely as Willy's knife sawed through the straps holding the chute. Chester's eyes cleared as the parachute whirled away in the wind, twisting and sinking into the maelstrom below.

'Jeez,' he tried to say, rubbing his neck. 'Goddam.' He sucked in another breath. 'The Major can't hear me on this thing, can he?'

'I think you'll find your headset went over the side with the chute and anyway even the Major would allow you a little freedom under the circumstances. Are you all right?'

'I will be. Willy, thank you. Guess that cleans our slate.'

'Make it Claud and I'll shake on that.' Willy peered over the side of the basket. 'Sorry to interrupt the joy ride,' he said, 'but we have to haul down now. That shell's left its mark on the cable.' He spoke into the mouthpiece. 'Down gently. Slow speed. There's a few strands gone.'

Chester looked over the edge. The winch truck was impossibly small and the wire curved down towards it but somewhere quite close, twenty or thirty yards down he guessed, there was a fuzzy star of wire, frayed and broken ends sticking out from the spiral winding. 'That looks bad,' he said. 'Will it break?'

'No, no, no — but just in case . . . ' Willy

unclipped his parachute line and clipped it on to Chester's harness.

'Hold on. Don't do that.'

'Have to. It's off-season for the American press. Considered most unsporting to kill one at this time of year. What do you suppose would happen to you if you jumped and the Germans got you?'

'Up in an enemy balloon? With my record? Can't happen.'

'Then keep your fingers crossed. We'll get down all right.'

As he said that, the basket jerked and a voice spoke on the phone. All Chester could hear was a harsh rattle of words but they brought a thoughtful expression to Willy's face.

'Understood,' said Willy and moved the mike again to talk to Chester. 'We now have another wee problem. It seems the winch motor has swallowed something nasty. These things are sent to try us.'

'You saying they can't haul us down?'

'There are other methods but they all take a bit of time. Trouble is, the wind is getting up. Look, I think the safest thing is for you to go down the quick way. I'll hang on here to sort things out.'

'The quick way?' Chester gaped at him. 'What is that? You mean *jump?*'

'Yes, and the sooner the better while the wind isn't too strong. You wouldn't want to have to walk too far back, would you? Particularly not from the other side. You go now and I'll just do a bit more spotting while I wait. There's that howitzer calling out for a touch more attention. No point in wasting the opportunity.'

'Hell no. I'll take my chances up here with you.'

'Jump, Chester. You have to.'

'No.'

'All right.' Willy shrugged in acceptance. 'Stay here but come and get into position so at least I can tell the Major I did my best. We need to swap sides. If you go out that side, you'll get in an awful tangle. Carefully now, duck under the sling and come and sit on the edge here then you're next to the parachute. Move slowly and I'll balance you.'

The American bent down under the canvas seat between them and gingerly pulled himself up so that he was half-sitting on the edge of the basket, facing inwards and holding on to the lines with white knuckles. Willy had wormed his way to the other side.

'I'm not going anywhere,' Chester said. 'Anyway, I don't know how to . . . ' which was when Willy hit him in the stomach, then, as Chester's hands moved involuntarily to shield himself, gave him an almighty shove backwards. He flailed his arms but there was nothing to grab but thin air and he heard a loud 'sorry' trailing off from above as the basket shot upwards away from him. He caught a glimpse of a thin stream of material being pulled from the cone before he was swung round by the crack of the canopy opening.

After his heart slowed down, he almost enjoyed the first part of the descent. The

246

parachute blocked his view of the balloon's plight but a strong wind was sweeping him towards the lines. He feared he was already halfway there but it seemed to lose its strength as he came down lower. He lost sight of the winch lorry then he looked down and saw that Belgium was suddenly rushing up to meet him. He fell, stiff-legged and scared, thudding down into the overlapping craters of a ruined field, saved by the softness of the shell-ploughed earth but still twisting an ankle as he hit. He lay there, winded, unable to get up without being immediately pulled off-balance by the half-collapsed canopy tugging at him in the breeze. As he started to wrestle with the cords he heard an engine and turned his head to see a Crossley tender bumping towards him across the field. Major Thompson and the driver jumped out, the driver bundling up the parachute and Thompson getting Chester's arm round his shoulder and dragging him towards the car.

'Shouldn't wonder if they don't send some shells this way in a minute,' said Thompson pushing him into the back seat. 'Juicy target, an observer on the ground, and you can be quite sure they watched you coming down. We were chasing you from the moment you jumped. That balloon of theirs can see you clearly enough.'

The Crossley roared out of the field and had just regained the road when a salvo of three shells burst behind them.

'Thank you,' said Chester.

'Did you have an interesting time up there?'

'Oh yes.'

'Sorted out this silly name business, I hope?'

'I'm happy to leave that one to lie, Major. Guess your man Taverner has his hands full enough right now.' He stared up at the balloon far above. 'Can you get him down?'

'Not much choice,' said Thompson. 'Not after he lost his brolly like that.'

'Brolly?'

'Umbrella. You know, parachute. Looked nasty from down here, not that we could see much. Lucky it wasn't yours.'

'It *was* mine. He gave me his then he pushed me out of the basket.'

'Did he now? He's always been a good man in a tight spot.' *Bloody fool*, Thompson was thinking — we need observers, not foreign journalists.

They pulled up beside the winch lorry. 'We'll do our best anyway,' said Thompson. 'The winch is napoo so it's back to the old-fashioned ways.'

In a scene of quiet, efficient turmoil, riggers were bolting a cage around the cable just above the drum. The cage held a large steel pulley hard up against the cable. A team of eight horses waited, stamping and snorting in the ever-increasing wind.

'Do you see?' said Thompson. 'His cable stays fixed to the winch lorry but the horses move off, pulling the spider — that's the cage-thing with the pulley in it — and that drags his cable down. He's still maybe half a mile up, so the horses trot along for half a mile and Bob's your uncle, he touches down on terra firma and off for a quick snifter, no harm done.'

'Sir?' called a sergeant. 'We've lost contact with him.'

'Oh dear,' said Thompson.

'Why's that happened?' asked Chester anxiously.

'Telephone wire's parted.'

'Is that bad?'

'It probably means that what's left of the cable is stretching.'

'Major, you got to bring him down. I owe him.'

'A lot of people owe him. Don't misunderstand me. He may be a bastard but he's our bastard.'

They stood in silence staring upwards and a faint sound reached them. A thin and distant trumpet playing the 'Marseillaise'.

'Ready, sir,' yelled the Sergeant.

'Carry on.'

The horses lumbered off, dragging down the first of thousands of feet of cable through the pulley, laying it down behind them on a line in the grass. They were slow, hooves slipping, labouring hard against the drag of the great balloon up there in the ever-increasing wind, a fat kite unwilling to give up its place in the sky.

'How long will this take?' Chester asked then he whooped as he saw the horses accelerate into a trot. 'That's more like it,' he said but he fell silent when he saw the expression on the Major's face. All the men around the balloon bed were running — getting out of the way of a half-mile flail of falling steel cable and everyone was staring up at the free balloon rising higher and higher, sailing on what had become a full gale eastward towards the edge of the Salient and the German lines.

'Oh Jesus Christ,' said the Major. 'Damn, damn, damn.'

'Do something,' yelled Chester in an agony of guilt.

'He's up there. We're down here. There is *absolutely nothing* we can do.'

'You could shoot holes in it.'

'Did you have to pass any sort of intelligence test to get your job?'

A headline appeared, unbidden, scrolling across Chester's mind's eye, 'Hero Saves Our Correspondent'. That wasn't too bad until it blurred into 'Correspondent's Free Ride Kills Hero'.

They all stood there, the Major, Chester and sixty silent men of the balloon crew watching it soar away. When it finally dwindled out of sight the men turned as one and began to attend to the coils of fallen cable.

'What happens to him now?' Chester asked quietly.

'At the very best he's taken prisoner when he comes down.'

'And the worst?'

'The balloon splits as it rises or it comes down too fast if he vents too much gas. Whichever happens, we don't see him again. Look, Mr Hoffman, the Balloon Service may seem to you like some sort of joyride but what you perhaps don't realize is that this is one of the most dangerous things you can do in this very dangerous war. No, don't interrupt. Listen to me. A shell can get you. An enemy scout can get you. A badly joined seam or a patched hole can split. Basket rigging ropes can fail. Your parachute can fail to open or rip to pieces or let you swing slowly over enemy lines where they use you for target practice. That's just the observers. You see all these men here? When you write your article, don't forget to tell your readers all the different ways they get killed too.'

'These men here?'

'Yes. Oh, I see. You think they have some sort of free pass out of the trenches too, do you? So let me reorganize your thoughts for you, Mr Hoffman. I had a new draft of air mechanics last month. That's what we call them. Twenty-six new men arrived to replace the twenty-six I had just lost when a German battery landed three shells on the winch. Popular target, do you see, a balloon winch? Now those twenty-six new men had gone through their training but they had never had to wrestle with a balloon when the wind gets up under combat conditions. They were green, do you see? I had to use them. No choice. The very first day they were all hanging on to the handling ropes like grim death when this big gust lifted a few of them off their feet. If they had all hung on it would have been no problem but three of them understandably let go. That's all it took, just three. The bloody balloon took off. Most of the rest let go at that point but ten of my best men hung on until they couldn't hold on any longer. Nine of them dropped off at a hundred feet and that was the end of them. One of them, my very best Sergeant, wound the rope round him and the last we saw of him was when the balloon went into the cloud at ten thousand feet.'

'So he might have lived?'

'Not one single chance of that. Come on. You're coming with me.'

Chester trotted after the silent, striding Major to a small hut in the far edge of the wood. Inside was a bed built out of rough timber, a chair, a table and a large wooden box. Thompson looked around then opened the box and began to root through the contents, pulling RFC uniform clothing out on to the floor.

'Damn,' he said. 'Where is it?'

'Where is what?'

'You are looking at the worldly goods of Claud Taverner,' snapped the major. 'Which appear to add up to more or less nothing. It should be here.'

'What should?'

'A picture. I found him looking at it once. I had knocked but he didn't seem to hear. It was a woman. I saw it before he put it away.'

'So he had a picture of a woman?'

'You are an execrable heap of worthless humanity, aren't you?' said Thompson, turning on him. 'I have to write to somebody. He has no next of kin I know of. Would you rather we all just forgot about him? Where the hell is it?'

'Maybe he took it up with him. He had some sort of bag. No next of kin, you say? I might have some clues for you there.'

'Don't go back there again, please. I know my

man. He's Taverner.'

'Just how long have you known him, Major?'

Thompson considered. 'Four months, give or take a week.'

'That's not so long.'

'Believe me, in this work, it's several lifetimes. Oh hold on now, let's see. What have we here?'

'Letters?'

'Obviously,' said the Major, riffling through a sheaf of forty or fifty envelopes. 'They look like they're all from the same person.' He slipped one out from under the rubber band, put the rest on the table and pulled out the sheet inside.

'From a woman?'

'Only if you know a woman called Donald Gilfillan,' said the major, scanning through it. 'So much for your Fraser nonsense. These come from some retainer from home and he calls his master Taverner.'

Goddam, thought Chester. How does that fit? He stared at the stack of envelopes on the table. A four-inch-tall goldmine of information. 'Can I take a look at those?'

'Certainly not.'

'Anything else in that box?' said Chester. 'Did you check for a fake floor? He might have made some kind of hideaway.'

'Ridiculous,' said Thompson, but he knelt down by the box and peered inside and that was all it took for Chester to slip a single envelope from under the band and tuck it out of sight in his pocket.

An hour later, in the back of a Crossley tender taking him away from the scene, he took it out and opened it with a sense of shame that surprised him. It began:

To our dear Willy,
I will address you thus one last time
because I find I cannot easily call you
Claud, although that is how you tell me I
must write to you from now onwards. I
will nerve myself to inscribe that strange
name upon this envelope. Morag shakes
her head at the sound of the name and
repeatedly asks me why you could not have
chosen something more suited to your
blood, to which I have no answer. You
have given up a great deal for the strange
privilege of fighting once again on the
Western Front. You have given up your
rank and your name and I do admire you.
Take care you do not give up your self.
Hold on to who you are and come back to
us and to your name with that intact. I do
not pretend to understand the reasons for
what has happened save that they gave you
a choice which was no choice at all. The
weasel of a man who represents your
mother has visited again. He has convinced
himself that you are dead and we are cov-
ering up the fact. It seems he has asked
among the regiments and been told they
have no record of you currently serving.
You have told me to tell no one so I pre-
sume I cannot reveal the truth but we will
protect Grannoch against him by whatever
means we can. Morag spilt an entire tray

of tea into his lap on this occasion and,
though she insists that her foot caught
under the rug, I see the light of battle in
her eyes and do not believe that man's dig-
nity will be safe in her presence from now
forward.

Chester put the letter away and stared into the middle distance, oblivious to the shells that bracketed them at the battery crossroads, frowning, thinking and deciding on his course of action.

16

Willy knew immediately that the cable had snapped. There was no mistaking it because the balloon leapt up, freed of the cable's weight, and the motion eased. Until then it had been diving, shuddering and soaring upwards as the cable fought the immense wind that was howling through the basket. Sudden calm arrived with the rupture of the remaining steel strands.

He had one leg over the side of the basket before he remembered the parachute line dangling from his harness was no longer clipped to anything. The whole balloon was now being whirled along, an integral part of the storm, and the bubble in the statometer tube told him he was climbing fast.

Good training firmly embeds knowledge you hope never to need and they had trained Willy well at Roehampton. He could vent hydrogen if he chose to but all students learnt to fly a free balloon in preparation for the day when they might have no choice. He could hear Captain Hawthorn saying it over and over again, 'Don't give up gas. Gas gives you choices. Rely on the valve.' He looked down and knew that he was already over the front line.

Venting meant capture. Failing to vent might mean death. Any breakaway balloon would swell as it rose because of the lower pressure outside as it went up and up. Every balloon had a built-in safeguard, an automatic gas release valve designed to open when the expanding envelope pulled a transverse line inside it too tight. So long as it was properly adjusted.

Otherwise the balloon would simply burst.

Willy excelled at choices. He was made that way. Once his father had granted him that special childhood spell against fear, the rush of urgent action that disables some men served instead to fuel his brain and body. On the wet autumn day when he was nineteen and he had run to his mother's scream, he had known where to find the nearest knife to cut his father down, still breathing that time. Correct and rapid choices had kept him alive through this man-eating war so far and now, for the first time he could remember, he appeared to have no choice at all. His only comfort for now was that, the higher he flew, the further he would be from the attentions of enemy aircraft and enemy guns. Why should they bother to attack? They had him in the bag. The wind was driving him across occupied Belgium towards Germany territory. With no parachute left and no other way of escape, his life hung on the correct and automatic operation of the gas valve safety line out of his sight inside the balloon and so far there was no sign it was working. The balloon had already swollen, bulging over the rigging ropes laced around it. He was far higher than he had ever flown before and it looked ready to split at any moment.

Death by bullet, shell or bayonet was the rapid toss of a gambler's coin. This was death stretched out and having time to think was the worst of it. Is this really it, he thought? Is the game over so soon? Is that all there was? It seemed absurd, a joke of a death to tumble out of the sky into some field far from the fighting. It seemed to him that for all the racing and the riding and the chasing and the loving, he had not begun to live yet and he heard Claude's voice in his head lecturing him on emptiness and its antidote, love. He yelled out in frustration and there was nobody to hear him.

For distraction he looked all around and there was Brussels ahead. At this unprecedented height it was quite visible and well inside his new expanded horizon. He checked the time to give himself back some illusion of purpose and control. Brussels was sixty miles from Ypres so at least he could use it to work out his speed. The balloon was still climbing into ever-colder air and he huddled down into the bottom of the basket, wrapping his leather coat around his legs to wait for Brussels and once again he was confronted by his own inescapable self.

For the past months of living entirely in the immediate and dangerous present there were only rare moments, just before sleep or on first waking, when he was still Willy to himself but in company he was Claud and there was no past. Gilfillan had questioned him in his letters at the beginning and Gilfillan was the only link that still mattered to who he had once been. Gilfillan's phrases came back to him as he sat, chilled, on the floor of the basket. *We whooped with joy when your letter came. Morag cried for an hour. She had dreamt you were dead. I still had hope*. Then during his RFC training, Gilfillan had taken the long journey south and Willy only found out what happened two days later in an overheard canteen conversation. *This bloody lunatic showed up at the gate, told us he was here to see his master. Some bloody Scottish name. I told him, no pilots here called Fraser; see, I said, you can look at the sodding list yourself, you old git. Took three of us to throw him out.* So Willy had written to explain that he now served under a new name and parried Gilfillan's incredulous reply with promises to explain when they next saw each other.

And when would that be? When this war ended if he was lucky.

It was best to forget that Willy Fraser had a past — easier that way until Chester had blundered in and brought that past right back with him, even into this balloon where Willy Fraser had no rightful place. He opened Claude's battered knapsack and took out Claude's trumpet again to fend off those thoughts, running his fingers over the damage to its bell. He had bribed a smith in some depot behind the lines to beat it back into shape and solder this patch over the bullet hole. He put the mouthpiece to his lips but memories were straining to get to him and he found he couldn't raise the spirits to blow.

A hissing noise above him startled him back to the present and told him the good news that the valve had finally opened under the strain of the balloon's expansion to let over-pressured hydrogen go whistling out. Would it close again? Yes. He heard the slight 'plop' of the spring-loaded disk clamping back home on its seat so that at least was working the way it was meant to. He would live. Could he evade capture? He stood up to look around the empty sky. North-west towards unthinkable England the sun gleamed on the long cylinder of a distant Zeppelin higher up and heading for the sea. A group of dark dots crossed the landscape a long way below him. Fighters. Ours or theirs? Probably theirs so far beyond the lines but anyway they were a mile underneath him and had no hope of struggling up to his height.

Brussels passed to his right after eighty-eight minutes and that meant he was travelling across country at more than forty miles an hour. The speed disturbed him but all at once a thought struck him and aroused the faintest of faint hopes. Could he travel far enough to get *beyond* capture? He looked at the charts on his boards but even the largest-scale map did not extend far beyond the old Belgian capital. What lay down there was now *terra incognita*, the stuff of forgotten school geography lessons and memories of glimpses at an atlas which had left little behind them but the vaguest impression. After Belgium, there was certainly Germany stretching out along the Baltic coast with the long finger of East Prussia but then what? Russia? Russia was an ally. Supposing this wind had the stamina to take him all the way to Russia. Was that remotely possible? He had no idea so he set himself to

260

following standing orders, tearing his useless maps up into tiny pieces, scattering them to the winds, cartographers' confetti. That occupied the next half hour then he inspected the stores in his knapsack. Half a canteen of water, two sandwiches and a bar of chocolate. He ate half a sandwich.

The balloon was no longer climbing and when he looked up, he could see a wrinkle in the fabric that should not have been there. All right, the valve had vented gas but the balloon showed no sign of descending so the balloon envelope should still be taut. He climbed up to stand on the edge of the basket, holding on to the rigging ropes, leaning out to inspect the curve of the balloon's flanks above him. The left side was intact but when he clambered round to the right he saw three small holes high up on the side and knew that the shrapnel that had released the parachute had also punctured the fabric. The holes were small but hydrogen must be escaping through them. At that moment he devoutly wished that Chester K. Hoffman had never come to the balloon unit but a voice spoke in his ear.

'Don't grow a wishbone,' it said. 'Grow a backbone.' His father's strong supporting voice from the good time of childhood before the broken years.

Hydrogen was lighter than air so nothing above the level of the holes would be affected. Could he get to Russia on two thirds of a balloon? There were things he could still do. A lighter balloon would travel further. He smashed the telephone headset against the butt of the

Lee-Enfield and threw the pieces over the side then hurled each empty map board after them, wondering what any dwellers below would make of plywood squares scything down from the sky. He went to throw the rifle after them but it felt like the last part of his warrior status and who could tell what change of fortune it might yet dictate? For the same reason he kept the lightest of the three pairs of binoculars and one of the five bags of sand ballast just in case that fortune offered him a small choice of landing places.

When there was nothing more to throw out, he studied the mystery of the scenery below. Woodland, distant villages, a small town off to his left but no more clue than that. A peaceful, rural landscape. An unlikely place for enemies to live. He sat down in the bottom of the basket again and reached for the knapsack. Would he be taken prisoner, shut away for as long as the war lasted somewhere deep in Germany? Could he possibly escape? They could hardly miss a balloon coming down. In that case, they would surely seize his belongings. Taking out the leather wallet from the knapsack, he carefully removed the torn and stained envelope inside it — that last letter written by Claude Tavernier to his young wife, written at De Panne, the day before Claude died in the rising water of the Yser inundation.

'Find her,' Claude had breathed with almost his last breath. 'Give her my letter,' but the first shell blast had buried part of the letter and a slice of the knapsack in his mutilated torso and the next shell had found Willy.

The Sergeant, terribly injured, had used the last of his strength to haul Willy up the embankment slope out of the water and when soldiers hurried over from the next detachment they had found the knapsack clutched tightly in his hand. When he finally recovered, Willy had kept it as if it were a holy relic. In those early days he had shown the mangled envelope to Belgian civilians and soldiers, hoping someone might make sense of the remnant of the address left on the front. 'It is somewhere near Comines,' he had told everyone who would listen in those first weeks. 'A farm near Comines close by the French border,' but most had shaken their heads and some had started to ask questions he did not want to answer and he had put it away from him for more than a year. Finally the random fortune of posting had brought him to the balloon section and then all at once Comines had been just there, at the edge of his range of vision from the balloon base for these past weeks, out there beyond Whitesheet and Houthem, sitting tantalizingly close so that if he had been further east in Plot's section and not his own, he might have scanned the farmland and the tiny figures moving on it, searching for a sign.

All that was left of the envelope had her first name on it, 'Gabriel . . . ' truncated by sharp iron and the partial address 'Pont V . . . ' below. The letter inside was chopped across in the same brutal way but he had taken it on as his sacred duty that one day he would find her and now all chance of that was whirling away on the west wind.

If they took the letter away then he would be relieved of his impossible task but they would also take the photograph and the drawing and he was no longer sure he could live without that. He put the letter back in the wallet and took out the two pictures. If Claude had been staring back at him, perhaps he could not have looked at the photograph in the way he did. Claude's eyes would have been fixed on him and he could not have stood up to their gaze while he studied Gabrielle. The flat light still robbed her face of any contours but he had begun to endow her with the beauty Claude had seen, adding back in the details from his drawing that were missing from the dull print. He could animate the images in his imagination, conjure a smile from that stern mouth, even watch her as she ran to tackle a fleeing thief, laughing, breathing, feeling.

Many of the women in his past would have shaken their heads in fond exasperation if they could have seen him then. They would have looked over his shoulder at the photograph in his hand, astonished that this foreign challenger had reached a part of him they had barely glimpsed. If some higher power had explained that she was an illusion, a hypothetical woman constructed out of sorrow and a lost friend's words, the wiser ones among them would have smiled in sad understanding, realizing he would only risk his own heart on a construct that was all his own.

Willy was alone with the photograph. Claude's eyes were not there to challenge him because that same sharp metal had sliced away that corner of the picture, taking Claude's head with it along with his life. He lost himself for an age staring at it, wondering about her, hoping she was indeed alive somewhere — the last relict of the man who had been his friend and shared more with him in a few weeks than most friends do in a lifetime. He had worked away at the bloodstains with damp cottonwool and the marks were a little less poignant now, streaks of dark brown that could possibly have been something else. Claude's face would have been full of love and pride before it was torn away. Only up here, in extremis, away from everyone in his life, could Willy admit to himself that he envied that dead love more than he could say.

He put the pictures reverently back into the wallet and let her walk in his head, hearing her talk in one voice and then another. To his surprise, he woke from accidental sleep, cold and stiff, to find darkness falling. As if he had neglected his duty and might be called to account at any moment, he scrambled to his feet. Back towards the west, a lens of yellow cloud framed the horizon where the sun had vanished. Below him specks of light gleamed from windows and to the south he could see the sharp white lights of a large, carefree city where there was no fear of bombs.

The ground below continued to move past at the same relentless rate as he was borne along on the gale that was racing across Europe. Cloud seemed to coalesce around the basket as it got darker, clammy, reducing him to the occupant of a silent sphere of dense grey. He sank back down and slept fitfully but jolted awake at some imagining and lurched upright to stare out at the same damp curtain. Once he saw moonlight on silver through a curling rent in the cloud below and was sure it was the sea. What sea? It had to be the Baltic surely, but all he could remember of the atlas suggested he must have been swung a little north of west. That must be the East Prussian coast somewhere down there unless fortune had swept him more northerly still. Where might that take him? Sweden? Would internment in a neutral country be any better than captivity in Germany? He had heard that the Swedes favoured Germany but there seemed no point in speculating. He would land wherever and whenever the leaking hydrogen made it so because even without shrapnel damage, any observation balloon was porous. None of them could stay up forever.

It grew still darker so he concluded that the moon had set and he went back to fitful sleep as the frigid night went on and on. When he became fully awake again, the luminous hands of his watch said it was half past five in the morning by some regional time that might not even apply any more. The sums in his head told him he had been adrift for eighteen hours. If the wind had kept steady that was seven hundred and twenty miles to the east, a long, long way — but was it far enough to take him to the Russian border? It had to be at least possible. He ate another half sandwich and stood up to stamp his feet and slap his hands together to manufacture moments of illusory warmth. Then the clouds drew back, or so he thought for a moment before he looked up and saw that the balloon was sinking through the base of an unbroken layer. The whole of the bottom of the envelope was now revealed, bagging into big wrinkles, and he knew that he was gradually and inevitably coming down as the slow escape of hydrogen passed some critical level. At first he could not make out any details of the ground below but the storm that still fuelled this wind offered a distant flash of lightning far off to his right and showed him a glimpse of barren country horrifyingly close and moving past at headlong speed.

All he could do was hang on, knowing he must soon hit the ground hard. He put the knapsack and the binoculars around his neck. One more flash showed the same bleak surface, broken with silver runnels of water chasing round scattered outcrops of rock. It was further below him now so he knew he must be passing over hilly, undulating land, then the solid earth rose abruptly to meet him and the broken end of the trailing cable came to his aid, dragging across the ground and slowing him as more and more of it trailed to bite into the surface. He threw out the last sandbag but it made little difference and he was reaching for the Lee-Enfield when the basket hit the earth with far too much speed. It tipped immediately, hurling him and the rifle onto the ground then, relieved of his weight, the balloon lurched back up into the sky to vanish into the dark.

It was a soft, wet landing. Willy found himself on his backside, sinking into black and sodden peat, soaking in to chill him through the seat of his trousers. He levered himself up with difficulty, rescued the rifle before it disappeared into the bog and used it as a crutch to work his way, one sucking step at a time, to the relative comfort of a flat island of rock sticking up out of the dark waste. There he sat, shivering and soaked as the first faint promise of dawn showed him the expanse of wild nothingness in which he had come down. Looking around, he could see only moorland, heavy with black peat-bog and the sun preparing the sky for its rising in entirely the wrong place. His usually reliable sense of direction had been swung off-balance by that last dizzying impact and that disconcerted him.

Could this be Sweden? It wasn't the way he imagined it. He thought he should head east towards the sun because Russia might lie that way if he was not already there and anyway east seemed to be more or less downhill. However absurd it was to think that a man in RFC uniform with only a rifle, a trumpet and one remaining cheese sandwich could walk to safety, it still seemed better than doing nothing. Perhaps this was Poland, he suddenly thought, that battleground where Russia was slugging it out with Germany. Could that be right? Or could it be that he was in the Baltic coastal provinces?

He got to his feet and trudged towards the brightening line of the still-hidden sun under the eastern horizon, sometimes on firm ridges of ground, sometimes jumping from tussock to tussock through dark bog and then occasionally on welcome harder sandy ground, always downwards towards a dark valley. The sun had still not come up over the horizon when its advance guard in the sky showed him an angled shape ahead, man-made, the roofline of a small hut or barn, something that might spell shelter, a place to get warm again.

Something that might also spell capture.

He stopped when he was thirty or forty yards away and stared at a primitive building of rough-hewn stone with what looked like a turf roof. He saw the walls of a yard and a dim light inside the building, a candle moving behind a small window. This must be a poor country, he thought. Should he skirt around it? He had the rifle. He needed food. The choice was taken out of his hands because a dog chained up somewhere in the yard scented him. It began to bark and would not stop. The candle moved sharply. He heard a door creak open and saw the dim figure of a man standing there peering around, then stiffening as he saw Willy.

'Supwiyo?' the man shouted and followed his incomprehensible challenge with a long string of angry-sounding words in a language Willy had never heard in his life.

'Ich bin ein Engländer,' he said slowly because there seemed no point in pretending otherwise.

17

Chester K. Hoffman arrived at Wing HQ in the village of Locre, courtesy of Thompson's Crossley. The Major had been glad to see the back of him because he had told him all he knew and avoided giving voice to the speculation that lurked behind it. Hoffman was now a man on a mission and it was not enough.

At Wing HQ, the Wing Commander was equally unforthcoming.

'Look, Mr Hoffman. I can't tell you how sorry I am to hear we have lost him. He was a fine observer and a very brave man but I have to say I don't have the first idea what you're talking about. I have his service record here and it really is as plain as a pikestaff. There's nothing here about the cavalry or anybody called Fraser. Look, you can see for yourself. He did his balloon training at Roehampton, March, April and May this year. Before that, it's all pretty straightforward. It says he joined the RFC in '15. Went through the usual flying training routine and had a few weeks in a squadron out here flying Sopwiths.'

'Scouts?'

'Oh goodness no. The one-and-a-half strutter. Do you know it? Too fragile to go dog-fighting if you have any sense. Bit of gunnery observation, spot of bombing, that sort of thing. Sort of kite that stooges around trying to have as quiet a time as possible if the pilot has any sense.

Doesn't seem to have stopped him, judging from his CO's notes. Kept putting in for transfer to a scout squadron but got no joy. Crashed three Sopwiths then put himself in hospital after he got shot up having a go at a Boche sausage.'

'A balloon?'

'Yes. Never a good idea, especially not in a Sopwith. Fokkers lying in wait and Archie all around them if the Fokkers don't get you first. Archie is what we call the guns that . . . '

'Yeah, thanks. I've been in this war quite some time now.'

'I see. Anyway they fixed him up and when he came out of the old sick bay it seems he decided the gasbag business was the life for him. Mad, but it takes all sorts.'

'What about before the RFC?'

'Civvy Street? Haven't a clue, old fellow. Nothing in the records. Doesn't really signify out here, you see? Not exactly a pressing priority. I expect it's all in some file back over there.' He trailed off and looked out of the window to the north as if he might catch a glimpse of some mythical kingdom.

'Next of kin?'

'Immaculate conception, I should say. It's all blank.'

'And he's definitely down there as Claud Taverner? No mention of any other name.'

'As I said, none whatsoever.'

'Do you by any chance know of any cavalry outfits round here?'

'Try over at Kemmel. All kinds of horse-wallahs there. Shall I whistle you up a lift?'

271

It took Chester four days shuttling from one cavalry unit to another around the Salient from Kemmel to Vlamertinghe, up to the Channel coast and out west to Hondschoote, chasing people who knew other people who might know part of the history. He became more and more determined as the gossip and the tiny fragments of precise, reliable detail began to coalesce into something believable, then his well-honed news instinct set his nose twitching as he started to smell the best story he had come across in a very long time. He found the main missing link in the chain of the narrative in a busy café full of soldiers ordering ham and eggs down a shelled side-street of Poperinghe, and from there he bummed lifts in staff cars and creaking lorries until he made it back to the balloon unit.

Bernard Thompson sighed when he looked out of the window of his brand-new hut and saw Chester clamber down from the cab of a Peerless. The American flinched away as the truck's over-burdened radiator sent a squirt of steam at his legs then he strode towards the Major's door.

'You had any news of him?' Chester demanded as he shook hands.

'No and I'm afraid we won't. Not yet. If he somehow managed to get down safely then he's certainly a prisoner of war by now. They'll let us know in due time. The Boches are gentlemen when it comes to that. I've posted him missing.'

'Who? Who exactly have you posted missing?'

'Lieutenant Taverner, of course. Who do you think I'm talking about?'

'Major, there is no such person. I can prove to you that I am right. The guy you posted missing is not and never has been Claud Taverner. He's William Andrew Fergus Fraser and what is more, he is a lieutenant-colonel with an MC after his name which stands, as I expect you know, for Military Cross rather than Mighty Confusing, though I do have to say the rank and the decoration came as a surprise to me.'

Thompson sat down slowly and waved Chester to a chair. 'Talk,' he said.

'Fraser was a cavalryman before the war. He quit in early '14. Someone high up didn't like him. I met him in Berlin and we both got caught up with the Germans on their way into Belgium. He dumped me, joined the Belgian army. Got hurt bad a few weeks later on the Yser. Serious injuries from a shell. By that time King Albert had promoted him in person to lieutenant-colonel.' He pronounced it lootenant but Thompson did not correct him.

'The Belgian Queen nursed him back to life then took him to the royal villa to convalesce. Those guys must have liked him a lot. When he could walk again he asked Albert's permission to rejoin the British side. You bet your life that your brass-hat, red-tab assholes didn't give diddly squat for his Belgian rank so they had him start over as a captain in the First Cavalry Division.'

'And you are quite sure this really is the same man?'

'I've spent eyeball time with men he commanded who won't hear a word against him but they all agree he upset some brass hats. They

273

kept the horses way back behind the fighting and sent the cavalry into the trenches on foot. Your man Fraser said that was a stupid waste and he couldn't abide fighting when he couldn't see a goddam thing. They gave him the medal for some crazy business storming a trench — promoted him to major. He told his friends he preferred to be out in the open. Got himself chlorine-gassed disobeying orders when he took his men to help the Canadians. You know about the big gas attack? Those Canucks stopped the German breakthrough and that was when he made lieutenant-colonel again. Why are you shaking your head?'

'Because it makes no sense to me.'

'Oh believe me, it does. I'm coming to that. He kept insisting that horses could break the German lines, even tried it one more time — horses against machine guns and the German gunners broke and ran away when they saw those goddam things charging at them. Some armchair-colonel was looking for a chance to cut him back to size. This part makes me want to spit. Your man saw all those fine chargers tethered back there behind the action, saw them getting fat and flabby and no good for anything so he had this smart idea. He sent to Scotland for a pack of hounds. Covered it up somehow. Exercised the horses chasing foxes round the back area and had them back in condition in a week. Clever boy, some said, but not the red tabs, not the brass hats. Like I told you before, his old Colonel the cuckold hated his guts. He poisoned the ear of a damn stupid General

274

who'd drunk too much port and together they got rid of him. You know what 'Stellenbosched' means?'

'Of course,' said Thompson. He was aghast at what he was hearing, aware that it all made some terrible sense. 'Comes from the South African war. It was a remount depot in the Western Cape. Officers who didn't come up to snuff were sent there where they couldn't do any harm. We use the word when someone's sent home for funk or sometimes drunkenness.'

'Or, in this case, inconvenient bravery and standing up for himself,' said Chester. 'So that's the true story of how Wild Willy Fraser became your man Taverner up there in the sky. They gave him the Stellenbosch choice. Back home to a training battalion for the rest of the war or stay at the front busted down to the ranks and sent to join a different unit under a fake name. Some choice for a man like that. What would you have done in his place, Major?'

'The same as him, I hope.'

'Exactly So, he joined your Flying Corps as a lowly lieutenant, crashed his plane one time too many going balloon-busting because he always hated balloons and here he is flying one or should I say 'was'. Major, have I somehow lost your undivided attention?'

'No,' said Thompson, looking out of the window, 'but I think 'is' was right after all.' He got up, pulled the door open and saluted. 'Lieutenant-Colonel Fraser,' he said to the man approaching. 'It is an honour to have you back, sir.'

★ ★ ★

Outside the moorland bothy, Willy had thought he was set for a stand-off. 'Letsayagleg,' the man said, walking towards him. He was holding a shotgun with both hands, down low, so Willy brought the Lee-Enfield halfway up, angled across his body. The other man stopped abruptly and raised his own gun to match.

Damn this, Willy thought, it must be Poland and I don't know a word of Polish. 'I am a Scottish officer of the Royal Flying Corps,' he said slowly and precisely. 'Do you understand me?'

The other man snorted derisively and looked him up and down in the first rays of the emerging sun. 'Art a balmpot,' he said. 'Thee baumed op.'

'I said I am an officer . . . '

'Bloddy officers I say.'

'What?' said Willy. 'You understand English?'

'Bogger, art daft? Whats tha think I'm speaking if not bloddy English?'

That was how Willy came to realize that this man was neither German, Polish nor Russian, that the soggy peat bog in which he had made his landing was on the edge of Kinder Scout in the Derbyshire Peak District and that the coriolis winds of a powerful low pressure cyclone had swirled him east, then north and finally west across the North Sea to bring him to earth in the next best thing to his own country.

He had dried out by the fire in the bothy, eaten a nameless stew rich in shotgun pellets

276

with stunned gratitude then walked down to Edale in the valley below on the first leg of a slow and difficult journey back to the war. It proved hard to persuade the authorities in Derby that he wasn't some sort of deserter until reports came in of an unexplained balloon carcass draped across the trees in a wood they called Marepiece. They gave him rail warrants and a little money to get to London where the surprised and overworked headquarters staff of the Balloon Service, squeezed into a tiny room in the top of Admiralty Arch, promised they would not forget to send a message to his unit before promptly doing exactly that.

That night he stayed in a hotel off the Strand and thought he should go out to enjoy himself but London was an unreal city full of disconcerting laughter and the wrong sort of noise. When a pretty girl asked him what he was doing in a way that implied she might enjoy doing it with him, he found she was altogether too real for him, too fleshy and undamaged, and he could not summon up any words that could convey where he had been or what he was going back to. Knowing Claud Taverner could never be at home in this odd city, he made some distracted excuse and left her disappointed and possibly poorer though that part had not been made clear. He tried a bar because that seemed the next obvious thing to do but everyone was talking of a different war to the one he knew, a fictional war of good versus evil where the worst thing that could happen was another Zeppelin raid. Instead he went back to the hotel. There, he lay down on the bed, took out the pictures and looked at the ravaged photograph long and hard. He discovered there was a comfort in Gabrielle's responding gaze that he could no longer find anywhere else.

He wondered who had told her of Claude's death and realized perhaps nobody else alive knew the details of it. He tried to imagine Claude's face filling the gap in the photograph, needing Claude to confront him and protect Gabrielle from him and the solace he sought. There was nothing left of Claude above the neck and all Willy had was his memory and his imagination, that same imagination which had worked alongside Claude's memory to draw his picture of her all that time ago. He went out early in the morning and found an artists' supplies shop near Charing Cross where he bought fine cartridge paper, glue, pencils, pen and ink. Back in his room, he doodled, drawing Claude's face, unsatisfied at first. He rubbed out the cheeks to make them thinner, lifted the eyebrows, narrowed the eyes until he had a face there that felt right. He copied it in a smaller scale to fit the photograph then he used the fine pen to outline it and when the ink was quite dry he carefully rubbed away the pencil marks. He stared at it for a long time, judging that he had somehow succeeded in conjuring the essence of Claude's face out of the past then he stuck the photo carefully down on to the cartridge paper and trimmed round the edges to square it up.

Now Claude gazed back at him, challenging Willy's right to stare at his widow.

The next day, he talked his way on to a destroyer for the short dash across the Channel and it was a relief to get back to the unvarnished world of war where people knew the worst and did not attempt to describe it. A series of slow trains took him to that place west of Poperinghe that represented the very last outpost of peace. 'Pop' seemed the most perfect haven when you were deep in the Salient but coming back from elsewhere, it was the war's front porch. When the town was being shelled, as it was most of the time, the train waited a quarter of a mile outside until the next thousand-pound cylinder of howitzer-launched explosive landed. Then, because the shells came at intervals as regular as clockwork, the locomotive chugged into town as far as the remaining undamaged rails allowed. Passengers burst out of every door, racing for the nearest cellar, and the engine driver reversed out, driving wheels spinning in a cascade of steel sparks, before the next shell curved slowly down the sky like a nail scratching on slate to land on what very little was left of the station.

It was dark by that time, so he spent a night in a deep cellar next to the ramparts where the Menin Gate had once been. He shared it with the utterly silent remnants of a Scottish regiment, staring at nothing in the candlelight with the unmistakable trench look on their faces. They were all comforted by the knowledge that the shells had already created a mound of masonry above them so thick that nothing more could reach them. In the morning he hitched a ride on a lorry heading south. Thompson's extraordinary greeting at the hut door was the very last thing he wanted to hear, especially with Chester K. Hoffman standing behind him grinning inanely.

'Major Thompson, *sir*,' he replied. 'Lieutenant Taverner reporting for duty.'

'I know the story,' said Thompson quietly. 'I will find it hard to accept a salute from one such as you.'

'In that case, sir, may I request an immediate transfer to a different section?'

'Look . . . Taverner, let's leave this for now, can we? I'm remarkably glad to see you. Mr Hoffman here insists he owes you his life and I'm sure he will be most discreet about anything he may or may not have learnt about your past military career.'

'Discreet?' Chester said. 'Goddam, I intend to make this man into the hero he deserves to be. Discreet don't even get a look-in.'

'Shut up, Hoffman,' said Thompson, swinging round, 'or I really will have you thrown out of a balloon. Please tell us exactly what happened to you,' he said more gently, turning back.

So Willy told them the whole story and watched unhappily as Chester scrawled notes. Later, he sat with Chester in his hut. A brand new observer had been turfed out. His box had been unpacked again and a bottle of cognac stood on the table between the two of them.

'So you don't want me to write you up,' said Chester. 'The best goddam story I got yet and you don't want me to make you famous.'

'No.'

'And I got to respect that on account of what you did for me up there.'

'Your choice. Not because of that. I had to do it. Duty.'

'Yeah.'

'Did you enjoy the jump?'

'Until I landed. Hell, you do it every day but that was my first time and my ankle is still twice the size I like it to be.'

'It gets easier with practice.'

'Willy . . . ' Chester noticed the minute flash of irritation. 'Okay, Claud. No, I can't call you that. This name thing. There's something going on here that I guess I'm not quite understanding.'

'It's nothing. They said pick a new name if you want to stay this side of the Channel. That's the name I chose.'

'Oh really? It's as simple as that? Not John Smith or George Jones? Claud Taverner? I don't think so. I talked to a woman up on the coast. She said something else.'

'What woman?'

'Easy, boy, easy. Cool down. A nurse. She was a Carolina Yankee, a real doll. The soldiers in the hospital call her 'Morning Glory'. Blonde, legs, blue eyes. That girl's a one-woman dose of the best medicine there is.'

Willy relaxed again. For a mad moment he had thought Chester might somehow have managed to talk to the Queen. 'Strange, I would remember anyone who fits that description. I don't recall her at all.'

'You would, brother. Believe me you would,

except she says you were raving at the time. Delirious, the way she told it. She got posted out to some field hospital for a spell before you got your senses back.'

'So what did she say?'

'Ah, now that is the whole reason I am interested. She told me you kept repeating that name over and over. Claud, Claud, Claud. Every time she tried to change your dressings you would grab at her arm and ask where Claud was, except she was damn sure you said it the French way like Clode. So my question is, who the hell was Clode?'

'That's my business,' said Willy, 'I might tell you one day but not if you write this story.'

'Why the hell not?'

'Why the hell should I? You want a good story. I don't want to be a good story.'

'I don't get you. Here's the way the world works. There are guys like me and we're kind of curious about everything so we have to go sniffing it out and sometimes we take big risks and that's because there's all the rest of the people out there who also want to know what's going on except they don't like taking the risks, do they? So they choose to spend a few cents on their paper and we get paid to go do the sniffing for them.' He paused and sighed. 'Then there's you,' he said, 'and you don't fit into either of those. Sure, you take the risks. You're the first one there when it all goes bad but then what do you do? You keep it all to yourself. I don't get it.'

Willy looked at him and thought of trying to explain but that meant finding words to fit something buried so deep that he knew only the shapes it made on the surface of his mind. He felt tired. 'It's called war, Chester.'

'Don't give me that crap. I'll lay you a thousand bucks you were like that before the war began. Hell, I know you were. I was there with you. You going to tell me about Clode now?'

'No.'

Chester poured another slug of cognac into his tin mug and topped up Willy's. 'Then here's the deal,' he said. 'I write the story of your latest exploit, including the fact that you saved the *Sentinel* the trouble of finding itself a new correspondent. I call it something like . . . ' He thought for a moment, 'How about 'The Gasbag Trumpeter'. Neat. You like that? I agree to use your fake name. I keep your real name out of it. I say nothing about the fact that you are really a highly decorated brass hat in the goddam horse army *but . . .* '

'But what?'

'You ain't going to stop me sniffing around this one. I plan to find out why you picked on Claud Taverner not Tommy goddam Atkins and when I do, I expect you to tell me if I'm right. Then and only then I will write your real story whether you like it or not because there are stories that have to be told for the good of the wider world even if they occasion some trifling inconvenience to their subject. Until that time comes I call you Claud. Do we have a deal?'

Willy thought of the handful of people who knew what had happened in his war so far. General Leman was a prisoner in Germany. The

Sergeant at the inundation? Probably dead. The King? Queen Elisabeth? He had grown very close to the Queen in the weeks of convalescence but it was beyond belief that she would ever talk to an American newsman. 'What happens if I don't agree?'

'I write everything I already know tonight and I wire it tomorrow.'

'Even though I saved your life?'

'You left me with von Emmich's goons, remember? You're not ahead. We're evens. Do we have a deal?'

'We have a deal,' Willy said.

'Just one more thing. Don't you ever want to be Willy Fraser again?' Chester said. 'There must still be people in the world who call you that?'

In the blizzard of casualty lists, no close friends still lived from that past life and of his family there was now only his mother left, cut off entirely by the Atlantic Ocean and a complete lack of motherly love. Gilfillan and his Morag, that was all.

'Nobody I ever see except you. Not that I usually see anyone outside the war.'

'Nobody waiting for you back home?'

'No one.' Willy's eyes drifted towards the unopened letter on his table and Chester followed his gaze. It was addressed to Claud Taverner and it came from Scotland.

'Someone,' said Chester and though he knew perfectly well who it was from, he couldn't help adding, 'You got a girl back there?'

'No girl. Just business.'

'What's with all this?' Chester asked. He was

still looking at Willy's table and the creased and annotated map spread out over half of it.

'Nothing. It's the terrain just along from here towards Comines.'

'Yeah, but you scribbled all over it.'

'I like to gather information. It might come in handy some day.'

'What are these written down on here? Names of houses? You telling me you need to know the name of a house before you blow it to pieces?'

'You never know.'

'A Belgian guy told me you were always asking questions back then. Looking for some farmhouse or other.'

'Did he?'

'Anyway, this map ain't your sector. This is up Polito's way. I've been there. What's with it?'

'I've had a hard day, Chester. I'm ready for bed.'

When Chester left, he slit the envelope open and read Gilfillan's weekly missive. Gilfillan told him of the sparse business of the estate, of his ingenious repair to the rotten beam in the stable roof, of the health of his one remaining horse and of Morag's cake which would be sent to him next week. The steward asked him for any news.

I know what you will say. You will tell me only that all is well with you. When I go to sleep at night I remember you in my prayers although I know you do not like to be prayed over but I still have no very clear idea of your daily life in a form of service of which I have no experience. I would wish to know more and should you choose to tell me I would of course pass it to no other, not even to my Morag if that should be your requirement. I mark that you are less able to make a joke of it all now and that should be no surprise with the duration and the damage of this terrible enterprise. Young Georgie Hamilton, the farrier's son, came home on leave two weeks ago but he chose to say nothing serious at all about his experiences. He said to me quietly that he could not, even to such as me who knows what it is like to be shelled. So be it. On another matter, I have sworn an affidavit today in Newton Stewart that I have direct knowledge that you are still alive. It was necessary for the frustration of your mother's weasel and I hope it may serve to keep him at bay for some time. Do they never give you leave? It would be very fine to see if you and the man could not argue with your corporeal presence in front of him though undoubtedly he will continue to try to overturn your father's will. Please remember that you should make a will of your own and send it to me, to frustrate him if for no other reason.

Willy thought of the first leave he had refused to take and the second leave, when Thompson insisted, and he had spent a week cycling pointlessly from St Omer to Hesdin and back again, unable to engage even with war-shadowed France.

★ ★ ★

Major Thompson seemed unsure how to approach him when they met at breakfast next morning. 'There was something you wanted to discuss?' he asked quietly.

'No, sir,' said Willy. 'Nothing that can't wait. Hoffman and I have sorted out the misunderstanding.' Better to keep on here, he thought, than have to start all over again somewhere else.

'Really? Well anyway, I have a nice surprise for you,' said Thompson. 'In your absence those munificent beings at HQ have finally found us some Cacquots. Wondrous beasties. We're last to get them as usual but never mind. Not only that but new Scammel winches which can haul them down, or so they promise me, at eight hundred feet a minute even in a high wind and, wait for it, better parachute harnesses that hook on properly and actually don't fall off when you most need them. It must be Christmas. Please don't look at me like that.'

The Cacquot was a new design of balloon, said to be much more stable in the wind than the *Drachens*, higher-flying and easier to handle. It had a fat tear-drop body with three rounded fins spaced around the narrower tail end.

'Cacquots look fine but the way they rig the phone cable is a death-trap,' said Willy.

'Captain Cacquot insists it is safe.'

'Captain Cacquot isn't flying it. I am. I don't

mind jumping. I do mind being hooked up under a bloody great burning gasbag.'

'Perhaps we can rig the phone cable a different way. We'll have a look at it this evening. Take it up and see what you think.'

'That's an order, is it, sir?'

Thompson considered him quietly and thought this might be a defining moment, sensing that this unreadable man facing him perhaps wanted it that way, to be ordered to do something he considered unsafe and do it uncomplainingly.

'Yes,' he said. 'And something else too. Wing tells us the Boche have a new scout. It's basically an Albatros but they've altered the top wing so the pilot can actually see out properly. Also it has some sort of airbrake flap arrangement so it can come hammering down at you then slow up enough to shoot better. Nasty piece of work. They've only seen one so far and he's a fellow with green and yellow stripes and he seems to know what he's doing. Two of the other sections had a visit from him yesterday. Barely got away with it.'

An hour later, the striped Albatros killed Bridges.

Willy had to summon up a few of his father's hundred heroes to climb into the car hanging under the Cacquot. The last flight had left some sort of mark on him and to make it worse, he didn't warm to the new basket's design. The sides of the basket curved inward at the top and that, he thought, would only make it harder to get out in a hurry. He looked down at the phone cable, angling unnecessarily down to the main cable some distance below, waiting to catch a parachute — just asking for trouble. Was this nerves, he wondered? Normal under the circumstances, surely? A cable break and a flight like that would test any man. He took two or three deep breaths and decided to smile.

There was cloud at six thousand feet and Bridges was flying his new Cacquot at four thousand. Willy was watching it with interest as his own balloon climbed past it a quarter of a mile further south. He looked across towards Bridges again wondering how they might best change the rigging and saw the German biplane drop vertically out of the base of the cloud above the other balloon. It fired a stream of smoking, glowing tracer bullets before it pulled up sharply and vanished the way it had come. The anti-aircraft guns never even saw it and Bridges gave no sign that he knew what had happened. For a moment Willy thought he might have got away with it but then bright flame curled along the back of the balloon. He spoke urgently into the mouthpiece. 'Tell Bridges to jump. Now. He's on fire.'

He saw the other man twist sharply around in the basket, looking up, unable to see the peril he was in. Willy gestured violently to him to get out and then, too slowly, Bridges began to climb over the side of the basket, losing another critical second or two as he dealt with the unfamiliar shape of it. Before he could drop away, the entire balloon was in flames, the fiery canopy slumping down over the man in the basket, wrapping him inside as the whole burning mass sank to earth leaving a long greasy streak of smoke to mark his passage.

On the ground, Chester was shouting at Thompson. 'Who's in that one?'

'That's Bridges,' Thompson replied tersely. 'Poor bloody Bridges. Don't worry, Mr Hoffman, you've still got your hero. He's . . . '

Three anti-aircraft guns opened up and drowned whatever he was about to say, field guns mounted on crude pivots to let them shoot nearly straight up. The green and yellow Albatros roared down past the surviving balloon, jinking and twisting as shells burst around it. Afterwards no one could be sure whether it was the German plane's machine guns or the defenders' shells that did the damage but a tongue of flame licked out of one of the balloon's upper fins. Hoffman, staring up, saw Willy clamber over the edge of the basket as the winch began to rev up. The combination of his weight shift and the sudden tug of the screaming winch sent him tumbling head-first out of the basket to spiral round and round the cable, wrapping his parachute lines around it like ribbons round a maypole. As he did so, the parachute canopy blew out sideways in the wind so that Willy was left hanging from one side of the slanting cable with the parachute flying out on the other, the twisted line in between keeping him from falling as the balloon's fin burnt furiously.

Thompson ran towards the winch lorry, roaring, 'Drive! Drive like hell!' at the top of his voice and the man at the wheel let in his clutch and bumped away along the track with the winch on the back still revving to wind down the balloon. Hoffman stared, slowly grasping what they were doing. The speed of the bucketing, swaying lorry and the rapid winding of the winch combined to drag the balloon lower in its wake and that kept the flames in the burning tail section streaming back away from the rest of the Cacquot's body. He could see Willy, high up there in the sky, twisting and swinging his legs around the cable, trying everything he could to unwrap himself.

Hoffman heard clashing gear changes and now the lorry had reached maximum speed and the cable stretched backwards at forty-five degrees to the balloon and the man caught up below it with his parachute streaming out behind. Despite the driver's efforts, a moment came when the fire erupted out of the main section of the balloon, writhing and shrinking as its gas gouted upwards in a cloud of flame. It began to droop towards the struggling man on the cable below but the driver had given Willy the seconds he needed. With one final twist, he forced himself up and over the wire and dropped free on the far side, swinging down below the liberated parachute as the burning canopy plunged past him. They watched him come down, drifting back towards them on the wind. Willy seemed to hang inert in his harness and crumpled up when he hit the ground but by the time they reached him, he was sitting up and blinking with blood running down the side of his face from a bullet crease across his scalp.

'I told you that bloody phone wire was dangerous,' he said.

18

Chester walked up to the door of Willy's hut, worrying that he might be intruding although he knew by now that peace and privacy were absurd ideas on the Western Front. Long before he had first been sent out on the New York crime beat, Chester had tended to put himself in other people's shoes and he had spent years doing his best to suppress that. He could still remember the first time he had been obliged to knock on a rain-washed door in a smoky night-time East Side street to ask a brand-new widow for a picture of her murdered man.

German guns were searching out a target somewhere to the south with whining blasts of shrapnel balls erupting from puffs of smoke a hundred feet up. A ragged salvo came in reply from a battery only two hundred yards away. They sounded like eighteen-pounders to Chester. More weapons by the dozen, by the hundred, probably by the thousand were firing along the great arc of the Salient in a ceaseless ragged roar overlaid with drum beats, staccato rattles and chest-beating thuds. It was the vast background noise of war, and even in the middle of it, he hesitated before he knocked.

He heard no response and pushed the door open, expecting to find Willy sleeping off his latest injury but instead found him, head bandaged, bent over a table, sketching a careful

292

diagram on a large sheet of paper.

'Can I come in?'

'What's that you're holding?'

'A gift from the Major. Half a bottle of his very special Scotch.'

'Then yes.'

'It's the least I can do,' Thompson had said as he thrust the bottle into Chester's hands. 'Should never have made him go up. Take that over to him and make sure he gets a drop of it inside him.'

Chester looked at the bottle's label and Willy watched his mouth moving. 'That some kind of typographical error?' he said in the end. 'Crazy name for hooch. How do you say it?'

'It doesn't really matter what it's called,' said Willy. 'La frog is close enough. You brought glasses? Just pour it out.'

Chester sniffed his glass, swallowed most of it in one go and watched Willy working. 'You mind telling me what that is you're doing?'

'I'm doing Monsieur Cacquot's homework for him, sorting out how to rig the damned telephone cable to make sure no one else gets caught like I did. Does the Major want any of his nectar back or is he joining us?'

Thompson had gone to see Bridges' belongings packed up and to write a letter to his parents. 'Neither,' said Chester. 'Okay now. Hear me out without yelling at me, will you? There's something I need to know.'

Willy looked sideways at Chester. 'What?'

'I heard a story from one of your old horse-army pals.'

'First law of military service. Never believe a cavalryman. They're worse than the Marines.'

'He gave me a tale about that horn of yours. Told me how you carried it round for months like a holy relic, all twisted up with a bullet hole straight through it before you finally got some guy to fix it.'

'Good trumpet repair men are few and far between in the front line.'

'So what's the story?'

'Story? I had a trumpet fixed. What's the second line of *that* story?'

'The second line? How about he also said you looked after it like a baby but you couldn't play a single note until you bribed some bugle-blower to teach you how?'

'And?'

'So I start thinking about why a guy carries a beat-up trumpet around the place with him through hell and high water when he doesn't even play the goddam thing and then I go on thinking about it and I wonder whether it has anything to do with another guy who just might go by the name of Clode.'

'I need some sleep, Chester. I had a busy day. You're making my head hurt.'

'That was a bullet from an Albatros made your head hurt, not me, my friend. Your life interests me more every day but I would prefer it if you were still breathing when I publish the facts so you can read all about it. I'm writing the first story tomorrow just like we agreed then I go back to work on the rest of it.'

'You'll be wasting your time, Chester.'

'I trust my gut. I can see you're a very interesting man but the bit I can't see is even more interesting. I know that horn has a story attached to it.'

'I don't care much for stories.'

'Yeah, I already got that. Like I said, for a man who needs to know what's happening you are one hell of a secretive son-of-a-bitch when it comes to telling anybody else.'

Willy looked him up and down. Chester had trimmed down to maybe only thirty pounds overweight. He was wearing sensible clothes, some sort of suit, but it was almost field grey and cut more like an officer's battledress. His face had changed. You could see his cheekbones and his eyes seemed larger. 'We can drink the rest of this together,' Willy said, 'but only if you stop asking me questions. Let's talk about something else.'

'Like what?'

'Like how's Ruthie, for example?'

'Ruthie? How do you know my wife's called Ruthie?'

'Just a lucky guess.'

'Yeah?'

'No, you told me.'

'I did? Hell . . . I guess she's managing. I've seen her a total of two months tops since I saw you last. She don't like that.'

'The paper didn't give you any choice?'

'They gave me a choice. Come back here or work for someone else. There's younger guys want my job. See, it's a hot topic stateside. Do we join in or don't we? Some of the competition, like the *Journal*, they're saying stay out of it but Webster — he's the guy owns my paper — he's on your side so he wants human stories, hero stuff. That's where you come in. That's what I'm here for, not for news — I mean, give me a break, there ain't any news. Your guys die. The other guys die. A bit of the line moves back half a block. That's not news.'

'So I'm still your story whether I like it or not.'

Chester sighed. He could never find the right words until he came to write them down but the idea that might with luck one day coalesce into his story was floating in pieces somewhere in the back of his head. It was about all the soldiers he had met who got through their trench time only by regarding themselves as already dead, by giving up on life and leaving it to fate. His editor would tear that up if he wrote it. His editor wanted to read about men who stayed alive all the way through to their core, who used their wits. His editor wanted heroes who put their lives in the balance but kept right on trying to tilt it their way. That was Willy and Chester wanted to explain it but in the end he just said, 'Guess so.'

★ ★ ★

Next morning Willy discussed his modifications with Thompson over breakfast. 'You'll be pleased to hear I've got rid of your somewhat crude American friend,' said Thompson.

'Chester? How in the world did you manage that?'

'Had the beggar woken at first light and told him if he was quick he could catch a ride. Got him in the car I was sending to Bertangles before he'd stopped yawning.'

'That's eighty miles. A whole day's travel. Why did he go?'

'I told him if he used my name, there was a very good chance of an interview for his penny-dreadful newspaper with our very famous Victoria Cross flying ace, Lanoe Hawker.'

Bertangles was an RFC aerodrome and Hawker's scout squadron was based there.

'I didn't know you knew Hawker, sir.'

'I don't, but there's a lot of people called Thompson and Hawker is a very polite man so you never know, the Yank might not work it out. Anyway, it succeeded. Now, listen. You're not flying today because you've left us nothing to fly. They're sending new balloons and a couple of new observers but we won't get them before lunch at the earliest and then we have to sort out the rigging changes before I let you go up again. You have a gentle day and get that head of yours better.'

'I think I might go for a wander, sir.'

'Then make sure you wander away from the shells not towards them.'

'Could I possibly take one of the P & Ms, do you think?'

The unit had two despatch-rider's motorcycles on its strength but one of the DRs was sick with measles and the other had taken a shell splinter through his thigh the day before. 'To do what exactly?'

'To find somewhere quiet.'

'I have a packet of forms to go to 9 Section. You can have the bike if you drop them off for me on the way.'

'What an excellent idea, sir,' said Willy, as a whole set of new possibilities dawned on him.

It was good to be back in the saddle of a motorcycle though the little P & M had nothing like the power of his old Thor.

The Sergeant at the neighbouring balloon section was surprised to see a despatch rider wearing officer's uniform. 'Mr Polito is in his hut, sir,' he said. 'He's going up in an hour or so, I believe.'

'Hello, Plot,' said Willy when the observer opened the door to his knock.

'Heavens above,' said the other man, staring at the bandage round Willy's head. 'The redoubtable Claud Taverner newly returned from the dead twice over, complete with stigmata. I watched your adventure yesterday. Wished I hadn't already bust the camera. Would have made a great series of snaps to sell to the penny dreadfuls. To what do I owe this pleasure?'

'I've brought you some bumph from Wing HQ.'

Plot opened the packet and ruffled through the forms. 'This should win the war,' he said. 'Jolly clever idea. They require that I appoint one of my precious officers to account for any surplus fat from the mess and send it back to the depot for rendering down. Oh yes, I have so many spare men with time on their hands that shouldn't be a problem at all. I don't know why

298

I didn't think of it myself. They sent *you* over here with *that*?'

'No, it was just an excuse. I have a favour to ask.'

'Then ask away.'

'I know you always fly by yourself . . . '

'As do you but the jungle telegraph tells me you broke the rules for our large American friend and then wasted a perfect opportunity. What on earth possessed you to clip the parachute on properly? I had the pleasure of his company for thirty seconds the other day immediately followed by another three thousand seconds which were no pleasure at all. You could have pushed him over the side without it. If you'd dropped him on the German lines it could have brought the war to a halt in an instant — much more demoralizing than a mine going up.'

'I know what you mean, but I wondered if you might make an exception just this once and take me up with you. We've used up our Cacquots after yesterday's adventures so Thompson gave me a day off.'

'And you can't wait to get back up there in the path of shot and shell?'

'It would be good to get a different view of the sector. I keep wondering about the dead ground. I promise I'll keep out of your way.' Their charts were marked with hatched areas to indicate the places that were hidden by contours or woodland.

'The dead ground is God's mysterious way of preserving the nicer Germans for future generations but for you, Taverner, it would be a privilege. I'll show you mine if you show me yours. Luckily you're not the heaviest of men.'

The Sergeant was astonished to be told to boost the hydrogen. 'You're flying with a *passenger*, sir,' he asked, to be quite sure he had understood.

'Yes, Sergeant. Give him the Verey pistol,' said Plot and the sergeant handed Willy a heavy brass flare gun. 'Wing has appointed him balloon security officer, you see. He has to burn the balloon if it floats away. New regulations.'

'Very good, sir.'

'I'm joking, Sergeant — up to a point.'

'Yes, sir.'

'Up to what point exactly?' Willy asked.

'Only up to you being appointed. New orders. Did Thompson forget to tell you? They're determined no Cacquot is to fall into the hands of the Boche though I'm perfectly certain they're already working on a copy. After all, we're not exactly invisible up there, are we? They can see all they need to know. So orders say that if the poor old gasbag's not already burning, you have to shoot a flare into it as you jump out, presumably while whistling 'God Save the King' and assembling a matchstick model of the Eiffel Tower with your spare hand. Today that's your job.'

Willy saw that they had already changed the run of the phone cable. Lessons were learnt quickly in the balloon corps. The Cacquot basket hung from a trapeze bar to let it swing backwards and forwards as the balloon soared or dived in the wind. 'If we have to jump, you go first, Plot,' he said as they climbed in.

'Manners, dear boy. Wouldn't dream of it, I'm the host after all. Anyway you're my lucky charm. What's the chance of having to jump twice on consecutive days?'

'Getting higher all the time. Don't rely on that.'

'Did you bring a gun of any sort?'

'No.'

'I took a Mauser pistol off a prisoner. Very useful. Huge magazine and all that. German design at its best. Might not stop an Albatros but it somehow makes me feel a lot better.'

All the twisting porridge of the front-line devastation opened up before them as they climbed through a thousand feet. Polito bent to examine a fly that had settled on the basket. 'Ah!' he said. 'Have you ever noticed, Taverner? These fellers are happy to come along for the ride but when they get to two thousand nine hundred, they drop dead just like that. Your grasshopper on the other hand, he's tickety-boo up to three thousand four hundred. Fascinating, don't you think? It's always so very *interesting* up here.'

They topped out at a little over four and a half thousand feet. 'Did you have a big breakfast this morning?' Plot asked. 'That seems to be as high as she wants to go.'

'Sorry. I can jump if you like.'

'No, no, wouldn't dream of it. We're easily high enough. There's a big gun our people call Clockwork Charlie. He's tucked away some-where behind a wood over there. It's quite made me lose my sense of humour. Keep a close eye. If you see any muzzle flashes . . . '

'I'll mark them.'

Willy stared through the binoculars at this new extension to his familiar landscape beyond the front line and there was Comines and its neighbour, Warneton, visible away in the hazy distance, right in the centre of his field of vision beyond Zandvoorde. From here, for the first time, the different contours of the low ridge allowed him to see parts of the countryside between Comines and Messines to the west of it, dotted with scattered farms and small woods, as yet largely untouched by shellfire.

There, perhaps, was Gabrielle.

The front line sounded different today. You could never tell. Sometimes the unending barrage, varying only in the intensity of the explosions, was muffled by layers of warm or cold wind. At other times, such as today, individual explosions lifted in sharp bursts to the balloon above and still retained their power to make even a seasoned man flinch.

They both wore headsets and he listened to Plot coaxing the battery towards the likely target camouflaged in the countryside beyond them. 'Forty minutes right', 'Line and short', 'Line and over'. Then after twenty shots or so, he heard a new note of satisfaction. 'That's found them,' Plot said and Willy followed the direction of his binoculars to see smoke rising as ammunition exploded. Tiny distant men were scattering from the wreckage of what had looked like a hedgerow beyond the wood but now lay strewn around a shattered gun. 'Battery fire! A dozen more just like that one,' Plot said into the mouthpiece then broke off and looked upwards. An engine opened up somewhere in the hidden sky above the balloon, the familiar rattling bass drone of a Mercedes.

A harsh voice broke in to Willy's ears. 'Albatros! Above you. Gone back in the cloud. Hauling down now.'

They craned out from opposite sides of the basket, trying to see upwards beyond the curve of the balloon and feeling the sharp jerk as the winch engaged. None of the section's anti-aircraft guns were yet firing. They couldn't hear the Albatros's engine any more. Plot put down his map board and took out the Mauser. They both shuffled closer to their parachute bags knowing that the German pilot must be planning his next attack somewhere up there in the cloud.

'If that's my striped friend from yesterday, he likes to dive straight down on top of you,' Willy said. 'That way, the guns can't get him for fear of hitting us and we can't see him to shoot.'

They heard the sewing-machine ticking of an idling engine above, then the rapid drum beat of two machine guns firing and the whine and smoky trail of a stream of incendiary bullets tearing down past them leaving stitchwork holes in the balloon fabric. Willy stared at the holes, watching for the first leak of flame as the plane flashed past, the Albatros pilot opening his throttle, turning hard as he climbed so they could see the whole plan view of the aeroplane with those same green and yellow stripes. A

303

solitary gun fired at him in their defence from the ground below. The shell burst shockingly close, a scatter of shrapnel clipping their rigging and slicing a long shard of wicker off the corner of the basket, but part of that shrapnel spray also hit its intended target. They heard the fighter's engine falter for a moment and saw a jet of smoke spurt from its cowling as the plane sagged out of its climb. Unable to reach the safety of the clouds above, it staggered around in a slowing turn as the other guns on the ground below began to chase it, their shells bursting behind it.

'He's not giving up,' shouted Plot. 'Bastard. He's coming back for us. Jump.'

'Only when you do.'

They had a head-on view of the crippled fighter, its engine burping and roaring and faltering again, so that it lifted and dipped as the pilot fought the controls. Willy's eyes were fixed on the two black gun muzzles swinging past him then back again. Plot levelled the Mauser, took calm and careful aim and fired off the whole magazine, one shot after another. It had no visible effect. A hundred yards away the Albatros lifted its nose and opened up at the balloon. Doing his best to disregard the oncoming fire, Willy raised the heavy flare pistol, steadied it with both hands and sent a bright red burning flare-ball straight at the attacking aircraft. As a signal gun it had never been intended to be an accurate weapon so it was a matter of pure chance that the flare went hissing into the centre section of the aircraft's upper wing. The doped fabric caught fire instantly and the pilot twisted away from the flames as they blossomed and roared backwards right by his head in the slipstream. They could see him leaning out of the cockpit trying to escape the heat, then diving steeply, either out of control or hoping perhaps to extinguish it in the wind. That was when all four wings slowly folded backwards and snapped off to flutter in the air as the streamlined fuselage plummeted down to bury itself in a field below.

'All right,' said Plot into the mouthpiece, 'Take us back up, please. I haven't done with that battery yet.' He turned to Willy with a grin. 'You've used the flare, damn it. They'll be cross with you at Wing HQ if the cable breaks and we can't burn the balloon. We might even have to fill in a report. In triplicate and block letters.'

'I'll burn it somehow. I can rub a couple of sticks together.'

'Might have to be pencils. I forgot to bring any sticks.'

It took Plot ten more minutes to walk the gunfire around the remains of the German battery until it unearthed their disguised ammunition dump, then as the pillar of flame and smoke was still twisting into the sky, they were winched back down. Willy had spent the time studying Plot's maps, pinning down names that turned the distant villages and houses into precise, identifiable locations. On the way down, a thought struck him. 'You won't let them make a song and dance about this, will you, Plot?' he said. 'I think I may have accidentally promised Thompson that I'd have a quiet afternoon.'

'It wasn't all that noisy, was it? I'll do my best,

old boy, but don't count on it. It was a little public after all. Which reminds me, back to that rather coarse Yankee fellow who was sniffing around — he was remarkably keen to know all about you. Couldn't really help him very much. Told him you were a dab hand at pointing a battery in the right direction and that was about it. No blasted use for anything much else as far as I knew.'

'Thank you.'

'But he did go on a bit about the trumpet. Asked if I knew why you carried the thing. I said 'why not?' but that didn't seem to cut it. Speaking of which, have you got it in that knapsack of yours?'

'Always.'

'Then why not give it a warble on the way down. The boys would like that. After all, we did get a battery *and* an Albatros.'

There were a hundred or so men around them as the basket bumped down. Half of them were hanging on to ropes so they couldn't join in the clapping but they cheered their heads off as Willy put the trumpet away after the last note of the French battle anthem. Playing it hadn't felt quite right. The trumpet was just for him and his memories up there in the thin air high above the battle but he had not felt able to refuse Plot's request. They had been hauled down at high speed and though he had kept his mouth open, his ears were popping and buzzing when they reached the ground. The ground crew received them as heroes but Plot claimed complete ignorance of the method of the fighter's destruction with such conviction that the congratulations died away to a puzzled murmur. 'Flare? No, must have been our Archie that got him,' he said. 'Top-class shooting. Tell them well done from me. Now, come on, Claud. We've got some work to do.'

'Yes, do you mind if I copy some details from your maps before I go?'

'Help yourself. I've got another one or two back in the hut if it helps.'

The huts were on the far side of the wood that sheltered the balloon bed. They were shrouded by a mock forest of camouflage netting and tree branches to hide them from enemy observers but even though they were three miles back from the lines, the shell holes in the fields alongside showed there was more action here than in Willy's section.

The maps weren't any help. Most of the buildings had been given simple descriptive English names: *Red Bam, Steeple Farm, White Chimneys*.

'What exactly are you looking for?' asked Plot then saw the look in Willy's eyes. 'No need to tell me if you don't want to,' he said quickly.

He began to shake his head then thought, if not Plot, then who could he possibly trust in this whole insane country? Who else had survived for as long as he had, a huge explosive target hanging in full view over the largest shooting gallery the world had ever known?

'I'll show you,' he said and reached into the knapsack. He opened the leather wallet inside it and brought out the remains of Claude's final letter. 'Don't try to open it,' he said, passing it to Plot. 'It's fragile.'

'Good heavens,' said Plot. 'That's had a hard life. Who's it to?'

'It was intended for Madame Gabrielle Tavernier.'

'Some Frenchified relation of yours?'

'No. That's a long story but she was the wife of a good friend. I made a solemn promise that I would find her.'

'He died?'

'Yes.'

'For heaven's sake, man, it has dried blood on it. You wouldn't give her this, surely?'

'Perhaps not, but I would tell her of his death.' *But would I really?* he thought. *Just how much could I possibly tell her and how? Could I persuade a scout pilot to drop a message?*

Plot looked at the shredded envelope again. 'Pont V,' he said. 'That's all you know?'

'I know it's a farm and I know it's near Comines,' he said.

'I don't have a clue but I know who might,' said Plot in the end. 'There's a Belgian battery only a mile or two down the road. I popped over for a snifter with them last week. Thought it might sort out a few communications problems. They've got some old maps from before the war. All kinds of ancient names on them. They prefer those to the grid letters but I must say it's jolly confusing if you don't know what they're talking about when you're halfway through a shoot. I'm sure they'll be happy to help.'

'Thank you.'

Plot looked at him curiously. 'If I didn't know better, I would say that this was tugging at your heartstrings in some way but then the whole Balloon Corps knows that Claud Taverner's nerves are made out of steel balloon cable and his heart is simply a double reinforced canvas air pump, so that can't be true, can it?'

'No.'

★ ★ ★

Plot's 'mile or two' was directly towards the front lines and Willy kept the P & M's throttle open for as long as he could. White puffs of shrapnel bursts were dotting the sky ahead. He disliked the whoop of the shrapnel shell explosion and the hissing wang of the spraying balls of shot that followed it but he couldn't hear them with the engine at full power. Then the shell holes began to join up so he could no longer curve between them and he was forced to slow right down for both the craters and the injured soldiers on the road, arms around each other's shoulders, limping their way back in shared pain to find a dressing station.

The Belgian battery was firing from gun-pits dug along the edge of a field, turf laid on planks to conceal the 75s below, with only a slot left for the protruding muzzle. Willy looked at the dark lines on the grass where the flame from the barrel had left its long mark and thought that any half-trained balloon observer would pick them up in a moment. Sweating soldiers were lugging shells from a ready-use pile along the north side of a hedge and handing them down to the gunners below who slid them into the breeches and sent them on their way with the sharp crack of a giant's whip.

'The balloon section sent me,' he explained to a surprised Belgian captain.

'This is not a good place to be,' the Captain said. He nodded south where a distant yellow sausage was rising above the frontline smoke. 'We are under their eyes. They are looking for us.'

'I'm told you have old maps. The Comines area from before the war. May I see?'

'You come here for maps?' The Captain shrugged. 'It is not the safest place for research. Next time try a library. In the trench there. The ammunition box at the end. Look all you like but do not take them away, please.'

Willy climbed down into the trench. The bottom was deep mud but the fire-step was dry and the box rested on it. He sat down and began to rummage through the contents and there was just exactly what he wanted. It was a Flemish cycle-club map with faded pink covers from that far-off carefree time of two years earlier when none of the lines drawn on it were lethal and there was no hurry and no danger in the air beyond the occasional wasp. He unfolded it and in a moment the air was full of earth, fire, screams and flying metal as the shells from a German battery burst on the Belgians. He ducked down, hearing the whine and the thuds of debris landing all around then with his heart racing, he looked over the parapet and saw

310

destruction nearby — one gun blown entirely out of its pit, split into its constituent parts with a gunner's armless body draped over the twisted barrel. The next shell overshot the field and he wondered if the motorcycle was safe, back there on the lane, then an entire salvo arrived on target and he curled down into the mud as the Belgian battery disintegrated under the accurate onslaught. Knowing the Germans wouldn't stop firing until they were quite sure of success, he stayed in the bottom of the trench hoping none of their shells would find it. When it was finally all over, the far end of his trench had filled with wreckage and not one gun-pit had survived. Four men were crouching under the only intact part of the hedge and apart from that there were only body parts and a single young gunner, as pale as death, who moved his head as Willy came up to him and whispered, 'Cigarette?'

Willy reached into his knapsack and took one out of the packet Claude had left half-finished. 'It's a bit stale, I'm afraid,' he said. He lit it with Claude's matches and placed it between the gunner's lips but by that time there was no breath left to inhale the smoke.

Back at his own hut, Willy spread the cycle map out on the table and began to search the area around Comines. All the roads had names inscribed in tiny writing and he had to peer closely to make out what each one said and there, wonderfully, leading north-west a little way out of the town was a lane and it was called *Pontveldstraat* in Flemish. He followed it with his finger, tracing it in the direction of Ypres and

311

stopping when he came to a rough outline of buildings around a square yard and there it was. *Pont-Veld Hoeve* said the inscription and *Hoeve*, he knew, was the Flemish word for farm.

He looked up sharply, staring south-east as if he could see through the tent and the wood and the incandescent smoke of the trenches to spot Gabrielle and the farm just six or seven miles away. Two hours of easy walking would have let him keep his promise if there hadn't been a hundred thousand men at war in the way.

19

At sunrise next morning, Willy sprang a mile into the sky in a brand new Cacquot, unpatched and drum tight. The basket was gleaming — fresh from the wicker-worker's hand. Who made these things, he wondered? He imagined an old woman sitting on a stool outside a Constable cottage, weaving his nest for him, far away from the bullets.

Time to get busy. Mornings were rarely the best of times for spotting. Staring towards the sunrise into the ground haze of the evaporating dew was all too often pointless. The Germans, with the sun behind them, liked this time of the day. He counted seven of their *Drachens* up between Geluveld and Messines alone and from the shell-bursts all along the front line he knew they were already well in to what the men in the trenches called the 'morning hate'. You could never be sure. Some days were sharp and clear enough to make him feel a little like a god inspecting the puny murderers below and choosing where to bring down his wrath. This morning visibility was poor but despite that, he thought he could see muzzle flashes beyond Torreken. He imagined the scene wiped clean of the war, drawing it in his head to wipe out the defiling band of churned earth below, putting cows back there instead of dead and dying men.

'I only have field guns available,' rasped the

chart-room officer into his ear, 'Heavies in ten minutes. Maybe fifteen.'

'We can have a go,' Willy replied, 'but I'm not likely see field-gun bursts, not in this.' The small puffs of field-gun shells at long range were hard to spot on the clearest of evenings, let alone a morning like this.

'How good's your fix?'

'Marginal B, probably C.' He meant he could not be sure of the target to within a hundred yards.

'Wait. I'll give you a countdown.'

Swaying there, waiting to direct more misery on the lethal world below, Willy looked up at a clear blue sky and saw an aircraft higher up, heading south. He recognized it, a BE2c plodding off on reconnaissance duties, slow and vulnerable. He looked up admiringly at the balloon's smooth flanks and something out of place caught his eye, a small lump where there should not be a lump. Clinging to a splice where two ropes met ten feet above his head was a field mouse, frozen by fear and the wind.

'Firing now,' said the chart-room voice. 'Thirty seconds flight time. I'll count you down from ten.'

Willy scrambled up on to the edge of the basket and it tilted under him. He held tightly on to a suspension rope with one hand and reached up as high as he could but his outstretched fingers were still five or six feet short. The mouse was staring at him with huge eyes.

'Ten,' said the voice, 'Nine, eight, seven . . . '

He lifted the binoculars with one hand and a

314

lurch sent him swaying out beyond the edge of the basket, his feet pivoting on the rim, held in place only by his other hand. That was silly, he thought, twisting to get himself back to safety. When the voice reached zero, he was still facing entirely the wrong direction.

'Didn't see a thing,' he said, clambering back in to the basket. 'Try again.'

The shoot went on with no discernible effect for another twelve minutes. Sometimes he could see faint swirls that might have been shell bursts and suggested corrections with little confidence, but between every salvo he stared up at the mouse, feeling there was one small life he might be able to save whatever else happened down there. He thought if he could shin up the basket suspension rope, he could probably grab it.

'The heavies are ready,' said the chart-room voice. 'Firing now.'

The big guns were based further back and the shell flight time was longer. They would give him ten seconds warning. An observer on a long shoot could not hold the binoculars to his eyes the whole time so this was a well-rehearsed cooperation designed to save his arm muscles. He looked up. It was a thin rope but certainly climbable and there were diagonals not far up to help him stretch sideways towards the mouse.

'Ten,' said the voice. 'Nine, eight, seven . . . '

This time there was a clear flash of bright orange in the target area just before the count reached zero. He frowned into the haze, trying to correlate it with his last dim view of the enemy muzzle flashes. 'Two minutes right and over,' he

315

said in the end. They thundered away for another ten minutes and he steered their shells all round that faraway patch of what had once been a meadow until someone in a German command bunker somewhere must have decided they had had enough of this. In an old quarry beyond Houthem, beside the canal, the Germans had just finished assembling a long-range gun designed for a battleship but diverted from the Kiel naval base to be pressed into duty at this edge of the Salient. In the night it had started bombarding the boneyard of Ypres with high-explosive shells, out of range of easy retaliation, but in the ammunition pile next to it were two shells filled instead with shrapnel balls and a bursting charge. Now, on instructions from the command bunker, they loaded the first of those.

It was a very creditable first shot and burst a hundred yards off to one side, with a howling bang that Willy had never heard before and a cloud of orange smoke.

'What the hell was that?' he said.

'Trouble?' came the voice from below.

'Unknown shell burst. A big boy. Take me down a hundred feet. Fast.'

It should have worked. The winchman was on the ball. The balloon was tugged down immediately and that brought it, by sheer bad luck, straight into the path of the second shot. Most of the shrapnel balls missed but the top slice of the spray peppered the Cacquot's round nose. The rest hissed past Willy, taking with them one side of the basket, complete with his

316

parachute bag. The balloon began to lose gas immediately, the nose dishing inwards under the gentle pressure of the wind.

Willy heard Thompson's voice in his headset. 'Jump, Fraser. Jump now.' He looked at the other parachute bag. The parachute was still inside but there were two rips right through the bag. It was anyone's guess what had happened to the chute.

'Not so simple,' he said. 'One chute's gone. The other's damaged. Haul down fast while I've still got some gas. I'll risk a jump if it looks like collapsing.' He looked up at the sagging envelope and saw the mouse still hanging on. 'Sorry, my friend, I can't help you right now,' he said. 'We're in the same boat.'

'We'll fly you down,' said Thompson in his ear. 'The winch lorry is turning now.'

Willy looked down and saw the truck lining up to drive down the lane. He understood exactly what Thompson was doing. If they could tow it fast enough, the deflating balloon, even without much gas, would billow out like a giant parachute and the truck would bring it slanting down to the ground.

'Don't worry,' he told the mouse. 'They'll get us out of here.' He fixed it in his mind's eye, thinking that when he got back down he would draw it in the quiet of his hut — making the balloon right again, intact, with only the tiny animal as the intrusion into order.

It all felt good for most of the descent but they were still five hundred feet up when he realized that the emptying balloon canopy was twisting in on itself and was now coming down uncomfortably fast. He could see Thompson perched on the back of the truck next to the winchman, staring up at him with a hand shading his eyes and shouting instructions at the driver.

This is going to hurt, he thought, then the mouse gave him inspiration. He climbed on to one of the surviving edges of the basket again and swarmed up the suspension rope until he was close to the tiny animal, wrapping himself into the network of ropes, hoping that the basket below would serve as a shock absorber when they hit. He reached across and grabbed the red ripcord with one hand and as the basket was about to strike, he tore open the vent panel in the balloon to spill the last of the gas. The basket cannoned on the wide verge, bounced on its side and dragged along the remains of a hedge, the balloon deflating to the sound of wickerwork splintering. Willy pivoted on the ropes, coming gently down on to the ground as the wind took the collapsing canopy off to one side. He reached out and freed the mouse, pulling its curled toes gently away from their tight clasp on the cord. He cupped it in his hands and put it down on the grass where it crouched for a moment then ran so fast into cover that he hardly saw it go.

A Crossley tender arrived with air mechanics to gather up the balloon for repair.

Thompson looked him up and down. 'Are you all right?' he asked.

'Oh yes.'

'Hate to say it but I need you up again as soon as we can. Do try to keep the next Cacquot in one piece. You're breaking them faster than they can make them. Also Plot's asking for you. He's the only one left in his section in full working order and they need two balloons up for a night job later on.'

'Why?'

'Cross bearings. I think they're trying to knock out the gun that brought you down. It was busy last night. They're bringing one of our heavies forward specially but it's a case of making sure we hit it before it hits us. Are you all right with that?'

'Plot knows what he's doing. If he's happy, I am.'

'We'll whizz you over there around dusk. Are you all right to go back up now? I haven't really got anyone else. Fifty-four Squadron have spotted a troop concentration. Brigade thinks there's an attack coming.'

Willy shrugged. 'I might as well be up there as down here,' he said. 'The air smells better.' He discovered that he meant it. It had once been a matter of being able to see for himself but now he no longer felt part of the war on the ground.

'Are you quite sure?'

Willy looked at his commanding officer. Thompson had very pale blue eyes and one of them had developed a twitch quite recently. He saw Thompson blinking to try to control it and understood that this kindly man, who was not at all cut out for war, felt some personal degree of responsibility to him quite unsuited to the random savagery of military life in the Salient. He smiled. 'I've had my ration of bad luck for today. Let's get on with it.' As soon as the words were out of his mouth he regretted them. He was still standing. That hadn't been bad luck at all.

'If you say so,' said Thompson and his mouth added 'sir' silently. 'Oh, one more thing. New issue from Wing. Forgot to give it you. You won't want it but never mind.' He took a small steel square out of his pocket and handed it to Willy. Willy examined it, puzzled. It was highly polished, two inches square with a hole drilled through the centre. A length of cotton tied to a smaller hole at one corner connected it to a second piece of metal, a flat finger of steel with another hole in it.

'It's for emergency signalling,' said Thompson. 'A heliograph mirror. What do you think?'

'How does it work?'

'Glad you asked. You hold the mirror up to your eye, like so — shiny side to the front, see? Hold the prong thing out in front of it, look through the two holes to line it up on the target then you catch the sun and flash it through the hole in the prong and . . . ' he trailed off and they looked at it in silence then at each other. 'I know,' said Thompson. 'Don't bother to say it. Needs at least two hands and something rock solid to stand on. Not to mention the sun in the right place. Absolutely bloody useless, right?'

'I don't know. Useful for a quick shave while you're up there.'

They were getting the remaining Cacquot ready for him. Another new basket, unmarked as yet, dangled beneath it, air mechanics hurrying to get everything done.

'There's only one chute ready, sir,' said the Sergeant. 'They're packing the second one. Ten minutes, they say.'

'There's only one of me,' said Willy. 'We can't spare the time.'

'Regulations, sir. We . . . '

' . . . are made to be broken. This appears to be an emergency. Up now.'

Two hundred feet off the ground, he put on the headphones expecting to hear the usual background static and there was nothing at all, just a sudden end to the background noise of war as the leather cushions around the metal disks covered his ears.

'Hello, chart room?' he said but he could hardly hear his own voice and nothing came back but silence. He looked down at the ground and saw a Crossley tender stopping by the winch. A passenger whose girth, even from this top view, could only be Chester Hoffman got out and Willy saw something trailing back behind the car, snagged on its chassis — a long loop of telephone cable. No one down there had noticed. The phone man by the winch was fiddling with the back of his box of electrical tricks as though the problem lay inside it. Willy shouted and tried waving to attract their attention, pointing emphatically at the Crossley to show them what was wrong, but the only person who saw him was Chester and Chester gave him a friendly wave back, quite unaware. Willy surprised himself by finding he was quite pleased to see the man. They should have been hauling him down again to fix the problem but no, the balloon was rising faster. Willy looked for the cork message container they would drop when all else failed but those weren't much used these days and in the rush, nobody had thought to put one in the brand new basket. He was now a lot higher and still nobody down below had thought to check the run of the ruptured cable.

He took the heliograph out of his pocket and wondered if its moment had unexpectedly arrived but it meant trying to angle the sunshine straight down at an impossible angle and anyway there *was* no sun, just a mass of thick cloud. He began to laugh at the absurdity of the idea and thought of throwing it down at the men below to attract their attention but decided it might easily kill someone so he tucked it back into his knapsack, feeling the shape of the trumpet and wishing he had given them a blast on that instead. Too late now, too high up. He put the bag down in the corner of the basket.

Now, finally, there were tiny matchstick men down below who had woken up to the true nature of the problem. They were gathered round the back of the Crossley, squirming under it to try to free the trapped and torn cable and when he reached four thousand feet, he heard the first brief crackle in his ears as they worked on the connection. Two or three words reached him. 'Can you . . . can . . . ' He knew there must be more internal damage inside the cable after its rough treatment but he was too far up now to see what they were doing. For heaven's sake, he thought. Just splice in a whole new cable. It can't be that hard.

The winch stopped. It was a calm day and the balloon was stable, its nose tugging upwards just a little in the faint gusts, like a yacht with its sails drying, snubbing at its mooring. Without the phone he had absolutely nothing to do so he picked up the binoculars and began to explore the whole area to the south beyond the lines for anything worth looking at. There seemed nothing to report. What looked at first like a streak of smoke from a train in the far distance was only a faint reflection along the slated roof of a trackside building. He turned the glasses further eastward and without any conscious decision, broke all his own rules. Gabrielle's face came into his head — her face as imagined in his sketch, freed of the two-dimensional limits of the photograph. He gazed towards what he could see of Plot Polito's sector as if some freak of refraction at that impossible distance could show him the dead ground and the farm where she just might still be living. He imagined her out there in the fields, sleeves rolled up. What was it farmers actually did on the battered fringe of war? He had seen Belgians herding cows on this side apparently unconcerned, then passed the same way a day later to find nothing but shell holes and carcasses.

Back in his quarters, using the gunners' cycle map, he had sketched out the place where he thought the farm must lie. He had carefully measured its distance from the nearest British batteries and decided it was more or less safe. It would take big guns and deliberate targeting to hit it at that range — that, or a random bomb from a passing aircraft. He pushed that thought away and went into a dream of Gabrielle again — the sort of dream he had warned so many other observers against, because it might take away a precious second of warning if they came under attack. That was why the first he knew of the all-white Albatros that now dropped out of the cloud above him was a *rat-tat-tat* and a smoky stream of bullets just wide of the balloon. It took him a moment to react consciously and by that time his body had taken over in automatic response, starting to climb out of the basket. He saw the pilot clearly as the fighter banked round, a man in a black leather helmet, a red scarf streaming back in the wind. His crew down on the ground must surely have seen the plane but they weren't hauling him down and nobody was shooting back. Why? The Albatros pilot was staring down at the ground as if he could not believe his luck either, then up at the sky above as if the silence of the anti-aircraft guns indicated the presence of protecting aircraft coming down to jump him at any moment.

The new baskets were indeed more awkward and Willy found himself momentarily stuck, one foot caught in something down there. He pulled it free but then he saw that the strap of Claude's knapsack was wrapped round his boot, and the bag itself was jammed in the outward-curving gallery intended to give extra foot-room around the base of the basket. Even as he heard the Albatros's engine roar into a climb for a second attack, he kicked his foot free then stared at the knapsack knowing that if he left it behind, the balloon would surely burn and he would never see her image again. Absurd, one part of him thought. It doesn't matter. Jump. Now. But the other part, closer to his heart, said no and, caught in the conflict between the two, he simply did not move, tensing himself for the impact of the bullets.

No bullets came. Instead he heard the Albatros drone unaccountably right past the basket without firing at all. He saw it begin to turn again but now it kept its distance, flying in a widening circle around him. He could see the pilot staring towards him. The slipstream from its first pass had made the balloon weave and duck and his position was so awkward that the movement threw him abruptly to the floor of the basket. At that same moment the guns on the ground below woke up and when he climbed back to his feet, the Albatros was jinking away into the distance, pursued by the white bursts of Archie.

Thompson's voice rattled in his ear. 'Sorry about that,' it said. 'All sorted down here. How did you persuade him to go away?'

'Nothing to do with me,' said Willy. 'I haven't a clue. I was a sitting duck. Now let's get on with it. Where's this target supposed to be?'

The next hour was business as usual. The chart room passed on a location for the supposed troop concentration in a distant wood. Willy could see the wood but nothing more, but he kept the batteries shooting at approximately the right place and when they had used up the allocated number of shells, they pulled him down.

For a mild man, Thompson was beside himself with anger. 'That bloody American,' he said. 'First the bloody car rips up the phone cable then he's so busy getting the crew to pose for their picture that no one's looking when a bloody Albatros appears.'

'What have you done with him?' Willy asked, looking around.

'Sent him to Wing HQ and told him not to come back until he has a proper written-out order in the King's English saying he has permission to be here. That shouldn't take him more than a month or two. Look, could you possibly consider the delicate state of my nerves and go up there without getting into some sort of trouble?'

'I'll do my best,' said Willy.

'Are you going to be all right for this night shoot? It is important or I wouldn't . . . '

'Sir, do stop asking me if I'm all right. I'll tell you straight away if I'm not.'

'It's just that you don't seem quite the man you used to be.' Thompson stopped and his face took on an expression Willy had never seen before. His cheeks slowly turned a deep red and he put both hands over his mouth as if to stop himself vomiting, then he began to shake. Willy looked on in surprise and was just about to look round to summon help when Thompson took his hands away and let out a whoop of laughter so uncharacteristic that all the airmen within hearing distance looked round.

'What?'

'Well . . . ' he couldn't stop laughing. 'You're . . . you're not, are you?' and then he was off again and Willy had to take his arm and half drag him away from all the curious eyes. When Thompson finally got back under control, he apologized. 'You've been in command of far more men than I have,' he said. 'I don't need to tell *you* what it's like, carrying their safety on your back.'

'You do the best you can,' said Willy quietly. 'We all know that . . . sir.'

'That American has done something to you, hasn't he?'

'He wants to take me back to somewhere I would rather not go. I prefer to be who I am now.'

Thompson stared at him, nodded once. 'I won't try to stop you,' he said and walked away.

For the remainder of the afternoon, Willy rested, preparing for a long night ahead. He lectured himself as he lay on his bed, telling himself he must never be so idiotic again. He should never take off the knapsack and he should never, ever allow himself to drift away into a dream world. He took out the photograph and the sketch and resolved that this would be the last time he looked at them until the war was over. With an effort of will, he drove Gabrielle out of his mind back into the flat and sterile surface of the paper, dismissing what was in his head as fantasy. After that he wrote a letter to Thompson, asking that he be transferred to a different sector, imagining how good it would be to start all over again somewhere where the past could not chase him. Even the Somme, he thought, would be better than this. He spent an hour drawing the balloon basket with the mouse clinging to the ropes then he went to sleep until it was time for the evening operation.

When the time came, a Crossley tender from Plot's section collected him. 'We're due there in thirty minutes, sir,' said the driver. 'Are you ready to go?'

'There' wasn't quite where Willy expected it to be.

A sentry directed them to a section of sunken road startlingly close to the front line where a winch lorry waited with a Cacquot hauled down as far as it would go into the dip, a crowd of nervous handlers hanging on as they watched the sky. Wattle camouflage screens had been nailed to poles along the bank above the road. They might hide the balloon, Willy thought, or they might equally serve as a huge sign to the German gunners that there was something interesting behind them. He hoped the darkness hid them.

'Good of you to come,' said Plot. 'We'll wait a few more minutes until this fella starts heaving hell and damnation at poor old Ypres. Let's not hang around on the way up. As soon as they notice us, they'll start chucking stuff our way so we'll go up as fast as you like. Look at this.' He held out a map board. 'We think he's somewhere around here, down in a hollow or maybe tucked away in one of the quarries.' He showed Willy a circle in an area far down the canal, much further away than any normal target. 'That's why I need a pair of eyes like yours,' Plot said. 'You could spot a muzzle flash on the surface of the moon. My gasbag's a quarter of a mile down that way. I'll give you a shout when I'm ready. Might as well go up together. At least we'll divide their fire.'

Plot's concerns were well-founded. The first minute or so of their ascent was peaceful. The front lines had gone into their night-time mode, flares rising from time to time at any suspected movement in No Man's Land and occasional bursts of rifle and machine-gun fire from nervous sentries. Despite that, the enemy artillery hadn't gone to sleep and the first shell burst near Plot as they passed through eight hundred feet, German gunners busily cranking their guns upwards to take on this unexpected target. Nothing hit them and above two and a half thousand, the gunners seemed to have given up on them. By three thousand feet, they were in their own pitch-black void, the light from the sporadic flares below nowhere near reaching them.

'See that?' asked Plot's voice in his ears and he had — a red bloom far away — the muzzle blast of a great gun. Plot's men had been hard at work. Laid out on the ground below them, two strings of lanterns stretched towards the front lines, shielded by cut-out oil drums so that they could only be seen from above and behind. One line pointed exactly south, the other south-west, so Willy used them to estimate a bearing for the distant muzzle flash and passed it to the chart room. Over the next fifteen minutes, they watched three more shots from the great gun in the distance. By that time, the chart room had averaged out all their different bearings, plotted the intersection of the directions from Willy's position and Plot's and passed the resulting location on to the gun crew waiting beside their own monster.

Afterwards neither Bernard Thompson nor Plot Polito was able to find out exactly who was responsible for what happened next. There was little enough time left in their working day to ask questions and for the next two weeks they got nowhere. After that, most of the people who might have known the answer were dead or wounded or somewhere else in the Salient.

What was known for certain was that the British gun had been positioned a mile behind the balloons, aiming to shoot through the wide gap between them. Balloonists, discussing it afterwards as the event passed into balloon corps legend, said the gun must have been in the wrong place. There weren't many landmarks in that part of the Salient, just a quagmire of temporary tracks, caved-in trenches and random arrangements of shell holes whose features changed with every barrage. Artillerymen insisted that the balloon chart room had given them the wrong coordinates. Realists thought it was possibly a bit of both. Whatever the reason, when the gun fired its first massive shell into the utter darkness, Willy's balloon cable was not safely off to one side but directly in the line of fire. He was deafened and disorientated by the focused blast of the gun and he was lucky that the shell passed some way below him. If the gunners had been trying to hit his cable they would undoubtedly have missed that tiny target but fate rolled the dice. Willy was lucky that the small percussion cap in the shell's nose missed the cable by an inch and the shell itself, travelling at vast speed, was completely unaffected by the encounter. However, the rest of the huge missile shouldered the cable out of its way and the kinetic energy it imparted as it did so was far more than the braided wire could stand. At the point of the momentary contact with the spinning shell, the cable heated to white heat in a thousandth of a second and then each of its strands burst apart in turn.

Willy was set on his task and for a few moments he thought the balloon's bounce was simply the effect of the shell's slipstream so he watched for its impact point ahead with all his attention but when he tried to call the chart room to correct the line, the telephone was dead. Only then did he look down at the ground and see that the guiding lanterns were already back there behind him. He was half out of the basket with one leg over the side before he remembered the new standing orders. Not wanting to be the first man to gift a brand new Cacquot balloon to the Germans, he climbed back in and crouched on the floor of the basket, feeling around until he found the flare gun. How could a man jump and fire the balloon at the same time before his spreading parachute canopy blotted out his view of it? It didn't seem possible. He looked south-east, inspecting the ground ahead and trying to spot how far away the front line lay but it was difficult to be sure. There were faint glows of light on the ground ahead, shielded torches, cooking stoves in trenches, the traces of lanterns shining out of dug-outs, but there was no pattern to them. They could have been in support trenches, saps, battery positions, dressing stations — there was nothing that clearly showed the front line. It struck him that the best plan was to vent hydrogen immediately and try to bring the balloon down before he reached the lines so he pulled hard on the valve-line and immediately felt the balloon dip. He let go but he could still hear the hiss of hydrogen escaping and knew that this time, the valve had failed to close. He yanked and released the line again and again, hoping to hear the plopping noise of the valve sealing, but no such noise came. Again, he craned over the side of the basket for anything that would locate him or tell him his height. The balloon's crude instruments were useless. In the light of his torch, the statometer told him he was descending which came as no surprise at all. The aneroid barometer seemed to be in some fantasy world of its own, implying he was already down well below a thousand feet and that was clearly impossible — or so it seemed until he smelt an utterly unmistakable smell.

At the usual observation height of four to five thousand feet, the prevailing south-west wind meant the air was wonderfully pure, blowing up from Amiens and Rouen and all the way from the distant sea north of Biscay far beyond that.

He could see the war from that height and sometimes hear the war but he could not smell the war. Now he did smell it and it took him straight back into the line in those first desperate battles to save Ypres, when he had lived in mud and blood and where the scorched and shredded trenches stank of burnt explosive. Even burnt explosive was preferable when it was strong enough to mask the far worse sickly stink of the decaying men, mixing in the soup of the mud around them or withering to scarecrow bones in No Man's Land. There had been a village of dead men immediately around their trench, a town in the barbed wire wasteland beyond, a city in the whole Salient.

That was the old and awful stench that rose to him now and told him where he was and just how low he was and then a German sentry, alerted by the dark and unusual bulk of the balloon approaching, fired a flare which burst into life above him and showed he had already left it too late. The front-line trenches were immediately below him, far too close to parachute, and he was crossing the cratered waste between them, crossing to the German lines on the rising ground beyond with no hope of return and bullets coming at him from both sides.

He began to throw everything he could over the side to gain height, hoping to clear the fighting zone and the trigger-happy men below. The Lee-Enfield went first, then the pointless binoculars until all he had left was the knapsack slung safely round his neck, the flare pistol and a pocket torch. The balloon lifted just a little and he crossed the German front line at a hundred feet as near as he could judge in the light of the dying flare, hearing men shouting and pointing at the strange sight, hearing also the *rat-tat-tat* of a machine gun and seeing the flanks of the sagging balloon shivering under the attack. Then the lines were behind him and he was drifting slowly down to earth over the motley trappings of the war's backstage. He drifted over a gun battery, the men around it waiting to shoot, lit by flickering oil lanterns on the ground around them and not one of them looked up into the darkness to see their strange visitor. He passed over a picket line of horses beyond them and the horses were far more aware of him, rearing their heads against tied halters to see upwards, then the consequences of gravity and the gas escaping through all the balloon's new perforations could no longer be ignored and the dark earth came running. The basket crashed through a sprawl of barbed wire and the collapsing envelope careered into a German supply depot, scattering a dozen men who were stacking wooden boxes into a neat pile.

The basket crashed into the crates and tipped Willy out. He cracked his head on something hard and staggered away from the balloon, clutching the flare pistol. Two of the Germans struggled out from under the balloon and began to shout at him. He raised the flare pistol and fired it straight into the wallowing mass of fabric. The remaining hydrogen erupted in a fireball, sending him staggering backwards followed by a series of blasts as the munitions in the wooden boxes underneath it began to go up. Something stabbed into his upper left arm and he turned, stumbling, and groped his way through a maze of barbed wire and out into the darkness.

Dawn found him in a ditch under the remains of a hedge, hurting through and through as he woke from a dream. His father had been holding him, smiling down at him. 'Be careful what you dream of,' he had said in his soft Scottish voice. 'In case the gods give it you.' No, Willy had replied, I wasn't thinking of her any more. He felt the knapsack next to him and knew that now there was nothing but German soldiers between him and Gabrielle's farm.

20

Willy had run limping from the fire, dodging through enemy soldiers racing to put it out. Unaware of the cause, they paid little attention to him and he had gone on as fast as he could, over a crossroads, heading east from what he could see of the stars until it hurt too much to run any further. Then he had found a deserted field, crawled into a dry ditch under a hedge, wrapped his coat round him and did his best to doze, though never fully asleep. While he was free there was still hope, he thought. He had stumbled past a farm in his flight but it was nothing like the fantasy farm of the fantasy woman he had so often imagined. It glistened in the eldritch moonlight, a burnt, abandoned ruin.

He crawled cautiously out of the ditch soon after dawn to spy out the land but a rising engine noise heralded the approach of a very low-flying aeroplane and he ducked back out of sight. As it rattled over him, swaying in the wind, he caught a glimpse of the cockade on the tail and cursed as he recognized the shape of a Nieuport scout — an ally, not an enemy. The pilot was rocking his wings, looking down one side and then the other. Willy stood up in the open far too late and all that was left was a spray of warm castor oil drifting down in the aircraft's wake to anoint his face.

Why so low? Because it was looking for him, of

course. He put himself in Plot Polito's place. Plot would have stayed up there, trying to follow his dark drift over the lines, seeing little from his basket until the sudden distant fireball on the ground and he must have immediately known that signified the end of Willy's balloon but not necessarily the end of Willy. Plot would have a good idea of the bearing so of course they would send a scout over at dawn to see what it could see. What exactly would it have seen? Only the blackened mess of the supply dump and a charred basket with no indication that Willy had survived the explosion.

This was not a good place to be found dressed in Royal Flying Corps tunic and leathers. The small field, pock-marked by a scatter of shell holes, was surrounded by a hedge and he could see through the gaps to where men were moving into the field beyond. Soldiers. He wormed his way back under cover and pulled the Belgian cycle club map out of the knapsack. Even in the darkness of last night he had kept his observer's eye for distance and direction. He could put his finger on more or less exactly where the balloon had come down on the dump. He could see the crossroads he had run past, named Les Quatre Rois on the map. How far had he gone after that? A mile? Two miles? Probably less.

There was a different noise in this part of the war. Willy was deaf to the background noise around the balloon section — the man eating rumble of the front, varying only in its intensity day and night — the crashes from nearby batteries, assaulting the ear for an hour on end and lapsing into silence only from shortages of shells or targets — the rising howl of enemy shells arriving to silence them. Here, the roar of the front-line trenches was muted by the rise of the Messines ridge in between. For the British and their allies there was no place in the wide basin of the Salient where you could pretend you didn't hear the war but on this side of the lines, safely beyond the dominating German-occupied rim of that unholy saucer, there was comparative peace to be found. That proved a presumptuous thought because it was immediately broken to pieces by a titanic eruption of noise and smoke from the next field. He flattened himself with his hands over his ears, realizing that he was immediately in front of a German battery perhaps only a hundred yards away, lying right in their line of fire so that the muzzle blast and the hot gases of their first salvo beat at him. It was impossible to stay there and equally impossible to move.

He thought how ironic it would be if this particular battery attracted counter-fire and put him on the receiving end of British guns. It would be sheer bad luck if the balloon sections were looking this way this morning. Except of course they would be doing exactly that. Thompson had joked about it in the Mess. 'If you wind up the wrong side,' he'd often said, 'just light a fire. We'll look out for the smoke and send the biplane boys across to fetch you.' He squirmed to the edge of the hedge and took a cautious look. There, far away, poking up into view over the ridge to the west were the small shapes of two Cacquots and he knew exactly what would be coming next.

The first British shells howled in six minutes later and they fell only a field's length short. He saw them erupt beyond the westward hedge and was grateful that they were high explosive. If they had been firing shrapnel, aimed to burst in the air above the batteries, he would have had no way of hiding from the wide spray of hissing steel balls. Here at least he could flatten himself in the bottom of the shallow ditch and hope the earth might save him. Someone good was up there in the balloon. Plot, he thought, then he knew it must be Plot because it only took the observer one correction to put his guns spot on target. He heard metal scream in the middle of the shells' eruption and a lump of steel scythed into the hedge line only feet from his head where it buried itself, hissing and smoking. He stared at the part still sticking out. It looked like part of the breech of the German gun.

Plot would have seen the hit. Plot would have spoken the brief command, 'battery fire', into his mouthpiece. Six British guns would now be trained on this precise, small corner of Belgium. Six lanyards would be pulled to send six firing pins hammering into the percussion caps of six brass shell cases. Six shells would be screaming out of the barrels towards him and they would be arriving in how long, twenty-five seconds? Thirty perhaps? Even now they would be shoving fresh shells into the smoking breeches, locking them shut, listening out for any more instructions to crank the barrel up half a turn of the screw or haul on the spikes to swing the gun a hair's breadth sideways. They would have already have fired the second salvo and Plot would have his big binoculars watching for the . . .

Willy's world went silent as an overdose of noise obliterated the field in a wave of heat, earth and metal. Pain lanced down his left upper arm and a hot, blunt hammer attacked his leg. Through buzzing he could hear distant men screaming but one of those screaming men was not nearly as distant as he sounded because he came crashing into the scrawny hedge, putting his boot and his full weight on Willy's injured leg as he did so. Willy yelled a yell he could hardly hear himself and turned to see a wild-eyed German gunner with blood all over his face staring at him in astonishment. The German's mouth moved and he still could not hear but he saw the man's eyes travel all over his clothing and then he saw the German reach to draw a pistol from his belt. The second salvo sliced away both the hedge and the German as if neither of them had ever existed. Willy felt another punch of heat and debris flail across him and then he was lying in his shallow ditch, now laid bare and with nothing around him still living. The German battery lay in scattered heaps of scrap steel and splintered wood speckled with the soft remains of men. A fireworks display of sparks and gouts of smoke flashed from the ammunition pile. Willy crawled across to the soldier's body. One of its hands still held the pistol but the man no longer had a head. He rolled it over, stripped off the long grey coat and put it on, tucking the Mauser into the pocket. Would Plot go on shooting? He was famous for not wasting shells. Could he see the job was done? Willy turned to look at the distant balloons and saw they had troubles of their own. One was just a streak of falling smoke and the other was hauling down fast with an Albatros after it. He wished them luck but not so much luck that the shoot would continue, then he got unsteadily to his feet on a left leg that seemed to belong to someone else.

No more shells came. Instead Germans came pouring into the field, leading horse teams to rescue the guns which were now far beyond rescue. One of them came to Willy and now he could hear a little so when the German asked him if he needed help he said in a polite shout that he was deaf and would go to an aid post. He remembered to shout in German. The other man shrugged and turned to more pressing business. Willy found a blood-stained forage cap lying in the carnage, jammed it on his head and limped eastward out of the field. He walked slowly for a long time, fending off offers of help from solicitous soldiers and turning down a ride in an ambulance. He passed two intact farms and that helped him fix his position on the cycling map. Their names were Flemish. His leg was painful enough to intrude confusingly on his thoughts and he considered knocking on a farm door to ask for help but memories held him back. Occupied they might be but he was close to the internal border between the Belgian Flemish speakers and the Walloon French speakers. Stories had spread through the trenches of Flemish farmers close behind Allied lines who would snipe at their English occupiers or pass obscure signals to the Germans pointing to a hidden gun battery or an ammunition dump — a sheet hung out to dry, a herd of cows penned in a field where cattle did not usually go, a new scarecrow. Queen Elisabeth had displayed a rare fury when she heard of these stories.

'Absurd and undeserved,' she had said. 'There may be spies just as there are spies in England, France and Germany. Remember there are Belgians alive today who are older than the country itself. We have been divided and owned and fought over for hundreds of years but for every spy there are one hundred thousand loyal Belgians. Look what our tiny army has done. Who can question that?' She had been unwrapping a dressing on Willy's chest at the time and she had seen him wince as she pulled away the last three inches.

'I am sorry,' she said. 'Did I hurt you? You should not get me worked up at a time like this.'

'No, keep on talking. It helps. That army of yours. They're wonderful soldiers but you must have noticed that all the officers speak French and half the men speak Flemish.'

'Do you want me to hurt you again? That is an exaggeration about the officers, though I confess I make the same complaint to my King.'

Now, hobbling along the lanes so far from that last vestige of all that had once kept Belgium unified, he was left with no choice in the end because he could simply walk no further. There was a brick-built farmhouse right on the edge of the road with old brick barns around the cobbled yard behind it. He walked slowly past, looking into dark windows, then stood so that he could see obliquely into the yard but there was no sign of anybody. After five minutes watching, he opened the yard gate and walked in. The first barn was completely empty, the centre part of its roof caved in by some past accident of war. The next was full of hay so he tucked himself into the corner out of sight behind the mound where he immediately closed his eyes and went to sleep.

He only woke up when someone prodded him with the muzzle of a rifle.

The man holding the gun was short and bald. Willy's first thought, born out of some sidetrack of pain and exhaustion, was that enough hair had gathered together to form his moustache to have covered his whole head quite well if it had been more evenly spread. The rifle with which he was poking Willy in the stomach was ancient and rusty. Willy recognized an ancient Belgian army Comblain — still potentially deadly despite its age. The man's finger was curled around the trigger and anything might happen. He barked something in Flemish which was enough like the German for Willy to understand it as 'What are you doing here?'

'I am hurt,' he replied in slow German. 'I had to lie down.'

'Get up,' said the man and added something else that probably meant 'Come with me,' because he stepped aside and waggled the rifle

343

barrel backwards and forwards between Willy and the door. Willy put the knapsack over one shoulder and levered himself upright, his leg giving way under him so that he had to hop along, dragging it behind him.

The man kept prodding Willy with the muzzle all the way to the farmhouse door. In a spartan parlour, he indicated a wooden chair with a frayed cushion. Willy sat down and without taking his eyes off him, the man shouted 'Helene!' The woman who came into the room was taller than the man, slender to the point of boniness. She was wiping floury hands on her apron. Something about her appearance prompted Willy to address her in French.

'Madame,' he said, 'I did not mean to disturb you and your family. I was hurt and I was only looking for somewhere to rest.'

He was right. She replied in perfect French. 'Why here?' she asked. 'You have a dressing station along the road. There is a headquarters not five hundred metres away. Why do you come to our dirty old barn? I do not believe you.'

There seemed no other way. 'Because I am not a German,' he said.

'Then what are you?'

'I am a British officer of the Royal Flying Corps.'

'In German clothing?'

'I took it as a disguise.' He went to open the coat but the man tensed and brought the rifle to his shoulder.

'Victor,' said the woman sharply. She gestured to Willy to continue. He held the coat open and

344

they both inspected the RFC tunic beneath. Victor spoke to her in rapid Flemish that Willy could not follow.

'He says that does not mean you are English,' she said. 'You have perhaps been sent to test us. We should tell the German headquarters. He wants to see what you have in your pockets and in your bag.'

The first thing they found was the Mauser pistol and that prompted a stream of Flemish invective. The woman took it and the old man retreated, training his rifle on Willy.

'If I had been going to use that, I would already have done so,' said Willy wearily.

The only other things in his pockets were a handkerchief and a mis-shapen bar of Fry's Chocolate Cream. The woman held the chocolate up as if it were proof of Englishness but the man shrugged, unimpressed, and kept the rifle levelled on him. Then the woman turned to the knapsack and Willy stiffened. 'Please leave that alone,' he said. 'That is personal,' but she had already taken out the patched trumpet, glanced at it curiously and laid it on the table. The next thing she took out was the leather wallet. She made a face at Willy as if to apologize, opened it and drew out the damaged photograph. She looked at it for a long moment saying nothing then she turned white and swayed. Willy found enough strength to lunge forward out of the chair towards her as her knees buckled. The farmer also went to catch her and let go of his rifle which dropped, butt first, on the floor. They collided, all three together as the gun went off,

345

blasting a bullet into the ceiling and bringing down a spray of plaster. Someone somewhere screamed. Willy's leg gave way and the farmer staggered under his wife's weight. Together they half fell, depositing her clumsily into the chair Willy had just vacated.

Willy sat down heavily on the floor. 'Get her water,' he said, then realizing he had spoken in English, tried again. 'Wasser? L'eau?'

The farmer shook his head, opened a cupboard and uncorked a small bottle. He waved it below her nose and the fringes of an acrid smell just reached Willy as she convulsed, flinging his arm and the bottle away with a sweep of one arm.

'Good God,' she said opening her eyes. 'Away with that.' Then she crossed herself.

'What happened?' said Willy.

She blinked, shaking her head, then stared at him as if she had forgotten him. She looked down at the photograph on the floor and gasped. 'It is real,' she said. 'Oh my dear sweet Lord.' She crossed herself again.

'Do you know her?'

'How would I not know her?'

A door in the corner of the parlour opened. There were stairs behind it and a woman stepped down into the room staring, blinking up at the hole in the ceiling. 'That woke me up nicely,' she said in French. 'If you wanted me, you only had to call.' Then she took in Willy, slumped on the floor. 'Who is this?' she said.

'A man who says he is English,' Helene replied. 'But he has brought some startling items in his bag, my dear. You must prepare yourself for a shock.'

Willy stared at the woman in front of him. The room began to spin slowly around him and he could see her still, then he couldn't as a curtain came across his eyes. He put his head down, shook it and looked again. This was not the woman he had imagined. Perhaps sorrow as well as the privations of war had tightened her face around cheekbones that had been hidden in that photograph from a happier time, but this was certainly Claude's Gabrielle and she had all her own beauty which was only a distant cousin to the beauty of Willy's fantasy.

Absurd words came to his lips. 'I didn't say I was English. I come from Scotland.'

'And how did you get here, bringing so much danger with you, Mr Scotsman?' asked Gabrielle. 'Are you an aviator? Is your aeroplane in our fields? If so they will see it.'

'No. I was in a balloon. It broke free. It came down and burnt. They will think I am dead. Do the Germans come to this house?'

The older woman, Helene, answered. 'Every day without fail. Sometimes twice or more. They oblige us to sell them our eggs and fodder for their animals. There is no end to it. They come to the back door but they do not often enter. Gabrielle, quickly now, take him upstairs to your room. It is safer.'

All this exchange had been in French and old Victor had been listening attentively. He had clearly come to understand his wife's language over the years even if he preferred to speak his

347

own Flemish. Now he said something that sounded to Willy like an objection.

Helene waved a dismissive hand at him. 'Pah,' she said. 'Don't be absurd. Look at the state of him.' Then she did look and looked closely. 'That is blood on the carpet around your foot,' she said. 'Are you hurt?'

'I am fine,' said Willy, struggling to his feet, which was a mistake because the room and the people in it began to rush away from him as if they were at the diminishing end of a long, long tunnel and when he opened his eyes again, he was in a soft bed.

21

'Hospital', his struggling brain suggested, then 'nurses'. Bathed in chemicals of pain, it found the best match in his memory until his eyes were able to focus on the face nearest his and the shock of Gabrielle brought him back.

'That's better,' she said. 'Be warned. Your leg is going to hurt quite a lot.'

He was astonished by the reality of her, right there a foot above him — an animated woman with colour in her cheeks who smelt of hay and lavender, not the flat, sepia Gabrielle of the photograph. Through the fast-fading anaesthesia of unconsciousness, he knew she was right. Waves of pain were washing towards him, sharper by the second. His left arm was sore above the elbow but his leg trumped that easily. He reached slowly down to touch it and found it wrapped in thick bandages.

'You are a little lighter now,' said Helene from the other side of the bed. She showed him a shard of curved metal two inches long. 'We took this from your calf. Is it part of a shell?'

He tried to answer but his throat was too dry so he nodded once and even that made his head hurt.

'I have work to do,' said Helene. 'Gabrielle will look after you.' She closed the door behind her. Willy looked slowly around the room. He was in a wide bed in an attic room right under the tiled roof of the farmhouse. There was a small dormer window up to his left, too high for him to see anything other than sky. Through the roof to the right, he could also see the sky in scattered chinks of daylight between some of the tiles. It would need work before full winter came. Gabrielle's face wore a set expression.

'Drink this,' she said. 'I will hold it for you.'

He sipped from a tin mug of a tepid infusion that tasted mostly of mint, swilling it around his mouth and throat to dissolve the crusted discomfort. She held the mug at his lips while he drank it down.

'Can you talk to me now?' she said when he had finished.

'Yes, I think so.'

'I do not want to press you when you have been hurt but there are some things I have to ask you,' said Gabrielle. 'I am sorry to say that my uncle is still very suspicious of you so he has searched through your knapsack.' She stopped. 'But is it really *your* knapsack?' she said. 'I think perhaps it was not originally yours because I can see it has two other initials inked on the inside. I have it here. Do you see? They are C and T and those are not your initials, are they?'

I borrowed them, he thought, but why complicate it? There was no possible route but the truth with her standing so close to him.

'It belonged to Claude,' he said, 'and he was my great friend.'

'My Claude?'

'Yes.'

'*My Claude* was your great friend?' she said.

350

'Then does that mean you are the Scottish person he wrote about?'

'You had letters from him?'

'One from Liège, six from Antwerp and a last one from De Panne before the Germans came here. He numbered them so I know there were eight more but those did not get through. I dream they may yet reach me one day.'

'And he talked about *me* in them?'

'He talked of little else. Claude did not like to tell me about the fighting so he told me about you, Monsieur Fraser, and the way you spoke and how he believed your strong hand would keep him safe . . . ' She stopped again and then gathered herself. 'And I know that in the end you were not able to do that but I do not know exactly how that end came. Now you have come like a trick of theatre springing up through a trapdoor with his pictures and his trumpet and even his knapsack, though they are all very much damaged and you too are damaged. I cannot tell if that is good or bad magic but I think you were sent here, perhaps to tell me how he died? Yes, I have been told that he is dead though only because a short message came through Switzerland. A few words to tell me such a big thing. Wait.'

She gave him another mug of mint tea. 'Are you well enough to tell me? I should not ask now but I admit that I have even hoped in the nights that perhaps he was not dead at all. I made a dream for myself he might be lying in some hospital for all these past twenty-four months and nobody knew who he was but that isn't

351

right, is it? You do know for certain that he is quite dead?'

'Yes, I do.'

'How did you come here?'

And then Willy did his best to explain that it was by chance and it was not by chance, that for such a long time he had tried all kinds of ways to identify the farm, that he had seized an opportunity to look this way from far off and in the end fate had delivered him to this side of the lines. 'Even then,' he said, 'I did not know this was the farm until I saw you.' He paused. 'If you have looked in the bag,' he said, 'you will know that there is a letter from Claude.'

'You do not need to say more. Helene has examined it and she says there is little left to read and it is a sad thing, to be looked at only when the years have passed. She told me also there is Claude's photograph of the two of us together. I have the same one here too.'

'You already have it? I am glad. Mine was damaged, you see.'

'Yours?' He saw a brief frown. Gabrielle stared at him. 'That photograph was taken just before Claude was called back. Mr Fraser, we had been married only three days earlier.'

'I know. He told me. That does seem . . . unfair.'

'Don't be absurd,' she said sharply. 'Did you say that because you thought you had to say something? All I know of you comes from the words Claude wrote but he was quite sure you were a realist. He said you had no room for sentimentality and in that way you reminded him of me. Was he wrong?'

'No.'

'Then don't talk to me of fairness. Where will
you find that in this world today? Perhaps in
places the war has not touched, if there are such
places? Do you know of any?' She sounded
genuinely interested in that question. 'America
obviously but what about Bolivia or Greenland?'

'So far as I know there is no fighting in Bolivia
or Greenland.'

'Then perhaps all the world's fairness has
gone there for safety but believe me, it no longer
lives here.' She frowned and stared hard at him.
'Helene has told me such a very strange thing,'
she went on. 'She said that someone has tried to
mend the photograph. They have drawn
Claude's face back in pen and ink.'

'Yes. That was me.'

'Why?'

'I wanted to remember him while his face was
still in my mind.' True enough, but what he did
not say was, 'I wanted him to guard you from
me, to remind me you are his, to bring back a
world in which Claude is next to Gabrielle and
all is right with that world,' but now he was next
to her instead and this was no longer just a
matter of a man and his imagination.

'Helene says it has been done very well. It has
captured the spark and the spirit of him and she
says that the same hand drew me also. How
could that be?'

'I had his help. He thought the photograph did
not do you justice.' And now he knew just how
true that was. 'It is not as good as the picture I

353

would draw now. He also asked me to take care of you.'

She smiled, she actually smiled at that thought. 'How did he expect you to do that?' she asked. 'He must have thought you were a very brave man indeed if you would come across the lines on purpose.' She looked at him and put her hand to her mouth. 'You didn't, did you? Did you somehow set your balloon loose?'

'No, it didn't need any help from me. Who knows? Perhaps it was given to him in his last moments to know I would get here. Gabrielle, if it is any comfort to you at all, I told your King and Queen all about Claude and his bravery.'

'My King and Queen? King Albert and Queen Elisabeth? How did you talk to *them* about Claude?'

It was Elisabeth mostly, Willy thought. I told her a great deal. 'We both served with them for a while and later on I told them everything that happened. The Queen said that one day when this is over, she will make sure that Claude gets a medal for what he did.'

'A medal?' She sighed and gave a little shrug. 'I don't care about medals. I would much rather ask you to be brave and tell me exactly what happened to Claude if you are ready.'

'If that is what you want. It requires us both to be brave.'

'It is what I need.'

For the next hour in the hush of the farmhouse attic room broken only by the passage of tramping German boots on the road outside, Willy told her of Liège and the fortresses, of

354

Claude using a damaged *mitrailleuse* to stop the Uhlans, of Claude's injury, the Zeppelin attack and his ragtime trumpeting. She listened, intent and silent, and he told of Gerard Leman, of the terrible wreck of Loncin and the road to Malines.

'He hoped to find you there,' he said. 'He looked for a woman called Anna. He thought you might be with her.'

'Anna? She had gone to Paris.'

'He wanted to marry me off to Anna.'

She managed another short laugh at that. 'Anna would not have suited you,' she said.

He went on to describe Antwerp and the forced retreat to the coast. He talked of Claude's determination and his gallows humour, of their closer and closer relationship to the King and Queen, of their promotion and of the way Claude defied all of Germany with his trumpet and then finally he told her, hesitantly and gently, all he remembered of Claude's death.

'You must understand,' he said, 'that I was injured at the same time. There was only one other man who survived from that platoon, a sergeant who pulled me out of the water though he was hurt too. I tried to find him later to thank him but it seems perhaps he did not survive for long.'

'Did they bury Claude?'

He had feared that question. He looked at her and slowly shook his head, remembering his fruitless trip back to the grim embankment when he had recovered sufficiently, an embankment now grown into a bizarre front line, a rabbit

355

warren of dug-outs and sandbagged emplace-
ments. It was a military village stretching miles
along the edge of the flood, tending its wooden
causeways, snaking out into the grey water to
serve the look-out posts and machine-gun nests
which kept enemy raiders at bay. The Captain
who had shown him what the inundation had
become had shaken his head when he asked the
same question.

'Bodies in the water?' he had said. 'It is half
water, half bodies. You do not want to drink it or
to smell it. Even now, a man who dies in this is
lucky if he sees dry land again.'

She looked at him and did not press him. Her
eyes were huge and shining with tears but, as if
by her willpower, they did not run down her
cheeks.

'Was it quick, his end?'

And there it was, the other question he really
did not want to answer. What could he say? He
looked at her face and thought now he must set
honesty aside for her sake rather than his own.
'Yes,' he said. 'I was with him, holding him in the
rising water. There was nothing else I could do.
He asked me to find you and then . . . he died.'
It was done and it was far from the whole truth
but he could not possibly have told her the whole
truth at that moment. 'He was thinking of you.'

'He wrote that you had been teaching him
how to stay alive, that you said he must not think
of me. You told him to concentrate on the war
and not think of anything else so that he might
live to see me again. Is that what made him die?
Did he think of me when he should not have?'

She stared at him intently, as if she might have somehow helped to kill Claude.

'Nothing could have made a difference, Gabrielle,' said Willy. 'I survived by complete chance and he died by complete chance and it was good that he was thinking of you.'

'Thank you,' she said. 'Let us try our best to pass to lighter things.'

'He talked so much about you,' Willy said. 'How you first met. How you tackled the thief in the market.'

'That? Oh, he did exaggerate. That was nothing. Anybody could have done it. He told me you were a little mad in the best possible way. He said William Fraser seemed bound for Valhalla but not for many years to come. Is that what I should call you? William Fraser?'

'Willy will do.'

'But you are here and not in Valhalla. I don't have a god but I hope that is where Claude is now.'

'He is brave enough to be there. He saved my life at Liège. I did what I could to save his. I am so very sorry that I failed.'

A shell exploded some way off, perhaps three or four fields away, and they both turned their heads towards the noise. 'They don't come this far,' she said. 'Not often. Two or three a week, no more.'

Willy realized how different everything sounded here. He heard boots on the road outside again, a voice barking time, and then a truck with a labouring engine, hard tyres crushing their way through the gravel. Realization came that those were German boots, a German voice, a German truck — unfamiliar sounds from the wrong side of the war. Living is such an insistent business. It roots you into where you are and who you are with and what you are saying, but sometimes that all combines to be so odd that an earthquake fault snaps and skids sideways in the head. For a disorientating moment Willy found it quite impossible to believe that he was really in this dangerous place with this woman who so far surpassed even his invented idea of her. Then the need to survive took over. It forced him to accept the reality of the enemy on the road outside and with it, the heady fact of her.

'Claude wanted to be as daring as you were,' she said.

'He became the daring one, Gabrielle . . . '

She waited for him, frowning. 'Why do you stop?' she asked and he could not possibly give her the truthful answer, that he had addressed his imagined Gabrielle in his thoughts so very many times but the impact of saying her name to her, the real her, had suddenly overwhelmed him.

They were silent for a while, staring at each other and she put a cool hand on his forehead. All those times when he had thought about her, had taken out the photo and dreamt life into the flat oval of her face and everything he had imagined had been far short of the truth. He should have kept Claude alive for her.

'When I first received that card and I hoped it might all be a mistake . . . ' Gabrielle's voice had a catch in it. 'I planned to walk all the way to the trenches and ask them to let me cross so that I could find out about him.'

'I am very glad you didn't. You're close enough to the fighting as it is. Have you been any closer?'

'No. We farm only the fields to the south and the east now. Would they have stopped me at the lines?'

'Oh yes, of course they would. You have no idea what it's like,' he said gently. 'In daylight they all stay in their trenches with their heads down unless they are commanded to attack. Snipers would have you in a second if you showed your face and the shells never stop. Well, you know that, don't you?'

Even here with higher ground between them and the front, the background thunder rumbled incessantly away out there, no longer attracting their attention except when punctuated by a sharper bang.

'I am sure I could have done it,' she said. 'I would have gone across at night. I know all the ditches and the hedges, you see. I could find my way between the lines. I thought I would walk to the other side and say loudly who I was before I got there.'

'Please don't ever try that. There are no more ditches and hedges. There are no gaps, no safe pathways. There is only barbed wire and shell holes full of mud to catch you and drown you and the stench of gas and flares that would light you up and raiding parties and nervous men everywhere with their fingers on the trigger.'

'So how will you get back there?'

He hadn't started to think about that.

'You came in your balloon. How exactly did you do that?'

So he explained to her all about the Balloon Service. She had seen them every day in the distant sky but she had no idea how they worked.

'And you chose to do this?' she said when he had finished. 'I think it sounds very dangerous.'

'Yes. They wouldn't let me ride a horse any more. I prefer to see what is happening.'

'The base you came from — could they not send a balloon to fetch you?'

His leg tore his attention away for a moment. 'They don't work like that,' he said in the end. 'They are held where they are by a long wire.'

'But I have seen the big German ones flying around.'

'The Zeppelins are different. They have engines and they can go long distances, wherever they choose. Ours are much smaller. If the wire breaks then the wind takes them wherever it wants to.'

'I have another idea. Two aeroplanes have landed in our fields since I came here. A Frenchman who had been shot and a German whose engine broke into pieces. Could they not send an aeroplane to get you?'

'If they knew where to send it, but they don't.'

She stared at him and he met her gaze, looking at her face, fully understanding why Claude had cared so much. 'Are you frightened they will find me here?' he asked.

She shrugged. 'I do my best never to let them frighten me. Different units come and go. They

360

do not really know us. They come to take our food. They have searched the buildings many times now. If they come, you will be my injured husband recovering from your wounds. They have released other Belgian prisoners to work their land for the German army.'

So I will be Claude, thought Willy. At Gabrielle's request. It shivered his throat and buzzed in his gut.

'This is your room,' he said. 'Is there somewhere else I can be?'

'No, not yet. I do not think it would be wise to move you. Your leg must heal first. I will sleep in a bed out there.'

'Out where?'

'In the south wing or perhaps the fifth guest suite. No, it is not a big house. There is a cot we can unfold on the landing and Helene and Victor sleep in the room beyond. That is all there is. They do not sleep well these days. Helene is brave but I know she fears that one day soon we will be in range of the British guns.'

'Why do you stay?'

'Where would we go?'

'Do you have family?'

'No, none any more apart from Helene and Victor.'

'Your parents from Namur?'

'Both dead.'

'Oh.' He stopped himself before he said anything she might have regarded as not fitting for a realist. 'You would be safer further from the fighting.'

'I am sure they would not let us leave. The

farmers are needed. Victor and Helene cannot work the farm by themselves. I must be here to help them but we do know that we might have to run. You see that bag?'

He looked where she was pointing at a battered leather Gladstone on top of a chest. 'That,' she said, 'is what we call our panic bag. It is for the day when the shooting comes too near. It has some money and our most precious possessions in it. If that time comes then we will take it and run.'

'You should go now, Gabrielle. Anything could happen here.'

'It is not so simple. We have to do what they say. Anyone on the road needs a permit. They want these farms to keep working. We are nearly the closest to the fighting but by the soldiers' standards it is quite safe back here. That is what they think.'

'It was safer before I arrived. Claude asked me to look after you. Instead you are looking after me. I don't want to put you in danger.'

'I have heard talk of one of your pilots who crashed near here and he walked all the way to Holland. Others have done it too. That is one way you could go. There is an electric fence on the border. They say that if you can climb over that you are safe.'

'Safe? Interned there for the duration of the war. No, I will find a way to get back and fight.'

'I need to dress your wound. Do you mind? I can ask Helene if you would prefer but she is better with animals.'

'Gabrielle, I have had wounds dressed many

times since this war began. It holds no horrors for me.'

He had spoken too soon. When she peeled the pad away from his calf he had to grit his teeth.

'It hurts,' she said. 'I can hear it in your breathing.'

'It's all right.'

'No, I fear it is not all right at all. It is infected. We tried to clean it out as much as possible.' She called for Helene and they conferred, then Helene went away and came back with a dish of brown, pungent liquid. 'We used this on the sheep when we still had sheep,' she said cheerfully.

'Did it kill them?'

'No, the soldiers did that.'

It stung enough to stop him talking but by the evening he had developed a fever and the two women were exchanging worried looks. They took turns to sit by the bed that night, sponging his forehead, but the fever bit into him ever harder. Before dawn, he was tossing, delirious, and in the morning they had a quiet argument outside the door. 'The German doctors might save him,' said Helene. 'We could tell them we found him unconscious in the barn. If he stays here he might die.'

'I will nurse him even if you won't.'

'They have powders and medicines for this. What do we have? Something Victor traded for a piglet four years ago in a bottle which doesn't even have a label.'

'I don't know much about him,' said Gabrielle, though as she said the words she felt

363

that they were already deeply untrue, 'but I know he does not want to be taken prisoner and we should give him the best chance we can.'

'He will end up a prisoner anyway. How can he escape? Do you mean to hide him for as long as this war lasts?'

'If I have to.'

'If he lives until morning.'

22

Chester Hoffman had only just realized that La Panne and De Panne were one and the same place, depending on which Belgian language you chose to speak. Chester's French was almost serviceable by now but his Flemish had a long way to go. The one-armed veteran guarding the front desk of the former *Hôtel L'Océan* addressed him in English but that was as far as his helpfulness went. No longer a hotel, it was still a grand building. It looked northwards over a sea patrolled by the Royal Navy's ugly river monitors now backed up by an ancient battleship bristling with guns and a flotilla of destroyers to keep German submarines at bay. The Navy's gunnery had preserved Belgium's tiny capital in the sand dunes, keeping the Germans pinned down to the east of Nieuport. The front held steady here on the coast.

'Monsieur,' said the veteran at the desk, 'Her Majesty is busy with her work here. She is with Dr Antoine Depage. They have important matters to discuss. In any case, monsieur, Her Majesty does not speak to newsmen. Not at all. Not ever. You should go to consult the King's *Chef d'Affaires*. He will convey any message if he thinks fit.' The veteran's quivering moustache said that he was quite sure the *Chef d'Affaires* would not think fit.

Chester took out a pen and began to write in

his notepad. He tore off the page, folded it and handed it to the veteran who shook his head.

'You do not pass a message on a dirty sheet of paper to my Queen, monsieur. That is not how such things should be done.'

'She will want to read this,' said Chester, 'I assure you. And if you want to stay on the right side of your Queen, I strongly suggest you get it to her right now.'

'Do not threaten me, sir,' said the other man. 'It takes more than one American to overcome my will. The German army could not do it and nor shall you.'

'Hercule,' said an American voice from behind Chester. 'Do not concern yourself. I will see to this. I know Mr Hoffman.'

Chester turned and was immensely relieved to see an American nurse, the tall, fair southerner the soldiers called 'Morning Glory'.

'Oh my dear,' he said, 'am I glad to see you again. Can we go talk somewhere?'

They sat on a bench at the far side of the lobby while Hercule watched Chester as if he would happily shoot him.

'Don't mind him,' said the nurse. 'He loves his Queen dearly and he has his instructions. What's your problem?'

'I need to talk to her.'

'Do you mind if I ask you why?'

'Because I have news of Willy Fraser and I think she would want to hear it.'

'Ah, that man again. You're still tracking down the valiant Scotsman? Has he won the war yet?' She saw the expression on his face. 'No, I guess not. Is he dead then?'

'I don't know that. All I know for sure is he has gone across the lines, carried there by a breakaway balloon.'

'Lawdie. I guess I can tell the Queen that for you.'

'No, please. I would like to talk with her myself.'

'Because you want to get a story out of this?'

Yes, thought Chester, but he said, 'Because I have an idea where he might have gone and I believe it may still be possible to get him back,' and the strange thing was that as he said it, he knew there was more truth in that than in his desire for a story.

Ten minutes later she showed him into an office where a tired woman stood by a window criss-crossed with paper tape, looking out at the ships patrolling. She wore a nursing uniform. Chester had seen her from a distance before and thought her elegant if not quite beautiful.

'Your Highness,' he said.

She flapped a hand at him. 'Stop there. It is just you and me in this room. Let us not have any of that nonsense. As a queen, I should not be talking to you. Could you please pretend I am a normal human being? Call me 'Sister'. Any small thing that helps me believe I know what I am doing here will encourage me to get through the rest of the day. Now for heaven's sake, sit down.' She stared at him in frank curiosity. Chester was aware that men of his shape and outward appearance were a rarity in this starved and uniformed world.

'All right, Mr Hoffman,' she said, 'I asked

them to bring you up here because of the message you sent but I am certainly not here to become a subject for one of your stories and anything I say to you is only for your ears. Do we agree on that?'

'Yes, ma'am.'

'Yes, *Sister*.'

'Yes, Sister.'

'Sit down, then. You had better keep your promise. Do you see those fine ships out there? At a single word from me they will turn their guns round and blow you to pieces.'

'Wouldn't that kill you too, Sister?'

'No. I am sure they are very fine shots and could deal with you without even scratching me.' She laughed. 'I would offer you tea but we are very short and the men need it more than we do. Now, let us be serious. I am putting off the moment when you tell me your news — so what has happened to our dear Willy Fraser?'

'The night before last, his balloon's cable was severed by a shell. The wind took him over the German lines. Another observer saw an explosion on the ground a mile or two behind the lines. A pilot reported the next morning that a small supply depot had been destroyed by fire and he could see the burnt remains of the balloon basket in the middle of the wreckage.'

She took a deep breath. 'Are you telling me that he is dead?'

'I am hoping it takes a lot more than that to kill Willy Fraser.'

'And why do you bring this news to me especially?'

'Because I came here recently to find out more about him and I heard that you nursed him, that you had formed an affection for him — you and the King that is.'

'My husband, you mean. Sisters are married to husbands, not kings. So what is your own interest in this, Mr Hoffman?'

'He and I travelled from Berlin on his motorcycle as the war started.'

'Ah, now I see. So that was you.' She looked him up and down and he knew what she was thinking, knew how Willy must have described him.

'I guess I lost a few pounds since then,' he said, hoping that was true.

'But did he not abandon you? I know he felt a little guilty. Why are you so concerned about his welfare now?'

Perhaps it's the way she looks at you, Chester thought. Something about her made him think harder. It stopped him making the smart reply. 'He's not like most of them,' he said in the end. 'I guess I meet a lot of brave guys out here and I meet a few clever guys but the clever guys do too much thinking and that can get in the way. The clever, brave guys are the special ones and it appears to me that Wild Willy Fraser is one of those.'

'Wild Willy?' she said and smiled. 'I did not know they called him that.'

'You knew he was a lieutenant-colonel?'

'Indeed. I heard that the King promoted him himself.'

'No, not a Belgian lieutenant-colonel, a real

one. Oh hell, Sister, I didn't mean to say it like that.'

'Oh, you mean a proper *British* rank?' He knew she was mocking him. 'Are you saying his people promoted him all over again? No, I did not know that but I am glad.' She thought for a moment. 'Please understand that I have not seen him since he recovered from his wounds here and that must have been, let me see, in March or April of 1915? So much has happened since then and I have heard nothing. He has done well, you say?' A high British rank and now this. She would have preferred him not to go back to his own army.

'I am making some enquiries in Scotland where he comes from. Did you know he lives in a castle?' Stupid, he thought. Most of her friends must live in castles. 'Only a small one,' he said. 'I already know he was shamefully treated.' Chester told her the whole story he had unravelled, of the old enemies in the cavalry who had taken the opportunity to take their revenge on a great soldier. He told her how he had discovered Willy masquerading as Claud Taverner, reduced to a mere lieutenant in the Balloon Corps, of Willy's daily acts of bravery there and his escapes from death or capture.

'Extraordinary,' said the Queen in the end. 'I do understand your interest and I am very grateful to you for bringing me all this news but you are looking at me as if there were something more I might do and I cannot think what that might be.'

'When I told you he called himself Claud

Taverner, ma'am, it seemed to me that you recognized that name.'

'Sister, please. I will not warn you again. I will call the ships and ask them to shoot you.'

'Sister. You nursed him. That American girl, a real Yankee doodle dandy doll if you will pardon my way of speaking — the very same girl who brought me here just now — she helped you, right?'

'Our famous Morning Glory.'

'That's the babe. She told me a while back that when Fraser was at his sickest he would cry out the name Claude over and over. Now why does a man do that and why does he take that very same name when he needs a new one? It kinda made me wonder.'

'I believe I can answer part of that for you,' she said. 'There was indeed a man called Claude Tavernier. He was a brave Belgian officer fighting with Willy Fraser in our own army first at Liège then in the battles all the way back here to the coast. Tavernier was killed here on the Yser River by the same shells which so badly injured Fraser. Tavernier was a gallant man, famous for blowing tunes on a trumpet at moments of great danger.'

'That old trumpet? That belonged to him? Fraser kept it. He played it from the balloon. They say he only plays one song, the 'Marseillaise'.'

The Queen nodded as if she was starting to understand something and Chester noted that to himself.

'When he was so sick,' she said, 'he was only concerned about the safety of that trumpet and

371

of a photograph of Tavernier and his wife and also, I think, a letter Tavernier had written. We had to reassure him all the time that we were keeping them safe. When he recovered he asked every Belgian he could find questions about the land beyond the German lines. That's where the girl was living, I think, on a farm somewhere?'

'I was getting to that,' said Chester. 'You see, Sister, I believe that is where he may have gone. His balloon was drifting that way. There's this guy who goes by the name of Plot, another of these insane balloon observers. He tells me that our mutual friend asked him a load of those very same questions about farms near Comines, one farm in particular called the Pont something Hoeve, the something beginning with a letter V.'

She shrugged apologetically. 'We have a lot of farms in our country.' He noted that she did not say 'had'. Then she nodded to herself. '*Hoeve* is the Flemish word as I am sure you know and Comines is a small town on the border between the two languages so it will be somewhere along that line but I cannot tell you any more than that.'

'Sister, I'm asking you to find out for me. Use your powers to locate this farm. Can you do that? Someone round here must know that area.'

'And what would you do if I did? Hold up a sign saying, 'I am an American neutral' and stroll across to fetch him?'

'I could try. We're not at war, not yet. It might be that they would still let me in to the front area if I went through Holland.'

'You think? I very much doubt it. Germany

does not believe your American neutrality is real any more. It will not last long now, surely.'

Interesting, thought Chester. What does she know? 'That's my back-up plan,' he said. 'But I got a better idea. I've met some crazy fliers in the RFC. One of them might go over and get him if I could only tell him where to land his aeroplane.'

23

For five days and five nights the two women nursed Willy with the only remedies they had available — cool well water to sponge him, spooned chicken broth, dressings made from torn strips of sheets and above all their constant attention. Gabrielle took on the lion's share of the work, sleeping just outside his open door. Whenever he raged in the night, shouting defiance and panic into the darkness, she would be next to him in a moment, calming him with the words she might have used to an animal, wiping his forehead until he subsided. German soldiers marched past the front of the house during the night on their way to and from the front lines and sometimes his incoherent ravings would turn into shouted English, easily loud enough to be heard from the road so that she had to hold her hand over his mouth. She couldn't understand most of the words he shouted but she could all too easily understand the one he repeated most often, *Claude, Claude*.

At noon on the sixth day, Helene went to Gabrielle, curled in exhausted sleep in the chair in the corner of the bedroom, and woke her gently. 'You must come,' she said.

Gabrielle jerked awake but she saw Helene's smile before she had time to feel fear and followed her to the side of the bed.

Willy's colour and his breathing had changed

so he looked the way any sleeping man looks. Gabrielle put her hand on his forehead. 'The fever is down,' she said in wonder.

'He has the strength of a plough-horse, this one,' said Helene.

It was another whole day before Willy opened his eyes to find Gabrielle smiling down at him. He sat up before she could stop him, looking about him in confusion, then slumped back down on the pillow. 'I thought you were a dream,' he said and reached out to take her hand. She sat down beside the bed holding it in hers and they stared at each other.

'This is not the time to talk,' she said in the end. 'Today I must work. We are rebuilding the chicken house to keep out the Germans and they need me to help or all our chickens will soon be gone. You must not try to get up. Really. Promise me that. Nobody must see you. An officer came prowling around yesterday. He was looking in the yard. We have not seen him before. He would not say anything to us at all. He just ignored us and opened all the doors to look inside. Such a rude man.'

Willy dozed through the morning and she came back in the middle of the day with a bowl of soup and a flat wooden box. She watched him drink the soup in silence.

In his delirium he had lived through wild dreams of her, accelerated years of life together in bewildering conjunctions. The detail had fled but left deep footprints all around his head. He could only focus on what had really happened and that gave him an overwhelming desire to tell her all his secrets. He wanted her to know how he had relied on her image to get him through these past months, how often he had looked at the photo and the sketch and the central part they had played in the life force that made it possible to think the phrase 'after the war' even when he knew he should not.

He could say none of that because standing there across the way to it was that other larger secret — the implacable facts of Claude's end. It silenced him.

She opened the wooden box. 'You need to do a little work now if you are able,' she said, 'in case the Germans come inside.' She took a letter out of the box and passed it to him. 'Victor has borrowed this from our neighbour Mathis. He was a soldier and he was captured when they seized Andenne. They released him to work the farm although he has lost one arm so his poor wife has to work very hard. This is their letter of permission.'

Willy looked at the letter, hand-written in Gothic script and stamped with a military stamp. 'What can I do?'

'You can write a letter like that for you. To protect you if they come. You speak German. I know you do. You were shouting in German as well as English in the nights. Can you write like they do? I have a pen and ink here.'

'Yes, but what about the paper? Look, do you see? If you hold it up it has a German eagle stamped into it.'

'Yes, I do see, but they are too efficient for their own good,' she said with a smile of satisfaction. 'They give us receipts for the eggs they buy and look at this, they use exactly the same military paper. We found two written in pencil and we have rubbed the words out.'

'And the stamp?'

'You just write the letter. Victor knows a man who is good with stamps. Farmers sometimes need such helpers.'

'And what name shall I write?'

'Isn't that obvious? You must be Claude Tavernier of course.'

Of course.

Within an hour, they had a very convincing document saying that Claude Tavernier had been released from the Coblenz Lazarett prison hospital for the purpose of returning to the Pont-Veld Hoeve to produce food for German war needs. The stamp had been carved from an old potato but only a man with a good microscope and some knowledge of potatoes would have been able to tell. 'I hope we do not need it,' said Helene as they showed it to her.

Willy lay in bed through the afternoon feeling the strength flowing back into him and reliving all those startling moments with Gabrielle until his memory had blurred them too much. He kept flexing his left arm, getting the muscles working, feeling the tight pull of the healing gash. The leg was another matter altogether. He levered himself up out of bed and persuaded it to move but it complained violently. He clung to the end of the bed, white-faced, then let go and lifted his foot to take a first step. When Gabrielle came in as the daylight faded, carrying a candle for him, she found him sweating in determination through a long series of knee bends.

'There is no point in telling you to stop, I suppose?'

'Thirty more, then I'm done,' he said. 'But please, if you have time now, sit and talk to me while I finish. It will distract me and there is so much I want to know.'

'What sort of thing?'

'Anything, like where do you come from originally?'

'My family you mean? Why?'

'I don't know. It seems to matter.' It matters because I don't want you to go away, he thought, and I do want to know everything there is to know.

'My father was Belgian. He was born in the city of Louvain, you may know it as Leuven, in a house close by the River Dijle but I never knew it and I don't suppose there is anything left of that now.' They both knew Louvain had fallen to the invading Germans and its medieval treasures had been gutted by fire.

'So where were you brought up?'

'In France but only just — outside a little town called Joeuf on the edge of the parts of Lorraine that the Germans stole forty years ago. That was where my mother was born. They met when my father moved there to work because I suppose I have to admit, with great embarrassment, that my father was one of those who helped to make Germany so hideously strong.'

'Your father helped Germany?'

'Yes. Don't sound so indignant. He was only a

very minor player. He was nothing compared to your two countrymen.'

'What are you talking about?'

'I am talking about the rise of Krupp and the creation of the military might of Germany.'

'And you're saying *my* countrymen are somehow responsible?'

'You do not know of Thomas and Gilchrist?' She pronounced the names 'Toe-mah' and 'Jeel-creest' then tried to say them again more in the English way but in the end she spelt them out for him, sighing when she saw that Willy still looked mystified. 'You should surely have heard of them,' she said. 'You came from the same place.'

'I don't know about that,' he said. 'They sound English to me and no, I have never heard of them. Why do they matter?'

'Germany was such a poor country once,' she said. 'The German soil was sandy and acid. Their iron ore was terrible, useless stuff. The English sorted it out. They invented a way to take the phosphorus out of the ore to improve the iron and that same phosphorus went into the ground to improve the soil. Krupp make strong steel today because of those two men.'

'You know a lot about it.'

'For a girl? Is that what you mean?'

'Yes.'

'Hah. My father was a chemist at the Joeuf factory. He would take us for walks through the mines and the chimneys and tell us what lay under the ground. You know about the Lorraine layer? No? Really?'

379

'No.'

'You are a very ignorant man. It is a huge deposit of iron ore. It goes all the way into Luxembourg and it transformed Germany once they had stolen all that land and of course once your people had done their bit to help. My father was most unhappy with his part in it.'

'Stop saying 'my people'. And I'm not ignorant, just because I have never heard of two obscure Sassenach chemists. What happened to your parents? You said they died?'

'They were killed.'

'I'm sorry.'

'My parents did not long outlive my Claude. Papa had retired to Namur. He would not leave. He took a rifle made with Krupp's steel and loaded it with bullets made by Krupp and then he shot three German soldiers dead from the window of his house. I am told they killed him immediately as a *franctireur* and I think he probably did not mind that, but then they shot my mother too for good measure and perhaps she did not mind that either.'

'You have had to deal with a lot of death.'

She surprised him by smiling as if she seemed to find that idea funny. 'We are not short of it, you and me or anyone else who was born to live in this place in this time. But, William Fraser, there is no point in dwelling on it, not when it is all around us. Grieving has its time but after that, we must always smile in death's face and seize hold of life instead because otherwise death wins. I think you must know that surely, a man like you.'

'Yes,' he said, reaching one hundred and sitting back on the bed gratefully with a leg that howled in reproach. He lay back down, gazing at her. Twilight was on them and the last of the sun was coming in from the west, highlighting the side of her face in curves of extraordinary beauty. He saw Claude sprawling in blood-stained mud and searched between the two for some way of being that answered to both.

Responsibility fought with something altogether softer in his head. 'Where will you go when all this is over?' he said. 'Will you stay here, do you think?'

'Here? Will there be a *here*? I think there is no point in guessing how this will end and I am a little surprised that you think it worth asking. If I am free to decide then, no, I will not stay here. And what about you?'

Until that moment, Willy had thought of Gilfillan and Morag as home but never of the castle itself. Grannoch was a heartless place and, but for Gilfillan, his mother was welcome to it. That felt abruptly different. In a single heart-bursting flash, he saw himself taking Gabrielle back there, seeing it through her eyes with the beauty of the sunlight on the hills, smelling the heather through her nose, hearing her breathe light and laughter into those cold stones. He saw Gilfillan welcoming her and Morag, a little slower to accept, studying her impassively before breaking into a small and cautious smile.

'As you said, I think there is no point in

imagining that,' he lied and responsibility came back — his two-year debt to Claude which was surely not to be repaid in so treacherous a manner.

'I have more work to do,' she said and when she had gone he found a pencil and a sheet of paper among the books on her table and he began to draw.

He must have dozed because it was dark when he woke again to find her sitting beside the bed, gazing at him. There were three candles flickering around the bed sending shadows dancing in the animal smell of tallow. She put her hand on his forehead and smiled. 'No fever,' she said quietly, holding his gaze.

'I'll get up later,' he replied. 'My leg needs more exercise.'

'There have been Germans here again,' she said. 'They will not let Victor in to the barn. He says they have brought wood and nails and canvas in barrows and now they have put everything out of sight and pulled a great tarpaulin over the barn roof. It is painted to look like the tiles — they even painted the damaged part to make it look as if it is a hole still. He wants me to ask you if you have any idea what they might be doing.'

'I don't like the sound of that,' he said. 'The disguise means they don't want our aircraft to notice anything different if they fly over and take photographs. They compare them, you see? Anything that has changed would stand out. That must mean they are planning to use your barn for something that we wouldn't like.'

'What is this?' she said and held out his drawing.

'I'm sorry. I should have asked you.'

'I can spare you one sheet. Did you see? It has a poem on the back. I wrote it down from memory last week before you came. I think I had a premonition.'

'Why?'

'It is by Charles Baudelaire. Do you know it? *L'Etranger?*'

'No.'

'*Qui aimes-tu le mieux, homme énigmatique, dis? Ton père, ta mère, ta soeur ou ton frère?* I think you are that *homme énigmatique.*'

'Does he answer?'

'He says he has neither father, mother, sister nor brother.'

'He sounds lost.'

'No, there is something he loves.'

'What is it?'

'*Les nuages . . . les nuages qui passent . . . là-bas . . . là-bas . . . les merveilleux nuages!*'

'The clouds?'

'Yes. You must have seen many clouds up there in your balloon. Are they not marvellous?'

Marvellous for hiding if you're an Albatros, he thought. 'Of course they are,' he said.

She turned the paper over again. 'So what is this place you have drawn. Is it a *château?*'

'That's my house in Scotland.'

'All of it?'

'It is quite large.'

'It is beautiful.'

He was surprised. He had never drawn it as

beautiful before. Perhaps, he thought with surprise, he had never drawn it at all — only the view from the turret of the surrounding wilderness that, with luck, might one day dismantle it.

'And who are these two people walking towards the door. I can only see their backs but I think they are young. Are they holding hands? Is this you and your girl?'

'My girl? No, I have no girl. Who knows? It is just two people.'

There was a shout from outside in the yard and it brought them both back from Scotland to this immediate danger.

'What did you mean when you said the Germans might use the barn for something we wouldn't like?' she asked. 'What sort of something?'

'Military stores,' he said but the word in his head was 'ammunition'. It proved to be worse than that.

'I will be downstairs. Knock with this stick if you want me. Shall I blow out your candles?'

In the early morning, a window-rattling explosion had him rearing up in bed, a loving dream evaporating into the flame-splashed room. He levered himself out of bed, wincing at the stiffness in his leg, and limped to the small dormer window that looked out across the road and the field beyond towards the distant rise that hid the lines. He heard querulous voices out on the landing. His first thought was that some random shell from a long-range gun had wandered badly off course but he saw a large fire in the middle of what had been an empty muddy field where there should be nothing to burn.

The moon was high and the field was bright and he could see fragments of an aeroplane scattered around the flames, including a whole tail section, broken off and far enough from the blaze to have survived intact. He was horrified to see that the rudder carried an RFC cockade. Beginning to pull on his clothes with some desperate idea of rescue, he heard engine noises approaching and saw a German staff car swerve into the field.

Watching intently, he was aware of Gabrielle coming in to the room, with Helene and Victor after her. He made space for them to look out, each in turn. 'It's one of ours,' he said. 'Looks to me like a BE2, judging by the tail. Two-seater. They don't usually fly at night. What the hell did he think he was doing?'

'Coming to fetch you?' suggested Gabrielle.

'Impossible. How would anyone know where to come? Anyway, who would be mad enough?'

24

Nobody in 4 Squadron *was* mad enough to fly one of their old BEs into an unknown field the wrong side of the lines in darkness but there had been someone else listening to a discussion with interest in the Abeele aerodrome mess hut. Lieutenant George McIntyre of 29 Squadron was kicking his heels in enforced idleness because the engine of his little Airco DH2 scout had packed up in mid-air on the way home to his own airfield, leaving Abeele the only aerodrome within gliding distance. The overworked mechanics there already had enough on their plates and kept promising they would sort out his fuel feed as soon as time allowed but time had not yet allowed. He had tasted their wine supplies, played all three tunes he knew on their piano and read last week's London papers from cover to cover so the unexpected arrival of a noisy American newsman surrounded by half a dozen questioning pilots was just what he needed to alleviate his boredom.

'How exactly do you know your man is holed up in this particular farm?' asked the adjutant. 'Do explain.'

'The Queen of Belgium told me,' said Chester with a tone of infinite gravity. 'She has a very soft spot for this guy. She made enquiries. I had a kind of rough idea where it was. She found out the rest.'

'But as I understand it, Mr Hoffman, you *are* only guessing,' said the adjutant. He had grey hair and his flying days had ended when he pranged a Shorthorn in '14 but he felt a need to protect the young men under his wing and he could see nothing but trouble on this particular front.

'It's a very good guess. If he survived the burning of his balloon, that has got to be where he went. I'm damned sure of it.'

'Because?'

'Because of a great story that you can read all about when we print it in *The Sentinel*. I'll be sure to send you guys a copy when it's public. Get your fingers out from under your butts, gentlemen. The man's a hero. He needs saving. I can guarantee I'll make the man who saves him a hero too.'

'I'll do it,' said a tiny pilot who looked all of sixteen. 'Sounds quite jolly.'

'When exactly?' said the adjutant. 'Monty, you're on spotting duty at first light. So is the rest of the squadron. Every plane that can fly except Hideous Hilda. There's absolutely no way that the Old Man will let you and he's not due back from Wing until take-off time so in his absence, I'm afraid I have to say no. No pilot from this squadron is to attempt this.'

'Then I'll do it,' said McIntyre and enjoyed seeing all their heads swivel towards him.

'And who exactly are you?' asked the adjutant. 'Oh, I know. You're the glamour boy with the broken Airco scout. First problem, as I say, it's broken. Second problem is that last time I

387

looked, a DH2 was a single-seater.'

'Just lend me one of your BEs,' said McIntyre, 'and I'll go over in the moonlight.'

'As I just told you, I don't have any BEs to spare. We have duties for the whole squadron from first light.'

'But, Adj,' said little Monty. 'As you said yourself, there's always Hideous Hilda. She's only slightly hideous really. No one's flying *her* tomorrow.'

'That's because you all still have a fingertip hold on sanity.'

Chester K. Hoffman walked over to McIntyre and pumped his hand. 'The Queen's going to give you a medal for this, young fellow,' he said. 'She and I will be very grateful.'

'Would that be the Queen Elisabeth Medal perhaps?' asked the adjutant. 'I think that's the only one she can actually hand out herself.'

'Then I guess that's the one.'

'Well in that case I should probably tell you that it's for nursing. She gives it to girls for sewing people up but I suppose a scout-jockey might be grateful for whatever he could get.'

'Sounds good enough to me,' said McIntyre, 'so long as a nurse comes with it.'

'Have you ever flown a BE?' the adjutant asked him.

'I was born flying a BE.'

And that was why, just before five in the morning, George McIntyre was grappling with an ancient, slow and completely unfamiliar aircraft of a type he despised and which he had never even sat in before take-off. It flew nose high unless he pushed the stick hard forward all the time and it crabbed right unless he kept one foot hard on the rudder pedal. He lurched through the darkness towards a field somewhere in occupied Belgium with a fierce and defiant grin on his oil-smeared face. George had no idea if this was how they always felt but thought on balance, probably not. He also didn't know what sort of noise a BE engine was meant to make but he was fairly sure it wasn't the intermittent screeching rumble he was hearing now. As pilots were fond of saying, any fool can take off — it's the last foot of coming down again that sorts out the men from the corpses. His take-off, down an improvised path of paraffin flares, had been interesting. The Airco always bounded up into the air but the BE 'Hideous Hilda' with serial letter H on its side had kept dropping back to terra firma in a series of violent bounces, the last one of which only just cleared the hedge. Take-offs — one, landings — zero, he thought. How difficult could it possibly be?

The adjutant had mixed feelings, watching him go. Getting rid of the worst plane in the squadron was a definite plus and McIntyre wasn't under his charge but he had a feeling that a lot of paperwork might follow this particular take-off. Until the last moment, it seemed the American newspaperman had been under the misapprehension that he was going too but when they explained that the old BE could barely be expected to struggle back into the air with two on board, let alone three, he gave up with a very good grace and made sure that McIntyre thoroughly understood whereabouts on the map he was headed.

McIntyre was a good navigator and he had pored over the map with Chester before taking off. He didn't have too far to go and there were quite a few signposts on the way. Dikkebusch Lake was exactly on his track and that was shining in the moonlight. After that it was simple enough. The six huge mine craters that had blasted the German defences to pieces last summer at St Eloi stood out, sockets of missing teeth, shining in the mud of the lines. The war was stirring sleepily below him. The moonlight was keeping the raiding and the wiring parties in their trenches. Nobody was wandering in No Man's Land. He saw glimpses of pale faces as sentries lifted their heads to look up at him, mystified by a night-flying BE, then he was past. After that he followed the line of the lanes he had memorized from Chester's map, looking for a farm that stood right on the road. He saw it ahead, scanned the fields around it to choose one for his landing then all at once he didn't have any choice at all because he closed the throttle much too quickly and the BE's engine did what they always did under such provocation. It cut out completely with one last backfiring bang.

George was the son of a vicar and was still disturbed by profanity on some deep childhood level but he yelled something he was immediately ashamed of. He would now have to try to fix a completely unfamiliar plane once he had landed. Adding to that, he would have to find a man who might or might not be at the farm over the road. A moment later those concerns ceased to apply because the plane fell out of the air and bounced hard. When it hit the ground again it ran into a drainage ditch George hadn't seen and cartwheeled, hurling him violently into the ground before the wreckage exploded into flame.

★ ★ ★

From the bedroom under the roof, Willy could listen to the German soldiers talking in the road just below.

'So much for our sleep,' said one. 'Old Rubber-lips is talking about searching the whole area.'

'Why? They've got the pilot and he's as good as dead.'

'It's a two-seater. Where's the other one gone? That's what the Feldwebel said over there. It could be a spy, he said.'

'Tell him to do the searching then.'

'You tell him. He's quick with his fists, that one.'

The flames had died. 'Back to our beds,' said Helene when Willy translated. 'Gabrielle, you stay in here.'

Victor bristled but she spoke sharply to him in Flemish and he followed her out.

Willy and Gabrielle stared at each other from opposite sides of the bed in the moonlight. It painted her face in silver and grey and for a moment she looked just like his pencil drawing. She took in a deep, shuddering breath and opened her mouth. 'It is for realism,' she said. 'They must believe in the papers you have made. Do not . . . '

She got no further. There was a violent beating on the yard door. They heard men shouting and footsteps going down the stairs then uproar in the room below. Victor's voice was raised and a German voice was yelling over him. Gabrielle slipped in to the bed. 'Quick,' she said, 'get in,' lifting the covers for him. Half of him was on full alert, listening to the sounds from below, racing through a limited array of possible responses. The other half was amazed by the intimate warmth of her body through her thin cotton nightdress.

'They will search the house. When they come up here, just remember you are Claude.'

They lay there, listening, lying side by side and only inches apart. The old bed tried its best to roll them together in its central dip but Willy found himself resisting that as much as he could. They heard Victor below, still complaining away at the top of his voice, then heavy feet climbed the stairs, a door opened close by and Helene's voice demanded what right they had to barge into a woman's bedroom.

'Hold me,' hissed Gabrielle and turned to him. He put his injured arm around her and she nestled against him so that despite the enemy at the door, he could only think of her and her scent and her body against his. As their door knob began to turn, Gabrielle wriggled right over on top of him, kissing him then looking round in astonished indignation as the door burst open.

'Who are you?' she yelled at the German officer in the doorway with a soldier behind him. 'Go away. Get out of our room.' She rolled back off Willy and sat up, gathering the bedclothes around her. 'You think it is all right to come in here like that? We are entitled to our privacy, my husband and I.'

The German officer was a young man, covering up uncertainty with an attempt at haughtiness. 'You will excuse me,' he said. 'I have instructions to search this house. I must look under your bed.'

'Under our bed? Why? There is nothing there but old rags and dust.' She let the bedclothes slip an inch or two and the German's eyes swivelled to the swell of her breasts revealed under the thin nightdress. 'Please look, then go. Not at me. How dare you. Under there.' He turned pink, bent down quickly and after a moment's inspection, left the room as fast as he could, closing the door carefully behind him, clattering back downstairs.

Willy thought for a moment that Gabrielle was crying but realized she was stifling giggles.

'I'm sorry,' she said. 'Are you shocked? It seemed the best thing.'

'Shocked?' Oh no, not at all.' Shock, he realized, was entirely the wrong word for what he had felt. 'It was very quick thinking.'

'I had to do something. Your uniform is down there on the floor. He was too embarrassed to know what he was looking at.'

'Wow. Do you think he will come back?'

'I hope so,' she said then put her hand to her

mouth and turned a little pink. She got quickly out of the bed, looking away from him, and he watched her go out, giving no further thought whatsoever to the German officer's visit.

He was woken in the morning light by Victor who came up the stairs, clogs banging on the treads, and stopped in the doorway speaking rapid Flemish to Helene. They both came into the bedroom.

'Victor says he has seen the same officer who came yesterday,' said Helene. 'He spent a long time in the barn, making notes in his little book and pacing out its length and its width. He has told Victor he must not go outside the house at all. Some story about a dangerous deserter who has shot a German officer. Victor is not at all happy about any of it.'

'A deserter? I do hope so,' said Willy. 'If I see him, I'll shake him by the hand.'

There was a place in the corner of the bedroom where he could stand on the chair with Gabrielle steadying him and push up a tile to peer across at the barn roof. A German soldier in overalls was sitting on the roof with the tarpaulin rolled back. He was working away at something and at least twice a minute he would take a long look around at the sky, watching for aircraft. Willy could not make out what he was doing but every half an hour, he climbed up to take another look and around mid-afternoon, he suddenly understood. They were building a long hatchway, a sliding section of the roof which could be pulled back to leave an aperture.

'Do you know what it is?' Gabrielle asked. She

had her hands raised to his waist, supporting him and though his leg was stronger now, he didn't tell her he could manage by himself.

He climbed down. 'I have an idea,' he said. 'If I am right then you really will have to leave.'

'What is your idea?'

He wasn't ready to say but he was fairly sure they were building a hide-away for a very big gun.

His suspicions were confirmed that evening. When darkness fell in late afternoon after a day in which he had forced his leg back towards working order by repeated exercises, trucks began to arrive with scores of men. Engines racketed away as they mixed tons of cement, wheeling barrow-loads inside the barn. Helene, Victor and Gabrielle clustered in the bedroom upstairs, taking turns to look out through the gap in the tiles.

'Telling us to stay inside indeed,' said Helene indignantly. 'In our very own farm, just as if it was theirs.'

Victor issued short, stabbing bursts of Flemish that made Helene cross herself almost constantly.

'We should sleep now,' she said. 'We will need it later.' She and Victor left the room and Gabrielle lingered for a moment, looking at their retreating backs heading into their bedroom and then at Willy with a question in her eyes. He longed for her to stay but was horrified by what that would bring with it. She seemed to find an answer for herself, pouted her lips in what might have been the sign of a kiss and went out, closing the door behind her.

He lay back, exploring her image in his mind, acutely aware that she was getting into her bed just the other side of that thin wall but he was exhausted and the body's natural processes of recovery brought deep sleep to Willy despite the noise outside. When he finally woke and pushed away the waves of grogginess, it was full daylight and he climbed on the chair to see what his ears had already told him. There were still Germans in the yard and judging by the light, it had to be well into the afternoon. Sleep had done his leg a great deal of good. He lay back on the bed, listening to the activity and realizing it was slowly dying down. Trucks were arriving one by one and he could hear the workers climbing on board. When he heard nothing more for a while, he climbed up again and saw Gabrielle, Victor and Helene walking cautiously across the deserted yard. He dressed himself in shirt, trousers and the German greatcoat and hobbled downstairs. Gabrielle was keeping watch at the gate and she turned, protesting, but he ignored her and limped towards the barn. Victor and Helene were staring at the floor of the barn, now half filled by a rectangular bed of concrete from which a series of thick steel rods poked upwards with screw threads cut into them. Gabrielle joined them as Willy inspected the concrete structure.

'Yes,' he said. 'I was afraid of that. Some sort of very big gun is coming in here. You see? They pull the hatch in the roof open, raise the muzzle to fire then they close it again if any of our planes come snooping over to take a look. Just a barn, nothing else as far as the outside world is concerned. They'll only shoot at night so the balloons won't see it. It's on the extreme end of our range of vision anyway.'

Helene translated for Victor and his response sent her into a frenzy of chest crossing.

'So much for our sleep then,' said Gabrielle.

'Oh come on. You simply can't stay here. It would be far too dangerous. At some point we will find it.'

'And then?'

'And then we will shoot back to destroy it with everything we've got or we will send acroplanes to bomb it. Either way, nobody here will stand a chance. Please, you have to listen to me.'

'Do you think they have left the other barn alone?' said Helene. 'What about the chickens?'

They crossed the yard and went inside. The chickens were clucking and shuffling in their wired cages. The heap of hay looked untouched. Victor poked around in the corner, inspecting a pile of old farm machinery as if the Germans might have stolen some.

'We will have to be very careful about you with so many Germans around,' said Helene. 'They will be here at all hours of day and night from now on, will they not? You do not look very Belgian, Monsieur Fraser. They might guess that you are a Scotchman.'

The three of them swung round as Victor yelped. They saw him step back from the machinery with his hands up. A German soldier came out from behind it with a pistol in his hand. 'You will tell her no doubt that the correct term is Scotsman not Scotch,' he said to Willy in perfect English. 'Please do not move, any of you.'

Willy froze, staring at him, noting that he wore officer's uniform. He knew he could not move anywhere near fast enough to jump him.

'Now please stand together where I can see you all while we discuss this most unusual situation. I have been waiting here for you for quite some time.' He turned to Willy. 'You are wearing a German coat with what appear to be English trousers underneath it. I wonder to which branch of the services you belong? You are indeed Scottish, are you?'

'You know very well I am,' said Willy.

Gabrielle said, 'Tell us what he is saying, please.'

Willy answered her in French. 'He is the deserter. German officers do not hide in barns by themselves to capture men like me. They send a squad of soldiers and watch from somewhere safe.'

The German smiled. 'It will be easier for everyone if I speak French. Yes. If you want to call me that, I *am* a deserter. I would prefer you to know that I have always been cursed by my father's nationality and only joined his army under the pressure of family expectations. I'm afraid my mother was not a Scot, Mr Fraser, but she was at least an Englishwoman and I feel more and more English every day. I was educated at Rugby and at Oxford and I think you will find that you already know my name.'

25

'What does he mean? How can *you* know anything about *him?* Do you believe him?' demanded Helene.

'As it happens, I do,' said Willy. 'This man's name is Otto and last time we met was in the Thomas Cook office in Berlin where he behaved magnificently. The time before that, he was on the other side in a cricket match, bowling rather well.'

'And if I may add one more encounter that I suspect you have forgotten,' said the German, 'we once hunted together with the Heythrop. I do like to remember my more English moments but I suspect Fraser may have forgotten because he had his mind on other quarry at the time.'

'Oh how perfect,' said Gabrielle. 'We already had one dangerous madman who must not be found here. Now we have two.'

'You are quite sure he is a deserter and this is not some trick?' said Helene.

'Yes, I am,' said Willy.

'Then let us go back into the house where it is a little safer.'

There was a cellar underneath the hall and Victor and Helene had disguised its entrance ingeniously in the early days of the war before the German army reached them, fearing the invaders would seize their valuables. Now Helene slid a hidden latch open and they lifted a wide trapdoor with irregular edges cut to look like the normal staggered joints of floorboards. The only valuables Willy could see in the gloom down below were racks of cobwebbed bottles and sealed glass jars of Helene's terrines but there was a space on the floor for the straw mattress leaning against the shelves and Otto nodded as he looked down at it.

'Absolutely splendid,' he said. 'Positively palatial one might almost say.'

Victor had his old rifle raised, pointing at the German's stomach, and he barked Flemish words at him.

'My husband wishes to know exactly why you deserted and why you came here,' Helene said. 'He also says that your answer must satisfy him if he is to let you survive. He does have a point, I think.'

'It is no coincidence that I came here,' said Otto. 'I had already arrived at a new conclusion about which side I should be fighting for. My Colonel was an absolute swine. He gave Prussians a bad name. We took some prisoners last week, Maorilanders. You call them Kiwis now, don't you? Brave lads. They raided our trenches and had a spot of bad luck. I was set to question them because of my English skills but he shot two of them in the head because they refused to answer his own questions. That was not at all surprising as he was shouting at them in German. When the aeroplane crashed here they brought the poor pilot to our headquarters up the road. Even our doctor, who is at best a most unkind man, said it was unacceptable to

400

interrogate him but the Colonel insisted.'

'The poor man could talk?'

'He could barely whisper and he was half delirious with the pain but the doctor would give him no morphine until the interrogation was over. The Colonel was convinced he had brought over a spy or perhaps come to collect one, you see.'

'The pilot told you something?'

'He gave me his name. He was called McIntyre, a Scot like Fraser here. He would say nothing else but then his reason began to slip away and he whispered to me that he had come to the farmhouse to collect me, that an American had sent him and so had the Queen of Belgium because they had worked out where I was hiding. His whisper was so faint that I had to hold my ear almost against his mouth. He called me Taverner. He told me I must get into the aeroplane with him and help to pedal it. The Colonel came back into the room and demanded to know what I had discovered and I told him nothing. The Colonel beat McIntyre on his injured chest with his swagger stick. I tried to stop him and he pushed me out of the way and so I took out my pistol and shot him. It seemed by far the best solution. I wish I had done it much earlier. You see, I may have been christened Otto Ebener Neumann but my mother called me Freddy and I have always felt much more like a Freddy somehow. I would really like to be Freddy Newman from now on. A new man in every way.'

'So in that case, why did you ever join the

German army?' Helene sounded unconvinced.

'Oh dear me. My mother died, you see. Life was good until then. She had left my father, so until I was twelve I lived with her in Wimborne Minster. Dorset, you know. A lovely part of England. Very quiet. When she died I had to go to live with my father in Munich. No choice at all, though I still went to school and to university in England. When the war broke out I joined the army to get away from him as much as anything else. I really thought nothing much would happen unless the French did something stupid. Do you know, they actually told us we were going to the French border because the French planned to invade us? Of course I knew it was Belgium as soon as we got there but the Generals kept telling the men they were in France. Would you believe it? So now here's a fine how-do-you-do. I've chosen to hide in a nice quiet farm that is about to be turned into a very noisy gun emplacement crawling with my former countrymen who would dearly like to shoot me. What do you suggest we do, Fraser? I don't really feel like giving myself up. The firing squad just doesn't appeal.'

'I suggest you stay down in the cellar,' said Willy. 'Don't come out unless we come to get you.' He looked questioningly at the others.

Helene nodded slowly. 'If you are convinced then that is enough for me.'

Victor lowered his gun.

'Just pop down there with me for a moment, would you?' said Otto to Willy in English.

Willy followed him down the ladder, pleased

that his leg allowed him to. 'What is it?' he said quietly.

'Time is very pressing, I fear,' said Otto. 'At headquarters they have a list of tasks and near the top of that task is a further investigation of the inhabitants of this now rather important house and a careful check of all their papers. Whether or not they find me, your presence here puts both you and them in immediate danger.'

'Will they come today?'

'Not today, I think. I left a false trail. That will keep them busy looking for me for some time yet but tomorrow, the next day. Who knows?'

'We could both hide down here.'

'When they come back, they will bring dogs. Being down here will make no difference.' Otto sat down on the floor. 'I confess I am too tired to think well. I need to sleep now then I will have a clearer head.'

They closed the trapdoor on him and Gabrielle beckoned Willy into the parlour. Helene took Victor away upstairs. He was grumbling.

'This gets more and more dangerous,' said Gabrielle quietly, facing him. The last of the daylight was fading and he could not see the expression in her eyes.

'Yes. I think I will have to take him away.'

'And go where? I don't know anyone who can help you. Can you get to the Dutch border, do you suppose?'

'I don't know yet.'

'There is something else he said that I do not understand. He said the pilot was sent by an

403

American and by the Queen of Belgium. Was the poor pilot out of his mind?'

'No. Not completely. I can see how that might be true.'

'So he was coming to find you?'

'I'm afraid he was.'

'In that case why by all the heavens did he say he was coming for someone called *Tavernier*?'

'No, not Tavernier. He said an English name. Taverner.'

'The same. Do not try to tell me that is a coincidence. He came to find a man called Taverner and you are Fraser but it was you he came for. You must tell me why.'

So they sat down side by side with a vast and complex tension keeping them apart and pulling them together and he finally found a great relief in explaining. He told Gabrielle in slow and loving detail how much Claude had meant to him, how Claude's death had freed him to return to his own army and inspired him in everything he did. He told how he was forced to give up his rank and choose a new name and how very natural it had been to become Claud Taverner. He still could not admit the depth of the place her pictures had carved into his life and the way he had used them as a crutch, nor the far more difficult detail of Claude's death.

At the end, she simply nodded silently, took his hand and they stared at each other, inches apart in the utterly dark room. She stood up and lit candles and as she turned away, he could see the shine of tears on her cheeks. She called Helene and Victor down from upstairs and they heated the iron pot of vegetable soup which stood on the stove and then, as the first lorry announced the arrival of the German work squads in the yard, Helene urged Willy and Gabrielle upstairs. Helene stopped on the landing and muttered something unintelligible to Gabrielle. Victor lifted his head, about to speak, but Helene caught him off with a sharp reply. Willy closed the bedroom door behind him, put down his candle, took off his shoes and got in to bed, fully clothed and ready for anything, but what he wasn't ready for was Gabrielle coming in after him and slipping into the bed.

'Helene's orders,' she said. 'She says it will raise questions if I am found to be sleeping outside there and not in here with my husband.'

Willy stared at her beside him. She had changed into a long cotton shift. She pinched out the candle and he could hear Claude's disconcerting voice in his head, intoning those same words that Willy had so often used to lecture him. 'Live in the present. Think only of the war. Don't just see. Look. Don't just hear. Listen.' In this present he was living in, Gabrielle's warmth radiated across the narrow space between them, Gabrielle's scent drifted to his nose. Her face was only inches from his and her eyes were wide open, shining in the moonlight. She traced a finger down the side of his cheek, then moved that last, small, inevitable distance towards him and kissed him on the mouth. She pulled back a moment later and her face showed dismay. 'Have I shocked you?' she whispered. 'I felt you go away from me. Don't

405

you feel what I feel?'

'What about them?' Willy whispered back.

'Don't think about them now.'

'I can't help it. They're right next door.'

'Listen to me. Helene gave us her blessing when she sent me in here. She will pay for it in Hail Marys when she next sees the priest.' Willy stayed silent and Gabrielle gave a small sad smile. 'She talked to me this evening. She sees everything, Helene. She said she believed that Claude had sent you here from the place he is in now. She said Claude knew you for the sort of man you are and knew that you and I would find some happiness in each other now that everything has been changed for us.'

She kissed him on the forehead and when her body moulded against him for a moment, his heart wanted him to wrap his arms around her and blow this kindling into a full flame. A part of him he didn't know he had and had never used before stopped him.

'I can't forget Claude,' he said.

'Oh.' She rolled away. 'You think I am a heartless hussy? You think *I* can ever forget him? William Fraser, let me tell you how this is for me. I have mourned my dear, dear Claude for two whole years now and perhaps in fine society in a time of peace that would not be nearly enough. This is *not* fine society. This is a farm where life goes on and the ruder forms of nature remind us of that every day. Not just that, my wondrously stupid William Fraser, but it is a farm in time of war, where every time I open my ears to it, I hear the massive noise of men dying brought to me on the wind and so time and love take on a different meaning. Don't think the death factory you inhabit has not reached its bony finger back to touch us too. So I want to feel love again while I am alive and at this precious moment I feel I do love you, William Fraser. I also know that you must leave this place somehow and very soon, though I do not know how. All my hope is that the world will turn to a point where you will be able to come back and that you will choose to do so. I pray that you and I will both be alive for that moment. Then we will sort out if anything happens between us next. Do you understand me? Am I making sense?'

He nodded.

'Now listen to me. It is not for us to know whether that time will come and I would not have you go away from here without loving you in the fullest way that this one short night can allow us, so please can you not just be glad that the doors are closed? What do you say to me, because there is only me and you in this world of ours and we should live in this moment? Will you love me?'

'Gabrielle,' he said and his arm went round her and she nestled against him, craning her head back as she did so to study his face. 'I have thought about you for a long, long time.'

'You have? How long? These few days? Oh come now, you were raving for most of them.'

'Far longer than that and yes, I am astonished to be with you because I do indeed . . . ' She waited but the other words would not come.

407

'But what? Is there some God wagging his finger at you?' she demanded. 'Did your mother warn you about foreign women? Am I too short? Too tall? Too thin? I am certainly not too fat.'

'No, you are not too . . . ' and that was as far as he got before she slid herself over him and kissed him urgently. Her fingers teased open the buttons on his shirt then pulled at the waist of his trousers. Her mouth smothered any objections he might have made.

Later they stared at each other, stunned and a world away from enemies and death. He sensed she was waiting for him to speak and he wanted to tell her of this entirely new feeling inside him, so different to anything he had felt with all those previous women that it was like comparing a symphony to a wavering solo. He discovered he still could not say it because there were three of them in the room. Claude's ghost was in his head. He took one arm from round her and reached behind him, holding the brass rail of the bed head. He found himself tapping out the message he could not speak, the way he used to practice Morse code back in training, one finger for a dot, two fingers together for a dash. She frowned, listened, looked up at his hand in the dim light and sat up abruptly.

'He did not tell you about that,' she said. 'He would not have.'

'About what?'

'About tapping.'

'What do you mean?' he asked as a faint memory resurfaced.

She looked at him and her eyes seemed huge

408

and shining then she sighed and lay back down away from him. She lay absolutely still for a time then gave another big sigh and turned to nestle against him. 'I think he is happy for us,' she said quietly. 'He made you do that.'

'Tell me.'

'When we first knew each other, before we were married, we had to stay with my parents. We had separate bedrooms of course, very proper, but the wall between us was nothing but thin board. At night he would tap on it just as you did, one finger or two fingers to make a different sound and I learnt to tap back. Weeks of tapping. When we were tired and our fingers were sore we would sleep but we would always finish with three letters, J and T and A for 'je t'aime'. Then we would sleep.'

'Ah.'

'I know what you tapped,' she said. 'I can still remember the letters. You tapped two dots which is 'I' then you tapped dot-dash-dot-dot which is 'L' and last you tapped dash-dot-dash-dash which is 'Y'. If you want to say it to me instead, Willy Fraser, I would like to hear your voice say it as well as your fingers. It is quite all right. You should be brave now.'

But he found it was not all right, not with Claude's ghost and the unshriven memory of that calvary flood beside the Yser River.

'There is something I want to say to you,' he said, 'but there is also something I have to tell you before that.'

'Then tell me quickly before dawn arrives and we have wasted the rest of this whole night.'

A brutal sentence hovered and he hunted for softer words but none came. 'Gabrielle. I killed Claude.'

'You mean you took him into danger? No, that was war. You had no choice. If he had stayed he would have died anyway, so would you both.'

'I don't mean that. I mean that I took out my pistol and I shot him dead because I had to. You see? You see why I can't . . . '

She sat up sharply, stared at him in horror then got out of bed and left the room, and he lay there looking at the door as it closed behind her, wishing this unknown voice in him had not insisted on the truth.

★ ★ ★

At some point much later in the night Helene knocked and came in. He was still fretting with it, turning it all over and over in his head, wondering if he could somehow mend it. There was plenty going on out in the farmyard, men moving and voices calling instructions, but he had paid it no attention.

'Is Gabrielle . . . ?'

'She is in our room,' Helene said. 'Asleep now in the other bed. I gave her some cognac. I will not ask you what has happened because I am quite sure there is no simple answer. Young man, I would have liked to say there is time for you both to resolve it but I fear there is not.'

'Why not?'

'Because you must now go down into the cellar with the German. Quickly. I will explain as we go. Put your clothes back on and come down the stairs. Leave nothing here. I will wait for you in the hall.'

Down in the cellar, Otto was sitting cross-legged on his mattress. He edged up and made room for Willy. There was a little chink in the stonework of the outside wall up by the cellar roof and it let in enough light for them to see each other.

'We must whisper,' said Otto quietly. 'If I can hear them outside then they might hear us in here. Do you know what is happening?'

'Helene says a new officer came to the door. She thinks he is from the artillery. He has told her they will install a gun here tonight. She and Victor told him in that case they would leave the house and he has forbidden them from doing so. He says they are to go on farming the land or face serious reprisals.'

'Of course they will be obliged to stay,' said Otto. 'In case your scout planes notice a difference. The farmers must still farm. If you are mad enough to stay, you will have to help them do it. I'm sure you can look like a farmer if you try.'

'No. You were right. He told her dogs are on the way to search the area for the deserter and they will also need to see all the household papers again. He has a list of the people living here and there are only three names on it. That is why Helene is afraid. He will check me much more closely. She says we must go as soon as we can.'

'Go? How? Where?'

'I really don't know, Otto. North to the sea perhaps? Do you know this area well?'

'Not well at all. Until last month I had spent the war at Dix-mude. You know where that is?'

'Yes of course, north of Ypres on the edge of the flooded area. Does that mean you know the inundation?'

'The Yser floods? Yes,' said Otto, 'every horrid stinking inch, though only from the eastern side.'

'And I know every inch of the western side,' said Willy. 'I even surveyed it when it was still dry land.'

'Really? Well now, Mr Fraser, in that case I am starting to think we might have a plan.'

'How would we get there? It's a long way.'

'I might have a plan for that too,' said Otto and they talked it through, but all Willy could think about in the silences was that he had broken something wonderful in this house and now he must leave this ruined Eden.

26

As soon as darkness fell, lorries came growling into the farmyard one at a time, laden with the heavy steel components of a very large gun. Each one stayed only long enough to offload its cargo. Willy pushed Gabrielle as far out of his mind as he could, telling himself over and over again that he could not stay and that only his escape could save her. He turned himself back into a military automaton, watching through the small glass pane in the back door with the cellar trapdoor standing open in case he needed to make a hasty retreat. He soon realized that the departing lorries could not be going far. One of the drivers had a distinctive red plume in his forage cap and he walked back into the yard to join the working party only ten minutes after he had driven the empty lorry away. Willy watched the next truck carefully and sure enough, the driver of that one also reappeared within minutes.

The farmhouse was silent. Gabrielle had not come down from upstairs. Helene and Victor were sitting quietly in the parlour. He went down to the cellar and closed the trapdoor behind him.

'What can you see out there?' Otto asked.

'I think it's a naval gun,' said Willy. 'A bloody great long barrel. I've just seen them hoisting it in.'

He told Otto about the lorries and Otto nodded. 'They'll be parking them up the road in case some nighthawk pilot spots them. That makes our life a lot easier.'

'It does?'

'Yes, my old pal. It certainly does. Can you drive a lorry?'

'Of course.'

'Then let us go and choose a nice one. You'll be the driver and I will be the officer sitting next to you, barking orders if we encounter any roadblocks.'

'Won't they be looking for you?'

'We'll cross that bridge when we come to it. Let's get out of here. Right now.'

'Give me a minute or two,' said Willy. He climbed up into the hall and, as if she had guessed he was coming, Helene was standing there.

'We're leaving you,' Willy whispered. 'We have to. It isn't safe for you if we stay any longer, not with all that going on outside.'

She nodded and opened a door into a front room full of furniture covered in dustsheets. Two windows looked out over the lane and they kept still as another lorry came out of the yard and rumbled slowly away but its lights were shrouded to glowworms and it barely lit them at all as it passed.

'I have to see Gabrielle before I go,' Willy said.

'No, I am sorry but you cannot. She was desperate, so bad that I had to give her even more cognac. It is much better that you are gone when she wakes. You must speak to me. She said some things. Why did you tell her what you did?'

'Because it is true.'

'I do not doubt that, but there are times to tell the whole truth and perhaps this was not one.'

He was aware of her eyes on him in the dim light of the moon but he could hear no tone of censure in her voice.

'Was it because you love her?' Helene asked and while the question shocked him to his core, he had to answer it truthfully.

'Yes.'

'So you needed her to know? How did that help?'

'I can't explain.'

'I think I can. You wanted to tell her that great truth but you could not while such a thing stayed hidden because that felt 'like a greater lie'?'

He was astonished by her acute understanding. 'Exactly that, Helene, and now ... ' He stopped. He, Willy Fraser, taken by indescribable war on a journey from flamboyant risk-taker to detached and quieter hero, had been brought back to what felt like a weakness in himself and his voice failed him.

She reached out and squeezed his wrist and stood there, her hand over his, until he got his control back.

'I don't have the first idea what to do,' he said. 'I don't want to go but I cannot stay.'

'There is only one thing you can do, William Fraser. I think you did not have the chance to tell her the whole detail of that truth so now you must quickly tell it all to me before you go and if the right time comes, I will do my best to make sure that Gabrielle understands it properly.'

So he did and she insisted that he spare her

nothing. In that dark room he pulled the veil in his memory away and went all the way back to Claude's last minutes in that pain-soaked Belgian flood, just as if he was there again and helpless to provide any other sort of comfort to his tortured, broken, dying friend.

'Before he died, he asked you to look after Gabrielle,' said Helene in the end. 'And in the middle of war, you came here to do that. That means everything. One day she will see that.'

'I can't pretend to you that I chose to cross the lines,' said Willy, 'but I often stared in this direction so perhaps I wished it.'

'Where are you going now?'

'We have a plan but it is better if you do not know it. We were never here.' Willy stopped. 'It worries me that the first officer saw me here. Will he not remember and wonder where I have gone?'

She shook her head. 'No. Another regiment has taken over this area. Victor's friends up the road say it is all new faces at the headquarters. All I want to know is, do you have a plan to get back across the lines?'

He nodded. 'Yes, I hope so.'

'Is it dangerous? Oh, absurd question. How could it not be? Is it better than going to Holland and spending the rest of this war in safety?'

'It is my duty to get back if I possibly can.'

'William Fraser. This war cannot last forever. When it is over, will you want to come back here to find Gabrielle?'

'Of course I will.' He frowned. 'I want to take

her to my home if she will come but I don't think she will, not after this.'

'You cannot say that.'

'In any case, I promise you I will come back here, but . . . '

'But?'

He looked out of the window towards the ridge that sheltered them from the lines. A staccato band of orange flashes reflecting off the clouds showed what lay beyond.

'The war has been chained up inside the Salient like a savage dog for two whole years,' he said. 'It destroys soldiers and steel but everything else is mud and there is nothing left to harm. Listen to me, Helene, one day that chain will snap. Unless we lose, and we will *not* lose, the war will spill over the edge and race towards you here, the first green fields in its path. Soldiers love fresh ground with walls to hide behind and firm earth under foot. They will revel in it. When you hear the guns getting louder, that will have begun. When they come up over the ridge their sound will change and then our tide will be finally flooding out of the Salient so that nothing can stop it. Then you must get away while you can. You must not stay here for a second longer because if they fight over you, you will not survive. This farm of yours will have a hard time of it. I fear there may be nothing for me or you to come back to.'

'Then how will you find us?'

'I don't know, Helene, but I will.'

'Will you go back to your balloons?'

'If they let me.'

417

'We will watch for you up in the sky and when we see the balloons, we will hope that you . . . '

She broke off as shouts erupted in the courtyard and someone hammered at the back door.

'What shall I do?'

'Fiddle with the lock. Talk to them. Hold them up. I'll get Otto out of here.'

Otto was up the ladder in a moment. They lowered the trapdoor and Helene pointed them to the front room. She had opened the window. They climbed out on to an empty lane and she closed it behind them.

Otto followed Willy across the road and they vaulted the gate into the field opposite, ducking down behind the hedge as another lorry came out of the yard then they ran along, crouched behind the hedge's cover, following it. The driver was in no hurry and they kept up with it until it pulled into a field a quarter of a mile along the road, joining twelve others already parked there. The driver climbed out, pulled off his jacket and put on a pair of overalls before he walked back towards the farm.

'No guards?' said Willy.

Otto had been studying the lorry park. 'No reason to guard them,' he said. 'We wait until he has reached the farm then grab that one. They won't hear anything from over there and his engine will be nicely warmed up.'

They crouched there for ten minutes, working out plans.

'Do you think we can get across the water?' Otto asked.

'The inundation? Yes, maybe. With a lot of luck.'

The Belgian soldiers called it the waterland. Two years had passed since the flooding had saved the Channel ports. It had separated the armies ever since from Nieuport on the coast down to Dixmude, halfway to Ypres. The Belgians still manned the fringe of that flood from the railway embankment where Claude had died. Here and there, small islands stuck up among the wind-driven ripples. On them crumbled the remains of the farms and the hamlets built in an age when higher ground was precious for different reasons, when every farmer valued dry foundations for his house. They were ruins now and they were the battlegrounds between raiding parties' hidden outposts. Both armies had built long boarded jetties, snaking out into the water past reed beds and mud banks, connecting them to island strong-points and sniper posts. In a furtive war of rafts and small boats, men on both sides joked that they had become amphibians and inspected their toes for signs of webbing in the rare moments when they could strip off to dry out.

'I know a good place,' said Otto. 'We can drive right to it. After that it's down to you.'

'Come on,' said Willy. 'The driver must be at the farm by now.'

There was nobody around to challenge them. Otto tossed Willy the driver's uniform jacket and a cap that was lying on the seat. 'Put those on,' he said, 'then I can order you around. All right,

419

let's get away from here before the next one comes.'

Willy studied the controls and decided they were simple enough. He flipped the switches, Otto swung the handle and the engine came to life. Willy backed it round and drove out on to the lane. There was nothing in sight.

'Don't go past the farm,' said Otto. 'Go left. With a bit of luck nobody will realize it has gone for hours. We will be well on our way by that time.'

Willy cast one long look back then locked the farm away in a sealed corner of his head. It throbbed at him and he forced it down again. The other way took them past the German HQ in the next farm along but all was dark.

'Turn right,' said Otto.

'Where are we going?'

'You'll see when we get there.'

'What do I do if we get to a roadblock. Drive straight through?'

'We'll be fine.'

'But they'll be looking for you.'

'My dear Willy, you would be surprised how silent my headquarters will be on the subject of an officer who has shot his commander. It might catch on, you see? No, they will have searched for me very quietly and only a few officers will know why. Even the men doing the searching will not have been let in on the secret, I promise you. However, I do have a plan.'

'Which is?'

'To fill up this lorry.'

'With what?'

'Trust me. An empty lorry is much more suspicious than a full one when you are approaching the front lines. Wait and see.'

They bumped along the rough roads of occupied Belgium for an hour and a half, sometimes reaching twenty uncomfortable miles an hour on the straighter sections. The villages on their way were jammed with military traffic, moving men and material under cover of darkness, and Willy took in all the details he could, imagining a time when he could help to target them. They found back roads wherever they could. Otto leant forward, scanning the road ahead and said, 'There, on the right. Turn in there.'

Willy saw a barrier across the road and a guard post. 'Otto. For God's sake. It's an army camp.'

'Don't argue. Do exactly as I say,' said Otto and Willy glanced across to see he had a pistol in his hand, half hidden under the flap of his jacket.

They stopped at the barrier and Otto barked orders at the guards who lifted the pole with alacrity and saluted him. Willy drove on into a wood filled with tents and huts in all directions. 'Turn round and wait here,' said Otto. 'I won't be long.' He strode into a hut with a regimental shield painted on the door. Dim lights showed when he opened it. Moments later a German NCO came running out and began shouting into the entrance flaps of the nearest tents. Before half a minute had passed uniformed men, wiping sleep from their eyes, began to emerge from the tents clutching rifles. Otto stood there urging them on as they clambered into the back of the truck and two more NCOs began passing up ammunition boxes and string bags bulging with stick grenades.

Otto jumped back into the front seat and shouted, 'Get going. There is no time to waste!' at Willy in German.

'Where are we going, sir?' asked Willy, also in German although he was almost sure the men behind couldn't hear him.

'To repel the raiders, idiot,' said Otto. 'Go faster. There is very little time. Straight on towards Dixmude and then we turn north.'

They skirted the ruins of the small town that marked the end of the flooding. Southward towards Ypres, they could see flares going up and the muzzle flashes of artillery. North, where the flood invigilated its long stand-off, there was nothing but darkness. German military police controlled the traffic in this congested back area but Otto's high-handed commands and the urgency in the eyes of the squad of keyed-up infantry behind them cleared the way every time they were forced to stop.

They drove on bumpy tracks through dark and unkempt wasteland for fifteen minutes more, Otto staring ahead. 'Stop here,' he ordered abruptly. 'Come with me.'

Willy followed him to the back of the truck where Otto issued sharp commands. The men were to block the track round a bend behind the lorry and let no one through. They must stop anyone approaching them from any direction. There were reports, Otto said, that a Belgian raiding party had infiltrated wearing captured German uniforms. He and his driver would go ahead to the German lines to report their arrival. The men doubled off and when they were out of sight, Otto rooted around in the toolbox bolted to the running board. 'Look along the ditch,' he said. 'Find the telephone wires.'

Willy scrabbled in the mud and pulled up a run of four wires. Otto cut through them with wire cutters. 'Come on,' he said. 'Do exactly as I tell you. Don't speak unless you have to. Behave like you're scared of me.'

'That won't be hard.'

He looked Willy up and down, twisted his forage cap to a different angle and shook his head. 'You don't look much like a German,' he said. 'A disreputable Hamburger maybe but by the time I've got them into a proper panic I don't think they will notice. Have you left anything in the lorry?'

And that was when Willy remembered the knapsack, his inseparable companion for all these months and even before he checked, he knew he had left it at the farm. That was as it should be, he thought for a moment. It was back where it belonged with Claude's trumpet, the letter and the photograph. Except that was not all. With a sense of dread he remembered there were other things in it too, objects that could incriminate Helene, Victor and Gabrielle. He thought hard. The English chocolate? They had eaten all of that. His clasp knife, did it have an English maker's name? It would say 'Sheffield Steel' on the blade, for sure, but a Belgian might easily have such a thing from before the war. Then his stomach clenched. The heliograph. No innocent Belgian would have a heliograph mirror with British military markings on it. If they searched and found that, they would know for certain that the farm had been harbouring an enemy and then what would they do? His head filled with an agonizing picture of Gabrielle blindfolded against a wall and soldiers raising their rifles.

Claude's voice spoke in his ear again — precise, real and urgent. 'Don't think of her now, Willy. If you want to see her again, put her right out of your mind just as you told me.' He could see Claude walking in front of him, just two steps away with his head turned towards him but then Claude fled away and it was Otto looking at him, gesturing ahead.

They had walked into a different world and he had not even noticed. He shook his head to clear the visions away. Their path had dipped into an artificial corridor of sandbags, iron and timber — a front line built into the riverbank itself and beyond it only the dark, dark water. Otto was talking urgently to a young German officer, gesticulating back behind them.

'They came through by Old Stuyvekenskerke and Den Toren,' Otto said. 'One hundred or more. The bastards are dressed in captured uniforms. They have got behind us. They will be coming up the road to attack you where you do not suspect it. Leave only sentries here. Take all your other men back to secure the rear while there is still time or we are done for. I will go forward to the outposts and warn them. Go now.'

'I must call the command post,' said the flustered officer. He was barely more than a boy.

'Yes, yes,' said Otto testily, 'but do it fast. I bring these instructions from the General himself.'

The young officer called orders to a subaltern sitting in a dimly lit sandbagged den. They heard him cranking a handle, calling for a response then cranking again. 'The line is dead,' he said in the end.

'They have cut the wires,' said Otto. 'Now, go or all will be lost.'

The young officer gave nervous orders. Men poured out of the sandbagged shacks that stretched along the line, thirty, forty, fifty of them following their officer back down the track. As soon as they were out of the way, Otto set off along the sunken way that paralleled the water. A hundred yards on, a nervous sentry guarded a narrow opening, staring out with his rifle half-raised. A narrow planked walkway snaked out into the darkness of the flood.

'Let us through,' commanded Otto. 'How many are posted out there?'

'Four from the machine-gun section, sir,' said the guard. 'All in the nest at the end of the causeway.'

'Good. We will return in ten minutes.'

Rifle fire crackled behind them. The guard swung round and peered back into the darkness. 'Keep a good watch that way,' Otto commanded. 'That is where the danger lies, not across the water. Our men have found the Belgians.'

He walked quickly out on to the planking and Willy followed. The causeway was two feet wide, a foot clear of the water, supported on posts every few yards. It creaked and swayed a little under their weight. Soon they could see nothing before them or behind, just the ribbon of planking, curving left and right, disappearing into the darkness. They could hear what now sounded like a pitched battle behind them. Something flashed ahead, out on the water, and a trail of sparks snaked up into the sky. In a moment Otto was flat down on the planks with Willy only a heartbeat behind him. The flare burst into light far above them.

'From the machine-gun post,' Otto hissed. 'They're getting nervous.'

The long jetty ended several hundred yards ahead at the hump of a small island. They could see nothing across the flare-lit circle of ruffled water except for the occasional clumps of reeds marking the shallower parts. They lay stock-still as the flare burnt itself out. The shooting had stopped. In its place, they heard an angry voice somewhere back on shore and the guard answering.

'They're on to us,' whispered Otto. 'They'll find us if we stay here. Come on, into the water.'

They rolled over opposite sides of the jetty into a shallow but shockingly cold layer of rancid liquid over only slightly less liquid mud. Another flare hissed up, this time from the landward end. Willy heard Otto's quiet prompt, 'Get right underneath the boards,' but he was already on his way. He floated on his back in the water staring up at the slats of wood just above him as a new flare lit up the sky directly overhead. Otto's head was next to his.

'They will be searching under the boards all the way along,' said Otto. 'That is standard practice when there has been a raid.'

'Then they will find us, won't they? We had better get away while we can.'

'No, they will see us all too easily out there. Don't worry. I came prepared. I hope you like the taste of petrol.'

27

Otto handed Willy a length of rubber tube. 'From the toolbox. Spare fuel pipe. One piece each. Get right down under the water, as deep as you can, and breathe through it. Go down now so the mud settles before they get here.'

Willy clamped his teeth round one end of the tube. It stung his lips with old petrol. He pulled himself down one of the supports into the layer of loose mud, blessedly just a little warmer than the water. His feet found a tangle of barbed wire deeper down and he hooked them into it to anchor himself horizontally. Reaching one hand up with the tube in it, he blew gently until a sudden drop in pressure told him it was clear of the water. Then he kept utterly still, sucking in air as quietly and steadily as he could. It took a constant effort to control his constricted breathing through this narrow pipe. The muddy water stung his eyes viciously when he tried opening them for a moment and he remembered what the Belgian officer had told him so long ago on the other side of the flood. This was not just water any more. It was the unpalatable soup of war — a hideous mixture of burnt explosives and what was left from human decay.

He hung in suspension, gradually chilling down in the sump of that November flood, the layers of his clothing helping to trap a little of his body's heat. He did his best to stay alert though he knew alertness could do nothing to turn away a bullet or a bayonet thrust from up above. Nothing was real down here. Time had made up new rules and, as if he were falling asleep, his mouth loosened around the end of the rubber pipe. That let in the vile water, biting into his throat and choking him so that he tried to rear up. Otto's strong arm grabbed his neck and hauled him back down. He had to gulp in some of the rank liquid then blew hard to clear the tube and subsided again. Fighting to get his breathing back under control and discipline his chilled limbs, he saw a pair of eyes looking down at him and immediately Gabrielle's face formed around them and he could look at her as if she were really there. Her voice came to him from the close intimacy of the darkness above and she spoke to him as Claude had done before. 'This is the time to think of me,' she said. 'I have not forgiven you so stay alive for me, William Fraser — you owe me that at least, damn you.'

Her face hung in the darkness, as detailed and mobile as the real woman, as if he had his eyes wide open. He could see every eyelash, every shadow of the curve of her cheek and he forced himself to suck in the air and exhale with deliberate regularity, struggling to hold on to her as she slowly, slowly faded away. He spoke to her in the same way she had spoken to him. Throw away the knife, he told her, trying to put a power into his thought that would let it cross space. Bury the heliograph mirror. Don't let the Germans find anything that will make them hurt you. Her face grew smaller and smaller and he did not think she heard him, then she was not there any more. He tried to pull her back, imagining her eyes, hoping her face would build around them again but she was utterly gone and then he missed her savagely.

An age later as he was slowly losing the fight to stay alert against the chilling of his blood, Otto's hand seized his arm, pulling him upwards. His face broke the surface under the planks and he took the pipe out of his mouth, breathing deeply. Otto put his mouth to his ear.

'There are sentries on the jetty now,' he whispered. 'They fire flares every few minutes but they don't know where we are. We must be gone from here before light or they will certainly find us.'

Willy's watch had not taken well to the water. 'How long do we have?' he asked.

'I don't know. Hours, certainly, but how many is another question. What should we do?'

'Use the hoses, stay under water and creep away from the jetty. Let's see how far we can get. Watch out for the dips.'

'Dips?'

'I was here before the flooding,' whispered Willy. 'There are drainage ditches everywhere. They can be yards wide. We'll have to swim some of the time.'

'Ah! Oh dear. I never learnt to do that. Cricket, yes. Swimming, no. I was hoping to wade.'

'You can't swim?'

'No. I joined the army not the navy. That was not a coincidence.'

'I'll get you out of here,' said Willy. 'You've done your bit. It's my turn now. We'll wade as much as we can. Get down below the surface whenever a flare goes up. Don't lose your tube. We've got the rest of the night so we'll take it steady.'

But it was soon clear that the rest of the night might not be nearly long enough. Every step was a challenge. They stayed under the cover of the jetty, inching outward, away from the German lines, taking infinite care as they heard the sentries pacing up and down just above them. The further they got from the lines, the closer they came to the German machine-gun nest at the end of the jetty. Fifty yards short of the gun team, they were forced to strike out sideways, their feet finding a firm, flat bottom under the mud. It was slow, heavy work, weighed down by their boots and their clothes, crouched awkwardly so that their mouths were just above the water. Wind-driven ripples slapped their cheeks and unpredictable softer patches put them under every few feet but with Otto holding tightly to Willy's arm each time they struggled on to shallower ground again. Then, when they were still far too close to the jetty for comfort, they waded into sharp spikes of submerged barbed wire, stabbing into their legs and throwing them both off balance so that Otto's flailing arm splashed the water.

They stopped, frozen, expecting a shot, a challenge or a flare but nothing came. Trapped, they took turns working the wire cutters with numbed fingers blindly down in the mud,

431

desperate not to lose hold of them, clipping out a way ahead a few inches at a time. Each click sounded startlingly loud despite the muffling water. For all Willy knew, the wire could go on for miles and this might be no more than a slow and hopeless path to discovery, but he rejected that thought as soon as he recognized the defeatism in it. He was snipping away, unable to move forwards or backwards, when he heard the hiss of another flare on its way up from the jetty. Before it burst into light, they both hunched down into the water, pressing into the savage pin-cushion of the barbed wire. The flare drifted in the sky for a pain-filled age before they could continue clipping their long, slow way through the barbed wire belt and the flood here was even more fetid. It had the same acrid smell of wet shell-holes on land where the burnt leftovers of explosives had changed the chemistry of the water, mixed in with rank decay. Then after one last strand, Willy's careful probing ahead met no more wire. Instead, there was something worse.

Some forgotten Belgian attack had ended badly against this stretch of coiled wire. His next step brought an acute stab in his leg and, reaching down, he found the sharp end of a bayonet still fixed to its rifle. He tugged it free and it came with a hand grasping the stock — bones and sinew held together by a twisted sleeve. One more step and his probing foot pushed into something that gave way with a crunch. A bubble of gas erupted to the surface just in front of his face and had him gagging for breath. He lunged forward to get clear but found he was now stampeding in slow motion through a tangle of rotting remains and a vivid image of Claude's death in this same water filled his head.

'Oh Jesus Christ,' Otto whispered. He gripped Willy's arm and pointed to the right. Only yards from where they stood in the churned and filthy mud, a patch of clearer water shallowed over some small rise in the drowned field. Just below the water a pale phosphorescent gleam outlined the shape of a head, a torso and one arm in a fuzz of light. 'Death in life,' said Otto quietly. 'Or is it life in death? Yea, slimy things did crawl with legs upon the slimy sea.'

Willy stared at the green body — a parody of a medieval effigy, moulded out of this putrescent swamp.

He tore his gaze away and they ploughed on, every yard they gained a silent struggle against more horrors hidden beneath the water. Otto disappeared below the surface time after time, with Willy clutching him as he swam them one-handed, feet kicking, to the next patch of firmer ground. This was a dark world of the dead between the lines. Out to seaward, towards the distant dunes, something was burning, the orange light reflecting on shreds of cloud drifting east, allowing them glimpses of the north star. Without Polaris, they would have been in trouble because the occasional humps of drier land gave them no clue for navigation. This landscape bore no resemblance to the fields Willy remembered from his exploration two years earlier. He looked back to see if there was any visible trace of the German lines and realized they could not possibly reach safety before daylight because a paler bar over the eastern horizon showed it was already on its way.

So far, they had skirted the islands, knowing any of them might contain a sniper post or a look-out from either side, but now they had no choice. They were exhausted and deeply chilled, teeth chattering. As the sky grew lighter, they could see the broken stubs of shattered buildings poking up from the water a hundred yards to their left and a small grassy island away to the right.

'The walls aren't safe,' whispered Otto. 'Head for the grass.'

It was a long, slow race against the light to reach the nearest hummock because it was surrounded by another submerged belt of barbed wire but in the end they crawled deep into the grass, huddling against each other for whatever body heat they could still generate. Willy didn't think it was possible to sleep but something which might simply have been unconsciousness overtook him and when he woke up it was full daylight. His injured leg, forgotten during their escape, was now alive with sharp pain. The grass was tall enough to block the view and Otto's eyes were still closed in a face that was grey with drying mud.

Willy parted the grass with his hands and crawled forward to the edge. The sun was behind him, so unless he had slept right through the day he knew he must be looking towards the Belgian lines. It still felt like morning and he could see the long line of the railway embankment in that

434

direction so that had to be west. More crawling took him twenty yards back past Otto to the other side of the mound, towards the sun. The shattered ruins of a village rose out of the water perhaps half a mile away. He tried to fit it to his memories but too much had changed. Beyond it was some larger ruin — a chateau perhaps? He had memories of a castle with a farm next to it. He twisted round at a sound behind him and there was Otto crawling towards him. They stared out side by side. Two ducks were paddling through the water as if it were still their natural habitat.

'That is the Kasteel Viconia,' said Otto pointing at the ruins. He kept his voice low as if the ducks might be enemies. 'And the village is Stuivekenskerke.'

'My God,' said Willy. He had last seen it as a small oasis of calm beauty in the beet fields. Now the little church and the trees around it had been ground to rubble and matchwood.

'Viconia is one of our look-out posts,' said Otto. 'At least it was last time I was here. We must not be seen. They have telescopes.'

'By 'our' I take it you mean German?'

'I must learn to stop saying that, mustn't I?'

'It would be a good idea,' said Willy. 'It's only a mile to go. We will stay here until dark then we should make it easily.'

'You're an optimist.'

'Of course. Haven't you found that's the only way of thinking that the war will tolerate?'

'Certainly.'

He would have liked to stand up and swing his

arms to fight the bitter chill but they had to lie low, pulling out armfuls of grass from the centre of the little island to heap over themselves, trying to persuade themselves that made them warmer.

'Can I ask you something?' said Otto.

'Why not. It will pass the time.'

'How long had you been at the farm?'

'Just a few days. I had a fever. I don't remember much of it.'

'The woman there, Gabrielle, she nursed you?'

'Yes.'

'Isn't that the wrong way round then?'

'What do you mean?'

'I thought it was the patient who was supposed to fall in love with the nurse.'

Willy was silent for a while. 'You hardly saw her,' he said in the end.

'I saw quite enough of the two of you to know what I'm talking about,' Otto said. 'It was like watching a short-circuit when a bullet hits a power cable. Do you feel the same?'

He was inclined not to answer but this island was a world between worlds and he had just shared so much with this enemy stranger who was becoming an allied friend. 'Yes,' he said.

'Well then, you are a lucky man indeed but your timing is truly terrible. What will you do about it?'

'I won't think about it. I will concentrate on one thing at a time. Staying alive while we cross that last mile comes top of my list.'

'And what do you suppose will happen when we get there?'

'We'll find some hot water and some dry clothes and a field kitchen with a big, big pot of stew on the boil. Then we will eat all of it.'

'You might, but what about me? You seem to forget that I possess the outward form of a German officer.'

'With me to vouch for you.'

'That might not be quite so helpful as you think. You are after all wearing a German jacket and your other clothes could have come from any army's rags store. Do you have any identification?'

No, he didn't. 'I served in the Belgian army for the first months of this war, Otto. I know them.'

'You can guarantee that someone who remembers you will be close enough to stop them shooting both of us?'

'I know the King of Belgium, for heaven's sake. I will tell them to take us to him.'

Otto began to laugh as a shell moaned through the sky above them from somewhere out to sea. 'That is really going to help. They'll certainly believe that. I bet our raiders use that trick all the time. Take me to the King of Belgium, they demand, and do you know what? It always works.'

The shell burst towards Dixmude — the Royal Navy doing its daily bit.

'We will cross that bridge when we get to it,' said Willy.

'A bridge? That's a good idea. I would give a lot for a bridge right here and now. A solid, dry bridge leading to the other side where we would be met by a big slice of buttered toast soaking in

Gentleman's Relish followed by an audience with this friendly king of yours.'

★ ★ ★

Chester K. Hoffman was waiting for just such an audience. The wire from New York had been quite clear. 'Go La Panne soonest. Palace agreed interview. Exclusive.' It sounded very good indeed but it was all much less clear when he got there. La Panne or De Panne or whatever they wanted to call the damned place was the usual crazy whirl of soldiers and ambulances and hospitals and even that was confusing because sometimes these Belgian guys called their hospitals 'ambulances' as if the whole mass of bricks and mortar might rev up a giant engine and go driving off some place. He had been to the right office where they said they knew nothing about any interview but he should sit there quietly while they made enquiries. That took an hour and they came back with polite regrets that nobody knew anything about any arrangement with any New York newspaper.

'Listen, buddy,' said Chester to the officer who brought the news, 'Go tell the Queen I'm here. I know her. She'll sort things out.'

The officer was openly disbelieving but he went away and he was gone for another half hour. When he came back, he looked annoyed. 'The Queen says she has never heard of you and she has certainly never met you,' he said. 'We do not like newspapermen who try to play tricks.

There will be a car here soon to take you back to Dunkerque.'

'I didn't come from Dunkerque,' said Chester, stung by Elisabeth's callous forgetfulness, but all he got in response was one of those eloquent shrugs that showed how little that particular Belgian officer cared and how richly the French deserved this irritant who would soon be arriving among them.

The car was typical of Belgium at war, a large Minerva tourer, quivering and steaming in battleship grey with two bullet holes in its doors and a long crack across the windscreen. Chester walked to it as slowly as he could, reluctant to give up, knowing he would face angry and uncomprehending telegrams from New York. Before he could climb in, a younger officer came running up.

'Monsieur Hoffman,' he said. 'The King sends his apologies. There has been a small confusion. Please come with me. He will see you very shortly. It has been a busy day.'

The Minerva took them to a villa away in the dunes and on the way Chester, vastly relieved, counted the days on his fingers. He made it eight days since he had talked to the Queen. She had forgotten him in eight days? No, of course, she hadn't forgotten him. It was a plain message. 'She has never heard of you and she has certainly never met you.' Elisabeth hadn't told Albert, had she? He had sat there talking to her about Wild Willy Fraser and she hadn't told the King. Well now, wasn't that something? But what exactly?

An equerry clicked his highly polished heels

and ushered Chester into a salon where the King and Queen of Belgium stood waiting for him, flanking an ugly fireplace.

'Mr Hoffman,' said the King in perfect English, 'it is a pleasure to meet you. May I introduce you to my wife, Queen Elisabeth?'

Chester bowed to them both. 'Thank you, your Highnesses,' he said and thought perhaps he had got that wrong. The plural sounded odd. The hell with it, he thought to himself, I'm a Republican.

'Mr Hoffman,' said the Queen. 'It comes back to me that I have heard your name before. You spoke, I believe, to one of the sisters at the hospital here recently, did you not?'

He smiled. 'Yes, ma'am, I did — a very impressive lady. I declare I liked her a whole lot.'

'We will perhaps discuss more of that later. I will leave the two of you to conduct your interview first.'

For the next half hour, the King did his best to elicit American sympathy for Belgium's rearguard efforts, suggesting more direct support would be very timely, while Chester tried to find out one single solid fact about the current conduct of the war. They were concealing their mutual frustration at the pointlessness of the process when the Queen came back in.

'Am I interrupting?' she asked.

'No, no,' said the King, 'I think we have probably got as far as we are likely to. I expect there will be a car waiting for our American friend here.'

'Before you go, Mr Hoffman,' said the Queen,

'I believe the sister you spoke to last time you came mentioned that you had some news of an officer who was very well-known to my husband? Is that correct?'

'Really, Mr Hoffman?' said the King, 'And who was that?'

'A British officer called Fraser, your Majesty. Willy Fraser.'

'No! Fraser? Of all people. I have often wondered what became of him. A most remarkable man. He did us great service in the first months of the war then he rejoined his own regiment. What news do you have?'

'Nothing good, I'm afraid, sir. He was in an observation balloon. It broke free ten days ago and took him across the lines at night. All we know for sure is the balloon exploded after landing.'

'Fraser? In a *balloon?* He was a cavalryman through and through. What was he doing in a balloon? Are you saying he is dead?'

'I have my fingers crossed, sir. There was hope that he had survived. We thought he might be hiding at a farm quite close by.' Chester glanced at the Queen. Elisabeth showed nothing on her face but polite interest as if she had no idea why that might be. 'I feel pretty bad about it, sir, because I talked a British kid into flying over there the next night but he never came back and the Boche dropped a message saying he was killed in a crash. His guys flew over and saw the plane wrecked on the ground the next day. Since then nothing.'

'I am most sorry to hear that,' said the King. 'I

441

pray that Fraser may be safe. He is a good man. I wonder why nobody else has told me. The British High Command knew of my interest in him, I am sure.'

'You should know, sir, that the British High Command did their best to get rid of him. They stripped him of his rank. They even made him change his name. He was going by an alias so I guess nobody in the High Command would have put two and two together. He's been calling himself after a dead friend — one of your own officers, a man called Claude Tavernier.' Chester was watching the King closely and he thought he could now sense some discomfort from the Queen. Albert looked at him, startled.

'I remember *that* name,' he said. 'I knew Tavernier. That was a terrible affair. Fraser told us all about it. He was . . . '

'My dear,' said the Queen. 'I expect Mr Hoffman is in a hurry to file his despatches.'

'No, not at all,' said Chester. 'Please go on, sir.'

'It is a very sad story,' said the King, 'and not at all the sort of thing you would want to write in a family newspaper but Tavernier was a true Belgian hero. The man did his very best at the defence of Liege and then in the fighting that followed. Do you know the story of the Battle of the Yser River?' Chester nodded. 'He fought there alongside Fraser right up to the point when the inundation saved us but he was shattered by a shell blast. Torn completely open. Ghastly. Far beyond any help and Fraser was badly hurt as well. The poor man did his best for Tavernier but it was quite impossible.'

'Mr Hoffman, you won't turn this into a newspaper story, will you?' said the Queen.

'Ma'am, I only want to make Willy Fraser the hero he deserves to be. I haven't told you the half of it yet.'

All thought of a waiting car had clearly gone from the King's mind. 'Please do tell us,' he said. 'Leave nothing out.'

So Chester told him of Willy's last escape, of the balloon ride back to England and then, when he was pressed to explain, the broad outline of the story of Willy's forced demotion.

'I have not heard this word 'Stellenbosched' before,' said the King. 'It is a very English way of doing things. But what I do not understand is why his commanders gave him such a very hard time when he was so excellent a soldier? Do you know?'

Chester squirmed a little. 'I should not say any more, sir, I believe it . . . ' He groped for the right words, tried to imagine a pompous British officer saying it, 'concerned an affair of the heart.'

'A woman?' said the King. 'They did all that to him because of a woman? In the middle of a war?'

'Yes, sir.'

'But fighting men, in war — well,' the King shrugged.

'I guess it was a question of which woman, sir,' said Chester. 'It was somebody kinda important. It was the wife of his commanding officer or something like that.'

443

The Queen said, 'Perhaps we don't really need details, my dear? If poor Fraser is dead then . . .'

The King cut her off with a raised hand. 'I wish to understand. I don't want to keep you from your duties if you would rather not be here. This is perhaps not a fitting subject for you.'

'No, I will stay. I want to hear.'

The King stared at Chester. 'His commanding officer's wife? How the devil did he have time for that in the middle of a war?'

Chester was uncomfortably aware that the Queen was watching him intently. 'It mostly happened a year or two before the war, I believe, sir. Some colonel in the cavalry. I believe his wife was much younger and she was kinda wild.'

'Fraser told you that? That's not very gentlemanly.'

'Hell no. I mean — no, sir. I had to prise that out of old friends of his. Took me days to find out what happened. The fact is people think it started up again while he was recovering. An affair of the heart, I mean.'

'Impossible,' said the Queen quickly. 'I mean how could that be? He was here with us.'

'Ma'am, I'm a little uncomfortable with this. I don't want to sound like some old tittle-tattling gossip.'

'I am sure you will keep it within the bounds of decency,' said the King, 'but now you have started, I think you had better carry on.'

'You might have met the lady in question. I understand she was based here for a short time a year or so ago. I believe she even stayed in your house on one occasion.'

'Oh,' said Elisabeth. 'I think I now under-stand. An English colonel's wife, you said?'

'Scotch, I believe.'

'Scottish,' corrected Elisabeth. 'Mrs McAlis-ter.' She looked at her husband. 'You remember her? She was at the hospital for a month training her young ladies then she came back to meet her husband.'

'The noisy woman?'

'Exactly.' She looked at Chester again. 'Are you suggesting it was the same person?'

'That's what people say. It was her first time round before the war then the Colonel got to hear it had started over so he confronted Fraser and reckoned he didn't get a straight answer. After that he wanted his revenge.'

'I suppose women would have found Fraser attractive,' said the King. 'Do you think so, my dear?'

'I cannot really say. The nurses were very fond of him, I believe.'

And perhaps some of the sisters, thought Chester, but held his tongue.

'All the same,' said the King, 'I have to say I think the worse of him for it. Loyalty to one's commanding officer is absolutely essential. I mean, I was his commanding officer once myself.'

'And he was absolutely loyal to you, my dear,' said the Queen.

'Of course. Well, well. I do hope he has survived. Do you know anything more?'

'Only one more thing, sir. I had a letter yesterday from Scotland, from the guy who looks

445

after his place there, Grannoch Castle. He's very concerned. He's asked me if I can pull any strings to get him out here. He wants to search for his master. Says he's a soldier himself and his duty lies with Willy Fraser. Nothing I can do to help.'

The Queen nodded. 'Perhaps we might be able to. May I borrow the letter, Mr Hoffman?'

'There is no time for such whimsies in war,' said the King to her softly but she ignored him and took the letter. 'Now, Mr Hoffman,' he went on. 'None of this is to appear in your paper. You understand that, I am sure.'

'Sir, he and I had a deal. He said if I found out everything that happened with him and Tavernier, he would confirm it and I could write it. The bottom line is now he has gone I can't check it with him but it feels to me like a fitting memorial to him and to his gallant friend, would you not agree?'

'Memorials are for the dead,' said the Queen sharply. 'There are quite enough of them without making memorials for those who may still live.' Her studied regal calm had slipped and the King looked at her in surprise.

'He deserves honour if not yet a memorial,' he said. 'He helped a great deal with the plans for the inundation and that is the only reason you are able to talk to the King of Belgium in his capital on Belgian soil today, Mr Hoffman.'

Chester failed to suppress a tiny smile in time as he looked around this room in a seaside villa in a small village and the King saw it.

'Please do not believe for a moment that we sit

here in this tiny surviving corner of our country and wait to be saved by larger nations, Mr Hoffman. If you cannot yet write your story, I will be very happy to show you one you may certainly write. You must however agree to stay here with us, incommunicado, until afterwards and I can tell you no more unless you agree to that.'

'I agree,' said Chester.

'In that case, tonight you may see for yourself how we hit back at them. We have planned a large raid and you will be watching its progress from our front line.'

'Thank you, sir.'

The King was silent for a moment, frowning. 'So,' he said in the end, 'Fraser took Tavernier's name, did he? I wonder why?'

'Perhaps it was a way to keep him alive?'

'I suppose that is true. He should have felt no guilt for what he was forced to do.'

'What was that exactly, sir?'

'You do not know that part? It was an act of the greatest gallantry. He . . . '

'My dear . . . ' said the Queen, 'I have some very urgent matters to discuss with you and I am afraid they cannot wait a single moment longer. Mr Hoffman, I do apologize but may I ask that you leave us now? I will take great care with your letter.'

Chester left the room taking with him the image of King Albert's astonished expression.

28

Otto and Willy shivered through a short November day that went on forever. The shellfire from the west intensified during the afternoon, most of the shells arching over them towards Dixmude but others bursting somewhere north along the coast. Otto said they would be aiming at the German positions east of Nieuport.

'They are busy. It was not usually like this when I was here,' he said. 'Now, do tell me more about how you plan to keep us both alive for this next bit?'

'Simple,' said Willy. 'We go as soon as it's dark, just like we did before. We keep heading west and when we get near the other side I start shouting.'

'And they start shooting. You don't speak Flemish, do you?'

'Some but possibly not quite well enough. I'll shout in French.'

'Then they'll take you for one of their officers and they will shoot you anyway. Remind me to stay well clear of you. On the slight chance that we might live through this, what do you really think they will do with me?'

'Would you sign up to fight?'

'Now that, dear Willy, goes right to the heart of the nature of war. If I could only shoot Prussian generals then, yes, I would take an English gun in my hand but there are ordinary decent people out there in German uniform. I spent much of my time trying to keep them alive. I would want to shorten this war as best I can but I would prefer not to shoot such men myself.'

'You set them on each other back there without a second thought.'

'Indeed there was a second thought and a third thought and several more after them but that was a question of our survival and I only hope most of their shots missed each other in the dark. They usually do. The wastage of ammunition in this war is simply incredible.'

'So you're suggesting ordinary soldiers are angels, are you?'

'I spent three weeks last year in the trenches south of Ypres. My Colonel lent me to a Saxon regiment that had run short of officers. He very much hoped they would get me killed but those Saxons were decent lads. Very English in their way. They threw messages in bottles across to your lines. I stopped one and made him show me what his message said.'

'And?'

'I can remember every word. It said, 'Look around you, my brothers. Do you see the harm we are doing to this land where neither of us has any business to be? Tell your officers you do not want to fight and we will tell ours the same.''

'What did you do?'

'I told him never to throw another one when an officer could see him.'

'I am not sure they would let you sign up anyway,' said Willy. 'Not to fight. It will be against some convention or other. More to the point, they will value your knowledge. That's what they will want to use.'

'For a short time, until they have exhausted it which will not take long. Then perhaps I will volunteer to serve in some exotic foreign place. Mesopotamia perhaps. I always liked the sound of Mesopotamia. It makes me think of a great beast wallowing in a mudhole. Exotic and far away. I would rather have fought men called Askari Bey in such places as Dujaila or Kut than men called Digby-Smythe in Ypres or Arras. At least, in theory. I think I would change my mind even in Mesopotamia when I saw that their blood was the same colour as mine. Look.'

A faraway grey blob had risen into sight above the elevated horizon of the tall grass surrounding them. It was almost due north. The all-seeing eye.

Willy studied it carefully then relaxed. 'That's a navy balloon,' he said. 'One of their Cacquots. How far is the coast?'

'In miles? Seven or eight perhaps.'

'He's high then. What's he after, I wonder?'

The answer came quickly and took away any of the brief comfort that came from being on the same side. A single, sonorous shell droned its deep bass like an airborne train, crossing right above their heads then plunging down with an anticlimactic thump into the marsh beyond. They wriggled a few yards through the grass to the south side of their refuge and saw a spray of mud still falling half a mile away.

'A dud,' said Otto.

'Only because it hit the mud. Not enough impact to fire the detonator.'

'Yes. They are aiming at Viconia,' said Otto. 'I would not like to be part of that garrison right now.'

'It's a small target and a long way off,' said Willy. 'That observer's working at the absolute limit of his spotting range. I wouldn't want his job.'

Otto snorted. 'I wouldn't want to be up in one of those things at any time or anywhere. What about you? Will you be back up in your balloon when we make it to the other side?'

'I expect so. It's the only thing they'll let me do these days and I quite like it.'

'You must be mad. I have seen so many balloons burning, men falling. It is not a guarantee of a long life.'

Another shell moaned across the sky. 'Nothing we do here fits that criterion,' said Willy.

'You have a lot to answer for, you people up there steering the war. We have guns big enough to wipe out a whole village with two or three shots from a place so far away that the villagers have never been there.'

'Why is that my fault?'

'Because without you people up there, the men with the guns would be firing blind and certainly my men were much more afraid of balloons than of aeroplanes because an aeroplane can only fly while it has petrol while a balloon can stay up there doing its best to kill you all day and night.'

'Don't lecture me, Otto. I didn't start this. I've been on the receiving end. I know how it feels to see the balloon go up. I would rather be up there directing it than down here receiving it.'

'Oh look. A water-rat. See it there? I wonder what it thinks of this war. Forgive me, Willy. It is the first time I have had the liberty to express my thoughts for a very long time. Don't you think all this is quite funny? Here I am, a mongrel — half English, half German, caught halfway between the Germans and another people who are themselves half French and something quite like German, talking to a Scotsman.'

'Better than that, a mongrel Scotsman. Half American.'

'Really? Even funnier. How on earth can any cook mix up such promising ingredients and manage to bake a war of all things? Such a shame that the recipe worked. What do you suppose you will do when all this is over?'

'I find it a very bad idea to think too far ahead. Tonight is far enough away for me.'

'Let us spend the daylight hours talking then,' said Otto. 'It is more fun than thinking of inconvenient matters like hunger and cold. So tell me how it is that you have managed to involve yourself so deeply with the mysterious lady of the farmhouse?'

'No.'

'Just no?'

'Just no.'

'She is quite beautiful and she loves you.'

'Still no.'

'All right. Do you wish to share any lascivious stories of your past conquests?'

'No again.'

'Would you like to hear my story of my landlady in Bad Godesburg and the remarkable things she could do with a cigar?'

'No.'

'I think I am sensing a theme here. Fine. We will lie here silently.'

'What did you mean back there when you said something about life in death?'

'Oh Willy, you ignorant savage. Do you not know the works of your own Coleridge, no — how delightful — now I can say *our* own Coleridge?'

'Some of them.'

'I was quoting from *The Rime of the Ancient Mariner*.'

'Of course, 'slimy things did crawl with legs . . . ''

''Upon a slimy sea.' Life in Death plays dice with Death and wins the soul of the Mariner? You must know that, surely?'

'I know bits of it.'

'Only bits? Shame on you. I know all of it.'

'All of it? Nobody knows the whole of *The Rime of the Ancient Mariner*.'

'I do.'

'It must have over a hundred verses.'

'One hundred and fifty-one. Some say one hundred and forty-three but I prefer the form of the earlier editions. Shall I recite it?'

'No.'

'You have a choice then. Either you tell me something interesting about the last woman in your life or I recite every word of it, whatever you do to try to stop me.'

'I will not talk about her, Otto. It is very difficult. I knew her husband.'

'Her husband? The husband of the fair farming widow? How can that be?'

'It is too complicated. Now leave it alone.'

'So there is something between you. I am right. Well then, my enigmatic friend, I won't trespass there. I am, after all, half of an English gentleman. What about the one before her? It is that or Coleridge.'

'Enigmatic friend' brought back a vivid image of Gabrielle's poem and her utter beauty in the intimate light of that bedroom. 'Why do men in the middle of a bloody war feel the need to talk about women?' he said.

'Because it is the only thing that can keep us going, you idiot. Love is the only antidote to this vast disease that surrounds us.'

Willy smiled despite himself. 'Claude would have agreed with you there.'

'Claude?'

'Her husband. I told him there is no time for such ideas in war.'

'Willy Fraser, you are in some ways a very impressive man but there may be just one thing I know more about than you.'

They both fell silent then Otto grinned. 'Go on, tell me about the one before.'

'The one before had a husband too — a rather high-ranking and dangerous husband, so I'm afraid it's Coleridge.'

'All right. First I will make a flute because Coleridge needs a little music in between the stanzas to keep hope alive in the listener's breast.'

'Make a flute? From what?'

'I have a wide choice. There are reeds or there are reeds. I think I will choose reeds.'

'Otto, if it keeps you quiet and happy, make a flute.'

The flute took up the next hour until Otto contrived something with the use of his clasp knife that could play three notes of surprising purity and two others of moderate ugliness. The seaward balloon had disappeared by that time but another had swayed up into the sky to their west. Somewhere near Alveringem, Willy thought. It attracted the attention of an Albatros but the German aircraft seemed content to inspect it from a distance, possibly because two other scouts, silver in a brief burst of November sun, were circling high above it ready to swoop on any attacker. Belgians, Willy thought.

'There is a story the Fokker pilots tell in the taverns,' Otto said, watching the Albatros fly away. 'They talk of a low English trick, of a dummy observer sent up in a balloon basket stuffed full of explosives, blown up by a switch on the ground when a pilot came too near. Is it true?'

'I haven't heard that one.'

'It is supposed to have happened somewhere south two weeks ago. The story has spread like wildfire. You would have heard if it had, wouldn't you?'

Willy thought of the Albatros that had circled him and flown away. 'I hadn't heard,' he said, 'so no, I don't think it happened but I think I may have benefited from the effects of the rumour.'

He told Otto the story. 'I was frozen to the spot,' he said. 'Couldn't bring myself to move one way or the other. I suppose he thought I was a dummy.'

'It has certainly made them windy about coming too close. That's what I heard. That man up there must have heard it too.'

'It sounds a pretty good idea to me.'

'Ah! Your navy friend is up again.'

He was right. The balloon spotting for the battleships was clear on the horizon. Within a minute or two, a salvo of huge shells curved down, howling out of the sky to burst around the German outposts beyond them in a barrage of unprecedented ferocity. They watched the rubble of the Viconia castle jumping into the air after the thud of each shell's explosion and tumbling back down in some new arrangement of destruction.

'The garrisons have boats,' said Otto, watching grimly. 'Flat-bottomed, like punts. If they have any sense they will have used them to get out. Those gunners are going to a lot of trouble for the sake of one small bump in the mud. I wonder if . . .'

A louder shriek stopped him, that blood-chilling note of a shell coming very close. The water a hundred feet in front of them geysered upwards and they flattened themselves with hands over their heads as they were drenched and pounded by muddy water, mud and vile-smelling lumps of decaying matter.

'Just as I was feeling dry at last,' said Otto. 'Has your balloon spotted us or did the gunner's hand slip?'

'Here's hoping some dozy munitions worker poured in too little powder,' said Willy. 'If not, it means something's changed in the atmosphere — wind speed, pressure, temperature. Or maybe the ships have drifted further off shore in the current. We'll soon know because if so, another one will . . . '

Another one did and then another, keeping their heads down until the far-off observer corrected their aim and the shells found Viconia again.

'*It is an Ancient Mariner and he stoppeth one of three . . . *' said Otto and looked questioningly at Willy who said nothing. It was better than listening to the precise arc of every shell.

Otto was ten minutes in, giving the poem all his skill and passion when he paused, prodding Willy to make sure he was listening to the next verse:

'*The very deep did rot, O Christ!*
That ever this should be
Yea, slimy things did crawl with legs
Upon the slimy sea.'

Then on he went, faultless all the way to the final realization of the Mariner's implacable task.

★ ★ ★

'That was a tour de force,' said Willy at the end. 'I admit it does fit. Here we are trapped in the wreckage while the artillery rolls dice for the possession of our souls.'

457

'I suppose I slew my commanding officer so he was my albatross,' said Otto. 'Is that what brought me here? But he was no albatross. It is supposed to be a symbol of hope. There was no hope to be found in him. Did you slay an albatross, William Fraser?' And absurdly, Willy realized that was exactly what he had done.

'With half the number of esses and twice the number of wings — yes, I did,' he said remembering those desperate moments with the flare gun when they were under attack. 'I shot one down so if I am the Mariner, what does that make you, the wedding guest?'

'I will gladly be a guest at your wedding, William, so long as you let me stop one in three and tell them your story.'

'There are quite enough people trying to tell my story already.' He looked up as a thick cloud front rolled over the low sun. 'It's nearly dark enough. What do you think? Shall we make a move?'

'Shall we crawl with legs upon the slimy sea? Have you got your tube ready? Let's go.'

They were so wet and muddy that creeping back into the water made no discernible difference to their body temperature. A strand of barbed wire stopped them twenty yards out and Willy was bending down to snip it when a loud German voice behind him told him to put his hands up. He straightened up slowly and turned to see three German soldiers, their uniforms ripped and filthy, squatting in a small punt. They had put down their paddles and each one was aiming a pistol.

'Put that down at once,' said Otto. 'I am a German officer and I am very glad to see you.'

'Why are you here?' demanded one of the soldiers, keeping his pistol raised. Willy noted that he did not say 'Sir'.

'Doing our best to escape, idiot. We were shot down. My pilot here breathed in the flames when we crashed. His throat is in a bad way and he needs help. That is why I am pleased to see you.'

The soldier said nothing but stared at Otto then at Willy, clearly wondering what to do.

'Please give me your rank and your name,' he said.

'I am Oberstleutnant Helmut Schiffer,' said Otto. 'Who are you?'

'Unteroffizier Aaronsohn, sir. You were shot down?'

'Yes.'

'Where?'

'Over there,' said Otto testily, pointing vaguely to the north.

'We did not see you, sir.'

'You have eyes to see in the dark? It was last night. Now help us in to your damned boat.'

They did so with some reluctance, all three staring hard at Willy and his filthy, nondescript clothing. He tried to look wounded. It wasn't hard to do. He was aware that Otto had awarded himself a startlingly high rank for someone flying around near the front and that he himself wore nothing remotely like a German pilot's clothing. Otto must have been thinking the same thing. 'We were on a mission of great importance and the highest secrecy,' he said. 'Now, what are you

459

doing out here and where are you bound for?'

'We were at Viconia, sir,' said Aaronsohn. 'You will have seen the bombardment, I am sure? We had severe losses.'

'Yes of course. And now?'

'We have orders to observe the Belgian lines from island 18. My officer believes the bombardment indicates an assault is coming. We are to install ourselves there and signal if we see an assault attempt.' He looked as if he knew his orders might be suicide.

'That is in accordance with my own mission.' Otto pointed into the bottom of the punt where a machine gun, three rifles and a box of ammunition were stacked. 'We shall be able to assist you should it come to a fight.'

Aaronsohn looked at him doubtfully. 'Yes, sir.'

'But I may also need you to take me back to make my own report if we are in any danger of capture.'

'Certainly, sir.' This time there was a tone of relief in the soldier's voice.

'Where is island 18?'

Aaronsohn pointed into the deepening darkness towards another mound to the north-west.

'Carry on then, man. Why are we waiting?'

The other two soldiers dipped their paddles at Aaronsohn's command and they crawled out across the water. It was a better way to travel and each stroke of the paddles brought them slanting slightly closer to the other side. Not a single flare went up from the Belgian lines. Something is cooking, thought Willy. First the barrage, then this suspicious nothingness. The punt nosed aground on to the mud of island 18 and the soldiers, crouching low, carried the machine gun and the ammunition up the slight slope to the line of rubble at the top. It was the remains of a wall. They busied themselves setting up the gun while Aaronsohn stared into the darkness.

'Do you see anything?' asked Otto in a low voice.

'I thought I did, Herr Oberstleutnant, but no.'

That was a step up from 'sir', thought Willy. He quietly picked up a rifle and checked the magazine. He thought of shooting all three of the Germans, wondering if he could be sure of them in the dark. Would Otto help? Would he kill his own countrymen in cold blood? They weren't Prussian generals after all. He checked a second rifle, stood up thinking of taking it over to Otto and threw himself back down as a hail of bullets came at him out of the darkness beyond the island.

One of the German soldiers setting up the machine gun collapsed in an instant. They all flung themselves behind the stones and the Unteroffizier, swearing, crawled to the gun. Bullets whined over their heads from out in the dark water and now the machine gun was firing back, aiming at muzzle flashes in the darkness. Willy heard a scream and the prolonged splashing of a flailing man. More shots came and the machine gun spat back, the Unteroffizier growling in satisfaction at another howl. Willy flicked off the rifle's safety catch, worked the bolt to push a cartridge into the breech and killed him. The other soldier, bewildered, shouted,

'They got him. Come and help,' then had a brief moment to notice Willy aiming at him before he too tumbled over. Willy flattened himself as more Belgian bullets chipped sprays from the top of the stone-work.

'Are they both dead?' shouted Otto.

'Yes,' said Willy, startled that he had shot the first of them in the back then thinking how poorly his upbringing had prepared him for moments such as this.

'Tell them who we are, quick.'

Willy chose French. 'Stop firing,' he shouted. 'We have killed the Germans. I am an escaping Scotsman.' That earned another fusillade of shots. Don't they know what *Ecossais* means, he thought. 'I am an English soldier,' he yelled. There were no more shots but something heavy thudded into the soft ground next to his foot. He twisted round to see Otto dive to get his hand under it and fling it away to burst in mid-air sending a shower of iron casing fragments back at them. A Mills bomb.

'English,' he yelled again. 'I am an escaping English officer. Can you hear me?'

A voice called back, 'Show yourself.'

'Don't be fooled. Stay down,' said Otto.

Willy stood with his hands up. 'I am a Lieutenant in the Royal Flying Corps,' he said. 'I am a balloon observer. I was escaping when a German unit found me. I have just killed the last two of them.'

A torch flashed on to him for a moment and then off again.

'Are you alone?'

Willy hesitated. 'No,' he said. 'I have a man with me who helped me escape.'

'Is he Belgian?'

'No, he is half-English. I will vouch for him. He has killed a German officer.'

'Let us see him.'

'Up,' said Willy and Otto slowly lifted himself into view.

'Do you have weapons on you?'

Willy kicked the rifle further away with his foot. 'No.'

'So how did you shoot them?'

'I'll explain to your commanding officer.'

'Walk into the water towards us with your hands up and stop when I say.'

They walked in up to their waists and could see the vague shape of a boat a few yards away. The torch flashed on and off again.

'Stay there,' said the voice. They heard the boat grate against the bottom in the shallows and men splashing ashore. Low voices indicated that they had found the machine gun and its crew. Willy heard the sound of men getting back into the boat then saw it loom out of the darkness.

'Climb in,' commanded the voice. 'You first.'

Willy was searched by rough hands. 'Get down on the bottom and do not move. Now you.'

Otto went through the same process.

This boat was a larger version of the Germans' punt and when a distant flare climbed into the sky to the south, Willy could see four men paddling and four more sitting staring at them with guns lined up on them. Fifteen minutes of zig-zagging between obstacles brought them to an embankment. They were half-pulled out on to a rough timber dock and marched forward over the rise and down into a bunker built into the reverse slope. A candle lantern lit a group of men around a table. The leader of the boat party explained to an officer what had happened.

'An RFC Lieutenant,' said the officer in French. He walked across to Willy, held up the lantern and examined his face. 'Possible,' he said. He turned to Otto. 'What have we here?' he asked, 'and what is your native tongue?'

'I speak English,' said Otto. 'My French is not so good. I was a German officer but I have, I suppose you would say, deserted.'

'A German officer and an RFC lieutenant. A most unlikely pair. I don't believe any of it.' He looked at Willy. 'You, he said. 'Go to the table and write down your name, your number and your unit. I will contact your unit headquarters and what you say had better be true. Do it in silence. If either of you speak, I will shoot you myself.' Willy went to the table. A group of men were huddled in the darkness beyond it, watching him.

He almost wrote his real name before realizing that would get him nowhere with the balloon unit so instead he wrote 'Claud Taverner' and the matching details on a sheet of paper lit by a dim candle.

The officer walked across to stand next to him, looked at it and silently wrote the words, 'Now write down the German's name.'

Willy realized too late what was coming. He dutifully wrote 'Otto Ebener Thiessen von

464

Neumann' then stood aside.

Otto was put through the same procedure then the Belgian officer studied the two sheets of paper.

'It seems I was right,' he said. 'You say you are Claud Taverner but your friend here says you are William Fraser. You should have got your story straight. You are certainly spies, I think.'

'I'm a British officer,' said Willy. 'Many of your senior officers know me well, as do King Albert and Queen Elisabeth.'

'Ridiculous. Under both your names, I suppose. Do you often have tea with the Kaiser as well?'

'They know me as William Fraser. I served as a lieutenant-colonel in your army in 1914.'

'And yet you gave me your name as Claud Taverner? You are absurd. Today I do not have time for this craziness. I am about to be very busy indeed.' He turned to a subordinate. 'Take them outside,' he said. 'Get them ready. Prepare the squad. You know what to do. I will be along shortly.'

29

Chester K. Hoffman had often been near the front lines but only *in* them twice and the first of those had been a brief visit to a quiet part of the German lines back in the early days when their High Command still cherished hopes of winning over American opinion. Not a shot was fired. No story. The second was arranged by the French for a few influential American pressmen to what was also described as a very quiet area. It had given him a startling understanding of what French soldiers meant by the words 'very quiet'. Deafening, lethal and terrifying would have been better descriptors especially when Joe Austin from the *Post* misunderstood their escort's shout and straightened up enough to show the top three inches of his scalp above the parapet. The way Joe wrote the story later, the sniper's bullet parted his hair and even Chester, envying the headline, had to concede that was only a slight exaggeration.

This flooded front line was like nothing he had ever seen before. They came from De Panne, driving fast until they came to a heap of rubble, the wreck of the village of Ramskapelle. 'This is where we stopped them,' said the Belgian Captain next to him in the back seat of the staff car. 'Here our glorious fourteenth regiment pushed them back into the floods on the last day of October 1914. We will leave the car here out of harm's way.'

They walked on for a mile into the night and it was just that — night. Whenever Chester had been within sight of the lines at night before, the horizon had been lit by a devil's firework extravaganza. He had once tried to learn the palette of war, which explosive was yellow, which one orange, white or electric blue. In the end he decided they all killed pretty much the same way. Then there were the flares that looped up into the sky, white to spot the creeping enemy, coloured to call for help, except here there were none.

'Why is it so dark?' he asked. 'Did the war go away?'

'The lines are too far apart. The flooding, you understand? We shell them from time to time but it is mostly a waste. Today the English ships bombarded them for a while to persuade them to draw back from their outposts. Now we hope they will sleep and while they are sleeping we will launch our attack.'

'How will you attack?'

'Fifty raiding parties on boats. Four hundred men. We will go for their listening posts and their causeways. We will take some prisoners and blow up others. It is good to keep them nervous.'

There were troops of men on the path, shuffling towards war weighed down with its hardware — ammunition boxes, wire and empty stretchers, men too tired to give Chester more than a single puzzled glance and who looked away again as if they had insufficient energy left to bother thinking about him. They came in the end to a linear shanty town — low huts of timber, iron and sandbags jostling along behind an embankment. Chester thought the first pioneers might have thrown up something similar in Sioux territory. Men squatted in entrances or perched on improvised stools, their cigarettes glowing orange to light up tired and muddy faces with every indrawn breath. He noticed how slowly they inhaled as if they were keeping count of the finite number of breaths left to them and decided to remember that for his story. He dismissed that thought immediately, imagining Bruiser Brewster on the Foreign Desk crumpling the paper in his hand. *Gimme facts, Hoffman, not this goddam fancy fairy dust.*

The Belgian officer escorting him asked a soldier something Chester could not understand and seemed surprised by the answer, asking again. The soldier gave him an emphatic reply this time, pointing along the embankment.

'The Major is busy,' said the Belgian. 'It seems he is about to execute two spies. Do you want to see that?' He looked at Chester as if he expected him to say no, which was what Chester wanted to say but he felt bound to rise to the challenge.

'I guess,' he said. 'Lead on.' It sounded like a story no one else would have.

They walked and slid on wet duckboards to a place where the shacks behind the embankment ended in a square compound surrounded by a sandbagged wall. Two blindfolded men, their clothes encrusted in mud, were tied to posts. Six soldiers waited with their rifle butts resting on the ground. An officer stood by the men, speaking urgently to them. Chester's escort listened.

'They were captured out there in the water and they are sticking to their story. They claim they have given him their true names but that is a lie,' the escort translated. 'He gives them one last chance to confess who they really are.'

The officer shook his head, walked back to the waiting squad and gave an order. The men slowly picked up their rifles, worked the bolts and aimed. One of the prisoners lifted his head at the sound. 'I tell you one last time,' he said defiantly. 'I am Lieutenant Claud Taverner of the Royal Flying . . . ' but the last word was lost in a fusillade of shots.

Faced by acute danger, the brain brings its vast unused resources into play. It starts by checking the memory for any similar situation that might suggest a way out. In the new and lethal world of ballooning, every observer had felt that sudden race of thought as time slowed down. Faced by fire at five thousand feet or bullets tearing through the basket floor, it was that chemical surge that kicked in the training and sent them over the side without a second thought. At worst, when the brain could find no helpful comparison at all, it simply replayed all possible circumstances along the way in the forlorn hope that one might contain an answer.

Willy's brain had run out of strategies while he was sitting under guard in a damp dug-out — separated from Otto and told to keep silent. Instead it sent him a long parade of all the events leading to this place where his allies would kill him simply because he had been saddled with two names. That took him to the shell burst on this very same railway embankment as the flood-water first crept in and to the hospital in the dunes where they had brought him back to life. He remembered waking one morning to take the usual inventory of the state of his pain and seeing a sight so bizarre that he took it for another hallucination — Marion McAlister dressed up as some sort of nurse, standing at the end of the bed staring at him in equal astonishment.

'Willy Fraser?' she said. 'That cannot really be you, can it?'

He could speak only in a whisper at that stage in his recovery so she had to come very close to hear his answer and the scent of her skin and her breath took him back to those wild, dangerous days at the barracks when she had not seemed to care whether the Colonel had found out what his wife was doing to render her days a little less boring.

She was in and out of the ward for the next few days, bossing young English nurses who got on with their job regardless of how she misdirected them. Willy watched her through the vast pain burning all the way up his left side and found he felt absolutely nothing for her any more. She in turn seemed disconcerted to find him less perfect, less vigorous. Duty of sorts took Marion away which was a relief but she reappeared when he was convalescing at the royal villa, sweeping in as a temporary guest, awaiting the arrival of her husband sent out from

England on a mission to the King. He was delayed, Willy was much recovered and when Marion knocked softly at his door in the middle of the second night, Willy had assumed she was somebody else completely. By the time he found out that the body in his bed was not the one he had been hoping for, there was no gentlemanly way of going back.

The King's staff, charged with rescuing the Colonel from his diverted ship, did rather too good a job. They got the Colonel back to the villa at two o'clock in the morning, twelve hours before he was expected. The Colonel's surprise at finding his wife in the corridor in her dressing-gown turned to barely suppressed fury when he learnt William Fraser was also a guest. He was hell-bent on revenge from that moment. In the next weeks, Willy recovered his strength and rejoined the cavalry and his exploits saw him promoted rapidly as senior officers were slaughtered around him. The Colonel was waiting for his opportunity back home, plotting from his comfortable office until his chance came. The story of the pack of hounds reached him and he twisted it to a disreputable shape and put it to the service of destroying Lieutenant-Colonel William Fraser. So it was that Willy had been given the Stellenbosch choice — all those steps on the long and absurd road to this death by Belgian bullets.

They came for him, took him roughly by the arms and led him to a wall of sandbags and he caught a last glimpse of Otto before they blindfolded him. A Belgian voice spoke in his ear. 'One final chance only. Tell us the truth and you live to be a prisoner. Who are you really?'

At that moment he felt much closer to Claude in his final agony than to Willy. 'I have already told you,' he hissed back.

'Enough.'

He heard the rifle bolts rattle and knew that time had run out. All he had left was to shout his defiance in Claude's name and memory and when the shots crashed out at him, he was astonished to find the transition to death so entirely painless that he could still hear and smell and feel even if the blindfold stopped him seeing. Footsteps approached. That same Belgian voice spoke in his ear.

'Blanks that time,' it said. 'Blanks to show you we are serious. Live rounds this time. Your last chance.'

'Go to hell,' said Willy in English and he heard Otto chuckle.

'Why does he laugh?' asked the Belgian officer.

'Don't worry,' said Otto. 'If we get there first, we will keep a seat warm for you.'

Again the bolts rattled but someone was yelling, someone with an American voice, someone who came rushing up to Willy and pressed his back against Willy's chest, screening him from the firing squad.

'Put those goddam rifles down,' the voice shouted. 'I know him. The Queen knows him. The goddam King knows him. He's a goddam authentic five-star Scotch hero, you goddam half-wits.'

'Chester?' said Willy. 'You can stop swearing now. Where the hell did you come from?'

'Let's call it magic. Hey, should I let them shoot the other guy? I can't stand in front of both of you.'

'No, no. He's on our side too. Could you persuade them to take this blindfold off?'

'We were not going to shoot you,' the Belgian officer said as he untied the cloth. 'It was just blanks to get information.'

'Understood,' said Willy. He walked across to the nearest member of the firing squad. 'May I?' he asked and took the man's rifle before he could object. He jerked the bolt open and a live round flew out and dropped on the ground. They all stared at it.

Chester's escort snorted and began writing in a notebook. He demanded the officer's name. 'Come,' he said. 'I will drive you to Furnes.' He pointed at Otto. 'Do you answer for the behaviour of this man?'

'Certainly. I would trust him, indeed I have trusted him, with my life.'

'Mr Hoffman,' said the escort. 'Do you wish to stay here and watch the rest of tonight's operation?'

'Hell no,' said Chester. 'I'm not letting this guy out of my sight. I take my eyes off him, he gets into all kinds of trouble. Needs a nursemaid.'

'Chester,' said Willy, 'despite your essential vulgarity, I could almost hug you. Meet Otto. He'll make a much better story for you than I ever will.'

Chester's escort led them back to the staff car.

473

It was a slow journey, Willy limping badly as the wounds in his leg complained. The car took them into a small town and stopped. 'This is Furnes?' said Willy. He looked around the shelled wreckage of the Grand Place and sighed. 'My God, I was here with the King. This was his headquarters in '14.'

'It is still a headquarters,' said their guide, 'but these days we live like moles. Gentlemen, please follow me.'

He led them between two guards and down steps under a heavy lintel. A bunker had been built in the remains of a medieval cellar, old stone arches on one side, concrete on another. He took them into a side room where they sat down around a table.

'Refreshments will come and perhaps a medic for your leg. Please be patient.'

'What's the story with you two?' Chester asked Willy.

'I was about to ask the same,' said Otto, so Willy tried to explain in as few words as possible.

'So you made it to the farmhouse?' said Chester. 'I knew you would, you old bastard. I nearly got you out of there, did you know that? The poor kid in the plane. I sent him.'

'I thought you must have done. How did you know I was there?'

'I kinda guessed and then I asked a friend of yours and she helped me pin it down.'

'A friend of mine?'

'Maybe we better not go there right now. She likes to keep things quiet. Let's just say she nursed you.'

Willy tried to imagine Queen Elisabeth confiding in Chester and found he wasn't up to it. 'So that pilot died trying to get me?'

'Hell, Willy. In this whole war I was never responsible for killing someone before. You may be accustomed to it, I ain't.'

Otto looked up sharply. 'You never get accustomed to it,' he said, 'but it's a lot easier when you can't see what you did.'

Chester rounded on him. 'You may think so, but I'm a writer, buddy. I spend my whole goddam time imagining stuff like that. Usually it's other people. This time it's me. I'll have that guy in my head for a very long time.' He took a deep breath and turned back to Willy. 'So did you get to meet Tavernier's widow?'

Willy didn't want to answer but he was afraid Otto might do it for him.

'Yes,' he said briefly.

'Did she look like her photo?'

'Who can say?'

'I suppose I can,' said Otto. 'If by Tavernier's widow, you mean a woman called Gabrielle then I can tell you that she looks like her photo only if her photo shows a lovely woman with a heart-shaped face, high cheekbones and long glossy hair, a little tired maybe but beautiful for all that and perhaps not sad enough to be taken for a widow, though that, I think, is only recent and since she met our friend here, she looks very happy indeed.'

'Otto,' said Willy. 'Please speak only when you're spoken to.'

'Boy, now that's what I call an ending,' said

Chester. 'Okay, big man, I guess I got your story sewn up now.'

'Do you really think so?'

'Remember our deal? If I tell it to you the way it was, you'll give me the okay to print it. That's what you said.'

'This isn't the moment, Chester.'

'Hey, I saved your life back there. I gotta go south tomorrow. This might be the only chance I get.'

'Shall I block my ears?' said Otto.

'You can listen,' said Willy wearily. 'Let's get it over with.'

'Goes like this,' said Chester. 'I been talking to a whole lot of people, even had a letter from your man in Scotland.'

'Gilfillan?' said Willy, shocked.

'The same. He didn't say much but he's worried as hell. You got to tell him you're alive. Anyway, this guy Claude picks you up at the frontier after you dumped me in the arms of the whole German army. You and he get on pretty good. Comrades-in-arms. You slug it out with the Germans right round Liège while the big guns blow the place to bits. You fight right through Belgium, right up here then something goes wrong. You both get hit by a shell-blast and you have to watch Claude die. Nothing you can do. He's too bad and there's no help. You find a letter for his wife and a photograph. Yeah?'

'Up to a point.'

'Time passes.' He put on a joke accent and pretended to screw a monocle into his eye. 'The limey generals decide they don't like the cut of

476

your jib.' He frowned and went on in his normal voice, 'They bust you down. They only let you stay if you change your name, so you choose to call yourself after your old friend Claude. You spend your time up in the air staring towards the farm where his widow just might be and when fate tosses you a hellish chance you blow over there and go see her. Final act, sounds like you and the widow might live happy ever after if this goddamn war ever ends.' He stared at Willy. 'So do I get to print it?'

'You got one big thing wrong, Chester. There's no happy ending. She hates me.'

'Don't spin me a yarn. Your pal here don't seem to agree with you.'

'Oh really?' Willy felt unaccustomed heat rising in his cheeks. 'Well there's something he doesn't know and it's no business of either of you. She hates me because I killed her husband.'

'Like I killed the pilot?'

'No, Chester.' He knew the moment had finally come to say it out loud, 'I took a pistol and I put a bullet in Claude's head.'

The silence was broken by a voice from the doorway. 'Gentlemen, have I arrived at a bad moment?' said the King.

Albert walked across to Willy and held out his hand. Willy lurched up to his feet to shake it but instead, Albert put both arms round him in a bear hug and held him like that for a long moment before helping him back down onto his chair. 'I am so very pleased to see you safe, my friend,' he said. He let go, sat down and turned to Chester. 'Yes, he shot Tavernier. The man begged him to. You look surprised, Mr Hoffman.'

'I got no clue what to make of that. That's one helluva thing to do, your Highness.'

'It is the bravest action of all,' said the King.

Chester stirred unhappily, shaking his head. He glanced at Willy and seemed about to answer but Otto beat him to it. 'You said you had an imagination just now. You said your dead pilot would stay in your head. Give us the benefit of that imagination of yours. Put yourself next to a dear friend who is dying in agony to a degree that really is far beyond your imagination. Look around and see that there is no possible chance of help and nothing else to ease his pain until his entirely inevitable death.'

'I guess.'

'You guess?' said the King sharply. 'Tavernier begged him to do it. Is that not right, Fraser? That is what you told the Queen, I know. Mr Hoffman, thank you for preventing a tragedy here. I have a car waiting to take you away to wherever you wish to go. My staff will need to talk to our German friend to decide what to do with him but rest assured that we will consult Fraser about that. I promise you will be treated well, sir. Fraser, the Queen will, I am sure, insist that she has the first say over any medical treatment you may require and do not concern yourself — there is no Scottish colonel's wife prowling our villa or our hospital.'

30

'Are you still intent on pursuing this war in your own eccentric manner?' Albert asked him three days later. Willy's leg wound had been opened up and cleaned out at the hospital in the dunes. He had spent the time there worrying. Gabrielle was his main concern but he could do nothing. He had fantasies of finding a team of airmen to rescue the three of them because he knew she would not leave by herself, but landing next to a German gun emplacement could only end in disaster. Then he worried about Gilfillan and Morag, realizing he had done nothing to protect their interests from his mother. He hadn't even made out a will. That at least was something he could change but before he did so, he was summoned by the King. A car had brought him, bandaged and recovering, to the Villa Maskens.

'What choice do I have, sir?'

'You could always return to your commission here in the Belgian army. We would very much like to have you back and all you have to do is say the word. I promise I will sort out any ensuing fuss.'

'Sir, I am fairly sure you would not join the British army even if our King invited you and I know for a fact that you refused to put your forces under the French flag.'

'Albert, do stop teasing the poor man,' said

Elisabeth. 'You know he never takes the easy way.'

'But I ask him for a purpose, my dear,' said her husband mildly. 'I think he may now have good reason to become Belgian. My sources tell me that he has lost his heart to a Belgian lady.'

A look close to consternation flashed across the Queen's face and was quickly suppressed.

'No really, my dear,' said Albert. 'My staff have been discussing recent events with his German friend and they have learnt something quite remarkable. It is a very touching story. It seems that by some strange, one might almost say occult means, Fraser wafted across the lines and then navigated himself directly to the farmhouse where the widow of the gallant Tavernier is living. Moreover, she and Fraser have formed a very strong attachment and . . . '

'Please don't go on with this,' Willy said.

'Fraser, that is not customarily the way you speak to a king.'

'It is when he sticks his nose into things that are not his business. It was not gentlemanly of Otto to discuss that either.'

Albert stiffened. Willy saw all the signs that he was about to become pompous. 'All things are a king's business,' Albert said, 'and of course your German friend has talked. He has been obliged to disclose everything because he is under interrogation. What did you expect? It is not a matter of social chit-chat. He has information that may prove of great value to the war effort.'

'Is he being treated well?'

'As well as any German officer can expect to

be treated in the middle of — '

'I vouched for him. I gave him my word and so did you. He made my escape possible. He — '

'Do not interrupt me.' The King was on his feet now, his cheeks reddening. 'You are treating me like some ordinary person. Let me remind you — '

'I'm treating you like that because you're behaving like a very ordinary person.' Willy levered himself upright and stood there swaying. He found they were standing almost nose-to-nose. 'What happened on the other side of the lines is my personal business.'

The King stared at him, his fists clenching, and Willy wondered for a moment what the rules of etiquette said about punching a monarch. Did it make a difference if they came from another country? Then his leg gave way and he took the table and the tea tray with him as he collapsed. Being lifted back into his chair by both the King and the Queen did a little to defuse the situation.

'You're not well,' said Albert as if that was the obvious explanation for what had just happened. He turned away and Willy looked at Elisabeth. She put her finger to her lips and shook her head slightly. There was a knock at the door and a young officer appeared.

'I beg your pardon, sir,' he said, 'but there is a car here from the Royal Flying Corps to take Lieutenant Taverner away.'

'You should not go yet,' said the Queen. 'You are far from healed.'

'I must get back,' said Willy quietly. 'This is not my war any more, not here.'

'Indeed you must,' said Albert hastily. 'Your duty calls, after all. That is the way of men in war. Go, go.' He made little shooing motions with his hands then met Willy's gaze and stopped. 'Ah, Fraser. What a long way we have come. You have your reasons, I am sure. Let us shake hands.'

He clasped Willy's hand and stared hard at him. 'Will you grant me one wish however? It would be a better way of parting, I think.'

'Yes, sir. So long as it is something I can agree to with honour.'

'It most certainly is. I would ask that you revert to your real name, your Scottish name. You have done your duty to Belgium and to Claude Tavernier with that other name and it is time to be yourself again. I will make sure your High Command accepts it.'

'Fraser,' said the Queen. 'You will always be Fraser to us and who knows, perhaps one day you will be Fraser to Madame Tavernier.' She studied him with one eyebrow raised. 'Whatever may have happened over there, and I am sure it was no small thing, time will pass and all may be possible again.'

★ ★ ★

The Crossley waiting at the villa's gate had an unexpected driver at the wheel, Major Bernard Thompson. He got out and saluted the King and Queen. Albert and Elisabeth stood waving as they drove away.

'My goodness, you have an everlasting

capacity to surprise me,' said Thompson. 'That really was who I thought it was?'

'Yes, sir,' said Willy curtly, 'and put your foot down. I'm very glad to get away from them.'

'You really must dispense with the 'sir' when it's just the two of us. For heaven's sake, Willy Fraser, call me Bernard.'

'Do you want me to explain everything? I'm quite tired of all that.'

'Not unless you want to. Your pet Yank has already been around and he's filled me in with his version of events.'

'Thank the Lord for short, fat mercies.'

'I suppose I would be repeating myself if I said I am very glad to see you and you must have nine lives.'

'Not any more. I have two or three left at best.'

'Even if only half of it's true, I take my hat off to you. Now, how are you feeling? Normally I'd take you for a slap-up meal in Pop on the way back. A good steak-frites at Skindles is the least you deserve.'

'But?'

'Ah! You noticed.'

'You're driving very, very fast and you said 'normally'. I noticed, so what is the 'but'? There's a balloon involved somewhere.' He stopped himself saying 'sir' but couldn't quite manage 'Bernard'.

'I hoped that might wait for later. We have a way to go.'

'Tell me now, but just slow down a bit so I can concentrate. It would be good to survive until you get to the end of your next sentence.'

'All right.' Thompson sighed and his hands clenched on the wheel. The Crossley responded by skidding as it hit a pothole and he spent the next hundred yards controlling a series of pendulum slides. 'Wing are jumping up and down,' he said in the end. 'The Boches have brought a new gun into play. It's creating havoc in the rear areas.'

'What are they aiming at? Ypres again?'

'No, no. If it was poor old Ypres I suspect my superiors wouldn't be turning a hair. Rubble is rubble, after all, however they rearrange it. No, the Germans have been doing their homework. They're hitting our HQs, nice cushy places that thought they were out of harm's way until now and would prefer to stay that way. They've flattened four this week.'

'How did they locate them? Aircraft?'

'Would that it were so. The word is that a party of top brass red-tabs out from Blighty on a sector familiarisation visit went the wrong way last week. Snobby lot apparently who reckoned they didn't need a guide. That was the last anyone saw of them so it's a sound bet that they blundered off into No Man's Land in the dark. The Boches must have snaffled them and persuaded them to spill the beans. I would lay odds they still had their maps with them.'

'So this gun is targeting the rear area HQs?'

'Absolutely. You can imagine how the Generals feel about that. Every squadron around the Salient has been out looking for it but the aeroplanes can't see any trace of it. All the signs are that it's a big naval gun and it's well hidden rather worryingly close by.'

German very-long-range guns were conspicuous targets usually kept well back behind the lines and that limited their effectiveness. With a sinking heart, Willy realized he knew exactly where this one was hidden.

Thompson had speeded up again. He just missed a despatch rider coming the other way. 'Next thing I know, Wing's on the phone telling me you've done your old trick again and popped up out of nowhere so can I come and get you straight away because you're needed.'

'Me? Have they run out of other observers?'

'I gather you brought some German officer across with you. Seems the Belgians have been putting the thumbscrews on him.' Thompson slowed down behind a line of trucks and looked across at Willy. 'Your German friend apparently told them enough to get them somewhat excited.'

Willy felt a chill. 'Do you know exactly what he said?'

'Apparently he kept saying, 'ask Willy Fraser' and he wouldn't change his tune whatever they did to him.'

'And how did anyone know he meant me?'

'Because your Yankee chappy was at Wing HQ and he knew the rest of the story. Anyway, seems you did very well to catch the Boche officer because although he's clammed up on that part, they're getting lots of other good stuff out of him. They say they'll get him talking about the gun in the fullness of time but Wing don't want to wait.'

'Jesus. They're putting him through it, are they?'

'Of course they are.'

'The man's a hero. I didn't catch him. He changed sides. Slow down. Turn in there on the right.'

Two sentries guarded a gate into a Belgian army camp. Willy barked commands at them and they lifted the pole. Thompson stopped the Crossley outside the command office. A Belgian officer looked up in surprise as they walked in, Thompson trailing a few steps behind. 'Get me High Command in Furnes on the phone,' said Willy. 'Immediately if you please.'

'Who in hell are you to come charging in here demanding that?'

'I am Lieutenant-Colonel William Fraser formerly of the King of Belgium's personal staff. Do it now.'

He did.

When they brought the officer in charge of Otto's interrogation to the phone, Willy was merciless. 'You will regard him as an ally,' he said. 'You can take that as the King's personal order and you may check it with him. If I hear he has been harmed, I will have you sent to guard some boggy island in the middle of the flood until next spring. What is your name?'

Thompson watched in wonder as Willy listened to the answer. 'Yes, I know he said that,' he replied in the end. 'Yes, I do know the likely location and yes I am on my way to deal with it now. Remember, I mean what I say and I will deal with you if necessary. Leave him alone. He is on our side and he will cooperate if and only if you remember that and treat him with courtesy.'

'Who were you talking to?' asked Thompson as they got back in the car.

'Matthieu, I think he said.'

'Some sort of lieutenant?'

'No, a colonel.'

'Remind me never to get on the wrong side of you,' said Thompson as he let in the clutch. 'So do you mean to say you actually know where this gun is?' and that was when it fully struck home to Willy that the gun in question was in Gabrielle's backyard and one way or another his own big guns would soon be shelling Gabrielle.

'Probably,' he said.

'We'll go straight to Locre,' said Thompson. 'You'll have to report to Wing first then it's a pound to a penny they'll want you to lead the shoot.' He glanced down at Willy's leg. 'Are you up to it? If not you can brief Plot to do it.'

Plot, the clear-eyed god of destruction, thought Willy. Plot, whose first warning to the little family trapped inside the farm would be the deafening arrival of death on their doorstep. 'No,' he said. 'I'll be doing this one, nobody else.'

$$\star \quad \star \quad \star$$

Wing HQ was on the hill they called Mont Rouge, behind the village of Locre. Willy had always found it an unsettlingly cosy place, granted some strange immunity from the nearby war. The Colonel and his adjutant had quiet, comfortable offices with proper bookshelves and

487

strong smoking chairs brought out from England. The small mess had plump sofas and a dining table loaded at mealtimes with strikingly good food cooked by a Belgian chef. A wide wooden balcony looked out south across towards the larger, altogether bloodier, rise of Mount Kemmel and the active edge of war. A telescope on a tripod stood there and jaundiced observers sometimes said that was as close as Wing HQ usually came to the travails of the men under their command. Willy knew that wasn't true. Colonel Peterson had done hard time up in the sky and did not advertise the fact that his missing eye had been taken by a fragment from the shell that blew his basket apart around him. He was a wiry man, a forty-year-old aged a decade more than that by the war's violent tannery.

'Taverner,' said the Colonel. 'I just heard you made it back again. That is a most unexpected pleasure. I really thought they had you this time. How did you do it?'

Thompson stepped forward. 'Sir, I suggest that may have to wait. Taverner knows the probable location of the Comines gun.'

'Tell me. Maps, please, George.'

The adjutant spread out a large map of the area between the front and Comines. Willy stared at it. He could see the farm but he knew that if he put his finger on the spot they would not need him and Gabrielle might as well be dead already.

'I have some difficulty identifying it this way, sir,' he said. 'I'll have to be up top looking at the landscape. I found the place while I was evading capture. I'm sure I'll work it out if I can see the terrain.'

'So can you tell me why the flyboys can't find it?'

'It is a long-barrelled naval gun, probably twelve inch bore or thereabouts. It is hidden inside a building.'

'Are you quite sure?' said Peterson. 'We'd ruled out buildings. There are barns all round there but if it's hidden in a barn, how do they aim it? They must be able to traverse it from side to side because the damned thing's been hitting targets left, right and centre.'

'I saw the building after they laid the concrete for the bed,' Willy said. 'They had built a quadrant to swing it round. There's a long, disguised hatch in the roof. They elevate the gun and the barrel must pass through the hatch at the halfway point so they can swing it round within reason. When they've finished, they straighten it up and lower away. The hatch closes and that's it.'

'You're telling me you *saw* the actual place?'

'Yes, sir.'

'And you can only find it again by looking? Really?'

'That's right.'

The Colonel pondered. 'It's a fair old stretch south of the lines for spotting,' he said. 'Where do you want to go up from?'

Willy fingered a spot on the map. 'There.' He stuck in a thumb-tack.

'Don't be ridiculous,' said Thompson. 'That's

489

barely half a mile behind the front lines. You'll be asking for it.'

'Put a couple of flights of scouts up to protect me. Have Plot up there somewhere a bit further back so he can knock out their batteries if they shell me.'

'Is Plot all right to fly?' the Colonel said to the adjutant.

'A bit singed,' said the adjutant, 'but he's been up again this morning.'

'What happened to him?' said Willy.

'The white Albatros got him yesterday. He jumped but the balloon passed him on the way down. He lost some hair. Someone needs to deal with that Albatros.'

'Make that three flights of scouts then,' said Willy. 'Can you get Hawker to come with them, sir?'

'Hawker's got his hands full at Bertangles,' said the adjutant. 'There's some new hot-shot Boche scout jockey down there. Feller in a bright red Albatros D11. Hawker's after him.'

'What time do you want to do this?' asked Peterson.

The clock on the wall said it was only 11 a.m. though Willy had lost track of what day of the week it was and realized he needed a large breakfast. 'It will have to be daylight,' he said, thinking that daylight might just see the family outside working in the fields. 'Shall we say two o'clock if we can get the balloons positioned by then?'

'See to it, Thompson,' said Peterson. 'Get them moving now. No time to spare. They'll be firing again as soon as it's dark. We don't want any more punishment like last night.' Thompson picked up the phone and began giving orders.

'Taverner,' said Peterson, 'when this is done, you're owed some leave I think. That's the very least we can do for you.'

'Actually, sir, there's one more thing I would like you to do.'

'Yes?'

'It's a request from the King of Belgium. He wants me to go back to my real name.' Willy expected surprise and a demand for explanation but Peterson only looked at him and nodded slowly.

'So that means the American's story *is* true?' he said. 'How very odd.'

'Has Hoffman been here again, sir?'

'You only just missed him. I thought the man had to be inebriated. Well, on balance I'm pleased. Welcome back, Wild Willy Fraser. I'm not quite sure whether there's an RFC form to cover this precise eventuality but we'll have sorted something out by the time you've finished this escapade. Do try to keep the balloon attached to the ground this time.' His tone was light but his eyes kept straying to the map and the thumb-tack, closer by far to the enemy than any daytime balloon had flown in the known history of the Salient. 'I'll see you there later on.'

'You're coming, sir?'

'As you know very well, there are times when you cannot order men into places you would not go yourself.'

They got back in the Crossley and Thompson

drove down the lanes to the wood that sheltered their balloon section. The Major braked to a halt just before turning into the entrance. 'Your friend's here,' he said. Chester Hoffman was standing on the edge of the wood talking animatedly to a sergeant.

'I don't really want to see him at this precise moment,' said Willy. 'Look, do you mind running me over to Polito's section? I need to go over all this with him anyway. I'll meet you at the balloon site in good time.'

Wing HQ had already told Plot that Willy was on his way. 'Fraser!' he said when he saw Willy. 'How very complicated. Taverner, then Fraser. I'm sure someone will explain sometime. I think I might just call you 'Lazarus'. It seems easier.'

'Plot, I need you to listen carefully to me and not ask too many questions. Can you do that?'

'I don't know but I'll give it a go.'

'You know we're looking for a target around Comines?'

'I certainly do.'

'You may find my actions up there a little strange.'

'Nothing new there. I'll do my best to ignore them politely.'

'No, Plot, I need you to go along with whatever I do. I'll identify the target but after that it won't be the usual shoot. If I have to go over the side at any point, I want you to take the lead from what you've already seen me do.'

'And how will I know what that is?'

'You'll be listening in and I think you'll work it out from what you see. Do you promise?'

'I'm a little mystified, old boy, but if you say so. I'll do my best to watch your back. You'll make a very juicy target for their gunners. Should be lots of fun. Don't forget our annoying new friend in the Albatros. He's horribly good at his job. Almost had me this morning.' Willy looked at him sharply. Plot's voice had lost its usual bantering tone in that last sentence.

He ate a second breakfast, found a spare cot in a tent and went to sleep. Plot shook him awake. 'It's one o'clock, old man,' he said. 'We've got out some togs for you. Sun's shining its little head off because it hasn't heard it's November but it's still cold enough to freeze your bits off up there.'

Willy pulled on the lined leather breeches and four layers of vest, shirt, fleece jumper and leather jacket. The boots were tight and his leg hurt as he hauled the first one on, but once it was on the pressure seemed to help and he could walk more easily. He put the gloves and leather helmet in a bag. A tender drove them towards the lines. He was silent, caught between worlds, coming back full circle towards that point in the high air where he would hang once again separated from her by nothing but space, imagining her as close to him as she had been — impossible to grasp now as anything but a manic delusion.

31

The tender bumped, rattled and tipped its way slowly through all the paraphernalia of the back area, the casualty clearing stations, the dumps of barbed wire and shells, the artillery batteries, cooking trailers and water bowsers. The shell holes clustered closer and closer and the mud grew deeper as they went, further than vehicles usually dared go and then there was Plot's balloon ahead of them, tethered to the ground out in the open, half concealed by a shallow dip and the ragged, shell-stripped trunks of three trees. They could see no German balloons in the sky and Willy took that as a blessing because his balloon, so close to the lines, would have been a sitting duck.

'The scout flight from 6 Squadron gave their gasbags a good going over for us,' said Plot. 'Sent one down in flames and riddled the other one. Good work. It should be a little while yet before they put up some replacements. Brilliant visibility. First sunny day for a fortnight.'

'All right. Now, Plot, you're clear about what I said?'

'Will I do what you said? Yes. Am I clear about what that is or why you said it? No, not in the least but that's war, eh?'

'I'd better get on with it,' said Willy.

Plot looked serious. 'When you're ready, give me the shout. I'll go up before you. I'll be a slightly harder target for them back here. That might distract them while you get up to a safer height.'

'Thanks, Plot.'

'Good luck, Lazarus.'

The tender lurched its way further forward into the ever-increasing destruction of the front line's backyard. It swayed over roughly filled-in shell holes then on to a newly laid roadway of improvised planking and bundles of sticks doing their best to fill in the worst of the holes. Now, just as Willy realized he had forgotten to make out his will, he saw his own balloon ahead, so obvious and so much further forward than they had ever attempted before that he was astonished it was not being shelled. Then he saw why. A thick cloud of smoke was blanketing the lines beyond it. The troops in the trenches had set off smoke canisters as they did before an attack. Up above, he could see scouts circling, six silver Nieuports, a trio of Sopwith Pups and an Airco or two. For the moment the balloon might be safe. Without their own balloons up, the Germans would not see him, not until he rose above the smokescreen into their vision.

A crowd of exhausted air mechanics were showing the effects of building the trackway and forcing their winch lorry along it. A small group surrounded the basket. Willy saw Thompson talking to Peterson and knew the Major and the Colonel hadn't wanted him to take this risk alone. Then he saw that one of the air mechanics with them was not an air mechanic at all.

Standing there in borrowed overalls bulging at the seams, his head covered by an ill-fitting and slanted tin hat, was Chester K. Hoffman.

Thompson came to meet him as he approached the group. 'Sorry about the Yankee,' he said. 'He talked his way through. It's a bit too late to get rid of him.'

'He can stay,' said Willy. 'He thinks it's my story but I suppose it's just as much his really. Give me a minute with him, would you?'

Willy saluted Peterson who saluted him back then he took Chester to one side. 'They'll start shelling us the moment the smoke clears. You should go back now while you can.'

'And miss the big story?' said Chester. 'I'm not going, Willy. I want to see what you do next. I guess I know the bit you haven't told these guys yet.'

'You worked it out, did you?'

'They gave me a few minutes with your friend Otto. You got a helluva choice, my friend. What happens now?'

'I'm making it up as I go along, Chester. You haven't said anything?'

'Willy Fraser, I know you think I'm a royal pain in the ass but you're my pal whatever you may think of me. I've kept stumm. Listen to me, I got the whole goddam story written right up to the last line. 'The Gasbag Trumpeter'. Worth the whole front page and then some. Do I get to publish it?'

'Do I get to read it first?'

'When you come back down.' He slapped his pocket. 'It's right in here. What do you say?'

'Let's get through this bit first, shall we? Chester, there is something you can do for me.'

'Whatever you say.'

'Get your notepad out. Can you write quickly? Promise me you will get this to Donald Gilfillan at Grannoch Castle near Newton Stewart in Galloway, Scotland. You know who he is. Have you got that address?'

'Yeah.'

'Put the date at the top then write this down.' Willy spoke slowly, staring up at the balloon. 'This is the last Will and Testament of William Andrew Fergus Fraser of Grannoch Castle.'

'Slower.'

'I hereby leave Grannoch Castle and all my possessions to Donald and Morag Gilfillan. Shall I spell that?'

'No, I got it. Go on.'

'That's all. Let me sign it. Now, you witness it. Don't lose it.'

'Jeez,' said Chester. 'That's short and down-right alarming. I got to say this.' He shuffled from foot to foot. 'I apologize before I say it.'

'Spit it out.'

'If you don't come back down, can I publish?'

Willy laughed. 'Oh, I'll come back down all right. The only question is how fast.'

'I mean it. If anything happens to you, I swear to you I won't publish unless you okay it right now.'

'I'm not a great believer in the afterlife, Chester. If I don't make it, I don't mind what you do. I promise not to haunt you so long as you get that will to Grannoch.'

497

'Time to go,' Thompson called. 'There's a bit of wind getting up. The smoke may clear.'

Willy swung his legs over the edge of the basket, clipped the parachute line to his harness, checked the map boards, binoculars and telephone. Peterson handed him another pair of binoculars. 'Try these,' he said. 'A Boche balloon drifted our way last week for a change. East wind. We found them in the basket. Higher magnification than ours. I liberated them but your need is greater than mine.'

'Thank you, sir.'

Plot's voice spoke in his earphones. 'I'm ready, Lazarus.'

'Hello, Plot. Up you go. I'll count to sixty and follow you.'

He looked backwards and saw the other balloon shoot up into the air half a mile behind him with the cable-drum running free. It was a dangerous way to ascend and it took a top-rate winchman not to break the cable. The Germans started shooting as he reached three hundred feet, machine-gun fire at first then the field guns came in on the act, firing high explosive but lagging behind the rising balloon.

Willy signalled to the ground crew and set off in the same wild style and it worked. Although he was a much closer target, the gunners weren't looking at him as the balloon burst into their view above the smoke. He was past a thousand feet before any shots came his way at all and then a single burst of machine-gun fire stitched the side of the balloon. He looked up at a group of small holes and shrugged to himself. They weren't incendiaries and he wasn't losing much gas.

He climbed more slowly now as the winchman began to control the drum, trying out the German binoculars, trying to get used to the extra magnification and the steadiness it required. He turned back to the more familiar British version as the balloon climbed high enough to let him see beyond the ridge.

He was used to selecting targets, staring down at a landscape that was only a little different from a map — a theoretical place where there were enemies to be dealt with by remotely guided elimination. Now, for the first time in his observer experience, there was nothing at all remote about the landscape opening up before him.

Familiar places showed themselves straight away. He located the site of the supply dump he had destroyed last time, glanced back to see Plot nearly at full height and the scout planes circling to protect both of them. He concentrated on the ground ahead once more, found the crossroads, moved on to the road and saw that he knew this land now. It showed itself as distinct shapes and patterns on a long slant below, but those shapes and lines sprang out to reality in his head, informed by memories of the feeling of the lane under his feet, of the smell of the hay and the chickens and the bed and the people because there, far away, was the farm and now it was a precious place.

It was his target.

He knew he should think only of the war, of

his job, of the task of surviving. He should not think of Gabrielle.

How could he not think of her? The sight of the farm brought her back to him in full and vivid detail. He picked up the German binoculars again, waited for a moment when the balloon was steady and braced his arm against the rigging ropes. The farm sprang startlingly into view. He could see the yard and the barn, sitting there, quite innocent. No sign of the gun and the roof hatch indistinguishable from the tiles. He needed a precise plan and he had only a vague idea. He had hoped to see some sign that they had taken his advice and left. Instead he got the exact opposite. A tiny figure walked across the yard towards the house. Victor? Helene? Gabrielle? More likely to be Victor, judging by the stiff gait.

Plot's voice said, '*Drachen* going up, sou' sou' west.'

Willy looked that way and saw a German balloon, deep orange-brown in colour, rising into the air three or four miles away. That meant they would soon be targeting his winch, delighted to have such a rare opportunity. Perhaps they had already guessed why he was there. He looked down at his map board. 'Chart room, I have coordinates for their balloon site. Plot, can you steer the guns in on that *Drachen* winch while I sort out the main target?'

'Go to it, Lazarus.'

He half-listened to the babble of instructions and corrections as he stared at the farm. Two more German balloons were now ascending further away. The six Nieuports peeled off and flew in their direction. Plot's voice sounded strained. 'Give me another battery,' he was saying. 'I'll get on to them in a minute.'

'Please wait,' said the voice from the chart room. 'Negative. No battery available for three more minutes.'

'For God's sake,' said Plot. 'This takes priority.' He went silent for a moment then came back on, sounding puzzled. 'I'm getting signals.'

'What do you mean?' Willy said.

'From way over there. Something's flashing.'

'I can't see it. Sun on glass?'

'No. Deliberate. Regular. Give me a moment.' There was thirty seconds of drawn-out silence and Willy stared into the occupied land but he could still see nothing then Plot came back on. 'Damned if it's not Morse code,' he said. 'Can't you see it, really?'

'No. Not at all.' How could that be? 'Can you read it?'

There was another silence. 'Six letters,' said Plot. 'Sent three times. A bit amateur. It's spelling something like 'P' and then 'TAILY'. Doesn't make sense. Same again. PTAILY? Surely you can see it now.'

No, he couldn't but he knew exactly why he couldn't. They had not buried his heliograph mirror. Whoever was using it in today's sharp winter sun had chosen one of the two balloons, sighted it and hoped for the best. Willy stared through the binoculars at the farm. He could see the window of the attic room and then a dazzling glare came straight at him. He put the glasses

501

down and had no trouble at all seeing the flashes now coming straight at him, focused on him now as the signaller changed her mind and switched targets.

He read the flashes and saw that Plot was wrong. The first letter was not a 'P' at all, but a 'J' — just one dash difference. The signaller was flashing slowly and irregularly. He spelt out the rest of it, J-T-A-I-L-Y and forgot the war entirely. J-T-A for 'Je t'aime'. I-L-Y for 'I love you'.

He let out his breath and clutched the edge of the basket and was sure of the truth. Helene had talked it out with her, had made her understand what had happened in the Yser flood and Gabrielle had forgiven him. She had put her trust in his escape and watched the sky for him. She must have believed that a balloon would only be so close if it had him in its basket searching for her. Why else would it be up in this unusual corner of the sky?

She would not imagine that it bore a man tasked with killing her.

'Those flashes. Is that our target?' asked Plot, then before Willy could reply he let out a cry, 'Bloody hell. Watch out. Look at this lot.'

Willy swung round in the basket, looked up towards the sun and saw an astonishing horde of aircraft diving on Plot and his defenders. One Albatros after another — a dozen of them. More. Two dozen? Impossible. A gaggle like that was unknown. He saw an Airco already tumbling down with black smoke trailing, another one stall and spin with its top wing fluttering down separately.

He tore his eyes away, studied his map and drew a deep breath, calling the first coordinates to the chart room. There was a moment before the gunnery liaison officer replied. 'Please confirm coordinates. We have open country at that position.'

'Do as I say. Four rounds,' barked Willy. 'Two-second intervals between each. I know what I'm doing.'

'If you say so.'

'Just do it.'

He looked back at the dogfight behind. The circling, diving fighters were drifting away from Plot's balloon, entirely engrossed in their task. He saw a white Albatros, quite separate from the melee, diving from far above. 'Plot,' he called into the mouthpiece. 'You're under attack. Get out.'

'Where from?'

'Above. The white one. Go.' He saw Plot leap, saw the balloon erupt immediately into an upwards gout of flame. He turned back in time to see the four shells burst and their fountains of smoke quivering in the air just where he wanted them to be, two hundred yards this side of the farmhouse. 'Up just a whisker,' he called. 'You're a hundred yards short. Two more only.'

'Received,' said the chart room but over the top of the reply came a burst of noise. He looked down over the edge of the basket and saw retaliation had arrived. Brown puffs of smoke were hanging in the air far below him. Brown meant German shrapnel shells bursting low over the winch lorry, sending their shotgun sprays of steel balls into the defenceless men who were now running and falling.

He glanced back at the other balloon and saw it shrivelling, twisting and dropping down from the sky in a smear of smoke, overtaking Plot's parachute below it, then movement to the right caught his eye and there was the white Albatros banking in a tight turn, bending its direction around to come at him next. Where was the anti-aircraft gunfire that should be protecting him? Of course it was miles away. They hadn't had time to bring up the guns. Where were the scouts? Fully occupied half a mile away, fighting for their own lives and losing.

A voice in his ear, Thompson's voice, said calmly, 'Hostile aircraft attacking you. Jump, jump. Acknowledge. We are under fire.'

He picked up the glasses, stared towards the farmhouse and saw two more shells erupt still well short. They must hear that and they must run, he thought. Surely they would understand. It was all the warning he could possibly give them. Gabrielle would know a full bombardment had to come next, wouldn't she?'

'Are we on target?' asked the voice from the chart room in his ear. 'Can we commence battery fire?'

Willy knew the man had been listening hard to the exchanges, that he had understood only Willy was left and was trying to give him the chance to jump. The battery fire command would flick a lethal switch. The guns would open up and would not stop again until they had obliterated

504

everything. In that onslaught, Gabrielle would die.

An engine roared above him and a glowing train of bullets hosed down past him as the Albatros hurtled downward and twisted into a violent climbing turn for another pass.

'Observer, report please,' said the voice in his ear. 'Can you hear us? We will commence battery fire in ten seconds.'

'Wait,' he said, knowing there was no time to wait. He would only survive if he jumped now. She would only survive if he did not. 'Hold fire,' he said. 'Do exactly as I say. Two more rounds just as before.'

There they were, the sight he had been longing to see — three tiny figures running through the farmyard, running from his shells. He stared through the German glasses and for a golden fraction of a second he saw Gabrielle with total clarity, down through all that air. She was running with their panic bag in one hand, turning her head to glance back. What was the range? Fifteen seconds flight time for the shells, maybe eighteen. He watched as she reached the field beyond the farmyard. 'Prepare to commence battery fire on my command.'

'Received.'

He snatched a look down at the winch but the smoke from shrapnel bursts blocked his view. He thought no one could live through that, so really what on earth was the point of jumping in to it anyway?

The Albatros opened up its engine again and its bullets cut through the balloon and the edge of the basket. He ignored it and picked up the more familiar glasses to watch the far-off figures now running through the field. They would easily be clear by the time the shells landed. 'Commence battery fire,' he said as the first flame licked out of the balloon's tail fin. He looked up at the fire then back at the distant figures.

One of them had fallen and the other two were running back to help.

★ ★ ★

The first shrapnel bursts had done for a dozen of the air mechanics and a shrapnel ball had made a long trough in Chester's helmet. He was huddled against the winch lorry, next to Thompson who had taken the telephone hand-set from the dead operator. Two men were carrying Peterson between them, hoping to get him back to a dressing station in time but Chester saw one of them fall when the next salvo of shrapnel arrived, mixed with an erupting column of earth from a high-explosive shell. And sane men are expected to do *this*, he thought. Thompson shouted a warning into the telephone — something about an aircraft — and Chester looked up to see the white Albatros diving on Willy. 'Tell him to goddam jump,' he yelled.

'Shut up,' said Thompson.

More shrapnel and Chester was knocked flat as the winch operator slid down the side of the truck and landed on him, blood spraying from his neck. He heaved the inert body off him, looked wildly around and saw men spread-eagled everywhere, some screaming, some silent.

'He's on fire,' said Thompson next to him. Blood was running down the major's upturned face. He followed Thompson's gaze and saw flame licking out of the tail of the balloon so very far above.

'Jump, for Christ's sake,' yelled the Major into the mouthpiece, then, 'Are you sure? Ripped? All right, stick it out. We'll tow you down.'

He climbed up to the cab of the lorry and leant over a moment later to shout at Chester. 'Get up here. I need you on the winch,' he yelled.

'Me?'

'You. They're all dead. It's just us left.'

'Jeez.' Chester climbed on to the back of the truck, out of its shelter into the cauldron of bullets and shrapnel. Thompson pushed the driver's body out of the open cab, didn't even watch it fall and edged into its place. The engine was idling. 'Pull that lever towards you when I tell you,' yelled Thompson. 'The one on the right. Got it?' The lorry set off, accelerating. 'Get it ready. Pull it *now*.'

Chester tugged hard and the winch screeched into action. He looked up and saw a long flame curling from the tail of the Cacquot then everything happened at once. The lorry began to move as a shrapnel shell burst above them. Balls whined off the winch and the rest of the truck. Something mighty ripped Chester's helmet off his head, the strap snapping as his head jerked back. Thompson crumpled and fell off his seat,

507

vanishing over the side of the careering truck.

Chester yelled, 'Help us, someone. Over here,' but there was nobody at all left to hear him. He looked at the spinning winch then up at the gasbag coming down and the fire gaining ground, eating through the fin towards the main body of the balloon and he knew exactly what the major had intended. The lorry was lumbering along by itself. He clambered across the winch equipment, half fell into the driver's seat and stared at the controls. This can't be that hard to do, he thought. I've driven an automobile. Once. Badly. The truck was still lined up along the trackway. He pressed a pedal and it slowed. He tried another and it jolted forward. He pressed harder. The engine was screaming so he did what he had seen drivers do. He pushed the remaining pedal all the way down and used both hands to thrust the gear lever in the direction he hoped was right. There was a crunch and when the pedals had sorted themselves out he found his speed had doubled. If any more shrapnel had burst above them, he had been far too busy to notice.

He accelerated again, managed another gear change with no crunch at all and suddenly he was juddering and bumping along the trackway at a speed that commanded his full attention with the steering wheel. The vast balloon was dragging at the truck, doing its best to hold him back as the winch fought to wind it down. He glanced behind and saw it was working, the balloon was angling back behind him and his speed had sent the flames streaming out backwards. Did he have another gear? He tried it, found one, and the truck leapt forward, bellowing.

He looked back again and saw two German balloons watching like fat brown eyeballs and exulted. 'You thought you had him, huh?' he yelled. 'Oh yeah? You didn't reckon on the good old US of A.'

A shell burst to one side of the track just ahead, showering him with dirt and sharp stones. He wiped his eyes, saw blood on his hand and shrieked defiance. He was racing the German guns now, terrified and thrilled, as their shells chased him along the trackway, bursting on one side then the other. 'Can't get me, huh?' he shouted. 'Can't handle a moving target, is that it?'

When he came off the end of the trackway, he reckoned the balloon was halfway down. The ground here was badly broken but he couldn't slow down without the flames starting to eat into the belly of the balloon. It was sinking faster and now he could see Willy up there in the basket, staring back at the inferno closing in on him.

Chester fought the steering wheel, careering over the ruts. He kept checking behind him. Another two hundred yards should do it. He had lost a little speed with the bumps and the steering and the wild wobbling. The balloon was falling too fast. He stiffened his nerve and forced the pedal flat on the floor again, his arms aching with the effort of holding the truck straight. One more rapid glance behind showed him the balloon a hundred yards up.

He looked forward again and wondered for a split second where the Salient had gone.

The way ahead was blotted out by a wall of smoke and earth as a vast shell exploded in the middle of the track. He lifted his foot as the cloud enveloped him then the smoke blew away in the wind to reveal an immense crater right in his path where the track had been.

A very clear thought came into Chester's head and he considered it. It seemed beautiful in its simplicity. Accelerate and Willy would live. Brake and Willy would die. To hell with that, he thought. It'll work out somehow. 'Goddam,' he said and put his foot hard down again.

★ ★ ★

Willy watched the distant scene unfolding below him in growing horror as he saw his team torn apart by the shrapnel. Through the binoculars, he watched Bernard Thompson tumble from the driving seat and he stared at the body, hoping to see him pick himself up but smoke shrouded him. The lorry slowed and a belch of flame came down at him from the sagging gasbag above. The heat crossed the border of what was bearable. His hair began to burn and he beat at it with both hands that were themselves scorching and crouched down into the basket in an attempt to escape. The basket lurched, tugged forward, and a blessed flood of cooler air swept the flame away from him. He clambered up and saw the lorry moving faster below, a lone man at the wheel, bare-headed. Despite the headlong speed, flames burst from near the balloon's nose and he was still much too high. The incandescent gas licked at him again and he flattened himself on the floor, curling for protection with his hands over his face. In that hopeless moment, he thought of Claude and wished there was a gun with a kind finger on the trigger for him now.

There was only one solution. Better to jump than to burn, he thought, so he stood up into the full heat, the canopy above him writhing as fire consumed it and he climbed out of the basket, clinging on to the rim with outstretched blistering hands as he prepared himself to let go. Looking down, he saw the ground now only two or three hundred feet below and rising fast towards him but there was no more time. There is nothing to keep me here, he thought, and he told Claude he planned to laugh as he fell all the way down. That was when Gabrielle shouldered Claude aside and appeared in front of him, mouth moving, angry. 'William Fraser,' her voice yelled. 'Do not give up, damn you. There is *always something.*'

She was wrong. There was nothing. He felt the fire reaching through the skin of his fingers to the tendons beneath, the sand of his life running out fast because the moment was imminent when his fingers would lose strength, however hard he tried to hold on. His mind calmed as he recognized the time for choice had passed and the picture of the mouse came to his mind — the mouse clinging to the rigging ropes. He drew himself like the mouse in his mind's eye, still holding on for dear life. He could see the picture clearly and wished he had time to complete it then Gabrielle was there again. 'Idiot,' she said, 'You have drawn it wrong.' His hair was scorching now, curling into carbon strands. He could not feel his fingers any more. He looked down to see what she meant and she was right — there was something.

The ground-handling ropes dangled down from the balloon rigging, all the way down below the basket, angling back in the wind so that one of them trailed just a body's length directly below his feet. He let go, arms reaching out, and willed his seared and screaming hands to grab it as he fell. The rope skidded through his grasp, tearing away burnt skin and flesh but he forced his fingers to close around it and braked himself to a bloody stop with only another six or seven feet still dangling below his feet, then he wrapped the rope twice around himself. Drawing in a gasping breath of cool air, he looked up to see the whole canopy alight, looked down again to see the earth still too far below and felt himself punched by the vast explosion of a shell in the middle of the track ahead. He saw the lorry disappear into smoke, emerge again and the driver look back at him.

He saw Chester's face.

The ground rose rapidly to meet him as the lorry careered into the crater. He unwrapped the rope from round him, holding on with both hands, bending his knees and rolling away as his legs crashed into the ground. The vast mass of flame passed over him, sagging to the ground as he bounced over and over, flailing along the edge

512

of the track until the stump of a wrecked tree trunk stopped him, head first.

*　*　*

Willy woke, who knows how much later. He was in a four-poster bed with a woman bending over him and first the woman was the Queen and then she was, without any change, Gabrielle, telling him he had served her husband well. He reached out to her but his hands were burning so she stepped back, blew him a kiss and faded into smoke. The bed grew harder and the bedpost by his head was a shattered tree-trunk by a stony track. He saw a second bed-post — smoke rising from the inverted wreck of a burning lorry, by Chester's body which was stretched out on the crater's rim. Another thick smoke column rose from the heaped balloon fabric, burning itself out beside the track. He lifted his head with difficulty and tried to stand to go to Chester but his legs would not move at all. A shell burst fifty yards away and then another and he thought how stupid it would be to die here helpless after surviving all that, marooned under the barrage, unable even to crawl. He turned his head to look back from where they had come to see salvation coming limping out of the smoke. Bernard Thompson, bloodied and determined, coming to his aid and behind Thompson, the final bed-post column rose into the shell-crossed air — a distant pillar of smoke climbing from a burning barn.

He remembered nothing at all of Bernard

Thompson's two-hour struggle to lift and drag him to the dressing-station, nothing coherent of the night-time ambulance ride to the first hospital and very little of his transfer to the coast.

Out of a violent turmoil of dreams, he tried to open his eyes but the lids would not part. He rocked his head from side to side and a voice said, 'Hush now, you're quite safe here.' A girl's voice. American.

'Am I blind? I can't see.'

'It's ointment for your burns. Kind of sticky. I'll wipe it off your eyelids.'

That hurt but not as much as his legs and his scalp. Cool fingers helped ease the eyelids apart on his right eye and he saw a blurry face with blonde hair tucked under a nurse's cap bending over him. The fingers moved to his left eye and soon he was able to blink both eyes clearer.

'Am I in England?' he asked.

'No, this is De Panne. They wouldn't let go of you that easily.'

'What's wrong with my legs?'

'Just a matching pair of fractures. They'll mend.'

'My hands?' They were wrapped in bandages. 'What about my face?'

'You got yourself grilled. It could be a lot worse. The ointment's good and there's morphine if you need it. You only have to say. Want some?'

'Maybe.'

'You got visitors waiting. I'll go get them.'

'Who are they?' he asked but she smiled and

went away. He looked towards the end of the long ward, memories of his rescue coming back, hoping he might see Bernard Thompson but his vision was very blurred. He blinked hard, trying to clear it and made out a tall nurse leading a man in uniform down the lines of cots. They reached the end of his bed and he could see the soldier was smiling at him but he still had no idea. The uniform was unfamiliar, of a plain and antique cut but he could not focus on the detail.

'I hear you're a hard man to kill, Mr Fraser,' said the soldier in a soft Scottish voice.

'Gilfillan?' he said, astonished.

'I would hug you, sir, but I see no part of you that would not hurt.'

'It is so very good to see you but how in the world did you get here?' That, he realized, was the uniform of the South African war, brought out of its retirement to give its wearer a suitable place in this new world of war.

'You may find this hard to believe but it was with the help of the government of Belgium. They sent a message to Grannoch in a grand motorcar and it transported me all the way down to Dover. I came at speed, greeted with opened doors at every stage of my journey. They brought me here in another grand car from the port of Dunkerque and it is such a very great relief to see you. The nurse here tells me you are on the mend. I think you are in very good hands.'

Willy looked at the nurse, blinked and saw her smiling for a moment before his eyes misted over again. 'What else has she told you?' he asked.

'We passed the time of day as we waited. I told

her a little of life at Grannoch and what a rascal you used to be. Now, this may surprise you but she told me that you are very well regarded in this country, that the King and Queen of Belgium, no less, both think very highly of you.' Gilfillan bent nearer and, in a stage whisper that carried around the ward, said, 'That is what my driver said, too. Indeed he said so much about how the Queen takes an interest in you that I wonder perhaps whether she might not be a little sweet on you?'

Willy smiled and it hurt his cheeks. 'Mr Gilfillan, you haven't been properly introduced to the sister here, have you?'

'A sister is she? I do apologize to you, ma'am, and there I was addressing you as 'nurse'. I'm sorry, I didn't catch your name.'

'That's all right, Mr Gilfillan. My name is Elisabeth.'

'And what might the rest of it be, my dear?'

'Queen.'

'Elisabeth Queen? Is that a Belgian name? Do you know, that could pass for a normal name in my own country.'

★   ★   ★

Three months later, Gilfillan was still unwilling to be reminded of that. He gave his attention instead to stoking the many fireplaces. His efforts sent a swirling, clammy smoke through the corridors that took an almost imaginary edge off Grannoch Castle's arctic soul. Morag sent away for different mutton recipes in the forlorn

516

hope of stimulating the master's appetite. The doctor called every second day to inspect the healing process. When Willy decided it was time for him to walk, both Gilfillan and Morag would drive him mad by shadowing his every move. Mrs McCann came to visit with the air of one prepared to surrender herself utterly to a wounded hero and Willy stared at her without comprehension then left the room and did not return. Young Lorna Wakeley was summoned, though Willy had no knowledge of that. His legs now worked again. His hands were still stiff though Morag worked oil into them daily and his face had healed with only faint and shining scars. Young Miss Wakeley walked with him in the garden. Two years of war, however distant, had brought her a surprising measure of wisdom so that he did not shun her company.

'You left something behind you,' she said and he seemed to nod. 'Was it companionship? You must have lost friends?'

'Friends?'

'You look surprised.'

He was. He had thought at once of Claude and only then of Chester who had saved him. 'Of course. It is the everyday business of war,' he said shortly.

'Not that then. Would you like to tell me?'

'No. There is no point.'

They turned and he looked at the bulk of Grannoch and remembered drawing it seen from just this spot, transformed by the young couple walking to its door. Gabrielle and himself. For all her intense, sweet kindness Lorna Wakeley could not for a moment fit into that picture.

'What will you do now?' she asked.

'Go back as soon as they accept I am fit.'

'Why? They would not make you. Not after all you've done.'

'It doesn't work like that. You don't get let off. Anyway, I think it is the only world I understand these days.'

The medical officer from the depot arrived and did not agree with his claim of his complete recovery. His mother's lawyer came from Glasgow, insisting rudely on proof of identity of the returned hero until Gilfillan escorted him to his motorcar with a twelve-bore tucked under his arm in a way that was just the right side of threatening. 'I will be back,' the man said sourly as he put the car into gear, 'with my senior partner.'

'Be it upon your own head,' Gilfillan said and fired over the roof of the car at an entirely imaginary bird.

The very next day a larger car arrived, an Arrol-Johnston also with a Glasgow registration. 'That must be the threatened senior partner,' said Gilfillan. 'Don't you disturb yourself. I'll see him on his way,' but he was back within two minutes and the man with him wore a colonel's uniform and an eye-patch with a long scar below to show he had earned it the hard way.

'Fraser?' he said, putting out his hand. 'Livesay. It is an honour to meet you.'

'Sir. May I ask what has brought you here? It is a slow journey from Glasgow.'

'Slower still from London, I assure you. You

look as if you need to sit down and I would quite like to do the same.'

Morag brought a tray of tea and seemed to want to tidy the room but Willy sensed restraint in his visitor and quietly sent her away.

'I hear you want to get back to war,' said Livesay. 'Is it true?'

'Yes, sir.'

'Leave out the sir. Do you mind where?'

'The Salient.'

'You *want* to go back to the Salient?'

Willy thought of a balloon basket, a mile up in the clean air. He thought of a pair of good binoculars and a distant farm. He nodded.

'I can't offer you the Salient,' said Livesay. 'Not yet, anyway. But I can offer you a trip across the Atlantic as soon as you are well enough to travel and I can tell you that it could have a direct effect on the outcome of this war.'

Acknowledgments
and Sources

I would like to thank Jo Dickinson and Victoria Hobbs from the bottom of my heart for their incessant support for all my writing and in particular for this book.

Every aspect of the war depicted here has been based on close research. Until I persuaded an intrepid hot-air balloon pilot to fly me over the Ypres Salient at an absurd height, I had no idea how fragile life felt, even in peacetime, in a basket that was nearly a mile high. Nobody was shooting at us. From that height, the 1914–18 cemeteries are everywhere you look, neat white patterns across trench systems that have still left their imprint on the landscape.

The balloon incidents depicted are all taken from real wartime episodes. I thank all of those few who left memoirs or fragments of memoirs and am fully aware that I am riding on their shoulders. I acknowledge them with gratitude. The key memoir is by Goderic Hodges — *Memoirs of an Old Balloonatic* (originally published by William Kimber in 1972). The fullest analysis of Great War ballooning is Alan Morris's *The Balloonatics* (Jarrolds 1970). For those who want to know still more, a bibliography is available on my website at www.jameslongbooks.co.uk.

We do hope that you have enjoyed reading this large print book.

Did you know that all of our titles are available for purchase?

We publish a wide range of high quality large print books including:
Romances, Mysteries, Classics
General Fiction
Non Fiction and Westerns

Special interest titles available in large print are:
The Little Oxford Dictionary
Music Book
Song Book
Hymn Book
Service Book

Also available from us courtesy of Oxford University Press:
Young Readers' Dictionary
(large print edition)
Young Readers' Thesaurus
(large print edition)

For further information or a free brochure, please contact us at:
Ulverscroft Large Print Books Ltd.,
The Green, Bradgate Road, Anstey,
Leicester, LE7 7FU, England.
Tel: (00 44) 0116 236 4325
Fax: (00 44) 0116 234 0205

Other titles published by Ulverscroft:

THE TWO OF US

Andy Jones

Fisher is fizzing with the euphoria of new love — laughing too loud, kissing more enthusiastically than is polite in public. How he met Ivy is academic; you don't ask how the rain began, you simply appreciate the rainbow. The two of them have been an item for less than three weeks — and they just know they are meant to br together. The fact that they know little else about each other is a monor detail ... But over the coming months, in which their lives will change forever, Fisher and Ivy discover that falling in love is one thing, while staying there is an entirely different story ...

THE GHOST OF THE MARY CELESTE

Valerie Martin

In 1872 the American merchant vessel *Mary Celeste* was discovered adrift off the coast of Spain; her crew were never found. A rather hard-up young writer named Arthur Conan Doyle hears of the ship and decides to write an outlandish short story about what took place. It causes quite a sensation back in the United States, particularly for sought-after Philadelphia psychic Violet Petra and skeptical journalist Phoebe Grant, who is seeking to expose Petra as a fraud. Then there is the family of the *Mary Celeste's* captain, linked to the sea for generations and marked repeatedly by tragedy. In salons and on rough seas, at seances and in the imagination of a genius, these stories converge in unexpected ways as the mystery of the ghost ship deepens. Will the sea yield its secrets?

WITHOUT YOU

Saskia Sarginson

Suffolk, 1984: When seventeen-year-old Eva goes missing at sea, everyone presumes that she has drowned. Her parents' relationship is falling apart, undermined by guilt and grief. But her younger sister, Faith, refuses to consider a life without Eva; she's determined to find her sister and bring her home alive. Close to the shore looms the shape of an island — out of bounds, mysterious and dotted with windowless concrete huts. What nobody knows is that inside one of the huts Eva is being held captive. That she is fighting to survive — and return home.

THE NIGHT FALLING

Katherine Webb

Puglia, Italy, 1921: Leandro returns home, now a rich man with a glamorous American wife. But how did he get so wealthy — and what haunts his outwardly exuberant wife? Boyd, a quiet English architect, is hired to build Leandro's dreams. But why is he so afraid of Leandro? Clare, Boyd's diffident wife, is summoned to Puglia with her stepson. At first desperate to leave, she soon finds a compelling reason to stay. Ettore, starving, poor and grieving for his lost fiancee, is too proud to ask his Uncle Leandro for help — until events conspire to force his hand. Tensions are high as poverty leads veterans of the Great War to the brink of rebellion. And under the burning sky, a reckless love and a violent enmity will bring brutal truths to light . . .

PEGASUS

Danielle Steel

In the German countryside, on the cusp of World War II, everything is about to change for two lifelong friends. As widowers, Nicholas and Alex are raising their children alone, but lead contented, peaceful lives — until a long-buried secret about Nicolas's ancestry threatens his family's safety. To survive, they must flee to America. The only treasures Nicholas and his sons can take are eight purebred horses. These magnificent creatures are their ticket to a new life, securing Nicolas a job with the famous Ringling Brothers Circus. There, he and the white stallion Pegasus become the centre-piece of the show. But as the years of war take their toll, Nicolas struggles to adapt to his new life, while Alex and his daughter face escalating danger in Europe. Then tragedy strikes on both sides of the ocean . . .